TIMELESS TRAVELS
Tales of Mystery, Intrigue, Humor, and Enchantment

Timeless Travels

Tales of
Mystery, Intrigue, Humor, and Enchantment

Joseph Rotenberg

gefen
publishing house בית הוצאה גפן
JERUSALEM • NEW YORK   Est. 1981

Some stories or essays in this compilation were previously published
in the *Jewish Link of New Jersey*, a weekly community newspaper,
and in the *Jewish Literary Journal*, an online venue of Jewish creative
writing. Some titles have been altered for this publication.

Cover Design: Dragan Bilic – Pixel Droid Design Studio
Cover image: "Joseph's Coat of Many Colors," painted
woodcut by Ben Avram, Jerusalem, 2015. Photo by author.
Typesetting: Raphaël Freeman, Renana Typesetting
Author photograph on jacket © 2016 Janet Joyner

ISBN: 978-965-229-915-4

1 3 5 7 9 8 6 4 2

Gefen Publishing House Ltd.
6 Hatzvi Street
Jerusalem 94386, Israel
972-2-538-0247
orders@gefenpublishing.com

Gefen Books
11 Edison Place
Springfield, NJ 07081
516-593-1234
orders@gefenpublishing.com

www.gefenpublishing.com

Printed in Israel

Library of Congress Cataloging-in-Publication Data

Names: Rotenberg, Joseph, 1949– author
Title: Timeless travels : tales of mystery, intrigue, humor, and enchantment
  / by Joseph Rotenberg.
Description: Springfield, NJ : Gefen Books, [2017] | Includes bibliographical
  references.
Identifiers: LCCN 2017008374 | ISBN 9789652299154
Subjects: LCSH: Tales. | Humorous stories. | Rotenberg, Joseph,
  1949---Voyages and travels.
Classification: LCC GR76 .R68 2017 | DDC 398.2--dc23 LC
record available at https://lccn.loc.gov/2017008374

To my wife
Barbara
who always thinks of others before herself

Contents

Foreword

In bygone eras, the *maggid* – the itinerant preacher – was a fix-
ture in the religious and cultural life of European Jewry. Much
like his entrepreneurial counterpart, the estimable peddler, the
sermonizer carried his intellectual properties from town to town
and displayed his spiritual and educational wares to appreciative audiences. Listeners could never be certain what theme or
teaching from the vast trove of Jewish tradition would be the
day's subject. But they would come away from the presentation
with a stronger sense of belonging to the Jewish people and an
intensified connectedness to what made Judaism special and
worthy of perpetuation.

Maggidim were, likewise, a popular presence within immigrant
Jewish communities in the early twentieth century. During long
summertime Sabbath afternoons, these raconteurs and moralists
would enthrall their audiences with their tales of tests of faith
that they had observed while traveling from the Old World to
America. And they would finish their orations with appeals to
the Jews downtown whose commitment to their faith may have
wavered to prove that Orthodox Judaism could survive in this
land of freedom.

Before you are the texts of a present-day *maggid*'s encounters
with the modern world. Imagine Joseph Rotenberg holding forth
at Seudah Shlishit (the third Sabbath meal) with accounts of his
own travels through America, Europe and Israel, adroitly linking

contemporary events with the timeless teachings of the Torah. This religious tour guide extraordinaire always feels the presence of the Almighty as his own consummate guide as he connects the past, present and future of the Jewish people to the sites and situations that he explored.

Rotenberg is aided in his efforts by his keen eye and ear for the stories people have related to him all along his way. Some of the accounts carry with them a legendary or fanciful tone. But no matter; such is the art of the storyteller who can be forgiven hyperbole in the service of strengthening faith.

Amid all the lessons imparted in *Timeless Travels*, many of them with humorous asides, others downright serious, two teachings will long stay with me. The first example of modern-day wisdom literature that Rotenberg dutifully records was tendered by "Uncle Malcolm," a man who was ironically by profession a travel agent:

> In our modern times, we question more and more what the meaning of life is. We strive and strive, follow all the guidelines our elders set out for us, achieve a certain status in our chosen profession, and question whether, in the end, it's worth it. What exactly does it mean to be a success, we ask.... Take all your inherent skills and instincts, your genetics, add all your acquired knowledge, and do the best you can.

The second enduring nugget – offered at the book's conclusion – reminds us of what my friend of long-standing is all about and wants us to remember (in the book, "Joey," as we knew him as a young boy, recounts his early educational days at Ramaz before transferring to the Rabbi Jacob Joseph School – I was one of his classmates):

> As we continue to interact with the broader world and with innovations to come, we, as Orthodox Jews, as *contortionists*, remember to infuse our actions with the morality and spirituality that they might otherwise lack, never for a moment

forgetting that it is we who ultimately determine whether those actions work for good or for evil. Being flexible while adhering to principle is the worthy challenge that we must be willing to undertake.

All told, *Timeless Travels* is an enjoyable and evocative read.

Jeffrey S. Gurock
Libby M. Klapperman Professor of Jewish History
Yeshiva University
October 2016

Prologue – Discovering
Timeless Travels

The bulldozer roared across the abandoned lot, smashing the remaining timbers, sharp reminders of the homes that had once stood there. Dust billowed up in staggered clouds, temporarily choking the immediate air. Progress had mandated that a garden apartment complex inherit several acres of riverfront property where, fifty years earlier, single-family dwellings had been carefully constructed. Young, eager families with children and pets, and older childless types had visited, viewed, inspected, contracted for, closed on, lived in, and died in these cookie-cutter, split level frame, brick houses for what seemed like ages. But neighborhoods change and Teaneck was no exception. A crew of five was finishing off one last section of the lot and preparing the way for the excavators.

One man, graying at the temple, stood off to the side watching the workers monotonously tossing debris into the dumpster that bordered the worksite. He was dressed in a faded suit, his expression grim; he appeared to be muttering words under his breath. He made no attempt to stop the workers; they in turn ignored him.

As the bulldozer was about to attempt another pass, one of the workers suddenly shouted: "Hold on!" The huge yellow vehicle lurched to a stop. "Just in time," added the warning voice. "There's something shiny down there, silvery," he said, pointing to a recessed area in the ground about to be covered by the bulldozer's efforts. "It may be valuable." By this time, the foreman of the work crew, alerted to the stoppage, had crossed the lot.

"What's holding you up?" the foreman asked. "We don't have all day!"

"He thinks he's found something valuable," said the bulldozer operator jumping down from his cab.

By now, the worker, Link, who had made the discovery was on his knees, then his chest, stretching down, reaching inside the earth almost up to his shoulder. "I've got it," he exclaimed, "almost, anyway. Just one more second – there – I've got it now!"

"Link, get up, show us what you have!"

"Come on, we haven't got all day."

"OK, OK, I'm coming."

Link slowly lifted his hand and arm out of the ground to reveal what appeared to be a small book or diary covered in silver plate. The metal of the book cover was tarnished in places. It was decorated with a border design of fruits: cherries, berries, pomegranates. A thin coat of dust covered it, but not entirely, so sufficient metal showed through to reflect the light playing off it – a key to its discovery perhaps.

"Oh, it's only a book," the foreman growled, turning his back to Link. "It's not really silver, probably, and we don't have time to waste. I don't want to stop unless it's real money, you understand? Back to work!"

Link walked over to his backpack, which was lying against the curb in the shade of the one remaining maple standing at the site. He unzipped the main compartment and slipped his discovery inside. He hadn't had time to even open the book, not with the foreman in an angry mood over the delay he had caused.

The bulldozer roared once more, the dust billowed again, and the man with the graying temples and faded suit stood silently, watching with a heavy heart the final leveling of a beloved site. He was no longer muttering, and the dust now burned his eyes.

The sun was setting, time for the workday to end. Link prepared to return home, tired as he was every day. Demolition work had little to offer him except regular wages, but in Teaneck, having a steady income was a necessity of life. Link's young wife came from the West Coast: the daughter of a longshoreman from San Diego, she was no stranger to hard work. Their baby daughter, now three years old, would urge Link to read to her all the time. Tonight Link wished to avoid that chore, so he tried – unsuccessfully – to sneak by her watchful eye.

"Mommy, Daddy's home," she squealed in her high-pitched voice. "Here, Daddy, read me this book that we got at the library."

It was no use. He was not going to escape. He grabbed Violet, lifted her up onto his shoulder, and together they collapsed in a heap on the sofa.

"What's the book called, Vi?" Link asked, forgetting that his daughter could not yet read.

"I don't know, Daddy, silly, but it has pictures of people working at jobs…"

This night Link didn't get past page eight before Violet fell asleep in his lap. Nursery school had tired her out. He gently lifted her out of his lap onto the sofa, covering her with a blanket he and his wife always used for that purpose.

After supper, Link went downstairs to his basement where he kept his father's old, battered desk and chair. A single, incandescent bulb just adequately lit a finished space about twenty feet long and half that distance wide. With his feet propped up on the desk, Link reached down somewhat awkwardly into his backpack; he slowly withdrew the object he had discovered that afternoon at the work site. It was larger than he remembered. He next reached for a tissue from the box he kept on the desk.

Link wiped some dust off the cover of the book and slowly opened it. On the first leaf, he was surprised to find the following inscription:

If you know Dr. Fishman, drop him a line
In Eldred you'll find the fishing is fine
Nature has found its way into your life
On Two Medicine Ridge it cuts as a knife
Escape to the suburbs where answers are found
To questions not asked yet where tea-mates abound
Michener as mentor; the process is fair
Meet all the cabbies; they're from everywhere
The City contains all you'll need for this quest
Historical progress not just for the blessed.

After a moment spent studying the page, Link determined that the verse was in fact some sort of curious, cryptic table of contents. He turned the cover page and found before him a list of ten headings, seemingly unrelated, but, as he began to read the first selection, Link knew that he need not make up his mind regarding that fact. The page on which the headings appeared was torn halfway down and several additional pages following also seemed to be missing.

We have to thank Link, our dedicated "archaeologist," for taking the trouble to not only save this book, but also to complete the table of contents to reflect the stories and essays contained in this collection. His efforts certainly allow the reader to better enjoy *Timeless Travels: Tales of Mystery, Intrigue, Humor, and Enchantment*.

PART I
THE PROMISED LAND

Jerusalem Tale -
A Modern, Mystical Moment

I landed in Tel Aviv or, more precisely, at Ben Gurion Airport, early one Friday morning. The late winter clouds only thickened as my driver drove up Highway One, past Sha'ar Hagay and the mountainous approaches to Jerusalem. The road was familiar, yet it always seemed somehow fresh no matter the familiarity. I was in Israel to visit old friends and new clients, but mostly to make my annual pilgrimage to my father's grave in Beit Shemesh. I had left my wife and kids back home. None of them could get away for even the week I had arranged: jobs and school proved too much of an obstacle. This year, 2001, the Second Intifada was raging, shrinking tourism as many in the States viewed even a short visit to Israel as too risky a proposition. Crossing a street where only the day before someone had blown himself up was too much for some to take. Bloodstains did not wash away very quickly; you only had to know where to look to make them out on the street crossing.

We entered the city at 9:00 a.m. Traffic was lighter than I expected. We drove to my hotel on Jabotinsky Street and I checked in without a hitch. I was tired from the ten-hour flight and I headed to my room to take a short nap. I might have slept the entire day, but I was awakened at about 1:30 in the afternoon by an alarm clock I hadn't set. Rubbing sleep from my eyes, I reached for my cell phone and called home to let them know I had arrived safely. I wasn't in the mood to unpack (I never am), but I needed to shower and get ready for Shabbat that would begin at sundown, a mere three hours away. Jerusalem, centerpiece of the Jewish homeland, had a special connection with Shabbat. The city, already a world spiritual center, only became more so on Friday evenings. A sense of peace and repose filled the streets and the population. The strife of the weekday routine, the conflicts – political and social – all took a deserved timeout. Too short though it was, the break was most welcome to residents and visitors alike.

The shower was hot and refreshing. As I dressed, I remembered I had promised to call Bonnie, my trusted Israeli guide and dear friend, as soon as I arrived. I didn't have much time for touring on this six-day trip; besides, it was winter and not all that warm in Jerusalem. Knowing my interest in military history, Bonnie suggested a visit to the newly established IDF Armored Corps Museum on Sunday morning. This new museum in Latrun, off Highway One, on the way back down to Tel Aviv and the coast, seemed a perfect outing.

The always attentive, veteran hotel staff was made up largely of Arab residents of Jerusalem. I recognized many of them from previous visits and they recognized me by name as well, something always appreciated when you're far from home. I would be dining at the hotel over Shabbat. But first, I had an important decision to make: where to attend Friday night services.

Leaving the hotel, I walked north up Keren Hayesod Street, a three-block uphill climb to the intersection with King George Street. This was the heart of modern, West Jerusalem and the silence grew as the last rays of the sun bounced off the stone facades of the surrounding buildings. In my mind the choice of where to pray that evening had narrowed to the massive Great Synagogue on King George Street itself or the small *beit midrash* (traditional house of study) adjacent to Hechal Shlomo, the seat of the chief rabbinate of Israel. The entrances to the two houses could not have been more dissimilar. The Great Synagogue was the product of the prodigious charitable efforts of American Jewry, its entrance doors tall, massive, and decorative, its interior breathtakingly large, ornate and well illuminated by countless chandeliers arrayed across the enormous sanctuary. The *beit midrash* seemed tiny by comparison, almost an afterthought by the builders. One could only reach its modest entrance through a back door off the main road. At the Great Synagogue a permanent chazzan, assisted by a choir, led the service; at the *beit midrash* an ordinary congregant would intone the prayers.

That particular evening, I quietly entered the smaller house of worship. Inside, several men were seated randomly, awaiting the start of the Mincha service. I reached for a siddur from the bookcase to my right, checking only to see if it was the appropriate *nusach* to which I was accustomed. I sat down on an open bench, leaned back, and waited. We needed two more men before we could start. I had a moment to survey my surroundings a little more closely, but my eyes quickly turned back to the siddur in my hands. Inside the dark blue front cover was an inscription, a simple dedication by a family to their child lost in battle:

> In loving memory of our son Gedalya who fell in battle to protect Israel.
> May his memory be a blessing to us all.
> – The Rosenbaums, 5733 since creation (1973)

The dedication was probably commonplace in this locale, I thought, but it made an impression on me. The everyday reality of conflict and loss in and around Jerusalem struck home profoundly at that moment. The chazzan began the service, jolting me from my thoughts and, for the time, contemplation of things sad and painful.

After attending the lengthy Shabbat service at the Great Synagogue the next morning, I returned to the hotel for lunch, where I befriended a couple from South Africa, the Lerners, and their son Gadi, a student for a year at a Jerusalem yeshiva. They were hosting their son for lunch, no doubt fearing that he was tired of the institutional-type fare served monotonously at school. After the meal we headed for the hotel lounge where we could spread out and relax. Steve Lerner looked to be in his mid-forties, lean and tall, his wife Chavi, a year or two younger, redheaded and friendly. Both were educated and educators. Our talk ranged from current events (a given in Jerusalem) to philosophy and garden care.

Steve: "It always amazes me to have the opportunity in Israel to walk in the footsteps, so to speak, of the characters in the Bible, to breathe the same air these historical figures breathed!"

Chavi: "I think it's sad though to realize that the age of miracles is over, maybe never to return!"

Steve: "Who really knows how miraculous those days were? Maybe they seemed quite ordinary to the people of those times. And who knows what tomorrow might bring?"

I certainly couldn't answer Steve's question nor add anything to the discussion, so after a while I left my new friends in the lobby and headed upstairs to my room for the customary Shabbat afternoon nap.

On Sunday morning, Bonnie, youthful and active, despite her sixty years, came to pick me up at the hotel at 9:00. The air was cool even for February, but the sun occasionally peeked out from the clouds above. We descended from Jerusalem on Highway One, reversing my initial trip from the airport. Within twenty minutes we reached Latrun where a sign pointed to the IDF Armored Corps Museum. A short ride down a newly paved road brought us to the entrance gate. Bonnie parked her van in a shaded spot and we hopped out.

"You know, Joe," Bonnie said, "this is one of the most diverse tank museums in the world. They have collected vehicles from over fifteen countries and dozens of actual models that you can examine up close if you want. But it's more than that. It is Israel's official memorial site for fallen soldiers from the armored corps of the IDF; right now they are completing a Wall of Remembrance to memorialize by name all those men and women who fell."

We viewed the displays laid out before us, row upon row of tanks, too many to count and each one looking suspiciously like the next. We soon tired of the displays and ascended to the upper level of the site where the Wall of Remembrance was to be erected in the spring. We found a nondescript building that we thought might give us shelter from the brisk, chilly winds blowing on the plaza. Entering the building, I needed a few moments for my eyes to adjust to the relative darkness. Soon I saw before me a sparsely furnished, low-ceilinged room with three or four computer terminals. Planks of lumber rested against the far wall; coils of wiring littered the floor. It looked like a project yet to be completed, but I approached the terminal at the center of the room.

gkuna/Shutterstock.com

"This must be where they are constructing the planned museum archives. I don't think it's open to the public yet," Bonnie cautioned.

Without hesitation I pressed the enter button on the keyboard in front of the computer, half expecting the blank monitor in

front of me to remain so. After a moment's pause the terminal
shook slightly. Suddenly before me appeared a screen inscribed
as follows:

> Below is the story of Sergeant Gedalya Rosenbaum who
> served with valor in the Armored Corps in the Golan and who
> fell in 1973 fighting to sanctify God's name. During a fierce
> firefight against enemy forces, he dragged five of his comrades
> to safety at great peril to his life. He paid the ultimate price so
> that his comrades would live. May his memory be a blessing
> to us all. He was twenty-two years old.

I stared at the screen, rereading the message as the full impact
of its contents seeped into my consciousness. I said nothing to
Bonnie about the Friday evening service at the *beit midrash* and
the inscription in the front of my siddur. On the ride back to Jerusalem, Bonnie apologized for the cold weather and the unfinished
nature of the memorial site.

"You know, while you were visiting the museum shop, I asked
the curator when she expects the memorial and archives to be up
and running," Bonnie said. "She told me, 'Not until the summer
at best; we don't even have reliable power to the terminals yet!'"

I sat in stunned silence at that remark and thought about
Gedalya Rosenbaum and my two encounters with him: Spirit
world, the departed reaching out to the living – who really knows?
The age of miracles may not quite have ended after all!

*

Several months ago I asked a *sofer* (scribe) I know in Jerusalem to
visit the *beit midrash* described in the story in an attempt to find
the siddur that contained the memorial declaration, or *hakdashah*,
I had read those many years ago. He was successful in that search.
Not to my complete surprise he reported back that the siddur I
had randomly chosen to use that Friday night was the only siddur
in the shul that contained a *hakdashah* for a fallen soldier!

On the Road to Jerusalem

Flik47/Shutterstock.com

Quintus Varus had spent too many years in the saddle. A newly minted Roman cohort leader, he counted ten years of service in the Imperial Roman legions, service with distinction and in too many battles, skirmishes, and sieges to remember one from the other. Varus had never seen Rome itself. He was a provincial soldier, born in Asia Minor to parents who themselves had not seen the Imperial City. It made no difference to him that he served such a distant master. Having survived the aforementioned conflicts, he was an important man in the military government that Rome had established in Judea by the year 100 CE. He could thus afford some of life's comforts that simple legionaries could not, including riding a horse or mule up the tricky, dusty mountain road leading to Jerusalem.

Though he regularly took this route from the coastal city of Caesarea to review the troops that occupied Jerusalem and its surrounding valleys, on this occasion he had a specific objective in mind. The Romans had heard disturbing rumors of unrest among the Judeans, had seen increasing signs of rebellion, and were concerned enough to try to get more detailed information about the leaders of these protests. Varus, who had served in Jerusalem for two years, had several friends among the locals. He was acquainted in a way few Romans were with a number of important Judeans, men of influence who could be helpful in providing important information. The destruction of the Temple had taken place thirty years before, but Varus knew that to all Jews who had lived through that devastation, Roman rule still remained a cause of great pain.

The road from Caesarea to Jerusalem took two days to travel. The difficult ascent began at Beit Shemesh and at times required nerves of steel to negotiate the twists and turns of this ascent of almost three thousand feet. Mudslides were just one of the dangers that the rainy season brought and it was rare to make the ascent without losing men or livestock or both.

Travel at night was precarious and so Varus planned to stop at a roadside inn nestled into a cleft in the mountain about halfway up the ascent. The inn was owned by a rather famous merchant named Zoma, rumored to be among the richest in Judea. Varus knew Zoma, not particularly well, but well enough to perhaps garner some important information to help Varus in his mission.

As the sun set earlier in the mountains, Varus spurred his horse and the men following him onward at a quicker pace and within ten minutes the flickering lights of Zoma's inn appeared ahead. The Romans soon arrived at a complex of two or three wooden buildings comprising the inn and the adjoining stables. Varus slid from his saddle, brushed dust from his cloak and tunic, and shouted toward a group of Jewish stable hands.

"Let your master Zoma know of our arrival, for we are stopping here tonight. Food for ten men and water for our horses!"

Varus opened the oak door to the inn and entered, his eyes adjusting to the large, torch-lit room. It was empty, except for a young boy, not more than twelve years old, and a large, fearsome-looking bearded man in his early thirties.

"Reuben, where is Zoma, I wish to talk to him," Varus addressed the older man. "Who is this young fellow?"

Reuben replied, "He is Zoma's son, Simeon, a rather bright lad! He's helping us around the inn."

"Looks like his father," Varus remarked.

Zoma entered the room at this point and strode toward Varus.

"What brings you to these parts, my Roman friend?"

Zoma, as the wealthiest Jew in this area, believed in making the best of life under Roman rule, though even he had his limits when it came to Roman violence against his people.

"Reuben, bring our guest some bread, meat, and drink, and make sure all his men have the same!"

Ten minutes later all the Romans were busy sating their hunger with all that Reuben had brought to their table. Varus, after eating and drinking, suddenly remembered his mission and motioned to his host.

"Come, sit down, Zoma, and join me," Varus said. "I have to ask you something of importance."

Zoma sat down across from Varus and inquired about what exactly had brought the Romans to his Judean hostel.

"Zoma, we have been hearing disturbing things about secret meetings among your people where, to put it simply, words of rebellion are being spoken, nasty words. You know we don't want to harm anyone, but we must maintain order – that is the Roman way!"

"What exactly is being said about the Romans that is so objectionable?" asked Zoma.

"We have heard of a master teacher, I think your people call him a Tanna, who has been preaching that the Romans are a stupid people, unwilling to learn from others; also, that they are a people incapable of controlling their impulses, quick to anger and slow to forgive. He is also preaching that we, the rulers of the world, are unsatisfied with our conquests, always wanting more and more; and finally, that we are unworthy of respect because we respect nothing but our own power! Taken separately this indictment of Rome is intolerable. Taken together it could set this entire region afire. Do you know, Zoma, of such a teacher?"

Zoma hesitated before responding, "I know of no one preaching such a message."

Zoma glanced toward his son, Simeon, but quickly returned his gaze to Varus.

He continued, "I think perhaps it is best to let a conquered people occasionally vent their frustrations. Certainly it seems preferable to open actions to overthrow their conqueror!"

"Oh, no, Zoma, we have learned over the centuries that words lead to deeds and provocative words to bloody deeds!"

"In any event, I have not heard of the express teachings that have disturbed your people, Varus, but I'll keep my eyes – or should I say my ears – open."

Zoma rose to return to his business, but something compelled him to sit down again.

"You know, Varus, my people believe that our Lord is the source of everything we possess, both as a nation and individually. You Romans pay lip service to your gods who are mere caricatures of the men who created their myths. Our God is God!"

"If your god is so powerful, is he not also the source of all your travails?" countered Varus. "Look at Reuben over there," said Varus, motioning at the burly attendant, filling the Romans' cups with more red Judean wine. "Could he not overwhelm one of my legionnaires in single combat? I believe he very well could do so! Why then with your powerful god of gods and your numerous, strong-armed men such as Reuben are my people rulers in your land?" He continued, "Forgive me, old friend. I think I know why we Romans, with our smaller numbers, have prevailed over your mighty people. We are united in our purpose and broach no division in our ranks and you, sadly for you, fight often and bitterly among yourselves. I heard this phrase once from an old Greek I knew, and it aptly applies to you Judeans: You are your own worst enemies!"

Zoma couldn't disagree on Varus's last point. It seemed on this evening long ago on the road to Jerusalem nothing would be resolved. Both the Jew and the Roman had spoken the truth as they saw it. Meanwhile, Simeon had seen and listened attentively to all that had transpired that night between his father and the Roman. One day he would draw the proper conclusions from that conversation and memorialize that dialogue in a positive fashion for all time. But that would only come about when he grew older and became a leader in Israel.

Jerusalem Tale –
David King's Singular Journey

My friend or, should I say, my acquaintance David King passed away last year. He had asked me to serve as his executor and I agreed. He left no heirs, so the administration of his estate went more swiftly than these things ordinarily do. Among his effects I found seven stories and a diary that I have endeavored to edit and bring to the public's attention. The following is the first of these stories, offered as a tribute to my departed friend.

In 2013, David arrived in Jerusalem on a hot August morning. His trip was a short one that year, highlighted by an annual visit to the graves of his parents on the road to Beit Shemesh to the southwest. As his plane made its way across the Atlantic, over Europe and toward the Middle East, a thought crossed his mind. As his youngest son would soon be celebrating his upcoming marriage, it would certainly be appropriate for the father of the groom to be generous to those less fortunate. David accordingly decided to dedicate this trip to donating charity to the needy of Jerusalem. On all his previous visits there, he had given generously to those who requested aid, but on this occasion he would be more active in seeking out worthy recipients.

Back home in New Jersey, the Orthodox community to which he belonged was inundated with requests from multiple charitable organizations. Mailings, phone calls, not to mention people ringing his doorbell – direct or indirect solicitations of all sorts – are a regular way of life. David decided on this occasion to commit to doling out twenty portions of charity to those in need in Jerusalem before anyone asked him for a contribution. "It shouldn't be difficult to find people in need," he thought.

Upon arriving at his hotel, David unpacked his luggage and decided to visit the Kotel (Western Wall) after a quick lunch in the hotel lobby. It was a Wednesday, and he soon found himself in a cab heading for the Old City. He walked from the entrance to the Rova (Jewish Quarter) to the steps leading down to the Kotel plaza, which was filled as always with a multitude of people moving in many different directions. Within minutes, he was standing in front of the Kotel, touching the cool stone blocks that contrasted sharply with the heat of the mid-day sun. He began to recite prayers of thanksgiving to God for allowing him to return once more to stand before the Temple Mount. Following his prayers, he looked around for people who were soliciting donations, but none appeared. Compared to years past, when a multitude of individuals would descend upon visitors to the Kotel, on this day there were almost no beggars. David asked a guard whether there was a new policy in effect that kept the needy away, but the man wouldn't answer him. Before leaving the Kotel, David duly donated the first two portions of charity to two younger-looking gentlemen who seemed appreciative of the contribution. There really wasn't anything scientific in how he chose the recipients. He just walked over to two shabby-looking men and dropped money into their hands.

David realized he would have to come up with a better plan if he were to fulfill his goal in any meaningful way.

Two days later, *erev Shabbat* morning, David set out for Kikar Shabbat in Meah Shearim to continue his quest. Soon he was instructing his driver to park the car and wait while he searched the neighborhood for the eighteen remaining recipients.

Good fortune shone on David that Friday morning as within ten minutes he located five local women who were sitting along the street actively collecting for their upcoming Shabbat needs. Next, David took to stopping people on the street and asking if they knew of any needy people who might require assistance. He chose six such people to receive a portion with the added instruction that they could use some of the gift donated for any efforts they expended in finding a worthy recipient. As a result of these efforts, eleven portions were distributed within the first half hour, leaving seven recipients yet to be chosen.

The hour was approaching noon and the street traffic was unpromising until, much to his surprise, David saw his nephew walking toward him.

"Netanel, what are you doing here?" David asked.

"I'm in Jerusalem for Shabbat."

"Perhaps you know locals who need *tzedakah*. I can give you money for three recipients."

"Done!"

David quickly said goodbye to Netanel and looked up and down Kikar Shabbat for the final candidates to complete his *tzedakah* mission. He saw a white-bearded elderly man walking briskly, carrying a leather briefcase. David rapidly crossed over the street and intercepted Rabbi Naftali Kaminetsky in stride. They spoke in Hebrew, David telling the rabbi of his desire to donate *tzedakah* to two remaining worthy recipients. The rabbi indicated he knew of two such families and would see that they promptly received David's gift. Before parting ways, Rabbi Kaminetsky, a Cohen, informed David, likewise a Cohen, that back in 1967 he had accompanied Rabbi Shlomo Goren to the Kotel when Jerusalem was reunited for the first time in two thousand years and that he (Rabbi Kaminetsky) was the first Cohen to lead formal *tefillah* (prayers) at the Kotel after the reunification. In parting Rabbi Kaminetsky told David to visit the Kotel once more before leaving Jerusalem as Hashem (lit. "the name," used to refer to God) had one more task for David to perform. David wished Rabbi Kaminetsky well and drove back to the hotel to prepare for Shabbat.

The following Sunday morning, bags packed, David made that last trip to the Kotel, as recommended by Rabbi Kaminetsky. As fortune would have it, a military induction ceremony was taking place in the plaza. Several dozen newly minted air force officers were milling around the plaza following their induction. David, after completing some prayers at the Wall, walked toward the officers. Suddenly, he realized why Rabbi Kaminetsky had sent him back to the Kotel that day. His mission apparently was not merely to donate twenty portions of *tzedakah* to the needy in Jerusalem.

David approached the first group of soldiers and asked them if they wanted him to recite Birkat Cohanim, the Priestly Blessing, over them. David told them he understood that they might not be religious or practicing Jews, but that many people throughout the world supported them and wished them peace and safety during their period of service to Israel. As one, the officers welcomed David's offer, and David intoned the blessings over and over that morning until nearly all one hundred soldiers received the blessing. There, in front of the Kotel, a simple Cohen blessed the army of Hashem with love as in days of old.

A fitting conclusion to David King's singular journey!

Golden Days – Gaza 1967 Remembered

It is undeniable that the Middle East has seen more than its share of conflict and war. Whether one looks back in time or just considers current events, the lands between the eastern Mediterranean and the Jordan River have been crossed by too many conquering armies and warring peoples eager to impose their will on the native populations. Throughout history there have been occasions when the opportunity to settle long-standing conflicts between those nations has presented itself.

One such time was the period between the Six-Day War in 1967 and the outbreak of the Yom Kippur War in 1973. On the surface, the triumph of Israeli forces in 1967 opened the door to a final resolution of Israel's disputes with surrounding Arab populations. In retrospect, hopes of imminent peace during those six golden years were merely a mirage, as events would sadly show. Yet the victory in 1967 did open a small window of opportunity for ordinary people to travel safely into Gaza and adjacent Egypt and get a sense of the potential for both peace and warfare between the defeated local population and Israel.

In July 1967, I arrived in Israel for the first time. It was an exhilarating moment in my life and, even more so, a time of great rejoicing for Jewish people throughout the world. My first visit to the Kotel was a transformative event, as I felt at one with the continuum of Jewish history as a living, breathing reality. My base of activity was to be Jerusalem as it was for many that summer. My stint in Israel was limited, however, to just three weeks – hardly enough time to even cover the basic sites. Fortunately, my older sister Judy had been living and working in Jerusalem for the previous six months, and she had established many contacts among the locals before my arrival. Judy had planned a partial itinerary for me, which helped me immensely. There was one special trip we took that summer, shared by very few tourists at that time.

Eli Yahalomi was a thirty-year-old Israeli whose family came from Morocco in the early 1950s. He drove a *sherut* taxi for the Nesher company, completing trips from Jerusalem to Tel Aviv several times a day. He had met Judy several months earlier, and together they planned outings with their friends when Eli was off work. He owned the large station wagon that he used as a driver, so it was available for the trips as necessary. Eli arrived at our apartment, where all the travelers had gathered. Our company consisted of my sister, two of her single friends, and me. Eli introduced himself to each of us. He had recently been mustered out of the infantry brigade, where he had served in the previous conflict. He had been sent to Sinai in a reserve role. Stationed there for two weeks, he thus had some familiarity with the Gaza Strip, through which we would be traveling. The entire distance between Jerusalem in the Judean mountains and El Arish in coastal northern Sinai was approximately 156 miles in a direct line. The one-way trip to El Arish from Jerusalem would first take us in the direction of Ashkelon on the Israeli coast. From there the journey would take about three and a half hours to traverse all of the Gaza Strip and arrive in the seacoast resort city of El Arish.

"Given the history of the places we'll be traveling, it really isn't that long a ride, you'll see. Heavily populated, but not that far to travel to cover the whole area," Eli explained after we had loaded up the wagon and boarded.

We soon entered the Gaza Strip, passing several Israeli military checkpoints on the way. The ancient city of Gaza was not yet called Gaza City as it is today. It was the first stop on our trip – multiple low-rise buildings extending in all directions as we reached the center of town. Eli pulled the station wagon alongside an IDF jeep and told us we could get out and stretch our legs.

"Don't be surprised if a bunch of Arab kids start crowding us, trying to sell you things. You don't have to buy anything if you don't want to," were Eli's instructions. As I stepped out of the car, at least a dozen boys approached me shouting in broken English "all for liras" (pre-shekel Israeli currency) and thrusting their wares in my face – everything from small drums, knives, and trinkets to unidentifiable Arabic beverages. I declined the offers and retreated with difficulty into the station wagon. The girls did the same, and after several minutes we continued on our way.

"They seem friendly enough, Eli," I said.

"They're happy that we've gotten rid of the Egyptians. There's no love lost between them," he responded.

"So for the moment we're viewed as 'liberators'?" I asked.

"Sort of," Eli responded, the irony of my remark not lost on him.

We drove on after five minutes with Eli continuing his guidance.

"Our next objective is an old caravan stop called Khan Yunis. Today it's a moderate-sized town where we can see the old buildings used as a stopover in Ottoman-Turkish times when the caravans from Egypt to Iraq followed this exact route. Actually the route dates back to even earlier times. The ancient pharaohs used this coastal road to carry them to battle against the Hittites at Megiddo in Emek Yizre'el to the north. The Romans called the route we are traveling on today Via Maris, as it connected their provinces of Syria, Judea, and Egypt by closely following the Mediterranean coast."

Khan Yunis was only fifteen miles south of Gaza City. As we entered the caravan town, we saw many remnants of disabled Egyptian military vehicles, tanks, trucks, and armored carriers. We stopped at the caravansary and got out to examine the old Turkish buildings that had housed camels and assorted goods in the past. In Khan Yunis we were spared the crowds of "salesmen," but when, after a half hour, we arrived at the final Gazan city we would visit, Rafah (Rafiach in Hebrew), we encountered the largest crowds of Arab children yet, armed with even more goods than we had seen in Gaza City. Large drums, small knives, and all sorts of nuts were proffered by the youthful throng. It was only with the greatest effort that we extricated ourselves from the crowds in Rafah and headed out of the strip into the Egyptian desert of Sinai. Eli pulled off the road after a mile or two.

"Make sure you all drink enough while we're in Sinai," Eli cautioned. "Dehydration is a real problem in the desert, and you may not be aware of it occurring."

We didn't have to be warned twice.

The landscape had changed rather abruptly from urban to desert wasteland. We resumed our drive west, and after an hour reached the ancient Mediterranean coastal resort town of El Arish, capital of northern Sinai. The people of El Arish appeared much more subdued than the Arabs we met in the Gaza Strip, as the residents here were Egyptian citizens under the control of the conquering Israelis. We drove along a stretch of the coastal road and the Mediterranean shone in the summer sun. Eli stopped at a scenic pullout, and we waded into the warm waters of the sea.

"We should start back toward Israel," Eli said after fifteen minutes. "We have a distance yet to travel." Eli turned our vehicle around, and we began the four-hour drive that would get us to the outskirts of Be'er Sheva by late afternoon. The desert roads we took on our return to this ancient, historic southern "capital" of Israel were not well maintained, and the bumps and curves took their toll on the driver and passengers alike. When we finally emerged from the desert into Be'er Sheva, we felt as if we had returned to earth from some foreign planet. We checked into the Desert Inn, the gaudiest hotel in town, and felt like kings as we lay on our beds in our respective rooms, exhausted, but with a sense of achievement. Be'er Sheva was a sleepy town, more a favorite of camels, donkeys, and Bedouin than Western tourists. The next morning, we arose early and returned to Jerusalem through the Elah Valley, past historic Nachal Sorek.

Over the years my recollections of the trip to the Gaza Strip and my impressions of its residents during those early months of direct contact with Israel have remained quite vivid. When one considers that the locals there viewed the Egyptians who had ruled them prior to 1967 as "occupiers," though also fellow Muslims, the Israeli ouster of the Egyptians could be seen as potentially having a positive effect on their lives. The hope that it might someday lead to self-determination for the Palestinians was real and palpable among the people.

The friendly, smiling children who had gathered around us and our vehicle in Gaza City, Khan Yunis, and Rafah offered no suggestion of the future tragedy and hostility that would result from the years of inertia to come. In retrospect, we all know the seismic changes that have taken place within the Strip in the decades following. It is sad and frustrating to contemplate what might have been. On that summer day of my visit in August 1967 it was in no way a sure thing that continued war and devastation would be the fate of Gaza. Yet it might be said that the Torah has always foreshadowed the future of the Gaza Strip, when Abraham is told that his son Ishmael's "hand shall be against every man, and every man's hand against him" (Genesis 16:12).

Sinai Journal

Tomos Konopasek/Shutterstock.com

To an Orthodox Jew, the image of the Sinai Peninsula conjures up vast stretches of endless sand dunes, mountains, and infrequent oases – essentially a trackless wilderness through which the ancient Israelites trekked during their forty-year journey to the Land of Canaan. I was to discover a different Sinai in 1969–70, when I spent my junior year of college as a student at the Hebrew University of Jerusalem. Despite a fairly heavy course load of nine subjects, I had plenty of time that year to sample life as an Israeli and took full advantage of the opportunities. Of all the activities I participated in, none quite compared in excitement and interest to the university-sponsored tour I took to the Sinai Peninsula during the mid-January intersession.

My friend Lev and I noticed the yellow flyer pinned to the student activity bulletin board located in the Kaplan Building in late December. It described in full detail a six-day trip to be led by guides from the university that would traverse the famed Sinai Peninsula from north to south. The tour would be conducted using semi-open trucks, all provisions would be taken care of, and all we had to bring were personal items, including a sleeping bag. This would not be a luxury bus tour by any means; rather, we would be traveling more off-road, in military style, with personal comfort being of little importance. The trip was scheduled to begin at 2:00 a.m. on a Sunday, when we were instructed to assemble near the university gate to board our assigned truck. Our return to the same location was expected early the following Friday morning.

Lev and I signed up almost immediately on the day the notice appeared, as did three or four of our other friends. All told, sixty students participated, representing seven nationalities – a true foreign legion. None of the student participants had ever been to Sinai before except for me, and my visit three years earlier had consisted of spending several hours on a single day's visit to El Arish in the far north of the peninsula. On this trip, we would be traveling the length and breadth of the famed territory, a detailed survey covering almost all the critical sites.

I waited expectantly for the appointed start date, assembling my required gear and supplies. On the Saturday night before our departure I had difficulty sleeping; I set the alarm for just after midnight, but I hardly slept a wink. I made my way to the designated site, arriving there forty minutes prior to the 2:00 a.m. departure time. As the minutes passed, I realized Lev was nowhere to be found. I located one of our guides and told him my friend had not shown up yet.

"We'll give him an extra fifteen minutes to arrive but no more. We're on a schedule, you know!"

Sadly, Lev, his alarm clock failing him, did not appear, and the three trucks roared off in the dark without him. I was disappointed at not having a close friend on the trip, but the sense of adventure soon overtook me, and I fell asleep in my place at the end of the bench near the back of the truck.

During the first leg of our tour we drove eight hours straight, toward the northern Egyptian desert. We traveled southwest from Jerusalem through Bethlehem, Hebron, and Be'er Sheva, through the Negev, and then west into Sinai and Egypt proper. It wasn't so much a matter of the sheer mileage we would be traveling, but the fascinating and sometimes forbidding terrain we would be passing through during our trip that was going to be so memorable.

I awoke with the rising sun at about 7:00 a.m. Situated as I was at the back of the truck, I had been separated from the outside desert winds by a canvas flap that I could move whenever I wanted a glimpse of the exterior. The vista was unchanging – sand dunes with an occasional disabled vehicle off to the side of the narrow two-lane road we were crossing. Our guide told us we would be stopping for some refreshments at about 9:00 a.m.

At the appointed time, the trucks pulled up along the side of a dusty road. I jumped onto the shoulder along with my twenty-odd fellow passengers. A small mirror was screwed onto the back of the truck, and I was shocked by my reflection. Though I had presumed that I was sheltered from the desert by the heavy canvas that enclosed us in the truck, my hair had turned from its normal dark brown to a light, sandy color in the course of the six hours of exposure to Sinai conditions. In the days to come, we would discover just how penetrating desert sand is and how thankless would be any effort to avoid sand getting into every object of clothing (as well as body parts and even food).

Following a fifteen-minute pit stop, we continued on to the site of an abandoned Egyptian dam project, originally funded by Soviet aid. The plan had been to develop a water irrigation project to rival what Israel was doing "next door" in the Negev, transforming desert land into fruitful, arable territory. The Egyptians under President Nasser were not as successful as their neighbors, and we saw that their efforts had been literally swallowed up by the timeless desert in a matter of several years.

That evening, we camped at the southernmost point of the desert sector, Sinai being divided roughly into three sections:

Saharan-type desert in the north, wilderness in the middle, and an extensive mountain range in the south. The mountains tapered off into a narrow coastal plain where the famous port city of Sharm El Sheikh was located.

As the sun set in the west, we gathered around a large campfire where we ate a hearty meal of bread and flavorful cholent. After dinner, we spread our sleeping gear around the fire, leaving room for everyone to maneuver in the dark. The desert night was cold and each of us had a quick lesson on how to handle all personal needs in the desert: use a flashlight, call out ahead of time, and walk at least twenty paces from the nearest known sleeping bag before taking care of business! Not unexpectedly, I fell asleep as soon as my head hit the ground. It had been a long day, and the total stillness of the desert night did not distract us as much as one might have thought.

The sun rose early on day two in the Sinai, a sun that was unhindered by clouds. As cold as it had been the previous night, the air at seven in the morning could only be described as stiflingly hot. We boarded our trucks quickly and soon entered the midsection of the peninsula, marked by the appearance of small, gnarled bushes growing randomly in clumps along the side of the road. On board the trucks, we began to familiarize ourselves with our fellow passengers and also discovered some surprises on board. Apparently, my truck was carrying a large supply of citrus fruits – oranges and grapefruits, primarily – and a hard salami, in the familiar shape of a policeman's nightstick. These food items were stored beneath the benches on which we sat. As we progressed south, we would learn to sample some of these supplies and, most importantly, use them as barter items when dealing with the indigenous Bedouin peoples we encountered.

That morning, we drove for about four hours in a southerly direction. Our immediate objective was a famous oasis to the southwest named Wadi Feiran. The term *wadi* refers to a dry river bed that during the short rainy season in the region carries a sometimes devastating torrent of water. For the vast majority of the year, all plant life depends on any precious moisture that it saved from these floodwaters. When we finally arrived, we were shocked by the size of the oasis and concluded that the volume of water that flowed through Wadi Feiran had to be enormous indeed, since the oasis that formed around it contained literally hundreds of flourishing date palm trees. It was a veritable paradise in the middle of a vast wilderness. Historically, it served as the most important civilized outpost to travelers passing through this arid region – from the Israelites of biblical times through Lawrence of Arabia to adventurous university students. We spent the better part of the day exploring the oasis, riding camels, and interacting with the Bedouins who called the *wadi* their home.

At about four in the afternoon, we headed into the mountains of Sinai just to the southeast of the oasis. Our route wound its way gradually upward through a series of narrowing valleys surrounded on all sides by peaks reaching as high as nine thousand feet. Steep cliffs of solidified lava towered above us as we continued for almost an hour toward the thousand-year-old village of Santa Katerina. Here, we would spend the night at the foot of the mountain traditionally believed to be Mount Sinai or, as the Arabs called it, Jebel Musa (the Mountain of Moses). No one knows for sure which of the many peaks in the area is in fact the mountain on which the Jews received the Torah, although it is believed not to have been the tallest.

Over the centuries, a rough-hewn "staircase," composed of 3,700 steps, was carved into the side of a mountain near a monastery in Santa Katerina, leading to a summit from which one can view a lower peak believed to be Mount Sinai (elevation 7,400 feet). Our tour guides informed us that in the evening we would be camping near the base of the staircase in preparation for a 3:00 a.m. ascent to the summit.

An early dinner was planned which, to our initial surprise and pleasure, consisted of cholent once again. Upon placing the first morsels into my mouth, I learned another lesson about desert travel. As I chewed the warm stew, I heard and felt the unmistakable crunch of grains of sand in my mouth. I spat out the cholent, as did several of my companions. It became clear that sand had infiltrated either our food supplies or the utensils in which the food was reheated. In either case, I lost my appetite immediately and decided to forego this and future cooked meals on the trip. However, we still had four days to go, so I had to come up with alternatives. I remembered the large volume of citrus fruits on board the trucks, grabbed an orange and a grapefruit, and that became dinner.

When bedtime came at about 8:30, we spread out our sleeping bags on a wide, rocky ledge at the base of the "staircase" with the clear starlit sky as our canopy. Never before had I seen the constellations of the Tropic of Cancer that run through the Sinai skies in such precise detail. This was truly one of nature's finest planetaria! From the brightness of the winter heavens above and the anticipation of our early morning ascent, we all had trouble falling asleep on this, our second night in Sinai.

It seemed as if I had just fallen asleep when one of the guides gently shook me awake.

"Time to get ready for the climb!"

It was 2:45 a.m. We all packed up our gear, loaded our bags onto the truck, and headed for the stone pathway to the top. It would take us just over three hours to reach the summit. It was not an easy climb because of the rough nature of the path; every step had to be taken carefully in the early morning shadows. Flashlights were essential, but in time, the sky lightened. Our plan was to reach the summit by sunrise. Once at the top, our group spread out on a flat stretch of rock and looked out to the east as the sun peeked out above Mount Sinai some three hundred feet below us in the distance. The view of the mountain was remarkable, the moment in time unforgettable. We lingered at the spot for only a couple of minutes, as we wanted to begin our descent before the full heat of the day was upon us.

The descent was more difficult than the ascent had been, but by 10:30 we were back in Santa Katerina. As a child I had read all of the *Believe It or Not* books by Robert Ripley, and I recalled an item he had recorded of a monastery called Santa Katerina where the monks followed a rather strange burial practice. Apparently, there were only six plots available at any one time in the monastery cemetery. Once a seventh monk died, the earliest monk to have been buried there was disinterred to make room for the new "occupant." This practice had been taking place for centuries. As Greek Orthodox Christians apparently don't dispose of the relics of their deceased, the monks of Santa Katerina designated a room in the monastery where the skulls and femurs of deceased monks were kept. I did not make the association at first of this *Believe It or Not* story with the monastery in front of me, until one of the French travelers confirmed to me that this was indeed the location of that macabre room filled with remains dating back centuries. I didn't enter the room, but I did make use of their facilities and must point out that the sanitation appeared centuries old as well!

At 2:00 p.m. we resumed our travels, this time descending from the mountain region toward the coastal strip and Sharm El Sheikh. Along the way we stopped for gas at one of the few available depots. To our surprise, a solitary Bedouin jumped on board and sat down opposite me at the back of our truck. Apparently, he had cleared his hitch ride with our guides and was heading for an intersection outside of Sharm. Since this was a trip of nearly five hours, I was soon interacting with our Arab companion, though I spoke little Arabic and he no English. I offered him an orange that he gladly accepted. His smile showed me he had never been to a dentist; though he was probably in his late twenties, he was already missing at least eight teeth. He cut up his orange neatly with the help of a small but functional knife. Hesitatingly,

I reached beneath my seat and brought forth the wrinkled hard salami hidden there. The Bedouin's eyes lit up at the sight of the savory cured beef truncheon in my hand. I offered him the meat and he cut off several slices without any difficulty. He devoured the tasty snack with relish despite his dental handicap. Well fed, our Arab passenger dozed off. On reaching his destination, he descended from the truck, clutching the remainder of the salami that we, by consensus, had given him as a parting "gift."

Another hour's drive brought us to the outskirts of Sharm El Sheikh and our first view of the waters of the Red Sea. In the waning daylight hours, the coastal plain before us shone in the reflected sunlight as did the turquoise-blue of the water. We drove toward the beach on which we would be camping, descended from the trucks, and spread out our gear. In the distance we could see a large radar station alongside an Israeli naval battery designed to guard the approaches to the famous Straits of Tiran to the east. Our guides suggested we not snap photos of the radar emplacement, and we complied. After dinner, again by campfire, we sang songs, both Hebrew and English, before heading to our sleeping bags and another night under starlit skies. Dinner for me that night consisted of citrus fruit slices – sort of "old" wine served in a "new" way!

Morning fully revealed the beauty of Sharm El Sheikh, particularly the expansive beach on which we had camped the evening before. The colors of the fine-grained sand that surrounded us reflected gleaming minerals of various hues of reds, blues, and gold. Years later, as I examine old photos of this site on the shores of the Red Sea, I'm amazed at the brilliance of that sandy beach before Sharm El Sheikh.

The day's itinerary consisted of following the coast of the peninsula to the northwest. We had reached the southernmost tip of Sinai; our way home would be by way of the road that followed the Suez Canal for half a day before turning northeast once again to the desert zone we had traversed on the first day of our trip. We got an early start toward the westernmost point of the coastal plain and then traveled north along the Gulf of Suez. This route led us toward the Suez Canal 220 miles distant, past famous coastal towns such as Abu Rudeis and Ras Sudr, known Red Sea resort spots frequented by wealthy Egyptians over the centuries.

At the time we traveled on this road it was under the control of the Israel Defense Forces. Taken in 1967, the area we were soon entering opposite the canal was protected by the famous Bar-Lev Line, considered impregnable by most military experts at that time. Sadly, the Yom Kippur War three years later in 1973 would prove otherwise. But at this time, the area was considered safe for organized tours. It was a rare moment in history for a non-military Jewish person to visit this historic and scenic location with any degree of safety. That moment in time lasted for a short six-year window. It cannot be safely traveled today due to radical Islamic fundamentalists and bandits freely roaming the peninsula.

That day, however, we rode up the coast continuously for at least four hours until in the distance we spied the southern terminus of the canal itself and the adjacent port city of Suez. We stopped for a moment at a large, ornate whitewashed compound stretching at least three hundred feet along the canal. This was the winter villa of the late deposed King Farouk of Egypt, known and hated by his people for spending money "like water." Nasser had led a successful coup against him in 1952. It was not known how often, if at all, this last king of Egypt visited his Suez villa.

At this point in our journey, our three trucks were within view of Egyptian military reconnaissance units on the other side of the canal. Accordingly, our drivers quickly turned onto the eastbound road that would lead us back to the desert and ultimately Jerusalem. The border with Israel at that point was only about 120 miles away. Because of the lateness of the hour, however, our guides decided to make arrangements with the military authorities to camp for the night at one of the captured Egyptian air bases that Israel utilized throughout northern Sinai. Our group was exhausted. We had seen and done so much in a short period of time, and we were amenable to getting to our camp area as early as possible.

When we entered the air base compound at Bir Jifjafah in mid-Sinai a little past nightfall, we were happy to be directed by some soldiers to a group of unoccupied barracks, where we unloaded our gear and set up a campfire. I was still loyally eating my citrus diet and an occasional candy bar gifted by a friend. On this night, as on previous nights, our guides handed out several old bolt-action Mauser rifles to those of us who wished to act as "guards" of our campground. The rifles were not loaded, and our guide informed us he had a limited supply of ammunition, but we could "yell for a bullet" if the need arose. (Not exactly a deterrent to unfriendly visitors!) As on the two previous nights, I was assigned the job of toting one of these ancient firearms; it got to be a habit, and I ended up riding "shotgun" with the unloaded piece the next day during our ride home to Jerusalem.

We lingered a bit longer that last night in Sinai in front of the campfire, surrounded by those friendly and brave defenders of Israel. Though we were not very far from Cairo on one side and Jerusalem on the other, we knew we had been truly privileged to have visited and viewed the Sinai during a time of peace. As the ancients and moderns who crossed its vast wastes drank from its oases replete with dates and cool water, climbed its high craggy mountains, and witnessed miracles, we felt the enormity of this land between two gulfs.

The next morning, we arose at 7:00 a.m. and were soon on our way through the desert toward the border with Israel. By late afternoon, our trucks pulled up to the gate at the university in Givat Ram. Later in my room, I stepped on the scale to discover that in five days in Sinai (on essentially a fresh fruit diet), I had lost seven pounds. A quick look in the bathroom mirror showed that I had also brought home to Jerusalem a sizeable amount of Sinai sand, as my hair had turned blonde once again. I couldn't begin to describe to my friend Lev where I had been and what I had seen; I didn't think it appropriate to even ask him what had happened to him on that early morning of our departure. A trip to Sinai such as the one I took that January in 1970 would not (some might say could not) be repeated if I lived a dozen lifetimes. The window of opportunity through which I traveled to this challenging land and sampled its historic mysteries was a narrow one indeed. Sadly, it may now be closed forever.

A Winter's Ride
Like No Other

Melissa Taub

Back in December 2002, I was assigned to train a team of young
American Jewish athletes who were scheduled to play a series of
"friendly" ice hockey exhibition games in Metula against the Israeli
junior national team. Upon our arrival, we were treated like royalty
by our hosts in this small, quiet border town in northernmost
Israel. We shopped and strolled practically an arm's length from
the border of Israel and Syria, the eyes of Hezbollah watching us
as we watched the Arab enemies going about their business on
their side of the border. As the competition at the Canada Center
played out, I discovered that on our third day in Metula my team
was only scheduled to play a single contest that evening. So, without any advanced planning, I decided to get into my rental vehicle
and drive wherever my fancy took me. With a general knowledge

of the geography of northern Israel, no map, no cell phone, but with a full tank of gas and a sense of excitement, I pulled out of Metula at 9:30 that morning.

The morning was misty, with gray clouds pointing to the distinct possibility of January showers. I headed south toward Kiryat Shmona, the largest town in the immediate area. From there, Highway 99 emerges as the northernmost east-west Israeli road extending along the border with Syria and ending in the Golan Heights, a mere thirty-six miles from Damascus. Highway 99 ends at the Druze city of Mas'adeh, itself only fifteen miles from Kiryat Shmona.

I drove along Highway 99 unaware of just how close I was to the Syrian border. On previous trips to the Upper Galilee I had visited the Golan, but always as a participant in a tourist group, being shuttled to and from various sites. This time I was going solo and could choose which places to visit. Along this short east-west highway were several spots that interested me in particular: the Nimrod Fortress, Mount Hermon and its ski area, and Mas'adeh itself, as it was one of only four Druze settlements in Israel.

First, I attempted to scale the dizzying heights of the Muslim-era Nimrod Fortress. The structure is actually built on a 2,600-foot-high ridge that is itself part of Mount Hermon. The Nimrod Fortress was constructed by a nephew of Saladin in 1229 to defend the road to Damascus from Crusader armies. The fortress extends over 1,300 feet in length and is five hundred feet in width. I began the ascent to the fortress with some concern as the road was wet, winding, and poorly maintained. About halfway to the castle, a switchback in the road revealed a rockslide about two hundred feet ahead of me. I decided that there was barely enough room for my Mazda CRV to make it past the blockage and would expose my outer wheels to a four-hundred-foot drop to the valley below. I carefully reversed course, realizing what a truly astonishing feat of engineering lay behind the construction of this fortress outlined against the sky above me. A part of me was thrilled that the roadblock had caused me to turn back, as I can't imagine how frightening the descent on this road would have been.

I drove on to the approach road to the ski area several thousand feet above me. On this ascent of Mount Hermon, I ran into a different sort of challenge. It wasn't the steepness of the incline, but the weather conditions that became an insuperable obstacle. The higher I ascended, the lower the outside temperature dropped. The higher altitude also brought more moisture. By the time I reached three thousand feet above sea level (about halfway to the base camp), I found myself in blizzard conditions! The wind-blown snow quickly covered my windows with an icy film. Here I was in Israel, a land known for its sun, beaches, natural aridity, and mild winters, and I needed all my skill as an experienced American Northeasterner to navigate a treacherous, mountainous winter driving situation. Again, unfortunately, retreat was the better part of valor in my situation.

Twenty minutes found me back on Highway 99, nearing the entrance to Druze country. Rainy conditions followed me into Mas'adeh. The village was populated by over three thousand Druze residents; however, all that was visible that wet morning were blurry, gray and black and white images, revealed intermittently through the motion of my windshield wipers. I hoped for better weather as I left Mas'adeh and headed south onto Highway 98 and the northern Golan Heights.

Soon, I saw something that, though common enough in mountainous areas, never ceases to amaze me. A mere twenty minutes and ten miles from the blizzard conditions of Mount Hermon, I emerged into the sun-kissed Golan, bathed in a golden glow, achingly beautiful. The road I was now driving on, Highway 98, is the primary north-south highway in the Golan. It roughly follows the ceasefire line with Syria and, as highways go in Israel, offers one of the true thrill rides of the Middle East as it begins at the Sea of Galilee in the south, at an altitude of six hundred feet below sea level, and terminates near Mas'adeh at a height of over five thousand feet above sea level – all this over a distance of only sixty miles.

Leaving the Hermon region, I drove toward the Israeli border checkpoint of Quneitra, where the UN had established the main observation point between Israel and Syria following the Yom Kippur War in 1973. On this winter morning, the area was particularly bereft of any signs of human activity, both sides hunkering down until warmer weather reached this location. From Quneitra I continued toward Katzrin, the Israeli "capital" of the Golan: a modern town in every respect, benefitting from the most advanced urban planning that Israel could provide. The 6,700 people of Katzrin spend their time producing fine wines and the best olive oil in the world outside of Italy. At the time I passed through, I observed the joint Israeli-Chinese solar electricity project that would create Israel's largest solar power station. My next stop, not far from Katzrin, was the Gamla Nature Reserve. In stark contrast to the futuristic look of Katzrin, Gamla represents Jewish history of the Roman period of occupation in vivid fashion. By now, everyone knows the story of the resistance of the zealots of Masada during the revolt against Titus and his legionaries. Fewer know the story of Gamla, a fortress redoubt that held out for years against the Romans near the Sea of Galilee. The camel-shaped fortress is surrounded on all sides by deep ravines that effectively protected the residents. Today, one can visit the site from which I observed the sea far off in the distant southwest of Gamla.

After returning to the main highway, I completed my trip to the Golan by choosing a direct route on Highway 91 toward the west and the Jordan River. I planned to cross the river at the historic Bnot Ya'akov Bridge about a half hour away. In the course of that time I would have to descend from an average elevation of 2,800 feet in the Golan to sea level near the Jordan River bridge crossing. Highway 91 is a most scenic east-west route that snakes its way in descending stretches of switchbacks, taking you from the dizzying heights on the Golan to the river valley below. As I drove the route that day at about 1 p.m., I saw the Jordan below as a shining strand of bluish water sparkling in the reflected sunlight. Rising to the west beyond the Jordan was a mountain range even taller than the Golan, from which I was descending. This was the Upper Galilee, hiding for the moment the famous, mystical city of Tzfat.

It took me a good half hour to descend to the Jordan, and as I crossed the Bnot Ya'akov Bridge, I sensed the historical importance of the place. I realized I was duplicating the steps of countless biblical and post-biblical characters who had previously entered the land of Canaan at that exact spot. On this winter's day, there were no other drivers around, yet, for a moment, I felt I was not alone. Whether members of the ancient Israelites in the original conquest, Romans traveling the Via Maris to Egypt, or caravans carrying their wares from Damascus to Acre, to name but a few, all were crossing the Jordan River with me that day as I slowly drove over the bridge.

Immediately after crossing the bridge, I began the ascent toward the intersection of Highways 91 and 90, the main Israeli road north to Tzfat, Rosh Pina, and, ultimately, a return to Kiryat Shmona and Metula. I had visited Tzfat (2,900 feet above sea level) on several occasions in the past and counted it as one of my favorite cities in Israel. My love for this home of Jewish mysticism and kabbalah came at a price, however. Driving to and through Tzfat involves curving mountain roads that challenge the best drivers. Many a person has difficulty handling the series of dangerous turns that lead into the city. Others fear the descent from Tzfat to Rosh Pina some 1,600 feet below. As if that weren't sufficient, one would have to descend another nine hundred feet or so to reach Highway 90 in the valley far below. In Tzfat itself I stopped at the Old City to visit some ancient synagogues and to buy some of the beloved colorful Havdalah candles that are family favorites.

As the clock struck three, I realized I had to return to Metula. Accordingly, I began my descent from Tzfat, covering my descent to Highway 90 in record time. The late afternoon sun was hidden from view by the cliffs of the mountains of Naftali and the Manara Cliff. I entered Kiryat Shmona and Metula to its north with plenty of time to join my team for dinner, exhausted but thrilled. According to my calculations, I had successfully traveled through the approximate *nachalot* (territorial allotments) of six tribes of Israel in the course of my winter ride like no other: Gad, Menashe, Zevulun, Issachar, Naftali, and Asher. I was able to traverse this compact territory in about nine hours with stops. Most astonishingly, I had ascended and descended a total of almost fifteen thousand feet in the course of my travels. Needless to say I didn't disclose the details of this trip to my car rental agency!

Jerusalem Tale - High Gear, Low Gear, No Gear!

My friend Lenny is an expert motorcyclist; he's been riding extensively for many years on the Tri-State metropolitan highways. Over the years, he's suggested I learn to ride, so, about two years ago, I finally purchased a shiny blue Buddy 50 cc motor scooter, only to let it languish in my crowded garage in northwest Teaneck. My wife is pleased that I have only occasionally taken it out for a spin on local roads since she knows my reflexes are not what they used to be and there's quite a small margin of error in avoiding a catastrophic accident. I often wonder what might have happened to me had I been successful in obtaining my scooter license back in my college days in Israel when, as a nineteen-year-old, I dedicated several months of study to just such an endeavor.

One of the first things I did upon the start of my junior year of college at the Givat Ram campus of the Hebrew University of Jerusalem in late October 1969 was to inquire how I could obtain a nonresident's license to operate one of those famous Vespa motor scooters so popular in Israel. Back home in New York no one in my crowd had ever considered owning or leasing one, but during previous trips to Israel I had sampled the thrills of being a passenger on one of those Italian gasoline-powered two-wheelers. I was determined to have a scooter at my disposal to avoid reliance on public transit between school and home in Kiryat Shmuel. My parents had no knowledge of my plans, nor was I going to discuss financing arrangements with them until I had my license.

The first step in obtaining my license was to select a driving school where I could find a qualified instructor to teach me how to operate a scooter. After an afternoon spent searching on foot in downtown Jerusalem, I came upon the Ramzor Driving School on Shamai Street. A large, brightly colored sign in Hebrew welcomed novices to sign up for driving lessons for automobiles, motorcycles, and scooters. I sat down at the reception desk, provided my US passport, and answered several introductory questions.

"What type of Israeli license are you interested in getting?" (Motor scooter.)

"Do you have an American motorcycle license?" (No.)

"Are you a tourist or a temporary resident?" (The latter.)

Tzadok was a tanned fellow about thirty years old who sported a brown moustache; he had a very low voice and a rather serious demeanor. After about a minute, he got down to the important details.

"We charge thirty lirot a lesson and we can start any time you want, Sunday through Thursday. We begin at seven in the morning and end at six in the evening."

I immediately followed up with the common American query appropriate to this situation: "And how many lessons do you anticipate it will take for me to pass the test and receive my license?"

At this, Tzadok came to attention and responded without missing a beat. "It's hard to say; in Israel, nobody passes the test on the first try."

I was shocked. I understood that each person had a different skill level that could account for differing results, but the notion that Israeli driving schools were not going to adequately prepare me to pass the test on my first try flew in the face of every American educational course of study I had ever undertaken.

"Well, I'd like to start lessons as soon as possible, and I really hope you instruct me so I pass the test the first time I take it."

Tzadok was silent on that point, but dutifully inscribed my name in his schedule book in three places, handed me a receipt for my thirty lirot paid in advance, and told me to arrive promptly the following day at 4:00 p.m. for my first lesson.

My last class at the Hebrew University the next day ended at 2:00 p.m., and I arrived at Ramzor at the designated time. I was introduced to Chaim, a tall, burly fellow who was to be my instructor for the day. He wore a light jacket and a helmet that looked too small for his large head. He offered me a helmet several sizes too small, but soon found one that was large enough for me. Chaim began the lesson by asking me how much experience I had riding scooters. After I claimed limited technical knowledge and no experience, he started a detailed explanation and demonstration of all aspects of operating a scooter. It was a lot to take in at one time. Ten minutes later, we mounted the scooter; I sat in front with Chaim behind me. It took a bit of time for me to master changing gears, but within a half hour we were on our way. We rode about ten blocks from the school, practicing stops and turns before returning to base.

Over the next two months, I took about seven or eight more lessons with Chaim, each time riding farther than before. Most notably, we rode south from Jerusalem on Derech Beit Lechem to Rachel's Tomb in Bethlehem, with me "at the wheel" and Chaim on the back. The route was hilly and twisting – not an easy trip at all, but memorably picturesque. I managed to do a credible job of driving and arrived back at Shamai Street all smiles.

"Chaim, I'd like to schedule my test for mid-January if possible; I think I'm ready."

Chaim didn't answer at first. Inside the office, he and Tzadok conferred for a minute or two and then advised me to take more lessons. I demurred.

"Please arrange for the test; after all, I'm only here until August. If I don't get my license soon, it won't be worth getting it at all!"

Accordingly, on a bright, sunny January morning at 8:00 a.m. I appeared at the midtown Jerusalem police station on Jaffa Street where I understood the driving test was to be administered. I had driven to the test site from Ramzor with Chaim at the controls as required. After processing some required paperwork, each of the sixteen examinees was instructed to board his bike for the start of the test. I, of course, had never been on the scooter solo at any time during the prep period. Once on board there was a pause during which time we heard the roar of a large Harley-Davidson motorcycle that appeared as if by magic from behind the parking area in which we were gathered. Straddling the Harley was a leather-jacketed Israeli police lieutenant wearing reflective sunglasses, who could have doubled as Marlon Brando in *The Wild One*. For some reason he was in a foul mood. He barked instructions at us in Hebrew; I caught only a few of the officer's words, hardly a promising sign for what was to come on the test itself. Unclear as to what exactly was required of me, I soon found myself following the lieutenant and the other fifteen candidates out of the parking lot, onto busy Jaffa Street and up King George toward the German Colony on Emek Refaim and the old train station complex. Traversing the route from the police station to the train station was a two-mile adventure for the novice riders and a challenge as well for the unlucky pedestrians who happened to cross our paths that January day. As we speedily passed by, many an early shopper frantically ran across the intersections at some risk to their lives, dropping bags of newly purchased produce in the process.

I picked my way through oranges, bananas, and apples haphazardly strewn across my path as I frantically steered my Vespa toward the objective. The "head" of our column was out of sight by now and it was only through my familiarity with the route to the train station that I managed to arrive at the examination site. Miraculously I was only five minutes late. The lieutenant had stopped, gotten off his bike, and was instructing several riders through a series of turns at the far end of the course. He didn't ask anyone for identification and to this day I have no idea how or if he knew one person from the other. Soon, I was instructed to stop, start, turn, and perform figure eights with my scooter, an exam of no more than five minutes, following which we were instructed to return to the police station to receive our verdicts.

At about 10:30, we were called to form a line at the licensing window. Just before me in line stood a tall, slender twenty-year-old prototypical Sabra with dark hair and a friendly smile. I had observed him going through the drills on his bike and, at least in my opinion, he seemed in flawless control of his vehicle. Soon, his name was called and he stepped to the window. He looked down at the paper he was handed and made a sound that was impossible to reproduce. He turned to me, tears streaming from his eyes. "Four times I've taken this test...four times!" he said in Hebrew.

I hesitated before approaching the window, any hope of passing vanishing in that instant. I stood immobile. But others behind me on line pushed me forward. I could delay no longer. I gave my name to the clerk and he passed me a yellow form across the counter. I peered at the paper and saw that it contained only four simple words. On one line it stated in Hebrew: "*nichshal*" (failed). Beneath that line were lightly penciled the fateful words "*tzarich yoter imun*" (needs more practice). What could I say at this point? Had I actually contemplated a different outcome?

I declined Chaim's offer to ride back to Shamai Street. I told him I'd have to think about taking more lessons with Ramzor. In the ensuing days, I thought hard about it. The licensing game seemed stacked against me and, ultimately, by failing to obtain my motor scooter license that January day in Jerusalem I had probably saved myself and my parents a lot of future grief, not to mention a good many lirot! I informed the school by phone that I was giving up my quest for the elusive license. I did, however, pray that time number five would do the trick for my young Israeli co-applicant. When I learned sometime later that the licensing official at the police station happened to have been the brother-in-law of Chaim, my Ramzor instructor, I finally realized how stacked against me the odds of obtaining my license truly had been!

The Amazing Mrs. Webster

American Jews of my generation have been truly blessed by having the opportunity to visit and live in a united Israel and, more particularly, a united Jerusalem, for much of our lifetimes. Over the years, in my several dozen visits to Israel, I have met many extraordinary people, some world famous and others unknown to more than a handful. In reflecting on my time in Israel, I realized that I have long been remiss in not recognizing one particular person, Dina Solte Webster, who welcomed me into her home when I first visited Israel many years ago. Her story is worth recording for multiple reasons. She not only opened Jerusalem's many secrets and joys to me, but, as I discovered many years later, she had also played a pivotal role in the early support of Orthodox Jewish life and education in New Jersey long before emigrating to Israel in 1956.

I was very lucky to be invited to fly to Israel with my uncle Alex for a three-week trip in July 1967. My uncle was engaged in charitable work outside Jerusalem, while I was scheduled to spend my time in Jerusalem itself. As I was only seventeen years old and had recently graduated from high school in New York, I had little experience of being on my own in a foreign land. Luckily, my sister Judy was living in Jerusalem that year, and she arranged for me to share a rented room in an apartment centrally located in the Kiryat Shmuel neighborhood of West Jerusalem. The room in question was being rented for the school year to an American college student attending the Hebrew University. The owner of the apartment, an elderly immigrant from New Jersey named Dina Webster, occupied the rest of the comfortable ground-floor apartment.

Mrs. Webster was the first person to greet me when I arrived in Jerusalem. She was a short woman with snowy white hair. Despite her age, she had the clearest blue eyes I had ever seen. She welcomed me in Yiddish-accented English to stay in her apartment "as long as you vant." Her accent seemed strange, since I later found out she had lived in America for over fifty years. As we got to know each other, she offered to cook meals for me, but I politely declined. I wanted to sample all the food Jerusalem had to offer – as a Diaspora Jew, I relished the opportunity to eat in numerous places throughout the Land knowing that the food was kosher. So I wasn't very interested in Mrs. Webster's offer.

Every Thursday evening, Mrs. Webster prepared to walk to the Machane Yehuda market to do her weekly Shabbat shopping. She took two empty canvas bags with her, and after an hour or two of bargaining, she returned lugging the bags, now heavy with the packages she had acquired. When you consider Mrs. Webster was nearly eighty-four years old at that time, her weekly shopping trips were nothing short of amazing. I accompanied her on one of these trips and can attest to the weight of the bags stuffed with the delicacies of the market.

Over my stay in Jerusalem, I learned how Mrs. Webster had barely escaped death at the hands of the Jordanian Army weeks earlier when an artillery shell scored a direct hit on her bathroom wall. The shell had, miraculously, failed to detonate. She proudly pointed out the exact spot above the commode near the bathtub where the shell had struck. The damaged wall had been plastered over, and you really had to use your imagination to recreate the scene she described, but the thought of it was absolutely unnerving.

My three weeks in Jerusalem passed quickly, and I sadly bade farewell to the city and to Mrs. Webster. However, my experience with her that summer led me to revisit her the next summer when, as a sophomore in college, I spent eight weeks in Israel. I met her great-grandchildren, themselves teenagers, and toured extensively with her family.

When I was accepted to the Hebrew University for my junior year (1969–70), it felt quite natural to call Mrs. Webster and ask if I could rent the room I had stayed in on my first trip two years before. She agreed without hesitation, and so I called 11 Rechov HaAri my home for that year of growth and education. The seasons came and went too rapidly that final school year in Jerusalem: the autumn of Succoth; the winter of cold, clouds, and coveted rain showers; the spring of warming winds and the festive Yom Ha'atzmaut celebrations; and, finally, the summer of hot days and cooler mountain breezes.

During the course of my stay, I developed a great respect for Mrs. Webster's indomitable spirit, her strength of character, and will to persevere that led her to make aliyah at seventy-four, an age when many are winding down their lives. The calendar sadly marched on without pause, and I reluctantly made my plans to return to the United States. I simply was not brave enough to do what I should have done – call my folks and tell them I wasn't coming home, but staying in Jerusalem. As I said my farewell to Mrs. Webster, I sensed I would not likely see her again. She was eighty-eight by then, and I was on my way to higher education in the States. I am sure I wiped away a tear or two as my *sherut* taxi drove down Rambam Street on the way to Highway 1 and the road to the airport.

In early 1971, I received a phone call from Mrs. Webster's great-granddaughter informing me that Mrs. Webster had passed away peacefully in Jerusalem, just shy of her eighty-ninth birthday. I was saddened to hear the news. I vowed to myself at the time that I would try to piece together all the facts I could find about this special "pioneer" woman and tell her story. Ironically, I was to discover that I knew much more about her than I realized, and that circumstances would bring me to live in a Jewish community that owed much to her philanthropy. As happened in the Torah with the story of Joseph and Pharaoh's wine steward, I too "forgot" Mrs. Webster and "didn't remember her." Now, after all these years, I present her life, that of a strong Jewish woman of valor.

Dina Solte Webster was born in Russian Poland, in Bialystok, in 1882. She immigrated to America around 1902, and by 1904, was living in the Yorkville section of Manhattan with her husband Samuel Solte. That year she gave birth to her only child, a son named Charles. By 1910, her life had changed significantly. She and Samuel divorced, and Dina faced the challenge of raising her young son on her own. And so, she embarked on an ambitious plan to create a life for herself and Charles outside of New York City.

Around 1920, she and Charles moved to Paterson in northern New Jersey, then home to a vibrant Jewish community of several thousand. There were many people in Paterson who hailed from the same region of Poland where Dina was from, so she found the transition to be an easy one. Paterson was a hub of textile manufacturers at the time, and many Jews found employment in this industry. In this regard Dina was no different from her neighbors. But she had bigger dreams than most. Through hard work, good luck, and imagination, within several years Dina succeeded in opening a two-story department store called the Junior Shop on a busy corner in downtown Paterson. Her thriving business provided her with economic stability and she became a well-regarded member of the Jewish community. On the personal side, Charles attended Yeshiva College when it opened in the late 1920s, and in 1928 married Sonia Kaplan of Brooklyn. The following year brought the birth of their son, Milton. As far as Dina was concerned, by this time, she had fulfilled all of her life's dreams and she was content.

She remained so for several years. Sadly, however, bad times were ahead. Just as Dina – and all of Paterson – was adjusting to the economic rigors of the Great Depression, a tragedy of mammoth proportions struck her small family: On a clear April night in 1934, Charles, Sonia, and Milton were returning from a family outing to New York City. They were driving on a country road near Paterson when one of their car tires blew out. Charles drove the car onto the narrow shoulder of the road, got out, and prepared to change the front tire on the driver's side. Sonia and Milton, then five, stayed in the car. Charles had nearly completed the exchange when a roadster came speeding down the lane. The inattentive driver did not see Charles and struck and killed him instantly. Dina was shattered by the death of her only child and never fully recovered. As is the norm in such situations, she became closely involved in her grandson Milton's life and education.

Rather than burying herself in mourning Charles, Dina became more and more involved in Jewish communal life in North Jersey. Over the next fifteen years, Dina contributed generously to the Talmud Torah of Paterson, the fledgling Yavneh Academy (established in 1942), and several regional synagogues. Numerous libraries were dedicated to the memory of Charles Solte and annual memorial tributes were made to Charles in the Yeshiva College *Masmid* Yearbook. Dina donated and dedicated the gates of the Bialystoker Synagogue cemetery in Hawthorne, New Jersey, in Charles's memory. It is almost impossible to find a Jewish charity in the Passaic-Bergen county region during those years to which Dina Solte did not contribute. Finally, with the establishment of the State of Israel in 1948, Dina, along with her second husband, Joseph Webster, gave up her comfortable life in New Jersey to make aliyah and realize the dream of building modern Israel.

Dina Solte Webster's biography is probably not a unique one among immigrant American Jews, but it is instructive nonetheless. This notable Jewish woman possessed and showed an indestructible drive to survive and flourish in a world where there were no "free rides." She faced many triumphs, but tragedies as well, and she somehow managed to come out stronger from the experience. In going through some of my papers recently in preparation for upcoming house renovations, I came across the following long-forgotten note and receipt, which Mrs. Webster received from Yeshivat HaKotel a few months before I departed for home in 1970:

21 Shevat, 5730

Dearest blessings and peace,

We had a wonderful and encouraging feeling participating with you in our recent meeting on Motzaei Shabbat, which was organized by the chapter of western supporters of the yeshiva held in the Old City.

The participants showed themselves to be role models in the realms of *tzedakah* and *chesed*. Many thanks for your contribution in support of the yeshiva and its institutions. We note your gift is being made in honor of Joseph Rotenberg. May God reward you according to your deeds; may God bless you from Zion and may you gaze upon the goodness of Jerusalem, all the days of your life.

– Menahel Hayeshiva (yeshiva manager)

It was clearly unnecessary for Mrs. Webster to make a donation to charity in my name, but that's just the type of person she was. She expressed her feelings of sadness and joy, of loss and kinship by giving *tzedakah* freely and generously.

Rest in peace, Mrs. Webster.

PART II
AROUND THE WORLD

A Letter from Lisbon

Gubin Yury/Shutterstock.com

Luc Kohnen/Shutterstock.com

In the past, millions of people have braved wind-tossed crossings to start new lives on one shore or another. The Atlantic Ocean has for centuries served as a massive communication link between continents. Its waves lap upon North and South America, Africa, Europe, and the Polar regions. Today, of course, planes cross the watery wastes in hours. But throughout history, some objects have taken much too long to make the crossing. This story is about one such case.

My father Maurice was a twenty-six-year-old private assigned to a Belgian infantry unit in northern France in May 1940 when war swarmed across western Europe like a plague of locusts, covering the victim nations over a period of hours, days, and weeks. As one would expect, those individuals more firmly established in their prewar lives were often least likely to possess the mobility to drop everything and run – the natural response to life-threatening action by an enemy bent on conquest. The elderly, small children, and young families were tragically in the majority of those unable or unwilling to flee.

With only the most basic training, Maurice was tasked with defending his country against elite German troops. Two weeks into the conflict, he awoke to his commanding officer informing him that the Belgian government had capitulated to the Germans and that all Belgian combatants were free to leave. It was 6:00 a.m. on May 24, and Maurice was stationed in the town of Abbeville, not far from the English Channel Coast. It was rumored that elements of the VII Panzer Corps were in the vicinity, so Maurice and some of his compatriots headed south on foot. It turned out to be a fateful decision to travel in that direction, as Panzer units arrived in Abbeville at 6:00 that evening. At that point, in a mysterious move still unclear today, the Germans stopped their advance. This allowed some three hundred thousand Allied troops to escape by ship from the French port of Dunkerque while the Germans dawdled.

Maurice did not dawdle. After barely escaping the Germans, he mapped out a plan to outrun the enemy (who were not, in fact, pursuing him) and headed in a southwesterly direction toward the Atlantic ports of Bordeaux and Bayonne-Biarritz. On foot, the trip of five hundred kilometers (three hundred miles) would take him more than a month, what with the narrow roads crowded with thousands of refugees heading south with him. While not advancing on the ground, the Germans harried the civilians with unending dive-bomber attacks; the Stukas controlled the skies over France and terrorized the many who were exposed on those roads.

In light of these conditions, Maurice decided to buy a bicycle to speed up his journey south. After a day of searching, he lucked out when a farmer offered to part with an extra bike he wished to convert into cash. Maurice mounted his new transport and set out the next morning in the direction of Tours.

In these early, chaotic days of the war, the Germans, though successful from a battlefield perspective, could hardly be said to "control" the lands they had conquered. They might have commanded important crossroads and accepted the surrender of combatant armies, but much of the infrastructure they had attempted to destroy remained in place for at least several months before the occupation began in earnest. Thus, Maurice, while in the French countryside, was able to communicate with his family in Antwerp as he made his way south. His mother instructed him, in no uncertain terms, not to return to Belgium. She sensed the danger even though she was unaware of the full scope of the destruction that ultimately awaited her. She knew Maurice's older brother Jos had arrived safely with his young wife in America in 1939, and that her eldest son Jack had left Antwerp as well, and she hoped he too would ultimately escape to America. Maurice heeded his mother's words and continued to advance toward the Atlantic coast of France.

After two weeks of hard pedaling, Maurice arrived at the bustling port of Bayonne. His first priorities were to find lodging and kosher food. The Jewish population of Bayonne totaled a mere three hundred souls, but that number had been hugely augmented by hundreds of French and Belgian refugees. Maurice was able to join a network of fellow escapees from Antwerp whom he found at the local synagogue. Several of the new arrivals had heard there was work available at the docks, since most of the young French workers had gone to the front to defend France. Maurice headed down to the busy wharves and soon found work toting forty-kilo (eighty-eight pound) sacks from cargo ships into adjacent warehouses. After two days of that backbreaking work, Maurice convinced the foreman that he had "office" experience and was assigned the job of counting the sacks that others carried into the storeroom. That daring move earned him several more francs a week in wages, and probably saved him from lifelong damage to his back.

After two weeks in Bayonne, it became clear that western France would not remain a haven for Jewish refugees for long. Maurice began to pay closer attention to the varied ships that came to the harbor, ships that were merely stopping at Bayonne and picking up supplies and fuel before continuing on to exotic

North African locations: Morocco, Agadir, Mogador, Casablanca, Marrakesh. Maurice had only read about these places in books, but they now appeared to be his only option to escape the continent. Having accumulated the steerage fare for one such trawler, one early morning in May, Maurice boarded the ship for North Africa and the mysteries of Morocco.

Eight days later, Maurice stepped ashore at Casablanca, the fabled port of intrigue and spies. All he knew of the city was from books and movies. The casbah, the Berber ruins, the myriad languages spoken in the *souq*, and the international flavor all made this city a unique travel destination at any time. In wartime, however, as a French colony, the city mirrored the country – the Moroccan populace was rapidly beginning to choose sides between those happy to collaborate with the Germans and those loyal to the "Free French."

Maurice inquired at the docks about where he might find a synagogue or, failing that, any representative of the local Jewish community. He was happy to discover that the main synagogue was just a short distance from the port area, and he immediately started in that direction. Within ten minutes he stood before a two-story building with a weathered sign in front that read: "Communauté des Juifs de Casablanca." The door was open and a tanned older man sat at a desk cluttered with papers. Maurice introduced himself, speaking in the French in which every Belgian was fluent. Eduardo Sasson was the director of the Jewish community of Casablanca, and he welcomed Maurice warmly. He apprised him of the situation locally for Belgian Jews and suggested he make the acquaintance of a certain Alphonso Sabah, who was a useful contact for a refugee such as Maurice. Sabah was a Jewish merchant from Tangier who was well connected at the highest levels of the Moroccan government. If anyone could assist Maurice, he would be the man. Sasson wrote a short note of introduction and handed it to Maurice, along with an address and phone number where Maurice could locate Sabah.

That evening, Maurice met with Sabah and they immediately bonded in those mysterious ways that one reads about in stories. Sabah, thirty-five years old, handsome, and a devoted Zionistic leader of the Moroccan Sephardic Jewish community, and Maurice, an Ashkenazic refugee on the run, from a family rooted in eastern European traditions, saw something in each other that resonated, and this chance meeting would flourish into a lifelong friendship.

"Maurice, you know we need educated Jews such as yourself here in French Morocco at this perilous time to help administer the country and assist our community," Sabah told him. "You may not be aware that while the national language is Arabic, the rulers of Morocco are Berbers, not Arabs, and our community is highly regarded by the king and his prime minister, El-Glaoui, the pasha of Marrakesh. Luckily, I am meeting tomorrow with the pasha and his captain of the guard. I'm willing to take you to this audience and introduce you to these important people. It would be useful for you to meet them."

Maurice didn't know what to say. He had hardly a couple of francs in his pocket and his clothing was threadbare. He didn't speak for a moment.

"I was told by my brothers that they were trying to arrange for a visa for me to the United States, which would be waiting for me in Lisbon," Maurice explained. "If you could help me contact them, I would be much obliged. And, of course, I would like to accompany you to meet the pasha!"

"You will stay at my house this evening," Sabah offered. "Meanwhile, here is some money so you can get something to eat."

The next morning after prayers, Maurice left with Sabah for the three-hour drive to Marrakesh and the foothills of the snow-capped Atlas Mountains. The weather was clear, the terrain alternating desert vistas and shrub-filled wilderness landscapes. If Casablanca was mysterious to a European, Marrakesh was stepping back into another time altogether.

This was a city of caravan routes, of oases and French Foreign Legionnaires; the city's minarets crowded the sky and dwarfed the ancient Jewish ghetto or *mellah*. The meeting with the pasha was scheduled for 3:00 in the afternoon, so Maurice had about two hours to wander the narrow streets of the Jewish Quarter and soak in the atmosphere. He felt transported back centuries in time when he heard the distinctive Muslim call to prayer of the muezzin from high above the city. He had to suppress the urge to run and hide from invisible assailants brandishing scimitars and knives.

Maurice met Sabah at the appointed time, and they entered the pasha's palatial offices together. After a brief security check, they were ushered into the office of the pasha's chief lieutenant, who embraced Sabah warmly.

"And who is this young man?" the official asked.

"He is the Belgian I told you about last night. He could be useful to us. Could you appoint him some governmental task so he will stay with us and not flee to America?"

"Young man, Alphonso here asked me to confirm with our connections in Lisbon whether you are on the list for a US visa. Our sources confirm that you are!"

Maurice was more than pleased.

"But that doesn't mean you have to go; if you agree to remain here, we could provide you with a place to stay, an easy job, and even a nice Jewish girl if you desire."

Maurice was flattered, but he did not readily accept the Moroccan's offer.

"I really want to join my brothers in the United States as soon as I can."

The Moroccan seemed disappointed by Maurice's response, but, after a momentary sigh, he changed the subject.

"Let's go in to see El-Glaoui."

They entered a large hall at the end of which stood a throne-like structure adorned with several large cushions. Atop one of the cushions sat the pasha in full Turkish-era dress.

He was surrounded by brightly colored wall coverings and guards armed to the teeth. Several veiled ladies sat on a divan behind him. Maurice thought he was on a movie set and expected the French Foreign Legion to burst into the hall at any minute. The pasha signaled for the three men to approach. It took a full minute for them to cross the hall and stand directly before the second most powerful man in all of Morocco.

"Hello, Sabah, my Jewish friend, how are you? Terrible things going on in Paris, *n'est-ce pas*?

"And who is this young man, may I ask?"

"He is a Belgian Jewish refugee; he was in the army and was lucky to escape the Germans."

"It must have been horrible, my boy. I'm glad you were able to survive! You know, we could use a good man like you. You could make a good life among us. We can provide you with everything for a good life. Morocco isn't half bad, you know!" the pasha joked.

Sabah and the lieutenant informed El-Glaoui of Maurice's earlier rejection of the Moroccan offer. The pasha smiled at the news and quickly addressed Maurice for a final time.

"I am, of course, saddened by your decision, but I also respect a man who wishes to reunite with his family. Good luck on your journey!"

The audience with the pasha over, the men withdrew, and Sabah and Maurice returned to Casablanca late that night. The next morning, a Wednesday, Sabah sat with Maurice to discuss how the situation could affect his departure from Morocco to Lisbon. Events locally were moving rapidly, and the collaborationist Vichy French government was sending their pro-German officials to all French colonies (including Morocco) to replace loyalist officials.

"It is necessary for you to leave for Lisbon as soon as possible, Maurice. Once the Vichy take over, you may find yourself interned in a camp by the Moroccan police, or worse, since you are a foreign citizen. I must call my friend in the immigration department to see how we'll get you out on the next boat to Portugal!"

After several phone calls, Sabah told Maurice to gather his few belongings and accompany him to see the chief transit officer in the center of Casablanca. Sabah took Maurice to the entrance of the white masonry building and bade him farewell.

"This is as far as I can safely go," Sabah said. "The building is being watched by unfriendly eyes. I hope we will meet one day in the future when things in the world are not so crazy. Maybe in the Land of Israel!"

Maurice could not adequately express his thanks to his Moroccan friend. He promised to never forget him and that they would meet again.

Soon, Maurice was sitting before the man who would decide whether he would be able to leave Morocco. The director was a man in his fifties, with a tan complexion. A tasseled fez sat on a chair near his desk.

"Remove the hat, Monsieur Maurice," he said, calling him by his first name, "and sit down on the chair, please. You have friends in high places; let me review your papers for a moment."

Maurice waited apprehensively.

"Ah, ah, they seem to be in perfect order! You can be on your way as early as tomorrow. One thing I should like to point out: We have a society in Casablanca that supports widows and orphans, and it is customary for departing visitors to donate some small token to this fund to facilitate departure."

Maurice was not sure what to say or do; he had only the one hundred francs on his person that Sabah had given him, and he had to book passage to get to Lisbon. Did the director think that perhaps Maurice carried Belgian currency of a different sort (diamonds)? Maurice had nothing of the kind in his possession. Finally, he reached into his pocket, pulled out a one-franc coin and placed it into the hand of the stunned director. Maurice quickly scooped up the signed and stamped exit visa, thanked the director, and hurried out of the office.

There was no time to delay, because the new Vichy director

of exit visas was arriving the next day. The only scheduled ship immediately leaving for Lisbon was a Panamanian trawler bound for Portugal carrying a large cargo of bananas. Maurice bought passage, and, at dawn, he boarded the ship for the northward trip of six hundred nautical miles. This trawler had absolutely no passenger amenities and, worse, no food to speak of – just green bananas. By that point Maurice had adapted greatly to his new life "on the run." Accordingly, he devised a plan to convert the inedible into the edible: each night of the eleven-day trip, he would take a bunch of green bananas and place them next to his body, where overnight his body heat would miraculously ripen the bananas enough to make suitable meals to get him through the days at sea. Finally, on a foggy day in August 1940, the trawler pulled in at the port of Lisbon, capital of Portugal, on the Iberian Peninsula.

Lisbon would be home to Maurice for the next three months or so. Communications with the United States were excellent, so Maurice was able to correspond with his brothers, who sent him details regarding his US visa status as well as traveler's checks as needed. The visa process was more complicated than he had anticipated, but finally, by the beginning of November, Maurice had completed all the necessary paperwork. He booked passage for early December 1940 on a ship called the *Serpa Pinta* (the Yellow Snake), a formidable five-decked vessel that ferried more war refugees and allied troops safely across the Atlantic throughout the war years than any other civilian vessel. Before he departed, Maurice decided to do one last thing to assist those he loved who were still captive behind enemy lines. The day before he was to leave, Maurice was walking from his hotel in the Baixa district of Lisbon when he came across a small store selling newspapers and sundries. He entered the store and approached the man who stood behind the main counter.

"Do you sell coffee, sugar, or chocolate?" Maurice asked. "And would you be willing to ship such items to other countries if I pay all the costs?"

The man nodded yes to both questions.

Maurice took out a list he had been preparing for this moment. The list contained the names and addresses of relatives in Belgium as well as more distant relatives in Poland. Even though the war had been raging for some time in the West and even longer in the East, there was hope that at least some of these posted packages would get through. Maurice made a second list of the items he wanted the man to ship. Maurice asked him to prepare such packages and mail them every two weeks. He gave the tobacconist the princely sum of two hundred dollars to cover present and future costs. Maurice had wisely saved a large part of the funds sent to him by his brother in America.

The next day, Maurice boarded the *Serpa Pinto* for the eleven-day voyage to Philadelphia, and though traveling through U-boat infested waters, arrived safely in the United States.

Maurice made a rapid adjustment to life in America. He quickly met the love of his life, married in February 1942, started a diamond-cutting business in Lower Manhattan, and began to raise a large family of daughters, all born while World War II continued to rage. He never forgot those individuals who helped him escape the Holocaust, his adventures in southern France, his Moroccan friend Alfonso Sabah, the pasha of Marrakesh, or even the director of exit visas in Casablanca who requested a "contribution" to the local kitty. The one individual he almost forgot was the Portuguese tobacconist and chocolatier with whom he had arranged to send packages into occupied Europe. Before she was deported to Auschwitz in 1942, Maurice's mother had written him in America that some of their relatives in Poland had told her they were receiving mysterious packages containing chocolate, sugar, and coffee. They had no idea where these desirable packages were coming from, but they were very happy to receive them, as was she. Soon all such communications from relatives in Europe ceased. The Germans had turned their war from military conquest to genocide.

It was early spring 1946, and New York was just starting to throw off the chill of winter. Maurice returned from work one afternoon and stopped at his mailbox to collect the day's mail. Among various bills and notices, he found an oddly marked letter with official-looking stamps. The crumpled letter had several Portuguese stamps affixed and a postmark dated April 5, 1941, alongside the following boldly stamped legend: HELD UP BY THE BRITISH CENSOR IN BERMUDA.

Maurice hurriedly opened the letter that had taken five years to be delivered. As he removed the contents, a piece of paper fluttered to the floor. Maurice retrieved it and read the message that was written in crude English print:

April 4, 1941

Dear Sir,

I am sorry, but I can no longer send packages to your family in Belgium and Poland. Packages are not going through any more. Enclosed is the balance of money that went unused. It is for forty dollars. Good luck!

Sincerely,
Arturo Cabral
Lisbon, Portugal

Maurice took the forty-dollar draft with him to work the next day, framed it that afternoon, and hung it on the wall of his office. He never spent that draft and was daily reminded that in the midst of all the horrors that had taken place during the war, man's humanity toward his fellow man had not completely vanished. It served equally as a reminder to him that he had been so fortunate during the war to have encountered many people – strangers (Jews and non-Jews alike), political and community leaders as well as every-day people – whose acts of selflessness contributed to his survival and to his lifelong belief in the ultimate goodness of mankind.

Homolka Hesitates

GreenArt/Shutterstock.com   Nataliya Arzamasova/Shutterstock.com

Thomas Homolka was an artist of renown. His was not, however, the realm of oil and acrylics, watercolor, and giclée. He couldn't tell the difference between a symphony and a concerto; he knew nothing of architecture, sculpture, or dancing. Homolka had a very special skill that few in his country could match. Thomas Homolka made the best cheesecake in Prague. His cakes were considered the best ever confected in the Czech capital, consecutive award winners for multiple years during the inter-war period. Homolka was particularly known for preparing the most intricate multicolored cakes, which were served in the finest homes in Wenceslas Square. Royalty demanded his cheesecake at state occasions, where wealthy burghers stuffed themselves on his product; he even saw to it that every week, a "run" of inexpensive cheesecakes came out of his ovens on Anenská Street to help feed the less fortunate who craved his creations, if only once a week.

Homolka had few rivals who could match his skill and imagination. He mentored younger bakers whom he hoped could replace him one day. He never married, so had no blood relative to take his place. At times, this bothered him, but he often took so much joy from his work that he scarcely had a moment to be concerned about not having a visible successor. Homolka was a "hands-on" baker – despite his fame, he worked long hours at his store, seeing to it that every cake was prepared to perfection. He kept such long hours tending to his shop that once, when he was invited by the mayor to see the famed Sparta Praha soccer team play, he fell asleep in the stands at Letná Stadium.

As mentioned, Homolka's customers were varied and came from all Czech classes. Of those, his most reliable clients included some of Prague's older residents, in particular two sisters: blond Katya Gruenbaum and brunette Magda Hasek. Each week, the sisters chose Friday afternoon to visit his store and Homolka liked to serve them personally if he could.

"Mr. Homolka," Katya would ask in her soft voice. "Have you any of your delicious cream cheesecakes? My sister and I would just love one."

Katya had been married for ten years when her young physician husband was killed by a British artillery shell while defending the empire in 1915. She'd been widowed for more than twenty years, and her regular visits to Homolka's bakery were part of the weekly shopping routine that helped her keep her sanity, allowing her to temporarily forget the pain and deep-felt loss of her husband. Her sister Magda had never married. She had moved into Katya's spacious apartment upon the death of her brother-in-law, and she accompanied Katya on her weekly visit to Homolka.

"And also your best chocolate cheesecake, please," Magda added.

Homolka was always glad to accommodate these refined ladies if he could. Though they always respectfully referred to him as "Mr. Homolka," he felt comfortable calling them by their first names and they didn't mind. There was a sweetness about them that was most endearing. Week after week he served them, and over time their visits became part of Homolka's routine. Once, when he thought about it, he realized he knew little about the sisters other than their cake preferences. However, one of the workers in his store knew them somewhat better.

"They live close to the square, I believe, a couple of blocks to the south," said Jan, the cashier. "They are Jewish, one is widowed, the other never married. They love our cheesecakes; I can tell you that! You can set your watch by their Friday visits," he added.

Homolka nodded in agreement. "That you can!"

On one particular Friday, the sisters came in to stock up on baked goods and order their regular favorites. When the time came to leave, Katya, burdened with more packages than she could handle, dropped several to the floor. Immediately, a tall, good-looking man with clear blue eyes who had been standing near her jumped to attention.

"May I assist you, Madam?" he said in accented Czech. Without waiting for a reply from Katya, the man bent at the waist, reached down and helped her rearrange her belongings so that they could be more easily carried.

"Thank you," said Katya. "You are so very kind."

"It is nothing, Madam," he replied.

The man held the door open so the sisters could be on their way. Homolka recognized the good Samaritan as Heinrich von Kleist, an Austrian embassy attaché, who was also a regular customer.

"Nice ladies," von Kleist said to no one in particular. "I see them here often."

"Yes, indeed," Homolka agreed. "Two of my most loyal customers, Jewish ladies, very proper ladies."

Von Kleist showed no visible reaction to Homolka's last comment. Under his breath, however, Homolka thought he could hear von Kleist say, "Too bad!"

Storm clouds formed over Prague as the calendar turned to 1937. Czechoslovakia had been a liberal republic since the Treaty of Versailles of 1919, and its people were adjusting to their newly acquired national identity. No longer were the Czech people legally subject to rule from Vienna and Budapest. That didn't mean that forces were not at work to reverse Czech independence. Clearly, Germany, now under the harsh rule of the Nazi Party, had express designs on the Sudetenland in the west and all of Bohemia, Moravia, and Slovakia. Homolka read the daily papers like everyone else and listened to the ominous-sounding radio broadcasts when he could, but he didn't care much for politics and felt he could do little anyway to affect the outcome.

On September 30, 1938, after more than a year of threats and negotiations, England, France, Italy, and Germany agreed in Munich on the cession of the Sudetenland section of Czechoslovakia to Germany. With this agreement, 66 percent of Czechoslovakia's coal, seventy percent of its iron and steel, and 70 percent of its electrical power were given to the Nazi war machine, not to mention the three million ethnic Germans who were included in this handover. The Czech government and its people were helpless to resist this illegal and immoral action. As events would show, the Germans were not interested in any compromises with the Czechs. Only total domination of the small nation by its much larger neighbor would do. And so, the next year, on March 15, 1939, under direct threat of a bombing raid against Prague, Czech president Emil Hácha granted free passage for German troops into and over the Czech borders. From that moment, Czechoslovakia was declared a protectorate of Nazi Germany, whereas it really needed to be protected from that evil nation.

The swift, bloodless conquest of Czechoslovakia in many ways reflected the Czechs' general attitude and culture of peaceful relations with their neighbors. Given the Czechs' desire to live in peace, Germany was able to defeat her neighbor without violence, guerilla warfare, or any popular uprising from the conquered nation. The native population had to get used to Germans taking up residence in Prague, where they began appropriating whatever they wanted. The Germans viewed Prague and the Czech nation as a whole as an efficient workhouse and profit center for the German Reich. In this regard, the German army, the SS, the Gestapo, and the Nazi Party officials all sought to enrich themselves at the expense of the Czech people.

For his purposes, Homolka hardly saw a fall-off in business from these sad political developments. In times of stress, people actually bought more of his pastries and cakes. Any reduction in local business was more than offset by orders from the new occupiers. Almost immediately, though, Homolka noticed that Katya and Magda, among others, stopped coming to the shop on their regular days. He heard about Germany's harsh decrees against Czech citizens of the Jewish faith, but as he didn't have much contact with Jews, he paid little attention to these rumors. Weeks passed and the sisters still did not reappear.

During the early summer, some four months after the occupation began, on a cloudy day just before closing, a woman appeared in the store in Wenceslas Square. She approached the side of the display case and weakly signaled to Homolka to come to her. Homolka advanced toward her, but suddenly stopped when he realized who she was. Katya Gruenbaum's features were so haggard and strained, sharp lines crossed her brow and face. Where previously she had looked attractive, even young for her age, now she was almost unrecognizable and appeared to have aged years since he had last seen her. "How could this have happened?" Homolka thought.

"Mrs. Gruenbaum, Katya, what is the matter? We haven't seen you for weeks. Are you all right? Have you been sick?"

"Can I talk to you in your office, where we can be alone?" Katya asked weakly.

"Sure," he responded. "Jan, take over for me for a minute. I have something I must discuss with Mrs. Gruenbaum. I don't want to be disturbed."

Homolka led Katya to his cluttered office, moving around some boxes to clear space for them to sit down.

"Would you like some tea, something to eat, perhaps?"

"No, thank you," she responded.

"How can I help, Katya?" he asked in as friendly a voice as he could muster.

"Things have been so difficult for us since the Germans came," she began haltingly. "As soon as they arrived, my sister and I attempted to apply for permission to leave our beloved Prague. The Germans don't want us here even though we've lived here peacefully for years as loyal Czech citizens." Tears filled her eyes as she spoke. Homolka had trouble avoiding tears himself.

"What happened when you applied?"

"The Gestapo told us we couldn't file our application until we made 'satisfactory arrangements' with Deutsche Bank and gave them full power of attorney over our property. My sister and I have a little bit of money saved and we own our apartment, but we're not what you'd call wealthy. We have cousins in England who we might be able to live with, but Magda is not well, and" – here she broke down – "I don't know what to do or who to turn to for help."

Homolka placed his hand on Katya's arm in a gesture of support. What could he do to help this poor lady? There didn't appear to be any easy solution to the sisters' problems.

"Mr. Homolka," Katya resumed after drying her tears with her handkerchief, "if only we had some place to hide, outside of the city. We hear the Germans are concentrating on Prague in their efforts against us Jews. Do you know of such a place where we might escape to or hide, or of someone else who might assist us in getting away?"

Homolka, in fact, had a country home in the mountains about sixty miles from Prague, toward the Hungarian border, but he hesitated to tell Katya about it. There was danger in helping Jews under the current conditions.

"Unfortunately, there is little I can do to help you at this time," Homolka answered. "And I know of no one else who can do so. I hope things will get better for you and your sister. Meanwhile, you should make sure you make no trouble for yourselves and follow all that the Germans request. I wouldn't rock the boat if I were you. In time things will improve."

Homolka felt sorry for Katya and her predicament, but he offered little in the way of concrete assistance. He felt somewhat ashamed that he couldn't offer her more hope, something to lift her spirits, but after all, what could he, one person, do?

"Jan," Homolka called out as he led Katya to the front, "see to it that Mrs. Gruenbaum gets whatever she wants from the store at half price, for old times' sake," he added.

Katya for her part left the store feeling worse than she had when she entered it twenty minutes before. She felt numbed by Homolka's remarks as she walked slowly toward her home under the setting sun.

While Homolka had been counseling Katya in his office, another of Homolka's most famous customers had been unable to decide which of three equally scrumptious cheesecakes to purchase.

"Ach, I simply cannot make up my mind which to choose!"

"It's really not that difficult, Doctor," Jan replied. "Take some of each if you'd like."

Jan had been addressing none other than the renowned Prague gastroenterologist Dr. Wilhelm Fessel, who had made a successful medical career out of instructing his patients not to consume the rich Czech cuisine they were used to, particularly cheesecake. He railed against consuming Homolka's delicacies as "a sure path to the grave." Yet he himself could not keep his hands off of Homolka's wares. He hid his addiction well from his patients, but he couldn't keep away from Homolka's bakery for any length of time. Dr. Fessel loved nothing more than a slice of Homolka's cherry cheesecake with a steaming mug of hot Bavarian cocoa.

"I'll follow your advice, Jan, and take all three cakes. Wrap them well, please."

Dr. Fessel hurried out the door and, realizing he was late for his office hours, sped down the street in a southerly direction, barely avoiding collision with Katya Gruenbaum, who had not gotten far down the street.

Katya finally arrived home at the apartment she shared with her sister.

"Is that you, Katya?" Magda asked.

"Yes, it's me."

"Was Homolka of any help?"

"No, he said we shouldn't rock the boat. I'm afraid soon there will be nowhere to turn and no boat left to rock."

Unfortunately, events soon proved Katya prescient. Several more months passed and the Gestapo began to increase their anti-Jewish activity. Random arrests of Jews became a more frequent occurrence in Prague. The SS promulgated regulations prohibiting Czech citizens from assisting their Jewish neighbors in any manner, penalizing violators with imprisonment or worse. Homolka followed all these events without being moved to act. "What could one man do to make a difference?" he asked himself. "Gestures, empty gestures. Staying alive till things get better is the way to go," he concluded.

But then one late winter morning, blaring sirens in Wenceslas Square broadcast a joint Gestapo/SS action several blocks to the south of the store. Jews of all ages and genders were being rounded up from their homes and apartments, driven through the square like cattle, and herded to the main train station, where they were shoved into cars for transport out of Prague to the east.

Homolka normally didn't go outside during these actions, preferring to stay in the kitchen and supervise the baking. On this particular morning, however, he exited the store and stood watching the sad trail of people walking toward the railway station. To his surprise, standing near a jeep parked in the square was none other than von Kleist, clad in the uniform of an SS major, surveying the marchers in silence. After a minute or so, Homolka noticed Katya and her sister walking haltingly along the square, dressed much more shabbily than he had ever seen them, their once blond and brown hair now gray. Homolka wanted to turn away, but he couldn't. A guard brutally menaced Katya with his rifle butt, shouting at her to move more quickly. She stumbled on the cobblestones and only with great difficulty got back on her feet and continued past the bakery without even a backward glance in Homolka's direction. Tears now filled Homolka's eyes and anger his heart as the two now-frail sisters shuffled to their fate without anyone raising a hand in their defense. Homolka suddenly felt sick as he at last realized the depth of his cowardice in the face of the evil being perpetrated in his beloved city. He reentered the bakery with a new resolve and, done for the day by the scene he had witnessed, placed the "Closed" sign in the window.

Spring 1940 brought an early thaw to Prague, and by the end of March the ice on the Vltava River had melted. For weeks, Prague had been filled with news of a big celebration for the fifty-first birthday of the fuehrer, Adolf Hitler. The Nazi governors had requested the finest chefs in Prague to create their specialties to be presented at a spectacular dinner to be held at the Grand Hotel in mid-April. Top German officials were to attend with the hope that this would be a most memorable event. Of course, on such an occasion, desserts must be served, and they must be varied and of the finest quality. In Prague, this meant only one thing: at the top of the dessert menu must sit a Homolka cheesecake. The officials in charge of the festivities personally called on Thomas Homolka to sample several of his more impressive offerings. They chose his cream cheese cheesecake and his chocolate cheesecake as their favorites. As his pièce de résistance, Homolka, however, suggested his royal cherry cheesecake be presented to the table where the highest Nazi dignitaries were to be seated.

"Most appropriate," the German dinner committee agreed.

"Perfect," concurred Homolka. "I'll see you in three weeks."

April 20 soon arrived. The birthday celebration went forward without a hitch. Dignitaries and high-ranking officials filled the large, ornate ballroom. Homolka, himself an invitee, noticed several of his best clients among the prominent guests. There at the dais sat Heinrich von Kleist with his clear blue eyes. Not far away from von Kleist sat Dr. Fessel and his large wife. The doctor was beaming. The four hundred happy guests dined on four delicious courses, fine Bohemian wines, and the best schnapps in Europe. Following the briefest of speeches by a high-ranking SS official, it was finally time for dessert. Homolka, who had been seated among the dinner guests until the soup course, was now in the kitchen supervising the dessert service. At the appointed moment the wait staff emerged onto the ballroom floor wheeling cheesecakes in every direction. Of special importance was the royal cherry cheesecake, which Homolka had personally prepared and baked. It was large enough to feed twenty and arrived at the head table, where it was greeted with applause. By now, however, Homolka was nowhere to be found. He was on his way back to Wenceslas Square, where he locked himself into his office, sat down at his desk, opened the locked drawer, and withdrew the World War I revolver his father had left him as an heirloom.

The next morning's *Prague Post* headline shouted: "Ten Die at State Dinner: Police Suspect Poisoning as Dozens Taken Ill, Seven Critical."

The story underneath gave the grisly details and concluded as follows:

> As a result of losing several top SS and Gestapo officers, the German Occupation government has threatened severe reprisals unless the perpetrators are brought to justice. The exact substance used has not yet been determined, but early speculation points to either arsenic or strychnine as the poison utilized, and cheesecake as the method of delivery.

Iranian Nuclear Fallout -
A Twice-Told Tale

Sergey Goryacheu/Shutterstock.com   EtiAmmos/Shutterstock.com

In the midst of the worldwide concern over the "Bad Deal" con-cocted by the Obama Administration with the mullahs of Iran, it occurred to me that had fate ruled otherwise, the entire issue of Iranian possession of nuclear armaments might possibly have been resolved a long time ago in a much less contentious manner. Accompany me back to the late 1950s for a couple of minutes and I'll explain what I mean.

It was October 1959 in New York City, after the High Holidays and Succoth. The members of the Stern family were preparing for the onset of Shabbat. The table was set with all the familiar finery, and the mother of the house was lighting the candles as her four children scurried about in last-second dashes to complete their tasks before sundown. The only figure missing from this scene was the father of the house. But of course, he wasn't really missing. As was his usual practice, he had left the ground-floor apartment moments before to attend Friday night services at the shul conveniently located around the corner on 103rd Street off Riverside Drive. Soon after his departure, the five other members of his family spread out in the modest living room, each of his three daughters choosing a different corner of the room armed with a book or magazine that she eagerly began to read. The nine-year-old son played with his toy soldiers on the carpet. Their mother sat in a sofa chair opposite her children trying to read the local paper without falling asleep. This scene continued unchanged for about thirty-five minutes.

At last a key turned in the front door lock.

"Daddy's home!" shouted the boy as he jumped up from the floor, knocking over most of his toy soldiers.

To everyone's surprise, it was not only Daddy who came down the hall into the living room. Walking behind him was a slightly built young man with a friendly, dark-complexioned face. Upon his head he wore a large multicolored skullcap. The men paused in the middle of the room.

"Folks, I want to introduce you to Eshagh Shaoul," the father began. "We met in shul this evening. He just arrived from Iran on Tuesday, and he's an exchange student at Columbia College. He doesn't know anyone in New York, so I invited him to have Shabbat dinner with us tonight."

The father introduced his children one by one to Eshagh, who greeted each in turn. Finally, he was introduced to Mrs. Stern, who welcomed him warmly. The Sterns' home was always open to guests, and they actually looked forward to hosting visitors who might need a place to stay or a meal to eat. But this young man from Iran, ancient Persia, the land of Purim, of Esther, Mordechai, and Achashverosh, was obviously someone special. After the introductions, Mr. Stern left Eshagh's side to prepare the silver cups for the recitation of the Kiddush. During dinner, as course followed course, the children watched their guest carefully, fully expecting him to reveal something of his foreign background and customs. But Eshagh simply smiled at his hosts, accepting their generosity in gracious silence. At last, the young boy asked Eshagh why and how he had come to America.

Eshagh responded promptly, and the story he proceeded to tell was special indeed. Eshagh explained that the Shah of Iran, who had come to power in his country with the assistance of the US government, was among the first world leaders to undertake a new program outlined by President Eisenhower called "Atoms for Peace." The program envisioned the proliferation of peaceful nuclear capability throughout the world. The Shah was eager to obtain these capabilities, perhaps as a buffer against the then Soviet Union with its extensive border with Iran.

As a first step in his nuclear quest, the Shah scoured Iran to collect the best minds in the country to study nuclear physics, mostly abroad. Ultimately, he chose ten of the most qualified Iranians to spearhead this program, of whom, quite incredibly, seven were Jews! Eshagh was the last selected, and he was assigned to begin his studies in the Physics Department at Columbia College in New York.

"My father died several years ago," Eshagh continued, "but my mother, two sisters, and three brothers are all still living in Tehran. There is a large Jewish population there, and we are treated pretty well by the government."

As the meal neared its end, Eshagh listened carefully to Mr. Stern singing his regular Shabbat zemiroth with occasional assistance from his son. When the singing ended, Stern couldn't resist asking Eshagh if he had any traditional Persian Shabbat songs he might like to sing for them.

"Of course," Eshagh said. "We have many songs. I will sing one from Tehillim, King David's song from Psalm 23."

Eshagh began to intone the words of the famous psalm *Mizmor L'David*, chanting the ancient words in a pleasant voice. The tune was somewhat dissonant to the ears of these American, Ashkenazi Jews, rising and falling in unexpected ways, highlighted by a loud choral part that surprised the listeners. Shutting one's eyes, however, a person could easily have been transported to faraway Persia, as the tune and Eshagh's accent conjured up images of perfumed gardens and desert-bound caravans.

The song ended abruptly, and the Sterns each in turn complimented Eshagh for his vocal efforts.

"It must sound strange to your ears," Eshagh said, "the music of Iran. But we like to sing and get together like you do in this country."

At the conclusion of dinner, Eshagh bade farewell to his new friends and left for the windy walk up Riverside Drive to his Columbia dorm some fifteen blocks north. He arrived safely and went to bed, pleased to have made such good friends and to have been welcomed into such a warm home so soon after arriving in America. In the weeks and months ahead, Eshagh became a regular guest in the Stern's home. In time, they "adopted" him and included him in their family gatherings and celebrations. As the months turned into years, the Sterns helped Eshagh bring his siblings over to New York from Tehran, opening their home to his sisters for extended periods of time until they could find satisfactory work and accommodation of their own. The Sterns even arranged for Eshagh's brother, David, to have delicate open-heart surgery in New Jersey; the operation ultimately saved his life. Subsequently, the Sterns became substitute American grandparents for the Iranian Shaoul clan, who treated the Sterns with respect and love.

In the midst of this modern American story of charity toward newcomers, important world and local events were taking place. First, US nuclear policy changed rather suddenly. In place of "Atoms for Peace," the focus in Washington shifted to the nonproliferation of nuclear weaponry, with the frightening realization that the peaceful development of nuclear capability could easily be converted or directed to warlike uses. The Shah's development program looked shakier and shakier. Aside from that, on a local level, as Eshagh became more and more integrated into American life, he began to consider changing his major at Columbia. Finally, in late 1960, the Iranian government informed him that they were ending the program and terminating subsidization of his nuclear physics studies. Eshagh announced his decision to study economics instead. The university, together with the Sterns, assisted him in continuing his studies at Columbia. Eshagh went on to have an illustrious career as the treasurer of a major American banking institution, where he supervised investments in the Far East.

As for Iran, the moment in time for the peaceful development of Iranian nuclear power passed into history just like that, barely noticed and with the slightest of fanfare. Imagine how different things could have been. Where would we be today had Iran in fact developed peaceful nuclear capability in 1960? Would a later regime change (as occurred in 1979) have delivered nuclear weaponry into the hands of a group of terror-promoting fanatics, as we fear might now occur? Or would a concerned United States have intervened more effectively to prevent such regime change, obviating the very debate we are having today?

Whatever one might say about these varying scenarios, the irony stands: Iranian Jews, such as Eshagh Shaoul, were a critical support element – really, at the heart – of the Shah's nuclear plans in the 1950s. Today, Jews worldwide are staunch opponents of Iran's nuclear aspirations and the declared targets of Iran's nuclear objectives. With world peace and Israel's security at issue, let's hope the current nuclear plans suffer the same fate as those authored by the Shah over a half century ago.

In Memoriam –
Heroes of the Skies

Lt. Jerome Lesser, US Army Air Corps

Front row, second from left: Staff Sgt. Murray Friedenberg, US Army Air Corps

Every year around Veterans Day, I look back at two of the mostly forgotten members of our family, who served with distinction in the US Army Air Corps during World War II. The war took the life of one of these heroes and forever transformed the other. Today, more than seventy years after the conclusion of hostilities in Europe and the Pacific, the sacrifices of these two Jewish airmen, among many thousands of others, should be recalled in as much detail as we can muster. Their examples serve to remind all of us of the great selflessness of these men and their devotion to duty.

Jerome Lesser (Yaakov ben Aryeh Leib, *zt"l*) of the Bronx, New York, and Murray Friedenberg (Moshe ben Yosef Yitzchak, *zt"l*) of Brooklyn, New York, never met each other. Jerome was born to American-born parents, Alfred and Martha (Spiegel) Lesser, themselves children of German immigrant parents who arrived in America during the 1870s. Murray's parents, on the other hand, Joseph and Hinda (Chapnik) Friedenberg, came to the United States in 1913 and 1920, respectively, from eastern Poland. Jerome was my wife's uncle and Murray, mine.

Jerome was born in 1917, the second child in his family. A good-looking, bright, and active boy, he loved sports and had great hand-eye coordination. Among his many achievements was a New York City–wide high school championship in sabre fencing in April 1935. Family legend has it that Jerome arrived home late one Saturday evening and went directly to his room, refusing to answer his parent's repeated requests as to where and with whom he had been socializing. To his family's amazement, the next morning there on the front page of the sports section of the *New York Times* appeared a photo of the Textile High School fencing team with Jerome Lesser listed as the winner of the sabre competition. They were duly impressed.

When the war broke out in Europe and the Pacific, Jerome was drafted into the Army Air Corps, which during World War II was still part of the US Army. Based on his abilities, he secured an ultimate commission as a first lieutenant in the 5th Air Force, 90th Bomber Group, 400th Bomber Squadron, seeing action in the Pacific theater as a bombardier. Jerome's unit was assigned to New Guinea, where they first saw action in December 1942. His crew took off from Port Moresby on January 22, 1943, on a solitary daylight reconnaissance mission over the Japanese airbase and headquarters at Wewak to search for the crew of a previous B-24 aircraft that had gone missing two days before on a similar mission.

The last message received from Jerome's plane was "intercepted by Zeros." The official record states that Jerome's plane was shot down by a squad of A6M2 Japanese Zero fighter planes. The following day, two B-24s flew armed reconnaissance over Wewak and unsuccessfully searched for Jerome's plane. These planes were themselves attacked by a force of thirteen enemy fighters, but were able to return to base despite suffering heavy damage. Postwar searches failed to locate Jerome's remains, and he and his crew were presumed dead on January 8, 1946. The entire crew is memorialized on the tablets of the missing at Manila American Cemetery in the Philippines.

Jerome's parents, siblings, and young fiancée were devastated by the news of his loss, compounded by the fact that his remains would never be located. In retrospect, the mission that took his life was essentially a suicide flight insofar as a single, slower-moving B-24 bomber on a daylight reconnaissance mission over a heavily defended Japanese airbase was too easy a target for a squadron of enemy fighters.

While Jerome Lesser was paying the ultimate price for America in the Pacific on that winter day in early 1943, another young Jewish man from Brooklyn was preparing to enter the Army Air Corps back home. Murray Friedenberg lived in Bensonhurst, the only son of Gerrer Chassidic parents. Murray was brought up in what would today be considered more of a Modern Orthodox home; he attended public school and Talmud Torah, grew up playing sports (especially baseball), and by eighteen was more Americanized than his parents ever became. Murray enlisted in the Army Air Corps toward the end of 1943 and found himself assigned after basic training to the 8th Air Force, 2nd Air Division, 14th Bomb Wing, 492nd Bomb Group (Heavy). During basic training he excelled at gunnery and, given his relatively small size (5'5"), made an excellent B-24 tail gunner. In that position, in the typical ten-man crew, it was his job to shoot down any enemy aircraft that approached his plane from the rear, a critical task. In addition, he acted as the crew's "eyes" from his turret position, which gave him a unique 180-degree rear view.

As fate would have it, Murray's unit found itself flying missions out of England and, today, detailed records of all thirty bombing missions he flew, including targets, aircraft used, and identity of the flight crews involved, are available online. Crews were known by the name of their flight officer or pilot. Murray's flight officer on almost all his missions was a certain first lieutenant Arthur Rasmussen. According to official Air Force history, the Rasmussen crew, including Friedenberg, flew twenty missions with the 492nd Bomb Group beginning on June 2, 1944, when, flying from North Pickenham airfield in England, they successfully targeted an airfield in coastal France. On their second mission just four days later, they bombed Caen, France, in support of the historic D-Day invasion. In the course of the rest of June 1944, they bombed five more targets in France and three in Germany. The targets included enemy airfields, oil refineries, and railroad bridges.

According to Paul Boos, the navigator on all of Friedenberg's flights, the worst mission they faced was the June 20, 1944, mission to Politz, Germany. One of their engines was shot out and the hydraulic lines were cut. Landing back at their English airfield would be extremely difficult without flaps or brakes. Rasmussen, the pilot, made use of a tail-skid maneuver to slow the plane down to a stop. On another occasion, the crew's bomb payload got stuck in the bomb bay, and Friedenberg, at significant risk, ventured out on the narrow catwalk above the open bomb bay to manually release the jammed bombs. He received an Oak Leaf Cluster Citation for that act of bravery.

In the five weeks that followed, the Rasmussen crew completed eleven more missions over the German heartland and France, including the Munich railroad station, the submarine base at Kiel (for which they received a Distinguished Service Unit Citation), and the aircraft manufacture center at Brunswick. The official history of the Air Force summarized the Rasmussen (and thus Friedenberg) crew's service record succinctly:

> The Rasmussen crew flew and survived some of the Group's toughest air battles. Their service with the Group was no picnic. It didn't take too long for them to be considered one of the older crews in the squadron.*

* Official website of the 492nd Bomb Group (Heavy), 14th Bomb Wing, 2nd Air Division, 8th Air Force, US Army Air Corp, www.492ndbombgroup.com, Rasmussen Crew R-02 [709].

On August 10, 1944, the Rasmussen crew was transferred to the 66th Bomber Squadron of the 44th Bomb Group, with whom they completed an additional ten difficult bombing missions, including notable targets in Hamburg and Dortmund. Friedenberg's combat service concluded with his thirtieth mission on December 4, 1944. He had seen significant, often heavy action for the period of June–December 1944, with a well-deserved six-week break for rest and recreation in August and September. Upon Friedenberg's return stateside, he was assigned the task of training recruits in the art of gunnery, not surprising given his extensive track record in the tail turret of a B-24. In sum, Friedenberg spent approximately three hundred hours in combat runs during the war when the might of the German war machine defenses was constantly aiming to blowing him from the skies. Of that time, at least 240 of those hours were spent crammed in the tail turret of a B-24, wearing an uncomfortable oxygen mask in very cold, unheated conditions: distinguished service indeed!

Back in America, Murray gradually returned to civilian life forever changed by his wartime experiences. Within four years of the end of the war, by age twenty-six, he had lost both his parents and his direction in life. Though he lived until the age of seventy-three (in 1995), Murray never married. Growing up, I was close to Murray, as he was my only maternal uncle. I was an inquisitive child; when I examined his war medals and citations and questioned him about the "war years," he always politely declined to discuss his exploits. "Everyone got medals," was his stock answer. I guess his memories weren't pleasant ones, and as a result Murray purposely chose not to talk about the war. Jerome sadly couldn't.

By no design of their own, both Jerome Lesser and Murray Friedenberg left no direct descendants to mourn them. Their wartime service recounted above thus largely defines them in history. That service links them to us forever. May they rest in eternal peace. *Yizkor Elokim et nishmoteihem.*

The Avenging Statue or the Last Victim of Hiroshima

As the *Enola Gay* flew toward Hiroshima on that early August day in 1945, the residents of that Japanese city were oblivious to the terror that would soon be unleashed against them from above. It would be little solace to them to know that many Allied soldiers' lives would be saved by the weapon soon to destroy their city.

"A million casualties avoided by not having to invade mainland Japan versus 250,000 casualties resulting from the atomic bombing."* So went the cost-benefit analysis that satisfied the strategists in the Pentagon, but did little for the man on the street at ground zero. It was over literally in a flash, a light so brilliant, a whirlwind so powerful that nothing human could withstand. The "end of days" was surely there for the residents of Hiroshima, yet some things did in fact survive.

The dust, the radioactive debris left after the clouds dissipated, revealed a bronze statue that had been merely grazed by the weapon of mass destruction that had been detonated around it moments before. Closer examination of the statute showed that it stood fifteen feet high and represented the image of a peasant wearing a hat and carrying a wooden staff in its left hand. If you were familiar with local religious traditions, you would have rec-

* President Harry S. Truman quoting intelligence estimates he received from General George Marshall at the Potsdam Conference during World War II, July 28–August 1, 1945.

ognized the peasant as none other than Shinran Shonin, the father of Japanese Buddhism. The statue's eyes were closed, unseeing bronze eyes that fortunately, perhaps, did not so much witness the devastation around it as "feel" its power. It survived essentially intact, however, and served as a silent reminder that the people of Hiroshima could survive as well and rebuild their ruined city. It would take time, but the statue would remain as a reminder of that terrible day of destruction.

As the years passed, the city did indeed slowly recover, but new plans were being made for the bronze statue, plans that involved moving it from ground zero and transporting it far away. A Japanese industrialist had come up with a plan to ship the statue to America as a gesture of good will, as a reminder to peoples around the world that conflict must be avoided at all costs in the future. New York would be the new home for Shinran Shonin. And so, in 1955, the statue was flown from Hiroshima to its new residence adorning the entrance to a small Buddhist temple in Manhattan at Riverside Drive near 105th Street.

While the plans for the statue were noble enough, time would tell whether it would have the benign effect on the local populace that had been intended by its Asian donors. Forces were at work in the world that would put Japan and its adjoining neighbors in the Far East on a collision course with the West; this time it wouldn't be missiles, guns, and bombs that would come between them, but rather trade wars that would cost many Americans dearly – including many from New York. Sadly, the statue on the Upper West Side would not be ushering in an era of good feelings, but would instead be witness to a kind of destruction different from the nuclear one.

By the time the statue from Hiroshima arrived on the Upper West Side in 1955, this neighborhood of wide avenues, tree-lined streets, and inviting parks had for many years acted as a magnet to many of those newly minted Jewish US citizens who had sought refuge from confining tenements and European shtetls. In the year of the statue's arrival, six-year-old Sam Katzman lived with his family in a ground-floor apartment in one of those massive fourteen-story buildings that line the east side of upper Riverside Drive. This particular 1920s structure had a main entrance on West 102nd Street and a smaller one around the corner on Riverside Drive itself.

Sam's spacious bedroom looked directly out onto the park. His room was filled more with books than toys, for Sam was a precocious reader. In particular, he loved pictorial world histories. For his previous birthday he had received a *Giant Golden Book* containing vivid descriptions of various ancient cultures, ranging from Mesopotamia and Egypt to China and Japan. The book became Sam's favorite. More than anything, Sam was fascinated by the illustrations of the Far Eastern civilizations. He was soon dreaming of the Great Wall of China, Japanese emperors, and colorful paper dragons. Sam's parents encouraged his burgeoning interest in all things Asian, even buying him a pencil case decorated with colorful scenes of China and Japan. Sam treasured the case.

One late autumn day, Sam's mother asked him to bring a Shabbat gift to his aunt, who resided several blocks north on 106th Street and at whose home the family would be dining the coming Friday night. Sam passed his younger sister on the way out the door. She wanted to go with him, but their mother didn't think it was a good idea. The weather was clear, and Sam embarked on the ten-minute walk to his aunt's home alone. The first three blocks were uneventful. However, between 105th and 106th Streets, Sam passed 331 Riverside Drive, where he came to an abrupt halt. There stood a fifteen-foot bronze statue of a man. He wore a big peasant hat and held a wooden staff. A low iron fence protected the statue, which perched atop an eight-foot staircase in front of the raised entrance to a small Buddhist temple.

Sam shuddered as he gazed at the silent figure looming more than twenty feet above him. The statue had eyes that could not open, yet Sam felt them staring at him, and he became frightened. He ran the rest of the way to his aunt's house. On the way back home, he tried to avoid looking directly at the statue, but something forced him to peer at it through the fingers of the hand he had placed over his face. When Sam arrived home, he did not mention anything to his mother about what he had seen, but from that point forward, Sam made every effort to avoid the Buddhist statue. When he had no choice but to pass it, the statue always evoked the shudder Sam had felt the first time he had seen it. He couldn't explain the terror he felt when he looked at it; he only knew he seemed unable to avoid its gaze.

As he grew older, Sam continued to enhance his knowledge of Asia, and Asia continued to have its hold on him. When Sam entered college in New York, he chose to major in Asian studies and became very knowledgeable about the languages, customs, and religions of that continent. On the rare occasion that Sam thought of the Buddhist statue, he would laugh at how silly his childhood fear of it had been.

"It's only a statue," he would say. "A large one, but nothing to be scared of!"

In 1968, Sam narrowly avoided the Vietnam draft. Upon college graduation, he started working in an import-export business owned by his beloved Uncle Phil, and though he needed to make a living, Sam still dreamed of traveling to the Far East one day, of reaching those distant lands that had always held such a fascination for him. Circumstances worked against him, however, when Sam's uncle got sick and relied more and more on his nephew to run the business. Soon, Sam had little time to dream of anything other than keeping the business afloat. He decided to develop a modular furniture business with some friends from school, and, with his uncle's blessing, acquired a small manufacturing facility in New Jersey. In time, the furniture business succeeded, and through Sam's hard work and acumen, even flourished. That is, until events in Sam's beloved Asia irreparably affected his life.

Sam's uncle died in 1998, and as sole owner of the furniture company, Sam looked forward to continuing that successful enterprise long into the new millennium. But within five years of his uncle's death, business sales began to plummet. At first, Sam was unsure of the cause of the drop-off, but soon his longtime buyers explained that new suppliers, new competitors had entered the furniture manufacturing business and were undercutting Sam's prices dramatically. Not only that, their product seemed at least as good as Sam's, at half the cost! To his astonishment and dismay, Sam soon discovered that his competition was coming from none other than Asia: the Japanese, Chinese, and Koreans had "rediscovered" America, or at least American furniture markets, and the Asian businessmen acted without restraint to displace America from its high perch in the economic chain. The objectives of peace and goodwill, despite the earlier promotion through Japanese gifts to New York City of famous survivor statues, were now transformed into Asian goals of economic domination through any means, legal or illegal. When he realized what was taking place, Sam was distraught; try as he might, he could do nothing about it. In a matter of months, his company ran out of money, and soon Sam was bankrupted by the Asia he had long respected.

Earlier, Sam had put aside a little nest egg to protect himself from the company going under, but nothing he had done prepared him for the deep depression into which he fell following his Asian debacle. Sam lived with his niece for a number of months, but, sadly, he soon took sick and, after a short illness, died. Unsurprisingly, an inventory of his personal belongings at his death showed, among other things, a gray suit and blue tie made in China, a dress shirt from Malaysia, underwear from Taiwan, shoes from Japan, and socks from Korea.

Sam's unfortunate case was not unique during this period. Looking back, it is now clear that a profound shift in the symbolism of the bronze statue from Hiroshima had occurred – a change from the promotion of a peaceful future for the world

to a reminder of the horrors of nuclear holocaust and a justification, however weak or debatable under wartime circumstances,
for a declaration of postwar Asian economic warfare against the
United States.

The Petrovs Speak!

The plane taxied through a light mist down the runway at Sheremetyevo International Airport on a late June afternoon several years ago. Among the hundred or so passengers on board the flight from Helsinki sat two American brothers, Daniel and Lenny Schiff. Daniel was thirty-one and his brother ten years younger. Almost on a whim, two months earlier, they had decided to visit Russia on a short vacation, with Moscow and St. Petersburg as their main destinations. The flight was uneventful, but the brothers wondered exactly what awaited them as the pilot guided the jet into its terminal berth. Neither spoke a word of Russian beyond *da* and *nyet*. It was the idea of visiting the former Soviet Union as private citizens that appealed to them more than anything.

Russia was not entirely foreign to the Schiffs. In fact, David Schiff, their paternal great-grandfather, though born in what is now eastern Poland, had served a four-year stint in the Russian army during the early 1890s, fighting with Czar Alexander III's southern army in the Caucasus against Chechen rebels. That service, more than one hundred years earlier, changed the fate of the family, as their great-grandfather, David, seeing firsthand the large, vibrant Russian urban centers such as Kiev, opted to abandon small-town Poland for Belgium and western Europe almost as soon he returned from military service. The boys thought it significant that even though over one hundred years had elapsed since a Schiff had last been in Russia, the Russians were fighting the same ethnic insurgents they had been fighting when David Schiff left the czar's service.

Change came slowly in Russia, at least more slowly than back home in the United States. Though the brothers had not planned a lengthy trip, there was one particular aspect of Russia they were very interested in learning about: Russian attitudes toward Jews. Growing up in a Modern Orthodox home in New Jersey, the brothers had been raised with traditional Jewish beliefs, but they had also been exposed to the broader world of ideas. They had synthesized these two streams of knowledge and felt prepared for whatever they might encounter – even in modern Russia (an oxymoron?) – when it came to anti-Semitism.

Moscow's main streets and avenues originate from the famous Krasnaya Ploshchad or Red Square, home to many famous buildings, including the Kremlin. The Royal Hotel, a relatively modern establishment, was to be the brothers' home for four nights. After checking in, the boys finished off a meal of candy bars they had "imported" from New York with glasses of cold water from their room, then quickly headed to bed to prepare for a busy day of touring the next morning.

Rising at 8:00 a.m., the boys recited their morning prayers and headed down to the lobby to inquire about transportation on their first day out. It didn't take long to meet Ivan, a taxi driver who chauffeured tourists to all the central Moscow sights. Exploring the sights in Red Square effectively requires a good deal of walking, and the visitors were prepared to spend lots of time on foot on their first day in town. They started out on a clear, cool day and within minutes stepped onto Red Square near the Kremlin and across the way from the GUM department store, a large, mall-like structure frequented by Muscovites and tourists alike. The scale of the square was enormous and took minutes to cross. In almost no time, the fundamental nature of Russia revealed itself to the boys. The monumental square dwarfed the individuals mingling within, even though they numbered in the thousands. That was the visual, the graphic that Russia projected from its core to these visitors. The boys visited several museums along the square before heading into the narrower side streets. Window shopping occupied their attention for the next few minutes.

At about the same time, the boys began to feel that despite the enormity of the place, they were being watched, a feeling they couldn't easily shake. In Russia there is an expression that "one often casts a shadow even when the sun isn't shining." They decided to pause after turning the corner ahead of them, and a large, balding man sped round the corner and collided with the taller of the brothers.

"Excuse me," he said in accented English.

"Have you been following us, by any chance?" questioned Daniel.

"Of course not," the man responded. "You are American tourists, are you not? Welcome to Russia!"

His smile revealed a number of gold fillings.

"I am Mikhail Petrov. Misha. You may call me Petrov. I guide tourists around the capital. I charge very reasonable rates. I know all the places you must see when you visit Moskva! For how long are you here?"

The brothers were unsure how to respond to the man who was obviously following them. They had heard that in Russia the people who offer to show you around are often planted to ensure that you see and meet only what and whom the government wants you to see and meet.

"We have very good guidebooks to help us during our stay. I am not sure we really need your assistance, though we appreciate your offer," Lenny finally responded.

"No, I insist!" Petrov continued. "I will show you *real* Russia! You know, I love Americans!"

The Russian glanced at his watch.

"It's almost time for lunch. Let's stop off down this block at the Gypsy Club for something to eat or drink."

Since the boys were feeling a little fatigued anyway from their morning schedule, and were tired of arguing, they agreed to accompany their newfound "friend" to the suggested destination.

The Gypsy Club was really more of a nightspot than a lunch place. The boys explained to Petrov that they ate a restricted diet and would only grab a drink to complement their candy bar lunch. They thought it better not to tell Petrov that they kept kosher or that they were Jewish.

The boys were therefore stunned when after Petrov ushered them inside and a waitress led them to a Formica-covered table, their new guide proclaimed, "You are Jewish, aren't you?"

"Yes," they responded. "Is that a problem?"

"No, not at all! In fact, I prefer American tourists who are Jewish. They're more interesting."

"Well, I don't know how interesting we are," Daniel said, "but I guess we'd like to know all we can about Russian attitudes toward Jews today."

"Ah, you've come to the right place, then. I have some insight into this subject, and aside from me and my opinions, my uncle Alexander – Sasha – former professor of sociology at Moscow State University, is considered something of an expert on this topic."

"You may not like to hear this, Petrov," Daniel began, warming up slightly to the talkative Russian, "but most Jewish people we know do not have very friendly feelings toward Russia; you might have heard of such things as pogroms, blood libels, the fabricated *Protocols of the Elders of Zion*, restrictions on where to live and what to do, among other things?"

"Of course, I have studied about such things in school, but these were reactionary events in the time of the czars. Russia rejected these actions after the Revolution, and currently Jewish citizens of Russia are prized for their contributions."

The waitress brought soft drinks, whiskey, and vodka to the table for group consumption. Petrov had ordered a sandwich containing two slices of black bread, an unidentifiable layer of processed meat, and lettuce.

In between bites, Petrov commenced his lecture on Russian attitudes toward Jews, at least how he saw it.

"First, I truly believe most people are unaware of how close the Jewish experience has been in both Russia and America over the last fifty years."

"You've got to be kidding," Daniel countered. "There's no way Jews have the freedom in Russia that they have in America!"

Petrov ignored Daniel's remark and began to quote a study by a Russian-born American university professor, one Yuri Slezkine, who wrote that in the 1960s the professional achievements of Jews in Russia squarely matched those accomplished by their American cousins. Though less than 3 percent of the population, Jews in Russia made up 27 percent of the country's law faculties, 23 percent of its medical faculties, and 22 percent of all biochemistry professors. In America, during the same time, of the seventeen most prestigious universities, Jews accounted for 36 percent of the country's law professors, 26 percent of its physicians, and 20 percent of its mathematicians.

"So you see, Jews succeeded in a similar fashion under Nixon and Brezhnev – not what most people think!"

Daniel disagreed. "Petrov, I'll concede that Jews in both countries strive for success, but clearly during that period, those who could escape to the West did so to achieve personal freedoms; those who couldn't or wouldn't leave became the 'best' Russians they could be or became refuseniks, leaders of the protest movement your government sought to brutally suppress."

The boys sipped their soft drinks while Petrov attempted to add some vodka to his almost empty glass.

"I sincerely believe you Russians don't really know or understand what it means to be a Jew, despite our peoples living side by side for centuries," Daniel continued. "Do you really think Jews have different goals from other Russians: a job, a home, some recreation, an opportunity to express themselves politically and religiously?"

"Don't make the mistake most people make, Daniel," said Petrov. "They think they can generalize about the Russian people. As in the past, we have as much ethnic diversity in Russia today as you have in America – many different peoples, cultures, languages, and religions all living under one roof, one flag!"

"But no freedom to express those differences," Lenny countered.

The boys noticed that an hour had passed since they had entered the Gypsy Club. They asked for the check, paid, and left with their new comrade.

Outside on the street, Petrov hesitated for a moment. "It was quite enjoyable, our discussion. You know, I will be visiting my uncle Sasha tomorrow. He lives in a suburb near Moscow, and it would give you an opportunity to see sights outside Moscow proper. You would enjoy spending time with him, I assure you!"

Realizing they would have little other opportunity to leave the city given their short scheduled time in Moscow, they agreed in principle.

"It sounds interesting," Daniel said, "but it has to be the day after tomorrow, because we have our itinerary set for tomorrow."

"Done," said Petrov. "I will pick you up the day after tomorrow, Wednesday, at 10:00 a.m. at your hotel. Prepare to meet the most well-informed man in Russia when it comes to Jews!"

The boys said farewell to Petrov as he turned the corner and disappeared among the lunchtime crowds entering the square. The boys walked back to their hotel, tired from their morning adventures, but appreciative of their chance encounter with Mikhail Petrov. Jet lag hit them hard and they slept through the balance of the day till the next morning.

A light rain greeted the boys when they arose around 9:00. They hadn't scheduled a full day of activities, so they were not really behind schedule.

"I'm exhausted," Lenny said. "Do we really have to tour today?"

"Well, there's one outdoor place I'd like to visit not far from here. It's called Monument Park, and the guidebook says we shouldn't miss it!"

"Is it far?"

"No, we'll take a cab and it shouldn't be more than ten minutes."

The former Park of the Fallen Heroes (now known as Fallen Monument Park) is located in the Yakimanka district of Moscow near the Moscow River, which winds its way through the central part of the city. There, the Russians have collected numerous sculptures, busts, and statues of former Soviet-era leaders and laborers. The scale of these works of art is enormous.

Men responsible for the deaths of millions are on display in monumental form, alongside some of the best Russian souls and common men as well. The boys posed for several photos with these famous marble Soviet giants: Lenin, Stalin, Brezhnev (the tallest), and the writer Maxim Gorky, who stood no less than twenty feet taller than Daniel. Finally, Lenny placed his baseball cap on the bare head of a statue of a Russian worker who stood mutely before him, his hand outstretched. Lenny justified his action as a "gesture of solidarity."

As they walked through the park, Daniel mused silently, thinking biblically: "Look at the enormous size of these statues; in Russia, the people really are seen as grasshoppers by their government, dwarfed by the state. No way you can confuse who's in charge – and it's not the people!"

The hours passed quickly that day, and soon the boys returned to their hotel to unload the souvenirs they had collected. A pleasant dinner followed at one of the new kosher restaurants nearby, and by 9:00 p.m. they were back in the room and, soon, fast asleep.

The next morning was sunny as the boys waited near their hotel for Petrov to arrive. After five minutes he appeared behind the wheel of a gray late-model Opel marked with a series of dents and scratches. The boys were somewhat apprehensive about what the day had in store for them, but they put on a brave face for their Russian guide.

"Sit up front if you like, Daniel. There's room for you to stretch out in the back seat, Lenny. Move those packages on the floor next to you."

They were soon on the highway, where traffic was moderate as they headed in a northwesterly direction.

"My uncle Sasha, you should know, lives in a section of Moscow known as Severnoye Tushino," Petrov offered above the noise of the surrounding cars and trucks. "It's a quieter life, a more relaxed atmosphere than living in central Moscow."

Petrov told the boys that his uncle had taught at Moscow State University for twenty-five years, but had never quite risen to the top of the ladder in the Sociology Department in which he toiled. Sasha had, however, specialized in Jewish issues in his studies, and he was eagerly looking forward to meeting American Jews and discussing his views with knowledgeable foreign visitors. The boys watched the unchanging landscape from the car windows. Clouds now obscured the sun and a slight chill entered the air.

"How far to Tuchino?" Daniel asked.

"Another twenty minutes or so," responded Petrov.

The rhythm of the tires bouncing off of the pavement soon rocked the boys to sleep. Just as they began to dream, Petrov braked the car to a halt.

"We're here, my friends. The only problem with this neighborhood is that Sasha's apartment building has very little space for parking. We'll have to walk eight blocks or so to get to the entrance."

The walk was quick, and soon they were in the elevator to Sasha's fifth-floor apartment. The hallway was starkly furnished with gray painted walls in need of a new coat or two. The letter *D* marked the door belonging to Alexander (Sasha) Petrov, former professor of sociology.

The sound of padded slippers preceded the door opening to

reveal a short, gray-haired, bearded man of about seventy years. Crumbs of uncertain origin dotted his cheek and open sweater. He smiled at his guests in welcome.

"Misha, my favorite *plemyannik*, it is good to see you! How long has it been since I last saw you? Six months, seven?"

"Too long, *dyadya*, but you seem to be in good health and spirits, and that is good!"

"And these must be your American friends. Ah – it's been a while since I've had visitors – not many since Katya died. Come, sit down, and I'll bring something for us to drink."

Uncle Sasha continued, "Misha has told me you are interested in Russian attitudes toward Jews, a subject that could take hours to discuss thoroughly and years to research. Let me start by telling you that life is changing for the better for Jews in Russia today. I did some research last night and discovered that seven new kosher restaurants have opened in Moscow alone in the last three years. There must be some demand for this food, if this information is correct!"

The boys sought to ask how many had closed in that same time period, but remained silent.

"Also, one of our most famous supermarket chains, Mosmart, has set up kosher food departments in several of its stores. In fact, I have some kosher cookies and herring I bought last week at the local store, if you'd like."

The boys politely declined, but agreed to a glass of seltzer. Misha drank something harder.

Sasha sat down across from the boys and began to speak freely on the subject that had brought the boys to his home far from the center of Moscow.

"You should know that my lectures at university were widely attended. Jews are a very popular subject in Russia, many different opinions. So I'll try to summarize for you. Interrupt with questions when you deem necessary."

Sasha spoke for thirty minutes without interruption. What he said went something like this: "Jews in Russia represent less than 3 percent of the four hundred million people of the old Soviet Union. Despite their relatively small numbers in the world, Jews generally seem to congregate near the centers of power wherever they live, including in Russia. Whatever happened in the past, today in Russia Jews can rise high in society as long as they don't bring their Jewishness along with them. There is some minor religious and economic anti-Semitism around, but ethnic or blood hatred of Jews is a thing of the distant past. Witness that the best friends and closest allies of Russian leaders from Stalin to Putin were Jewish! Who can forget Mikhail Kaganovich, Stalin's right-hand man for thirty years! So we've had Jews at the highest levels in Russia."

Daniel reacted to that last remark. "So, to what do you attribute the commonly held view of Jews around the world that the Jewish experience in Russia has been marked for centuries by systematic repression of Jewish culture – not to mention outbursts of violence, pogroms, blood libels, visits to the gulag, and disappearances without a trace!"

"What you describe, my friend," countered Sasha, "is the old Russia. Also, you, as many other Americans do, erroneously combine atrocities perpetrated against the Jews by other European peoples, notably the Germans and Poles, with more benign treatment received by Russian Jewry. I'll point out some major differences you may have overlooked; I think you'll agree with me after you hear what I have to say.

"First, in order to distinguish between Russian and German attitudes toward Jews, for example, one must note some differences between the two peoples. The Russians, for one, cultivate a reputation of being 'wild men' – hard-drinking, rough, and uncultured – when in reality they are quite rational, calculating, and accomplished. Giving the image of being out of control, they are in fact always deliberate in their actions."

"Aren't you generalizing too much?" interrupted Misha. His uncle ignored him.

"The Germans, in contrast, cultivate a reputation of being in control, an educated, intellectual people, yet they have often in the past acted collectively as true 'wild men' – an angry people who cannot tolerate the 'other.' Hatred of foreigners is a German fundamental, while perhaps a grudging diversity characterizes the Russian."

"An interesting point," Daniel finally said, while the professor paused to drink some more vodka.

"I'll tell you something even more interesting that sort of proves my point," Sasha continued. "Have you ever considered what would have happened to the Jews if the Lord above" – here he looked upward for a moment – "had chosen Stalin with his personality to be the leader of Germany before WWII and had chosen Hitler and his uncontrollable passions to head the Soviet Union: what a different outcome the world would have seen! It is easy to imagine Stalin with his controlling temperament using his notably loyal German-Jewish citizens – scientists, engineers, doctors – to spearhead the German war effort and likely conquer the world, while Hitler and his ungoverned passions and hatreds were wrecking any chances Russia had of victory!"

"And Stalin might have rewarded his loyal Jewish allies by eliminating them from German society after he had achieved his goal of world domination with their help," added Daniel, somewhat sarcastically.

"Perhaps," the professor finally had to admit. "Perhaps… It's all so complicated, isn't it?"

After a few moments, Uncle Sasha sighed and concluded, "I'll confess to you I really secretly, no, now openly, admit to liking and admiring Jews – especially American Jews. You have two things going for you. First, you are Americans; and second, you are Jewish. America has provided your people – all of its citizens, actually – with huge advantages over every other culture in the world. Take Russia, for example. In Russia, we have some of the greatest thinkers on the planet developing breakthroughs in many spheres. Practical development of those ideas is where we break down, where we are not so successful. In America, in contrast, the ideas you come up with you readily succeed in implementing. Maybe those ideas are often less important, less consequential conceptually, but you can consistently achieve your practical implementation. The net effect is you live in an environment of achievement, a culture of translating ideas into accomplishments; one, by the way, that you as American Jews have helped to create. And I'll also concede that in America, Jews are often catalysts of positive social and cultural change."

A final sip of vodka for the professor.

"Which brings me to what it means to be Jewish in the eyes of a Russian. No one said it better or more positively than Gorky did in 1916: In my early youth I read the words of... Hillel [the Elder], if I remember correctly: 'If you are not for yourself, who will be for you? But if you are for yourself alone, wherefore are you?' The inner meaning of these words impressed me with its profound wisdom.... The thought ate its way deep into my soul, and I now say with conviction: Hillel's wisdom served as a strong staff on my road, which was neither even nor easy. I believe that Jewish wisdom is more all-human and universal than any other; and this not only because of its immemorial age... but because of the powerful humaneness that saturates it, because of its high estimate of man."

The professor fell silent after the Gorky remark.

"By the way, didn't Stalin kill Gorky after his usefulness to the regime ended?" asked Daniel, breaking the silence.

"Let's talk of happier times," Misha said to no one in particular.

"On a lighter note, I forgot to mention one other major distinction between the Russians and the Germans," Sasha said. "We are a people who can laugh at ourselves and frequently do. The Germans on the other hand have absolutely no sense of humor. I know I'm generalizing again, but I simply cannot help myself."

This led to twenty minutes of each man trying to top the other with a joke about Russians and life in Russia. Of course, the boys did not know many jokes about Russia; yet, in the end, it was agreed that Lenny told the best joke of all: "In Russia, all calendars consist of three pages, and it has nothing to do with paper shortages. One page reads 'July,' the second page reads 'August,' and the final page reads 'Winter'!"

The clock in Sasha's living room read 4:00. Somehow the meeting had lasted for nearly five hours. The boys rose, said their goodbyes to Sasha and thanked him for his insights, candor, and hospitality. Soon they were motoring toward the center of Moscow, this time struggling through heavy traffic. When Petrov pulled up in front of the Royal Hotel forty-five minutes later, he turned to the boys to bid them farewell.

"So, you are off to St. Petersburg tomorrow night; you will love it. I am truly sad to see you go."

The boys offered this to Petrov: "From our perspective, it seems one must always be on his toes in Russia, ready to move and change at a moment's notice. Survival demands it. Be careful."

Upstairs in their room it didn't take the boys long to discover that several hundred dollars in traveler's checks were missing from the drawer where they had been hidden beneath layers of underclothes. Petrov had warned them of the tendency of Russian hotel staff to "go shopping" in guests' rooms. The boys had put most of their valuables in the hotel safe, except for the traveler's checks. Now, apparently, these modern Jews were being exploited in the "new Russia" much as their ancestors had been in the old, an unauthorized transfer of assets, if on a smaller scale. In light of the theft, the boys decided they would leave no tip for the chambermaid. They would soon be "escaping" Russia for home and a refuge in the West, so the loss bothered them little.

From Moscow to Riverdale –
A Spy among Us

Back in 1982, a young Russian scientist found himself posted to the Russian embassy in New York City. Technically, he was assigned to work as a physicist in the UN Center on Science and Technology for Development. From 1974, as a matter of course, Russian diplomatic staff members were offered housing accommodation at the Russian Compound in Riverdale in the Bronx. At times, as many as several hundred Russians were housed on West 255th Street near the fast-moving Henry Hudson Parkway under the watchful eye of their government. This included the diplomats themselves along with their wives and children. Very few exceptions were granted allowing personnel and their families to live outside the compound. However, one exception was Gennadi Fyodorovich Zakharov, whose story is particularly compelling because of where he chose to live and whose house he shared. You see, Gennadi Zakharov was a Russian spy, and his home for three years was that of an Orthodox Jewish family, wholly ignorant of his true character. The story also highlights how the Russian intelligence services thought nothing of secreting an agent among the very people identified with anti-Russian activities in support of refuseniks and in favor of free Jewish emigration.

Our story begins simply enough. The Berger family – father Max, mother Michelle, and their two sons, Adam and Seth – lived in a three-story stone structure, rising high above Brighton

Avenue and 260th Street in Riverdale. A flower garden enclosed the building on three sides. Inside, a staircase to the right of the double-doored entranceway led to two separate apartments above the ground floor. In October 1983, the top-floor apartment, complete with its own kitchenette facilities, was unoccupied. The Bergers, in need of extra income, placed a "For Rent" advertisement in the *Riverdale Press* and eagerly awaited responses. They did not have to wait long. The very first day the ad ran, Michelle Berger received a call from a gentleman with a Russian accent who told her he represented a young couple who were interested in the apartment. Michelle agreed to meet the couple that evening, and at the appointed time, four people appeared at the door to the Berger home.

"Hello," Michelle greeted them, "please come in and make yourselves comfortable." She ushered her guests into the adjoining living room, where they all sat down.

"My name is Michelle Berger. This is my home," she said, making a sweeping gesture, "where I live with my husband, Max, and my two sons. You are interested in renting the third-floor apartment we advertised?

The older of the two men, broad-shouldered and gray haired, responded: "These are the Zakharovs: Gennadi is the father, Tanya his wife, and their daughter is Irina."

At each introduction, the named individual smiled with head bowed in Michelle's direction. Michelle smiled back.

"Nice to meet all of you," said Michelle, guessing as she spoke that Zakharov appeared to be about thirty-five, his wife about the same age, and Irina approximately ten years old.

"Could we possibly see the rooms?" Zakharov asked. His voice was accented, but his diction and manner were precise and clear.

"Absolutely, just follow me up the stairs."

Michelle led the group past the second floor, containing several bedrooms and a bathroom that her family occupied, to the almost self-contained apartment on the third level, where one could live privately except for the shared staircase to the outside. A separate bathroom and kitchen were available on that floor, along with a private phone line.

It didn't take long for the Russians to make up their minds. The third floor of the Bergers' home would be ideal both for the Russians and the Bergers – the Soviet Union was paying a reasonable price, and the apartment provided just the quiet, clean, and comfortable haven in which the Russians would be happy to live during their stay in America.

All required paperwork was completed over the next few days, and it was decided that the Zakharovs would move in on November 1, 1983. A day or so after the lease was signed, Zakharov came over alone to go over the few requests he had. This time Max was home, and he took the opportunity to get acquainted with Zakharov. Max was a very friendly man with a broad sense of humor. He suspected Zakharov might not be aware that the Bergers were Jewish and, in particular, Orthodox. But Zakharov had seen the *mezuzot* on the doorposts throughout the house and entranceways and the Berger men wore *kippot* all the time. And despite his mild manner and diffident smile, Zakharov was a highly trained scientist who lived by his refined powers of observation.

"Yes," Zakharov thought, as he contemplated moving into the Berger home with his family, "a religious Jewish family might be the perfect place for Russians to live hassle free."

If the particular Russian in question had something to hide, it might be ideal if he lived with and befriended the very people who might have complaints about Soviet policy, that group of Americans who spearhead the refusenik movement – the Orthodox Jews.

"'Hide in plain sight' is a good strategy," Zakharov thought as Max invited him to sit down to a snack of cookies and soft drinks in the Berger dining room.

"Mr. Berger," Zakharov began, "I've been told you are a science teacher of children, that you have started a program where the best students get an opportunity to work in the laboratories of top scientists, even Nobel Prize winners! This is very impressive, indeed. I hope you are compensated well for your efforts."

"In American public schools," Max said, "teachers are not highly paid, neither as a group nor individually. They get job security after a certain point, decent benefits, and lots of vacation. Just not a lot of cash."

"Too bad," Zakharov countered.

The two men talked a little more that day, and it appeared to Max that Zakharov was an intelligent, affable man who, along with his small family, would make ideal tenants for their vacant third-floor apartment.

In the months after they moved in, the Zakharovs easily established a comfortable routine, with the father going to work every day by commuter bus to Manhattan and his UN job. He was well liked there, given his sense of humor, diligence, and pleasant manner. Meanwhile, Tanya was getting used to life in New York, arranging things at home as the manager of the domestic "front" for her family. Her main efforts were in seeing that Irina's educational transition went smoothly. Irina was placed in a Russian-language school program specially made available to the children of diplomatic personnel. There, she was taught English as a second language and soon, with the help of the Berger children, Irina became quite fluent in the local language.

Over the following months, the Zakharovs and Bergers had numerous opportunities to socialize in the stone house on Brighton Avenue. On Friday nights and Saturdays when the Bergers celebrated the Jewish Sabbath, they would often invite the Zakharovs to share dinner or lunch with them. On the occasions they accepted, the Zakharovs would watch the rituals carefully performed by the Bergers with interest, often questioning the basis for a particular blessing, prayer, or song. Max, master teacher that he was, enjoyed explaining the practices they followed and, for their part, the Russians appreciated his explanations. On special occasions such as birthdays, bar mitzvahs, and anniversaries, the Bergers invited the Zakharovs to attend and treated them as close friends. Over time, the Bergers' extended family got to meet the Zakharovs and took every opportunity to question Zakharov and Tanya about what life was really like in the Soviet Union. One time in particular, Michelle Berger's brother, Jack, had a memorable discussion with Zakharov concerning Russian attitudes toward how they were portrayed in spy movies, specifically James Bond films.

"Oh, we think these portrayals as, uh, bad guys, yes, it is very entertaining. In Russia, we enjoy it very much," Zakharov responded quickly at the time.

Zakharov wouldn't elaborate on the subject and Jack let the matter drop.

As a result of their own efforts and those of the Bergers, by the end of the summer of 1984, the Zakharovs could be said to be firmly established in their Bronx home, a contented family living an unremarkable existence. Then, on one unusually warm September day, Michelle Berger received a phone call that shattered that peaceful picture.

"Mrs. Berger, Mrs. Michelle Berger?" said a very official-sounding voice.

"Yes, I'm Michelle Berger. What is this about?" Michelle responded.

"I'm Special Agent Mark Stone of the FBI, and I'm calling on official business," the voice continued. "May I have a moment of your time?"

Michelle assented to the agent's request. He told her he had an important matter to discuss with her and Max and asked if they could possibly meet the agent at a mutually convenient time and location. It was agreed that the agent could stop by the Berger home the next morning at 9:30, a time when only Max and Michelle would be around. When the agent got off the phone, Michelle quickly called Max to alert him of the meeting and the agent's firm warning that they not discuss the matter with anyone.

"What's this all about?" Max wondered. He couldn't fathom why the FBI would want to contact them.

The next morning at the appointed time, the doorbell rang. Michelle opened the door to Special Agent Mark Stone and his partner, Agent Pat McCarthy.

"Come in, officers or agents – what exactly should we call you? I'm not sure," said Michelle as she showed the men to the dining room table, where Max was awaiting their arrival.

"Mark and Pat would be fine," Stone responded, sitting directly across from Max. "Here are our credentials showing we are who we say we are."

Stone and McCarthy slipped their badges toward the Bergers so they could examine them.

"Everything seems to be in order," Max said, returning the items to the agents. "What seems to be the problem?"

Stone slowly began to explain the reason the FBI had contacted them. It boiled down to this: Gennadi Zakharov was under strong suspicion of spying for the Soviet Union; under the guise of being a physicist, he had one mission only in New York, and that was to steal and transmit back to his country any US naval armament secrets he could obtain. The FBI believed Zakharov had reached out to several potential Americans sources to provide him with the desired information. He was offering significant amounts of money to entice those individuals to participate.

"Are you in any way aware of these suspected activities of Mr. Zakharov or his wife?"

"Are you kidding, absolutely not!" responded the Bergers. "I don't believe it," added Max. "He's such a quiet guy, very friendly, and with a good sense of humor. A spy? Wow!"

"As you know, this is a serious matter and requires absolute secrecy on your part. At this point, we need to gather more evidence against Zakharov and find out more about his comings and goings. Accordingly, we would like you to agree to permit us to tap his private phone line in his third-floor apartment. We believe this would help us greatly to impede Zakharov's activities and foil his espionage mission."

The Bergers listened intently to Stone's words, and, without responding directly to his request, interjected with concern, "Are we in any danger from Zakharov; is he armed?"

"We don't believe you are in any such danger at the moment," McCarthy responded. "Will you help us?"

"Of course, we want to help our government in any way we can," Max finally said.

"It'll just be the Zakharovs' phone that you'll tap?" Michelle asked.

"Yes, I promise," Stone said.

"Well, then, do what you think is necessary to catch him," Max concluded.

Having obtained the Bergers' agreement to permit the Zakharov wiretap, the agents thanked the Bergers and prepared to leave. At the door, Stone turned toward the Bergers and made a final request.

"We may from time to time ask you for additional assistance in this case. For now, remember, mum's the word!"

Throughout the following year, Zakharov quietly and deliberately cultivated likely candidates for help in collecting the desired naval secrets, but he fell short of obtaining the sort of data he was after. The Bergers, meanwhile, didn't know exactly what information on Zakharov the FBI was collecting through its wiretaps, although every so often they thought they heard a clicking sound on their phone line. Was the FBI tapping them as well?

For the most part, outwardly life continued unchanged at the Berger home during this surveillance period. However, one day in February 1986, Agent Stone called Michelle with an additional request. He offered her a 1986 Cabbage Patch Doll calendar on which he suggested she note Zakharov's comings and goings each day. Michelle expressed concern that Zakharov himself might read those notes.

"It's too dangerous," she responded, and Stone withdrew his request.

In the summer of 1986, the Bergers departed for a month-long trip to Israel for a well-deserved vacation. The Bergers let the FBI know of their plans before departure. On July 25, they boarded an El Al flight to Ben Gurion Airport and arrived the next morning without incident.

Zakharov used that month to finalize his espionage plans. Over the previous years, he had targeted a Guyanese student living in New York as his main source of important classified naval secrets. However, unknown to Zakharov, the former student, code-named "Birg," had been working as a double agent with the FBI. Birg, through his current employment with an American defense subcontractor, had previously provided Zakharov with nonclassified information in exchange for thousands of dollars. Now Birg and Zakharov arranged to meet on a Queens elevated subway platform to exchange classified documents dealing with the design of military jet aircraft engines. The agreed-upon price for the information was one thousand dollars.

On August 23, 1986, just two days before the Bergers were to return, Zakharov left the Berger residence in Riverdale for his rendezvous with Birg. That evening, the late-edition headlines screamed: "Russian Spy Arrested on Queens Subway." As soon as he accepted the package of classified documents from Birg, Zakharov was taken into custody by the FBI, who had been tailing him throughout the day. The story of his arrest had international reverberations as the KGB soon arrested American Nicholas Daniloff in Moscow, where he was serving as chief correspondent for *US News and World Report*. While both the Kremlin and Washington denied any link, both men were soon sent to their respective home countries in what appeared, for all intents and purposes, to be an exchange of one for the other.

With the completion of this successful FBI endeavor to stop the espionage activities of Gennadi Zakharov, the Bergers briefly found themselves in the international spotlight as many television stations and newspapers descended upon them for interviews. Zakharov himself had an opportunity to speak to Michelle Berger while in custody. He told her he was "framed." When called upon after Zakharov's arrest to describe the years that the spy had lived in his home, Max remembered him blending in very effectively, a friendly and helpful neighbor and tenant, willing to help out around the house when possible, essentially a very "unremarkable" man.

"If I needed medicine or something, he would pick it up; or I'd go on an errand for him," Max remembered.

As one might expect, talking politics with Zakharov was more difficult.

"He was open, but he realized we have our own point of view, as Americans," Max said. "He admitted there was a problem with Soviet Jews, but we didn't go into depth, because we both realized we didn't want to get into deep political issues. I was hoping, however, that he would see the way we lived as a Jewish family, see that we pray at home and observe the Sabbath, and take something of it home with him to Russia."

For all we know, Gennadi Zakharov – who despite other trappings was in fact a highly trained Soviet KGB intelligence officer, sent to the United States for the sole purpose of spying – may have taken home something of value from the three years he spent living among Orthodox Jews in Riverdale. The Bergers surely did what they could to present their warm and principled Jewish way of life to the Cold War face of the Soviet spy who secretly lived among them.

Samovar or the Magic Teapot

For the last four centuries, the samovar functioned as the quintessential hot water boiler used throughout eastern European homes, Jewish and non-Jewish alike. Originating in Russia, it was made of various materials, from the cheapest metals to the most precious. Some were simply designed, while others were intricately crafted by the finest metalsmiths. Most were crowned by a teapot used to brew the hot tea so essential to the often frigid winter conditions found in Ukraine, where our story begins. Magical powers have been attributed to the samovar throughout the years, as the following story illustrates.

The samovar we are concerned with began its life somewhere in Russia around 1750. By the time we find it, fifty years have passed and it has traveled one thousand miles to the town of

Brody in northwest Ukraine. In the early nineteenth century, the town of Brody, vibrant home to over ten thousand Jews, was part of the Pale of Settlement prescribed by the Imperial Russian government as permissible for Jewish residents. The Jews lived in close proximity, if not always on the friendliest terms, with the largely Ukrainian peasantry surrounding them. Despite the generally restrictive Czarist regime, the Jews were permitted to engage in a full range of activities and occupations within the Pale.

While many Jews lived in difficult straits, during the period of June 1804, Chaim Chait was among the wealthiest residents of the town. The source of his wealth was a factory that produced the largest quantity of vinegar in that section of the Ukraine. Chait employed almost fifty laborers at his vinegar works, Jews and Ukrainians alike. He was considered an exemplary employer, paying the best wages in Brody. He and his wife, Golda, gave charity generously to support the less fortunate in the community, and they were widely regarded as model citizens.

In this period of awakening national identity, however, the native Ukrainians surrounding the Jewish community in Brody occasionally made trouble for their Jewish neighbors. Aside from the difference in religious beliefs, the Ukrainians, primarily wage or field workers, resented the perceived economic success that the Jews were believed to be attaining at their expense. The reality of course was that in the Pale of Settlement most Jews were eking out a rather meager existence, which doesn't justify Ukrainian jealousy from any perspective. But the outstanding success of individual Jews such as Chaim Chait in accumulating wealth from his economic activities stuck in the collective throats of several of his non-Jewish neighbors.

The leader of this "anti-Chait" faction was a local hetman named Vova Budnik, who had worked in the Chait factory for a period of time before leaving under somewhat mysterious circumstances. On Friday nights, when Budnik and his friends met at a local inn for some music and drinks, talk would often turn to the Jew Chait and the fine house he lived in with his wife and five children. On one particular Friday, the following conversation took place.

"The Jew is making more money in a week than ten of his workers!" began Budnik.

"I wonder how he does it," added Egor Lutsky, Budnik's brother-in-law.

"It's not fair these Jews are so well off while we struggle to make ends meet," again Budnik.

"Is there some magic or special power these people have that gives them an advantage over us?" continued Lutsky.

"We should put these people in their place – their proper place," threatened Budnik.

Lutsky demurred, "I'm more interested in figuring out how they do it and copying them!"

Budnik shrugged his shoulders at Lutsky's remark. He got up and pulled Lutsky toward him. They emerged onto the now darkened street in front of the inn.

"Let's go pay our friend Chait a visit. Maybe we can finally discover his special secret, Lutsky."

It wasn't a long walk to the Chait home, and by the time Budnik and his brother-in-law neared their destination, their resolve to physically confront Chait had weakened. Instead, they decided to approach the building carefully and attempt to peek through the curtained windows to see if they could uncover some of Chait's secrets by their reconnaissance.

Since it was Friday night, the Chaits had just ushered in the Sabbath as the Ukrainians appeared. Budnik carefully moved the shutter covering a side window to look into the dining room. The Chaits were sitting around a dining table illuminated by two large candlesticks in which burned the simple white Sabbath candles lit at sundown by Golda Chait. Mr. Chait sat at the head of the table, his two sons and three daughters around him. Mrs. Chait was serving pieces of boiled fish to each family member from a large serving dish. In an adjacent breakfront stood a gleaming silver menorah alongside a silver spice box shaped like a turreted castle. These silver objects caught Budnik's eye, but he wasn't ready for what he saw next. On a table behind Chait sat a larger, shiny object. It was the most magnificent silver samovar he had ever seen!

"Lutsky, take a look at that!" Budnik nearly shouted to his brother-in-law.

"Quiet, Budnik," Lutsky cautioned. "I don't want us to get caught spying on the Jews." Lutsky couldn't resist peeking in to see the object of Budnik's excitement. His brother-in-law was right. The Chaits' samovar was the most beautiful object he had ever seen. The craftsmanship was exquisite. It had to be priceless!

After a minute, Budnik and Lutsky decided it was time to go, and they rapidly but silently left the Chaits in peace – that Friday night, anyway.

As the weeks passed, Budnik and Lutsky couldn't agree on whether or not the Jews of Brody, and Chait in particular, had any special powers that contributed to their material success. What they did agree on was a plan to "relieve" Chait of some of his wealth to even out the Jew's economic dominance over them. Two weeks after spying on the Chaits, the Ukrainians perfectly executed a diversionary theft, which involved Lutsky throwing a rock through a back window of the Chait home, drawing everyone's attention away from the dining room, with Budnik simultaneously forcing the front door, entering the house, and scooping up the samovar into a large sack he had brought along for that purpose. The theft took no more than two minutes to carry out, and the thieves got away without being caught.

Now, the aftermath of the theft was as you might imagine. The Chaits were crestfallen at losing a family treasure, while Budnik couldn't really announce that he was the proud owner of a priceless samovar. At best, Budnik could draw the shades in his home and brew endless cups of tea for his family and occasional friends. Needless to say, the theft didn't lead to any great, "magical" improvement in Budnik's or Lutsky's fortunes. As the years passed, Budnik took ill and died, as did Chait. The silver samovar was inherited by Budnik's son, Bogdan, and later his grandson, Alex, who knew nothing of its origins.

In 1895, Alex left Ukraine for the United States. He had trouble adjusting to life in America, but after some time had success working as a carpenter in the uptown neighborhood of Harlem in New York City. Unfortunately, following a particularly harsh winter, his young son took sick with pneumonia and had to be hospitalized. At the new Beth Israel Hospital in Manhattan, he was treated by a young doctor named Samuel Chait, a great-grandson of Chaim Chait, the old vinegar maker from Brody. In the era before antibiotics, the Budnik child's case was extremely grave. Compounding the situation, the Budniks informed the doctor that they would have difficulty paying the medical bills that were accruing from the treatment. The doctor repeatedly assured them that they should not be concerned about the bills. Dr. Chait worked hard to get the child through his medical crisis and, after a harrowing week, helped the boy pull through.

Budnik and his family were overwhelmingly relieved by their son's recovery and were greatly appreciative of the young doctor's efforts on their son's behalf. However, since they were unable to pay him directly for his services, they decided to make a special gift to him of one of the few family heirlooms they possessed. Accordingly, one early spring day, Budnik came to Dr. Chait's office carrying a burlap sack. Inside was a silver samovar of the finest construction. On top of the samovar sat a shiny teapot. Dr. Chait was touched by Budnik's generosity, but at first he did not want to accept such an obviously valuable gift. Seeing that Budnik was insistent, the doctor reluctantly accepted the samovar. He took it home later that evening, never imagining that he was carrying it back to its rightful home after so many years away.

Food for Thought

Melissa Taub

As the days grew shorter and the air got crisper, my thoughts
turned to things that keep me warmer and, ultimately, happier. I
was sitting in front of my fireplace not long ago with my friend
Steven, and the conversation turned to what the ideal meal would
be and, more specifically, what our favorite dish was. It wasn't long
before Steven, a Jewish philosophy lecturer at Columbia, raised
the level of discussion: Could we possibly determine among us
that night what the most universally popular dish was? We had
both recently finished reading Professor Bernard Lewis's famous
essay "Middle East Feasts," where the author convincingly connects distinctions in dietary forms with differences in culture
and politics. Specifically, he cites how the differing uses of dairy
products in a given country may have determined varying devel-
opmental outcomes:

> One can, in a sense, divide the civilizations of this planet into
> three zones: the sweet-milk zone, the sour-milk zone, and the

no-milk zone. The sweet-milk zone is Europe and the Americas; the sour-milk zone the Islamic lands and India; the no-milk zone China and Japan, where they neither drink it nor use it in their traditional cuisine – no milk, no cheese, no butter.*

With Lewis's observations in mind, we quickly dismissed pizza, our personal favorite, from consideration as the world's most universally liked food – the Chinese simply will not eat it. Even with pizza out of the running, as tenured companions, Steven and I still felt uniquely suited to make a determination. That evening, we read the following notice in the newly arrived, winter quarterly edition of the prestigious *Journal of Culture and Cuisine*:

Inaugural Competition: World's Most Popular Dishes
Geneva, Switzerland (November 12): The International Cordon Rouge Society is pleased to announce the first annual competition to determine the universe's most popular dish. As people around the world are becoming more and more aware of the art of cooking, the society feels it is past time to study the world's cuisines more closely and most appropriate at this time to hold a contest to determine annually which dishes should be considered the most universally appealing and popular. Recognizing how subjective such a determination may be, the society is impaneling a tribunal of twenty-five of the world's most experienced culinary experts to judge all submitted entries. The entries may take the form of actual food sample entries and/or research briefs in support of each entry. The deadline for all entries will be May 1, 2016. The ruling of the tribunal will be made on July 1, and its decisions will be final. Check the Cordon Rouge Society's website for official, detailed rules for the competition.

"Now that's something!" Steven shouted. "Our little exercise may have international repercussions. Warms one to the task, no?"

* Bernard Lewis, *Babel to Dragomans: Interpreting the Middle East* (Oxford, UK: Oxford University Press, 2004), 37.

"Absolutely!" I responded. "Let's get to work right away."

First, we each made a list of our choices, five in all. To our surprise, Steven and I agreed as to the most universally popular dish: it was some kind of beef stew, some dish comprising meat, potatoes, an additional starch, and spices simmered in a pot for hours. As Orthodox Jews, we of course recognized our choice as cholent, that savory stew mixture served piping hot for Shabbat lunch throughout the year.

After a little further discussion, we realized we had greatly oversimplified the task.

"Every cuisine I know contains some kind of stew or cholent," Steven noted.

"But shouldn't we define what constitutes a stew before we run off and select cholent as a single dish?" I countered.

"Good point," said Steven, "but that's pretty easy. Cholent is made from beef, potatoes, and barley; throw in some spices and stew it overnight in water. Simply add an appetite!"

"Not so fast," I said. "Your cholent is incomplete by a mile! What about beans? Cholent without beans isn't cholent!"

Steven had no response. It dawned on both of us that we needed to study the problem more carefully. Accordingly, over the next two weeks, we researched the matter and discovered there were so many different forms of cholent, each almost unrecognizable from the other, that it was impossible to consider cholent a single dish but rather a class of dishes. For instance, while it is true that the basic Ashkenazic Jewish cholent consists of beef, potatoes, barley, and beans (for some), the Sephardic Jews of Mediterranean origin substitute chicken for beef and rice for beans/barley in their cholent recipes. Further research revealed the following cholent variations with these ingredients:

- Smoked goose, duck, veal, kishke (a sort of sausage, sometimes made with flour instead of meat), and even frankfurters instead of beef or chicken
- Chickpeas, rice, hulled wheat, potatoes, and whole eggs

- Macaroni (!), chicken, and potatoes
- Vegetables including carrots, sweet potato, tomatoes, zucchini, and onions as well as Middle Eastern variants containing fruit
- Spices such as salt, peppercorns, garlic, beer, whiskey, and baked beans
- Condiments such as barbeque sauce or ketchup

Based on the foregoing review, we disappointedly concluded that the sheer multitude of variants disqualified cholent from consideration as a single dish. Frustrated that our favorite dish would not likely be accepted as a distinctive, universally popular dish, we decided to choose chicken soup as our entry.

"It's clearly a very popular dish and, unlike milk [referencing Lewis], almost everyone in the world eats chicken soup," Steven concluded after hours of research at Columbia's Butler Library. The facts bore out this view, as no fewer than twenty-five cultures happily include the tasty soup in their cuisine. The list contained countries as diverse as Bulgaria, China, Colombia, and Denmark. France, Germany, Greece, and Hungary also favor it, as do Indonesia, India, Italy, Japan, and Korea. When further research uncovered Mexico, Pakistan, Peru, and the Philippines as chicken soup devotees, we knew we had uncovered the winning ticket in the competition. Steven's parents added Portugal, Brazil, Romania, Russia, and Ukraine to the soup list.

I further raised the point that chicken soup was a worthy choice since it was very popular in the United States, Canada, and the United Kingdom, not to mention Israel.

"You're aware of course, Steven, that hot chicken soup has been known as 'Jewish penicillin' for years," I concluded.

With our research completed, Steven and I wrote up our findings and forwarded our supporting brief to Geneva as required, satisfied we had the winning entry.

The weeks and months flew by, the spring semester beginning and ending before the big announcement came from Geneva.

To our great satisfaction we received honorable mention for our chicken soup submission. The blue-ribbon tribunal had indeed chosen soup as the *second* most popular dish, and, remarkably, beef stew in the third spot (including cholent and its variants as one class of dishes). First place, however, went to a dish that we had somehow overlooked. With its simplicity, ease of preparation, nutrition, and tastiness, it should have been on the top of our list, but somehow escaped our attention. Dozens of countries and cuisines recognized this dish's attractiveness and desirability. It was none other than that ancient staple of kitchens worldwide: stuffed cabbage rolls!

According to the tribunal, cooks in over forty countries world-wide are accustomed to taking a vegetable leaf of some sort (typically cabbage), stuffing it with some form of meat, boiling it, and serving it. What clinched it for stuffed cabbage was the common name the dish is known by in many unrelated countries: in Lithuania, Russia, and Poland stuffed cabbage rolls are called respectively *balandeėliai, golubtsy, and golabki*. These names all mean the same thing: little pigeons. Belarus (*halubcy*), Ukraine (*holubtsi*), and the Czech Republic/Slovakia (*holubky*) all call stuffed cabbage rolls by substantially the same name as do the first countries mentioned. Ashkenazic Jews throughout the world call them *holishkes* or *prakas*. In Israel, they are known descriptively as *kruv memuleh*.

It shouldn't come as much of a surprise that Jews are quite familiar with the world's most popular foods. It's obvious that, with our history of living among many different cultures through-out our far-flung Diaspora, Jews have acquired an affinity for the most popular dishes if available in kosher form. As a footnote, you might have guessed that the next time Steve and I hosted a dinner party at Columbia for our friends and family, we served the top three items chosen in the Cordon Rouge competition. Our guests dined on a stuffed cabbage appetizer, chicken soup, and beef stew. All the dishes were delicious, and it mattered little which had been determined to be the most popular. There were no leftovers!

Note: For readers who may be interested I have included below in no particular order the list of additional "stuffed cabbage" countries and regions that appeared in the official competition results of the Cordon Rouge Society.

Armenia (*kaghambi tolma*); Argentina, Chile, Dominican Republic, Ecuador, and Mexico (*ninos envueltos*); Austria and Germany (*kohlroulade/krautwickel*); Azerbaijan (*kelem dolmast*); Bosnia-Herzogovina, Bulgaria, Croatia, Macedonia, and Serbia (*sarma*); Brazil (*charuto de repolho*); China (*bai cai juan*); Estonia (*kapsarullid*); Egypt and Sudan (*mashi kuronb*); Finland (*kaalikaaryleet*); France (*chou farci*); Greece (*lahanodolmades*); Hungary (*toltott kaposzta*); Iran (*dolmeh kalam*); Italy (*involtini di cavolo*); Japan (*roru kyabetsu*); the Levant (*malfouf mahshi*); Malta (*bragioli*); Moldava and Romania (*sarmale*); Parana/Santa Catarina (*aluske*); Quebec (*cigares au chou*); Turkey (*lahana sarmasi*); and even Vietnam (*bap cai cuon thit*). Stuffed cabbage rolls invaded North America, as well, where almost every immigrant group brought the dish with them to the East and West Coasts. From there the dish spread throughout the land.

The Inquisitive Swiss

girafchik/Shutterstock.com

Of the most privacy-conscious people in the world, there are few that equal the Swiss. Sure, their scenic, mountainous country with pristine air and quaint villages attracts tourists worldwide and year-round; their decorative cuckoo clocks, melodic music boxes, pungent cheeses, and savory chocolates have few rivals. But aside from all these attractions, the Swiss are known to keep secrets better than most – particularly when it comes to financial matters. The Swiss may not have invented numbered bank accounts, but they have certainly perfected the system of hiding the identity of account owners from public scrutiny. In recent years, some nations have objected to their citizens attempting to evade local laws and taxes through the medium of a Swiss bank account, but the Swiss have been reluctant to transform themselves into a truly open society, that is, except for one rather strange, somewhat intrusive habit that amuses many new travelers to the country while annoying, or even shocking, others.

Among this latter group was the family of Jake Rabinowitz who, along with Jake's best friend, George, arrived in Geneva several years ago for a long-planned summer vacation in Switzerland. Jake, his wife Brenda, and their three kids, Yoni, fifteen, Daniella, thirteen, and Ariel, nine, planned to meet up with Jake's old college buddy George for a day-long train excursion to the capital city of Bern, high up in the Swiss Alps. Along the way they would traverse fifty different mountain bridges and spy glacial vistas without equal in Europe, even having time for a ten-mile boat excursion on Lake Thun, gliding by numerous picturesque, gingerbread-like houses along the perimeter. The varied greenish hues covering the surrounding meadows and mountainsides were unequaled in beauty and clarity to anything they had seen before or since.

On arrival, the Rabinowitz clan reached the center of Bern, a town noted for its fixation with all things "bruin." Statues of bears, variously costumed, lined the downtown streets; sculptures of bears peopled the clock towers, appearing at regular intervals to mark the quarter, half, and full hour. Of most interest to our visitors was the famous medieval Bernese Bärengraben. This noted tourist spot consists of a sizable open pit, a mere twelve feet below street level, with six large Eurasian brown bears living in relative equanimity. These bears were probably chosen by the municipality for their willingness to beg for food from the bystanders who came to observe them. Several of the beasts had been trained to place their paws together in a religious pose and genuflect in the direction of anyone who flashed their favorite food – grapes – from the parapet above. If five minutes passed without a treat, the bears as a group began to growl and make menacing gestures with their paws, ensuring a fairly steady stream of grapes from the crowd.

After ten minutes, the Rabinowitzes grew bored and continued toward their second objective in Bern: a visit to the home where Albert Einstein lived in 1903 when he formulated his world-famous theory of relativity. Jake arranged to meet George at 1:00 at 49 Kramgasse for a tour of the Einstein Museum. At the appointed hour, Jake and his family greeted George as he came up the street from the direction of the Clock Tower.

"Hi, guys," George offered. "I got lost, sorry I'm late."

"It's OK," Jake countered. "You made it in time."

They climbed the stairs to the second floor landing where the entrance to the house was located. The door to the museum was firmly bolted, and no amount of knocking opened it. Jake and George checked their watches to confirm the time; it was 1:10 p.m. and the museum was supposed to be open.

"Maybe we're at the right place, but it's the wrong time," Jake offered scientifically, "or maybe Einstein's playing a joke on the Swiss, and his museum is open in another dimension!"

After several more minutes of bad relativity jokes, our tourists gave up on Einstein and began their walk back to the Bahnhof (train station) for their scheduled trip back to Geneva. It was there that they got a bit of a surprise and George found himself in more than a little trouble. As is the case with families who travel together, it is often necessary to schedule pit stops on the way. In this instance, the Rabinowitzes sought a comfort station as soon as they arrived at the train depot.

"Does anybody have to go?" Brenda asked. "This may be your last chance before we board the train to Geneva."

Jake reminded her that there were facilities on the train, but who knew in what condition they would be. Accordingly, they followed the signs to the bathrooms.

They soon found themselves standing in front of a brightly lit glass and aluminum storefront with a neon sign reading "McClean's" across the top. Etched on the glass was a menu describing the services and fees for each of several personal "activities" available at the futuristic-looking comfort station.

"Mommy, it looks more like a fast-food store or hair salon than a restroom," Yoni quipped.

George was the first one through the automated doors. He started to walk past the desk, which was manned by a burly guard.

"And where do you think you are going, sir?" the guard asked George in accented English.

"I need to use the bathroom facilities, if that's all right with you," he replied.

"You have to pay to use the facilities," the guard continued, pointing to the menu with "price list" attached. "It's two Swiss francs for use of a *pissoir*, three for a *toilette*, five for a shower, et cetera. So what will it be?"

"Excuse me," said George, obviously displeased with what the guard had said to him. "I'm an American citizen and you have to be crazy to think for one minute that I'm going to tell you what I am going to be doing in your bathroom. There must be some sort of international right of privacy that covers this. Our train's going to Geneva, after all – there must be some kind of convention governing this!"

Within minutes, two Swiss gendarmes entered McClean's and asked George to stand down. He continued to refuse to either divulge his plans or pay the required fees.

"Listen, I want to speak with the American consul if there is one in this town; I know my rights!"

Jake attempted to intercede on George's behalf, but events had gone too far. The gendarmes insisted George accompany them to their office, where a proper hearing would be held. They informed George he would probably be charged with disturbing the peace. In the end, George didn't get to use the facilities at the train station. As he was lowered into the police car, George told Jake not to worry since George had adequate funds to cover any fines.

"Take the train back to Geneva as soon as you can, Jake; I'll be OK as soon as I straighten out this mess. As if I'm ever going to disclose anything to the Swiss! God bless America!"

The Rabinowitzes got back to America shortly after that episode in Bern. Weeks later, Jake spoke with George about the incident.

"I spent two nights in detention, but I never told them anything," George insisted. "Of course, the bathrooms in the police station were free of charge. For people known for their habits of secrecy, the Swiss sure are nosy when it comes to personal functions."

Just a cautionary tale that you should consider the next time you travel abroad on vacation. If you find yourself in Switzerland, remember that customs values may not be the only things you're going to have to declare!

PART III
ONLY IN AMERICA

Suburban Succah

Fona/Shutterstock.com

Of the many holidays in the Jewish calendar, Jacob loves Succoth best. From his earliest days as a boy growing up in the city, he looked forward to that time of year when his father would build the small, traditional canvas succah in the narrow courtyard of their Manhattan apartment building. Jacob loved the ingenious ways his father devised to transport the linens, utensils, plates, and food from their fourth-floor apartment to the succah fifty feet below. One year, the family rigged a laundry basket to slowly lower the needed items from their kitchen window to the ground below. The basket would sway back and forth, frightening any neighbor who happened to be looking out his window as the basket passed by. His father's recitation of the Kiddush on the first night of Succoth, with a slight chill in the air, was among Jacob's earliest and most pleasant memories.

While many things change as a person ages, this wasn't the case when it came to Jacob's love of Succoth. This love extended to his studying in detail all the laws pertaining to the holiday. He knew the rules of constructing a succah – all the regulations on how, when, and where to enter this temporary structure, and the order of the blessings required to be recited in the succah. He even mastered the rules of when a person is exempt from the commandments of the succah. In particular, Jacob knew that one was not required to eat or otherwise dwell in the succah if heavy rain was falling. In fact, each year Jacob would nervously scan advanced weather maps to try to predict whether rain was forecast for the first days of Succoth.

After graduating from law school, Jacob met the love of his life, Hannah. They married a year later and moved into a small apartment in the city. Their life together was idyllic, but with the arrival of their son Benjamin, the cramped apartment had clearly outlived its usefulness. In time, the couple saved enough for a down payment and purchased a pleasant home in northern New Jersey. The closing on their new home was scheduled for early August. Jacob realized that for the first time in his life he was going to be able to construct a proper succah in his own comfortable backyard.

A week before Rosh Hashanah, Jacob bought a sturdy, paneled succah at his neighborhood Succah Depot, arranging for delivery of all the necessary parts to assemble his prize. Once it arrived, Jacob immediately completed the frame, topped the structure with the *s'chach* (the natural covering), and set up the electric lights for the interior. Hannah decorated the ceiling with plastic fruit, birds, and multicolored hangings. She covered the inside walls with colorful holiday-related artwork. It was a joy to behold. Jacob and Hannah were very pleased.

There was only one thing troubling Jacob. With one week until Succoth, the weather reports turned ominous: a late season tropical storm, approaching hurricane status, was creeping up the East Coast from the Caribbean. Based on its current trajectory, the storm was on track to arrive in Jacob's town on the first night of Succoth! It was not a question of whether Jacob and Hannah would be eating in the succah that night, but whether Jacob's sturdy succah could even withstand the driving winds that would surely accompany the storm. Jacob was greatly distressed by the dire weather forecasts that each successive day brought. It seemed so unfair – his first opportunity to observe the holiday in his own succah rained out!

As people often do in times like this, Jacob prayed that somehow the storm be averted. And as so often happens, Jacob's prayers appeared to be answered at the last minute. On the morning of Succoth eve, a sudden change in the weather occurred in the form of a blast of cooler but drier Canadian air pushing the approaching storm far out into the Atlantic Ocean, sparing New Jersey the predicted downpour. Of course, Jacob was ecstatic; at the last minute, all his plans to properly celebrate the holiday were back on track.

It was now evening on the first night of Succoth. The table inside the succah was set perfectly, the sparkling Kiddush cups arranged in a circle, the challot covered by a spotless white cloth. Jacob and Hannah brought Benjamin's yellow and white high chair into the succah and carefully placed him in it. Four guests, attired in their finest clothes, admired the decorations. Jacob poured the wine into the cup, opened his siddur, and began to intone the blessings. Suddenly, a high-pitched whirring could be heard and a burst of rain streamed into the succah, interrupting Jacob's chanting! Had the weather reports been wrong? The succah's occupants were being heavily showered upon. Jacob rushed outside and to his amazement realized it was not raining outside at all. It was only raining inside the succah! Everyone and everything inside was drenched. Where was this shower coming from? Jacob finally figured out what was happening, though he could do nothing about it. After ten additional soggy minutes, the sprinkler head, around which Jacob had inadvertently built his succah, and which he had forgotten to deactivate, turned itself off. Obviously, Jacob, succah savant though he was, still had much to learn about suburban succahs.

The Name

The man carefully steered his car into the designated parking space. It was a bright, sunny day in early July and he had just finished playing a tiring softball double-header with his over-the-hill gang of friends (average age forty). Leaving the car, he walked toward the two-story apartment building he occupied with his young wife and two children. His right knee ached a bit from the hard-hit groundball that had ricocheted off his leg on the decisive play of the second game. It stung, as did the loss.

He rang the doorbell as he often did, even though he had the house keys in his pocket. His wife answered, and he immediately saw her tear-filled eyes and the tension etched on her face. She sat down slowly on the nearby couch as he entered the living room; he closed the outside door without looking back.

"What's wrong?"

She hesitated. "It's my father," she said. "He suffered a heart attack this morning. He woke up early and wasn't feeling well. He's in the hospital in Far Rockaway.

Her words momentarily stunned him, but they triggered an immediate response. "Let's call someone to come over and watch the kids so we can drive out to the hospital." He hurried to the bathroom to clean up, hoping that his father-in-law would be fine. "Are you OK?" he shouted over the sound of the water filling the bathroom sink. His wife was pregnant, one month into carrying their third child; he worried how the news about her father might affect her. She came into the room and said quietly in her calm manner, "I'm very concerned, but hopefully everything will be all right."

An hour later, standing in the hospital room where Grandpa lay intubated, the man and his wife learned of the severity of the attack. The doctors informed them that the damage had been significant and that it could be days before they'd know if he would survive.

Grandpa was a fighter, a survivor, known for his quiet strength. His family hoped and prayed for the best.

A week passed and to everyone's relief, Grandpa won his battle. It appeared the crisis had passed, and with proper care Grandpa could return to a normal life. The woman was overjoyed because she loved her father dearly, as did the man. Everything seemed to return to normal in their household as well. For the woman, however, one thing remained to be discussed with her husband, something important to her and of import to her unborn child.

"Last week, when Dad got sick, I prayed so hard that he would survive. I was so deeply concerned that I told myself, if he pulled through, I would give our baby a name that would reflect our great thanks to God for sparing Dad's life. I really want to do this! What do you think?"

"It's a great idea," he said. "We've got some time to decide on the exact names and – don't forget – we'll have to choose two sets of names 'cause we don't know if it's a boy or a girl!"

That suited the woman just fine. Time would show, however, that fulfilling this vow would not be as easy as making it in the first place.

Time went by, lists of names were made, some names added, some crossed off until some measure of agreement began to emerge. The man and woman concluded that whatever name they chose should express their thanksgiving for the successful birth of a healthy child as well as for saving Grandpa's life. Ultimately, he and his wife concurred that if a male child were born to them, he would be named Jonathan, which means God's gift; if a girl, she would be called Daniella, meaning God has rendered favorable divine judgment. Either name would be most appropriate, they thought. Both wanted to give the child a middle name as well, and on that subject the man and woman still could not agree.

"My mother's father was named Aryeh ['lion' in Hebrew], and we could use that as a middle name," said the woman.

The man countered, "I prefer the name Asher; it means 'fortunate' or 'lucky.' Asher was one of Jacob's sons mentioned in the Torah, you know."

Weeks passed and they stopped discussing names altogether. The man started studying the holy books specifically to find some sign that the middle name of Asher would be acceptable to fulfill the woman's vow. It became something of an obsession with him, he would later admit. But he felt there was precedent for what he was doing. Since early times, people had sought confirmation for important steps they were about to take, for omens and portents that the powers around them approved of their actions. Even though the man and woman were educated, literate, and modern, they too sought this confirmation. Somehow the man believed he could find a connection.

In fact, the books he researched offered some support for the use of the name Asher. In the Bible, Asher's descendants had inherited the most fertile portion of Canaan upon the conquest of the land by the twelve tribes of Israel: the Jezreel Valley, west of the Jordan River. The sons and daughters of the tribe of Asher were considered "lucky," became wealthy, and were chosen as princes and princesses in biblical times. The man could find no direct evidence or link that naming the baby Asher would fulfill the woman's vow, but that did not deter him from trying. When continued research proved fruitless, the man despaired of ever finding such a link, if it existed.

The months passed rapidly and, as winter progressed, the woman reached that time she had long awaited. On a sunny, crisp day in late February, a baby boy was born. He was a long, slender child with dark hair and strong lungs. His parents were overjoyed at his birth, and the man made preparations to welcome home mother and child. The father realized that the time had come to make a final decision on what to name their child. The first name, Jonathan, was certain, but the middle name was not.

Early on the morning following the birth, the man sat nervously alone at home waiting for his car pool ride to work in the city. He finished his breakfast cereal, rose abruptly, and walked over to the bookshelf. He reached up and pulled down a volume from the shelf; somehow he had overlooked this author in his prior searches. The book was the famous *Yalkut Me'am Lo'ez*, literally *A Compendium of a Foreign People*; its author, Rabbi Yaakov Culi, began this compilation of Midrashic and Talmudic analyses of the Bible and Prophets in 1730 in Turkey. Pressed for time, the man quickly read from the volume, selecting the verse from Bereishit where Jacob names his newborn son Asher. What he read was disappointing, since it was by now a familiar summary of all the sources the man had uncovered in his earlier researches. Frustration at failing to find a decisive clue gnawed at the man; he had mere moments to spend before the car horn's blast would tear him away. At that moment, the man's eyes fell on the last few Hebrew words in the paragraph he had reached, which, when translated, read: "and he [the biblical Asher] was born on the twentieth day of the Hebrew monthof Adar."

"I had no idea we know the birthdates of Jacob's sons!" the man exclaimed.

Immediately, another thought entered his mind. He placed the book on the table in front of him and went into his kitchen where a calendar hung conveniently on the nearby wall. There, in front of him, was the proof that he and his wife had been seeking, the proof that the vow would be deemed fulfilled, for their son had been born on the twenty-fourth day of February, which that year coincided with the twentieth day of the Hebrew month of Adar!

The man quickly dialed his wife's hospital room.

"Don't ask any questions, dear, the baby's middle name is Asher! I have it on very good authority. Short of our receiving word from a heavenly messenger or a rainbow appearing outside our window, naming our son Asher will fulfill the vow you made those many months ago."

And the woman, absorbing what her husband had just told her, knew that this was true and that the child, blessed from birth, would grow to be a fine young man and good fortune would shine upon him.

The Ambiguous Reward

Oleg Ivanou IL/Shutterstock.com

The High Holidays are considered by most people to be the ideal time for contemplation and reflection on how we lead our lives. Frankly, any time of year might do equally as well. In recent times, with scandals of infinite variety – moral, financial, and otherwise – we have almost unlimited opportunity to confront age-old dilemmas of righteous deeds going unrewarded and evil-doers seemingly profiting from their anti-social activities. While reviewing the daily goings-on in this realm might push one to cynicism and then shortly to clinical depression, I recently recalled an apparently minor episode in the life of one of my friends that leads me to conclude that things are in fact seldom what they seem and are often ambiguous. So don't worry too much if you don't have all the answers; you may not be seeing the whole picture!

Spring 1967 was a time of uncertainty. On a macro level, conflict in the Middle East was reaching a climax, the world anxiously awaiting the resolution of the then Egyptian existential threat to the State of Israel. On a personal level, more mundane events were taking place – of most significance, my friend Isaac's upcoming graduation from Yeshiva University High School in Manhattan. The years he spent as a student at various Orthodox day schools followed by four years at a yeshiva high school were coming to a close at a time of great turmoil and change in Jewish and American cultural history.

Since childhood, Isaac had been completely absorbed by one Torah ritual above all others: reading the weekly Torah portion in the synagogue. He was obsessed by every aspect of the process, the repetition of the cantillation notes, the memorization, the recital itself. He approached the best readers in the synagogue and asked them to teach him special methods of reading and any techniques they had mastered that would help him perfect his style. The consequences of Isaac's zeal for reading soon became apparent. Unlike most kids, once his 1962 bar mitzvah celebration was over, Isaac immediately set to work teaching himself new *parshiyot* (Torah chapters) to read, his zeal for the performance of this mitzvah unwavering.

Soon, out of his love of Torah reading (and a growing adolescent need to supplement his allowance), Isaac expanded into teaching others their bar mitzvah portions. The process began easily enough. First, he taught his younger cousin Mark to read his portion, then Mark's classmate and another neighborhood boy. For the then-handsome sum of one hundred dollars, Isaac would work with the prospective bar mitzvah boy for six months or so, preparing him to read both *parashah* and *haftarah*. Around this time, Orthodox boys from the West Side began to celebrate their bar mitzvahs at weekend galas in Catskill hotels. Isaac was invited and accompanied several of his students to these festive events. By 1967, Isaac added high-tech to his training methods and materials. He began to record the required readings on a state-of-the-art portable cassette player to enable his students to study and review the readings at their convenience. Isaac was getting comfortable in his routine. All seemed perfect to our youthful bar mitzvah teacher, himself only seventeen.

That is, until Isaac met Mr. Roth of West End Avenue. Roth was a close friend of Isaac's Uncle Manny. Roth's son David, a rather slight boy of twelve, was in need of a bar mitzvah teacher. It was early 1967, and David's bar mitzvah was scheduled for midsummer. Isaac met with Mr. Roth, quoted his price, and Roth agreed to Isaac's terms. They worked out a mutually convenient schedule for the lessons over the coming months. As usual, Isaac prepared a tape recording of the required portions.

The lessons and months of teaching passed quickly. Global events likewise passed like a blur: the Six-Day War, the long-awaited reunification of Jerusalem, events far-reaching and of truly historical import. On a personal level, Isaac graduated from high school and dreamt of starting college, the self-absorbed teenager that he was.

Isaac had been carefully reviewing David Roth's progress at their weekly meetings, and David was doing well. So well that Isaac turned his attention to finding additional opportunities for summer employment, but no job could be obtained at that late date, and Isaac was forced to face a summer unemployed. In mid-July, however, Isaac received a phone call from his father telling him some remarkable news. Another of Isaac's uncles – this time Uncle Alex – was inviting Isaac to accompany him on a three-week trip to Israel. They would be staying in Jerusalem, visiting the Kotel, Bethlehem, and Hebron – all the holy sites Isaac had dreamed of visiting appeared suddenly, unexpectedly within reach.

"Do I want to go with Uncle Alex? Are you kidding?" Isaac thought. "My first trip to Israel! Is there any question?"

There was, however, one problem: the Roth bar mitzvah! Mr. Roth was furious when Isaac told him he was accepting his uncle's travel invitation.

"You're coming to the weekend bar mitzvah," Mr. Roth told him. "It's on August 5, and we expect you to be there!"

"But I'll be in Israel then," Isaac meekly protested.

"Our agreement was that you'd attend the weekend bar mitzvah."

"We never really discussed that."

"We want and expect you to attend!"

Isaac kept his disagreement with Mr. Roth to himself and left for Israel at the end of July. David celebrated his bar mitzvah in the Catskills as scheduled. Mr. Roth never again spoke to Isaac. He also never paid him the one hundred dollars Isaac thought he was owed. Since Roth was a good friend of Isaac's uncle, Isaac had limited options to protest and, ultimately, Isaac despaired of ever being paid.

Over the ensuing years, Isaac would occasionally catch a glimpse of Mr. Roth walking on West End Avenue or Broadway and a twinge of anger (and maybe some feeling of guilt) would overcome him. Even though Isaac had not attended the bar mitzvah celebration, he felt entitled to some payment for his months of effort. But the pull of Israel had been too great, and Isaac had in fact failed to appear at the hotel as required. The moral ambiguity of Isaac's situation became clearer to him. He had made his choice – possibly not the right one – and would have to live with it.

Isaac soon turned to more important things: becoming a lawyer, marrying, moving to the suburbs, and raising five children. In no time, Isaac was charging more than one hundred dollars an hour to his law clients and had almost forgotten the one hundred dollars that Mr. Roth hadn't paid him – at least until May 1997, when he was reminded of the incident quite definitively.

Isaac and his wife were driving to the Spitz bar mitzvah at the Homowack Lodge in upstate New York. They arrived late Friday afternoon, hurrying to complete their pre-Shabbat preparations. Isaac's wife lit candles and they headed to the combination shul/ *beit midrash*. Sitting in the front row waiting for Mincha to start, Isaac noticed a short, vaguely familiar man sitting facing him, no more than ten feet away. Next to that man sat a younger man in a charcoal gray suit. Just then Isaac's friend Gene sat down next to him. Gene knew the extended Spitz family better than Isaac did.

Isaac whispered to Gene, "Do you recognize... do you know the name of that short man sitting across from us? Is it by any chance... Roth?"

Gene nodded. The thought of that unpaid one hundred-dollar bill briefly crossed Isaac's mind. Roth had noticeably aged; he must have been in his late seventies.

"What about the other guy?" Isaac continued, referring to the man in the charcoal gray suit.

Gene's words sent a chill up Isaac's spine: "Oh, that's his son, David. He's considered the best Torah reader in all of Queens!"

I'm not sure how Isaac took Gene's revelation, but it is safe to assume that Isaac was finally at peace with the matter of his "unrewarded" efforts. There was no report whether Mr. Roth or his son had recognized Isaac after all the years that had passed or, if they did, how they felt about him!

Highway 49 and the Vision Quest

Throughout American history, when Jews went west, the adventures and travails they faced on the road were not unique to them. In our own times, this continues to be true. Witness the following tale of a Teaneck family who heard the "call of the wild," and answered it, sort of.

Back in 1989, my friend Jack, prone to assuming he knows more than he actually does, decided it was time for an unusual family summer adventure: the outdoor type. They set out on a two-week trip to Montana: national park visits, fresh air, and happy trails under the stars. Jack's family of seven brave, if somewhat misguided, Teaneck travelers were determined to ride the Lewis and Clark Highway, crisscrossing the Continental Divide near Canada. The cast of characters in our tale were not out of the ordinary: Jack was a self-described compulsive father, aged thirty-nine, who was living out childhood fantasies by taking his family on this trip out west. He prepared for the adventure by studying multiple mile-by-mile guides, leaving nothing (he thought) to chance. There was his dutiful wife, Beverly, who, despite serious misgivings, agreed to accompany him on condition that they "have a good time" and "do things that everyone likes," and she was glad to get away from home for a while. There were five children: the boys were fourteen, eight, and two; the girls twelve and six. They would fly to Calgary, Alberta, in the Canadian West as the jumping-off spot for their trip. Once arriving, they would lease a thirty-foot-long RV that would be their home for their western family adventure.

Food, water, and shelter are the three essentials on any western wilderness trek. Our easterners planned to stock up on provisions in Calgary before setting out toward the Montana border. They phoned ahead to order kosher food for the trip, and upon their arrival in early August, they dutifully picked up their RV on the outskirts of town and motored to the Jewish Community Center to collect their food. Our travelers had never even been inside an RV before and marveled at all the details of their new "home on wheels." They quickly learned how to convert couches, seats, and tables into sleeping areas and back again. They wondered why there were locks on the cabinet doors and how exactly to read all the gauges that measured water, refuse, and fuel levels. The short orientation session at the rental agency was woefully inadequate, but they had little time to waste. They loaded the RV with their belongings and started out for the JCC fifteen minutes to the south. As they approached the center and Jack attempted a left-hand turn into the parking lot adjacent to the building, the red engine light came on and the RV stalled. As he pressed on the gas pedal, all the contents that his family had carefully stowed in the unlocked cabinets went flying through the interior of the RV, a missile attack on a grand scale! Jack's wife was upset with the mess, but Jack was busy trying to restart the engine and he ignored her.

"I'm really concerned that the engine stalled," he said. "It's one thing for this to happen here in town, but what if we're on a mountain road and we lose power on a turn? It would be a disaster!"

"Well, try to get it to work," Beverly exclaimed.

Jack carefully restarted the engine, but as he was negotiating it into a parking space, the RV stalled again.

"Do you have the number of the rental place?" asked his wife.

Jack descended from the cab and went inside the center. He called the rental agency from a pay phone and was informed that they would replace the defective vehicle. It would take about a half hour to bring the replacement, just enough time for Jack to settle accounts with the food people inside the center. Luckily, the latter had everything packed and ready to go. Kosher hamburgers, hot dogs, steaks, and rolls were neatly frozen and packed in convenient boxes. The kids were impressed. Soon, the new RV arrived and the family unloaded the first RV and loaded their belongings into the new one.

Jack took the wheel and headed south out of Calgary toward the Montana border. The terrain started changing and large individual mountains began to appear to the southwest. The first major sign they spotted declared they were entering Chief Mountain Road near the Canadian-US border. The family was struck by the stark beauty of the view. They were traveling south on a road that contrasted the easternmost border of the Rocky Mountains with the absolute end of the vast prairie that extended from Minnesota to the middle of Montana.

"It's amazing!" Jack shouted over the roar of the diesel engine powering the RV.

The mountains towered above the road like so many giant, cowled figures. Row upon row of mountains stood silently as far as the eye could see, blocking the setting sun to the west. To the east, the rolling prairie extended to the horizon. But one disturbing image marred Jack's vision. Massive clouds were forming over the adjacent mountains they were passing, by far the blackest-looking clouds he had ever seen.

"Is it going to rain?" Beverly nervously asked.

"Not likely," said Jack. "This is what they call a 'dry' thunderstorm out here," he opined, suddenly becoming an expert on Rocky Mountain weather systems.

Within the hour, our travelers were ascending the mountains to the west in the most horrific "wet" thunderstorm any of them could remember. Night had fallen as Jack maneuvered the RV around twists and turns of the ascent, straining to see the dark road ahead through the windshield wipers and the driving rain. They had been on the road from Calgary for about three hours when they arrived at the first of the many campgrounds they would visit on the trip. They were all relieved to reach their destination, but Jack's job wasn't complete until he backed up the RV into its designated slot and properly hooked up the electrical, refuse, and water attachments. Jack had no experience hooking up RVs and because of the storm raging outdoors it took him a half hour to complete the job. In the meantime, Jack's family undertook the conversion process necessary to sleep. It took quite some time to figure out who would sleep where, locate the bedding, and get comfortable. The exhausted travelers were all under their covers by the time Jack removed his soaked clothing and tried to squeeze into the "master bed" already occupied by his two-year-old son and his wife. Emanating from behind the curtained bed perched directly above the cab came the voice of his fourteen-year-old son. "I don't care if I have a good time on this trip, all I want to do is get home alive."

Jack thought his son might have added, biblically, "Were there no graves in New Jersey so that you took us to die in Montana?"

Jack assured his son that everything would be all right.

The next morning, Jack awoke early, dressed, and went outside. The thermometer read forty-five degrees, a cold contrast to the afternoon August temperatures in the 80s. The sky was crystal clear, the air clean and fresh. What a contrast to the previous night's stormy conditions. A pattern was forming in his mind:

when things are tough in the mountains, they can be exceedingly so; when things are good, nothing really compares. Jack walked to the front of the RV and got his first surprise of the day. No more than ten feet from where he backed up the RV in the dark last night was a ravine at least forty feet deep. Incredibly, they had avoided a huge disaster. He decided not to discuss the matter with his family. Instead, after breakfast he carefully maneuvered out of the space, and they took off to tackle the day's itinerary.

They spent the morning hiking in Waterton Lakes National Park, the afternoon in the prairie visiting Browning, Montana, the center of the Blackfeet Indian Reservation. The Blackfeet were the only tribe never to have been forcibly subdued by either the US Seventh Cavalry or the Royal Canadian Mountain Police. Their existence as a "border" tribe made all the difference. Whenever the US Cavalry approached, the Blackfeet promptly left for Canada and, similarly, they headed back to the United States whenever the RCMP appeared. Ultimately, Teddy Roosevelt ceded one million acres in Montana to the tribe and purchased another adjacent one million acres that belonged to the tribe to create Glacier National Park. To this day, the Blackfeet live where they lived in the days of the fur trappers, raising beautiful horses under the Big Sky of northwest Montana.

The Blackfeet Reservation was a beehive of activity with ritual demonstrations and tribal dances the day Jack's family visited. Our Jewish "pioneers" participated in one memorable friendship dance with about twenty costumed tribesmen. Following the dance, Jack befriended a young Blackfoot man named Wade Manyfeathers who agreed to guide the family around the reservation. Wade wore an authentic Indian costume, colorful and complete with beaded headdress. Jack instantly knew what to do: Wade's belt had a perfect space for the small, turquoise-handled camp axe Jack had purchased back east at a sporting goods store. As many a Jewish trader had done a century before, Jack offered the axe to Wade in exchange for guide services. Wade gladly accepted the gift and fulfilled his duties admirably. Through Wade the family learned about many Blackfeet rituals and how the tribal members tried to cope with the modern world surrounding their reservation.

At the next campground, in the prairie around St. Mary, Montana, Jack prepared an outdoor barbecue whose centerpiece was comprised of the meat provisions from Calgary.

"Who wants a hamburger, who wants hot dogs? Come and get it!"

Everyone gathered round, plate in hand, and commenced to eat. The hot dogs weren't bad, but the hamburgers were somewhat rubbery and had little taste.

"That was really good," said Jack, sitting by the fire in a folding chair near the RV door. "I was hungry."

The kids picked at their hamburgers, but could only manage a few bites. Jack's twelve-year-old daughter made the discovery of the night: "Daddy, the hamburger wrapper says 'Best if eaten by November 15, 1988.' It's August 1989! Yech! No wonder it had no taste!"

Jack didn't feel so good all of a sudden. He swallowed hard.

"Don't worry, guys, the meat was probably frozen all this time and was OK to eat."

Another restless night followed for our travelers. Except this time Jack was sleeping above the cab by himself, exiled in punishment for leading *his* tribe to tainted food.

"Was this any different from what must have occurred more than a century earlier to every wagon master who brought greenhorn settlers from back east over the Oregon Trail?" Jack thought. "Even Moses in the desert had to deal with rebellious followers!"

The next morning broke to reveal Jack trying to figure out how to rebuild confidence in his leadership. At breakfast, he revealed his plan for the Rocky Mountains' aftermath. "How would you all like to go to Southern California after we finish our mountain exploring next week? We can go to Disneyland, Universal Studios, and all the sites."

The response was unanimous: "Let's go now!"

"It would be crazy to leave Montana now, just before we explore Glacier Park," Jack pointed out. "This is the highlight of the trip. We're going to cross Logan Pass alongside the Continental Divide. It's the highest point on the Going-to-the-Sun Road."

"What's the Going-to-the-Sun Road?"

Jack was ready for that question! All the guidebooks he had studied now came to the fore. "Well, that's a road that winds fifty-three miles across the width of Glacier Park; it's an impressive road that is usually open only from June to September each year because of avalanche hazards during the winter," Jack said. "It's impossible to keep the road open when you consider the amount of snow that falls on this road. During a normal springtime, it can take ten weeks to clear away the snow drifts; they reach a depth of eighty feet sometimes!

"Also, because of the narrowness, we can't take our RV onto the road; there are special 'jammer' buses we need to take to do the tour."

After parking the RV, the family boarded the red bus waiting at the tour assembly point and soon began the ascent up the scenic road. Twenty minutes later, they arrived at the visitor center, where they enjoyed the spectacular view. Jack began to feel ill rather suddenly and explained to Beverly that he didn't feel up to continuing the scheduled round-trip tour. Instead, he wanted to take a bus directly down the road to East Glacier, a town farther away at the southeast corner of the park. From East Glacier he could rent a car to bring him back to St. Mary and the family. In this fashion, he would avoid interrupting the family's trip through the park. On the following day, they could return the rental on the family's way west out of Glacier Park.

Reluctantly, Beverly agreed to Jack's proposal, but she sure wasn't pleased.

"Where's Daddy?" the kids asked.

"He's not feeling well, so he's going to meet us at the RV later," she responded. She suspected that Jack had an ulterior motive for this "side trip." Maybe he really didn't feel well or maybe he just needed to get away from the group after days of too-close proximity in the cramped RV. That was a sentiment Beverly shared with him at that moment.

About two hours later, Jack rolled out of the car rental parking lot steering a late-model Chevy Cavalier onto Montana State Highway 2. He had consulted his map and, feeling better, decided to look for a shortcut that he could take to rejoin his family. He didn't want to now descend all the way down from the mountains to the prairie before traveling north only to reenter the mountains once more to reach his family and the RV.

"There has to be a shortcut through the mountains," he insisted to himself. His fingers traced the outlines of a road that led from East Glacier to Highway 49. This road in turn rejoined the main road at a town called Kiowa. It would be a short jog from Kiowa to St. Mary, the RV, and his family.

What Jack didn't know was that the twelve miles of Highway 49 that he was about to traverse were even more precarious than the Going-to-the-Sun Road he had just traveled along. Unbeknownst to him, Jack was ascending to the Blackfeet Indian's most revered and sacred part of the mountains, the place known as Two Medicine Ridge, visited by the locals since ancient times on their vision quests. That quest was the initiation rite or rite of passage all members of the tribe would undertake, seeking spiritual insight, guidance, and purpose. A person would spend between one and four days secluded in nature in order to achieve a deeper understanding of one's life purposes. Jack, concerned about getting to his family quickly, was taking an unscheduled side trip into his personal, Jewish vision quest whether he liked it or not!

Highway 49 started innocently enough with forested mountains on either side of the road. Soon, however, the road veered to the east and began to ascend rapidly. After an abrupt switchback, Jack saw stretched before him miles of the steepest, narrowest, and most winding road he had ever seen. He immediately thought he had seen this before and just as suddenly recalled that it reminded him of the children's book illustration of the yellow brick road stretching to infinity on the way to the distant Emerald City in the Land of Oz. The present road had no guardrails, and from the distance Jack saw that it was prone to landslides. The straight drop from the road to the valley and lake below as it clung to the side of Two Medicine Ridge had to be at least one thousand feet (it was in fact 1,288 feet).

Jack was terrified as he realized there was no turning his car around. He couldn't turn back and the road ahead was frightening. He was angry with himself for getting into this predicament, but that emotion was of no help. He had to keep his nerve up, proceed slowly, carefully, braking at every turn. The road at this point became even wilder as he was ascending one foot for every fifty feet he was driving. The section he was now entering was called Looking Glass Hill Road and it was a stretch unmaintained by the state and (he later learned) impassable in the winter. As Jack drove ever closer to the ridge wall, he barely missed scraping the Cavalier's right fenders against the exposed granite. At this point, he stared straight ahead, not daring to look at the abyss below and the oblivion a wrong move promised. Would his rental car survive this ordeal?

The minutes passed so slowly, but Jack still felt out of breath. Here he was, traveling on a perilous road that few people on the planet had ever seen, let alone driven on. Here was a discovery, a place he hadn't known about, where God tested people, inspired people if only they survived, a "shortcut" that would forever end a person's search for shortcuts in life and maybe lead one to deeper deliberation on life's meaning: a western Mount Moriah for those seeking to find evidence of a supreme being if they needed such evidence.

Clearly, this was more than Jack had bargained for as he'd sat peacefully planning the trip back home in Teaneck. He was being sorely tested and, like his ancestors, he was given no advance warning. Finally, mercifully, after several more minutes, the road ahead leveled off, even descended a little as the terrain evened out somewhat. A sign ahead heralded Kiowa Junction: "One Mile Ahead." Jack had survived Two Medicine Ridge.

A half hour later Jack arrived at the St. Mary parking area, where he quickly spied his children playing near the RV. It was 4:00 p.m. and Jack was in no mood to talk. When he saw Beverly in the RV, Jack paused.

"I've just been someplace I can hardly describe," he said. "Crazy as it may seem, I felt and saw the presence of Hashem on this treacherous mountain road."

"Why didn't you come back with us?" she interrupted. "After all, it was your idea to take this silly tour. And the cost of the rental car, was it really worth it?"

"You had to be there, I guess, to appreciate the experience," he said.

The family trip west continued the next morning, and over the next week Jack led his people to British Columbia, the Canadian Rockies, and back to Calgary, where the Rocky Mountain expedition had begun. The family happily boarded their flight to Los Angeles as Jack had promised and soon checked into their hotel on Pico Boulevard. It is rumored that unlike the rest of his family, Jack remained locked in his bedroom for the next three days refusing to come down from the mountain he had ascended in Montana and dilute his experience through exposure to "civilization." Vision quests – even Jewish ones – can be funny that way.

Torah and Teepees – A Comanche Friend of the Jews

"There's nothing new under the sun." We've heard those words of Kohelet (Ecclesiastes) so often that we assume they are an accurate description of reality. The following story shows that sometimes King Solomon's biblical observation isn't necessarily so!

Back in the 1850s Sam Bennett left his home in Lodz, Poland, for the distant shores of the United States. Back in Europe he was known as Shmuel Benovits, an aspiring rabbinical student, who somehow had also mastered the carpentry trade. Political unrest in Lodz had led to attacks on the Jews of that city, and since he had been orphaned at a young age, Shmuel's uncle and aunt arranged passage for him on a train leaving from Lodz to Warsaw, and ultimately on to a ship bound for Philadelphia from Germany. He arrived weeks later in America, speaking the language with difficulty, and with just enough money to sustain himself for two weeks. No one was there to greet him, but after inquiry, he was guided to the home of a rabbi in the port area and so made his first friends in his newly acquired domicile. In a few weeks' time he made more friends, got a job helping a master carpenter build wagons, and in every respect started to build his new life.

This was a period of great change in America, and soon talk of the West reached even the sections of Philadelphia in which Sam (Shmuel) lived. As a single fellow of twenty years, Sam was fascinated by the stories he heard about the West: the hostile and peaceful native tribes, the buffalo, the cavalry, and the hordes of settlers who clamored to leave the urban East where Sam lived for the wide-open spaces of the West. Soon the call to try his fortunes out West became too great, so Sam gathered up the courage to leave Philadelphia and head to Missouri, where he planned to open a trading post to sell all kinds of general goods to the new settlers arriving there. It took him three months to get to St. Joseph in Missouri, the jumping-off point for trips across the continent. To Sam's chagrin, St. Joe, as the locals called it, had an abundance of trading posts and general stores and didn't need Sam's store at all. What was really needed were brave and hardy individuals who could carry supplies out into the wilderness to reach those distant smaller settlements and army forts that relied on these shipments for their very existence.

Sam decided to save his money, and he did so with a passion. In the next six months, by taking on numerous odd jobs, he accumulated a sufficient amount of capital to equip a sturdy wagon, four horses, and a supply of sundries to begin his life across the Mississippi River as an itinerant peddler. Whether you needed pots, pans, small tools, linens, or blankets, Sam the peddler was the man for you. He started out visiting smaller towns and villages in Iowa and Nebraska, always making sure he didn't venture too far from the larger trading posts, where he could replenish his stock of goods and take some time off the road when he got tired. As the months and then years passed, Sam found himself traveling between US Army forts and encampments, often befriending cavalrymen and their families as the government expanded the American footprint on the prairies.

Of all the sights Sam beheld on his travels, nothing quite compared to the mammoth buffalo herds that regularly migrated from north to south across his path. The herds seemed endless and, in fact, were rumored to contain a million beasts in a single herd. When the buffalo departed, Sam quickly felt the loneliness of the prairie, a sense of the vastness of God's creation that had few parallels. At such times, Sam keenly felt the absence of other humans. In his western wilderness, Sam prayed on a daily basis, referencing the almanac he carried in his wagon that told him what day of the week and what time of year it was, and utilizing the worn prayer book he always kept nearby.

In the summer of 1858, Sam found himself as far west as he had ever traveled – in the Texas panhandle near what is today Lawton, Oklahoma – when he had the misfortune of running into a war party of Comanche Indians, themselves traveling farther east than they had ever been before. The Comanche tribe was given their name (meaning "enemy") by the Ute Tribe, with whom they were not on speaking terms. In fact, the Comanches, though not the most numerous tribe of Plains Indians, had no natural friends to speak of. They were known as the most adept horse soldiers in the West but were also regarded as the most capable horse thieves. Add to this their expertise in kidnapping for ransom any poor soul they might find out on the plains, and it is easy to see why Sam was in a great deal of trouble on that day in August when twelve Comanche horsemen entered his camp.

Now, Sam had met Indians of a less warlike nature at various forts and trading posts over the years. He didn't know it at the time, but he was fortunate that this particular group of Comanches belonged to the Quahada or Antelope group headed by Chief Bad Eagle, a fairly advanced young man who was fluent in several languages, including English and Spanish. Comanches were sort of "equal opportunity" kidnappers in that they would take captive Mexicans, Texans, and other Indians almost without exception. They would trade them for horses, their most prized possession. As a result of this "trade," the Comanches were rumored to have accumulated close to 250,000 of the finest horses on the continent. Sam's team of horses was of great interest to the war party, as was Sam himself. Accordingly, the Comanches promptly sent Sam under guard to their larger encampment some two days away to the northwest. They didn't physically harm him; there was no need to lessen his potential ransom value.

It's worth noting here that the Comanches had never met a Jew before. As was their custom, they treated everyone they captured pretty much the same, and they made no exception in Sam's case. After Sam was led on horseback into the Comanche camp, he was kept bound and blindfolded for three agonizing days during which he feared the worst. Finally, on the fourth day, two of his captors entered the tepee where he was being held and brought him before three of their leaders, including Chief Bad Eagle. His blindfold finally removed, Sam studied the chief: he was fairly tall with long dark hair and brown eyes, and looked to be in his early twenties. Bad Eagle sized up Sam very carefully and spoke to him slowly, in accented English: "You don't look like you're a Mexican. My braves told me you were Mexican. *Habla Español?*"

"I'm an American, not Spanish," replied Sam.

"I myself was captured by the Mexicans and lived and fought with them for five years before being recaptured by my Comanche brothers," said Bad Eagle. "My men say they examined your wagon and contents and found rather strange objects among your trade goods. I am curious to know what they are. My Mexican captors taught me about their Catholic religion, but your objects I am not familiar with."

The Comanches brought forth a blanket in which they had wrapped Sam's tallit, yarmulke, and tefillin, and laid it on the ground in front of him. Sam knelt down and carefully lifted the items from the ground. A Comanche attempted to restrain him, but Bad Eagle intervened.

"Let him be!" the chief declared. "What are these things you hold so important?" the chief asked Sam.

Sam paused before describing in detail each of the items used in his daily prayers and beliefs.

"And so you pray three times a day, every day, to your god?" asked Bad Eagle, almost incredulously.

"Even four times on our Sabbath," added Sam.

"These are strange customs. You don't appear very strange from your looks and your clothes, hat, and beard. My men also found books among your things, written in a language I do not recognize."

"It is Hebrew, a language spoken by my people far away and long ago. It is only the language of our prayers today. Hardly anyone uses it for daily conversation."

"Our Comanche language I fear will one day soon fall into such disuse," the chief said. "We are hemmed in on all sides by the Americans, Mexicans, and other more numerous tribes. Perhaps we could learn from you how to keep our language alive if only to pray to our Great Spirit Tetonka."

Sam was weak from having eaten little since the day of his capture. He had been given plenty of water, but he had a gnawing feeling in his gut that water alone wouldn't satisfy.

"Give him some of the tamales and buffalo meat to chew on," Bad Eagle ordered.

In his duress, Sam had no choice but to take what his captors offered. After his meeting with Bad Eagle, things went better for him in the Comanche camp. The tribe was interested in exchanging him for something of value. It was just a matter of what opportunity would arise for such a transfer and how soon it would occur. In the meantime, Sam learned more about the Comanche way of life. Chief Bad Eagle sought him out on several occasions to discuss Jewish customs.

"Can Jews fight against other Jews?" the chief asked him one day.

"We are not a warlike people; we *can* fight of course if we have to, but we *don't*, generally."

"Comanches are forbidden by custom from making war on other Comanches, but we are surrounded by many enemies and there are no restrictions on killing them."

On another occasion, the chief asked Sam if he believed in many gods, as the Comanches did. They thought every object had its own spirit, but that the buffalo embodied the great universal life-giving spirit. Sam by observation understood easily why the buffalo was central to the Comanche belief system, essential as the animal was to every aspect of life on the plains, but he tried to explain to Bad Eagle the concept of one god from which all emanated.

"My people, the Jews, believe that heaven and earth were created by the one, all-powerful, all-knowing god or spirit," Sam explained. "There are no other gods. Our god *is* God. All of creation, including the buffalo, is his creation. We cannot see or touch God, but He exists just the same."

Bad Eagle had much trouble at first with the concept Sam described, but seemed to accept the possibility.

"I'm not sure I understand you, Sam, but I sure am glad your god created the buffalo."

Sam remained under Bad Eagle's "supervision" for about four months. One early winter morning, however, he awoke in the Antelope camp to discover that his captors had left rather abruptly on some kind of mission, leaving him on his own. He never quite discovered why they had abandoned him, it being their general habit to never leave something of value behind. Food had been scarce, and perhaps they didn't want to continue feeding him. Even more extraordinarily Sam found that they had left a pony tethered to a nearby tree. Sam rode toward the rising sun, and in a day or so saw the smoke of a farmhouse in the distance. The settlers who took him in were fascinated by Sam's story of captivity, and were amazed he had survived his ordeal with the Comanche. Soon, Sam was on his way toward Fort Sill (in Oklahoma) and a full return to his old life.

Sam heard little over the next years about Chief Bad Eagle and his band of warriors. He had lost a lot of weight during his ordeal, and his hair started to gray prematurely. In time, Sam gave up the itinerant life, settled in St. Louis, opened a large general store, married a woman of his faith, and raised several children.

He became a successful and proud member of his community. His grandchildren often asked him about his pioneering adventures and his days among the feared Comanches.

"What ever happened to the chief who spoke with you, Grandpa?"

"I heard that many years after I was his captive, maybe around 1874 or 1875, Bad Eagle and his group finally surrendered. They were the last of their tribe to give up. You see, their empire had fallen. Their numbers were dwindling, and white men were overrunning their land. Band by band, the Texas Rangers hunted them down until one small group remained, and I read that Bad Eagle and several other chiefs persuaded the last group to travel peacefully to Fort Sill. They had run out of options, since the buffalo were gone and they faced starvation in the coming winter months, always a hard time for the Indians."

Soon enough, Sam's memories of his Comanche captivity faded. In 1909, within a week of each other, both Sam and Bad Eagle died – Sam of a fever, surrounded by his many loved ones in St. Louis, a pillar of his growing Jewish community; and Bad Eagle of a stomach ailment, apparently after eating a tainted can of sardines, a suspected victim of tribal enemies. Unlike Sam's fading memory of his days with the Comanche, Bad Eagle never forgot that strange American captive with his customs of the one God and his prayerful life. He told his children and grandchildren of this man and they didn't forget the words of the old Comanche chief. In fact, one descendant of Bad Eagle did more, much more, than that.

On a late December night in 2013, I was surfing the Internet when I happened upon a website created by a Dr. David A. Yeagley, a great-great-grandson of Comanche Chief Bad Eagle. Yeagley was a former professor of humanities, psychology, literature, music, and philosophy. He espoused quite conservative political views on the site, but it was not his political and Native American activism that caught my eye. Among the many features of the site were

Yeagley's take on matters spiritual and musical. He had obtained
academic degrees from Oberlin College in music, Yale Divinity
School in religion, and Emory College in liberal arts.

What struck me as unusual was that the website contained
a series of serious articles written by Yeagley over the years on
Jewish subjects, including dissertations on tractate *Berachot* of
Talmud Bavli. Titles include "Midnight in the Talmud," "Talmud
in the Night," and "Talmud, Time, and Temptation." The most
impressive of all was an article entitled "Neusner, Mishna, and
the Talmud: When to Recite the Shema," which he published
on May 11, 2013. This article included a picture of Rabbi Adin
Steinsaltz whom Yeagley apparently met at Yale. It was quite a
surprise to find a Comanche Indian, albeit a highly educated
one, studying Jewish texts. Additionally, further research showed
that Yeagley's interest in Jewish scholarship and issues extended
much deeper. In addition to these essays, Yeagley had undertaken
a serious initiative to bring lessons in Chumash (the Five Books
of Moses), or "*shiurim*," as he called them, to a broad audience
on YouTube. In fact, he recorded ninety five-minute *shiurim* over
several months in 2012 in which he studied individual verses
from Bereishit. His introductory video is quite enlightening and
includes his explanation of why the descendant of a famed Indian
chief would undertake such an endeavor:

> I think it's important for everyone . . . the *goyim*, the Gentiles,
> to realize the Torah came out of the Jewish mind, its shape
> is Jewish. I believe that it is supernatural, that the instrument
> through which scripture came is the Jewish mind. I think
> that is very important. . . . I believe the Torah was divinely
> inspired. . . . The fact that it was communicated through the
> Jewish nation gave [the Torah] a uniquely Jewish flavor and
> character. . . . These [YouTube] lessons . . . are comprehensible
> by anyone with or without formal training and might hold
> interest for those who have training, whether it's at the level

of *aleph, bet,* or *gimmel* I cannot say.... The lessons are not meant to offend anyone, especially Jewish people. Hopefully [they] might find an interest in how a half-breed Indian views Jewish things.... *

Asked why he had such a close affinity for Jews and Jewish issues, Yeagley responded that the first time he actually met a Jew was at Yale in the late 1970s. The ability to meet flesh and blood descendants of Abraham, Moshe, and David after years of his studying the Bible was a life-changing event for him. Whatever the source of Yeagley's philo-Semitism, it permeated his life's work. Aside from his religious scholarship, Yeagley composed several classical music pieces on the Holocaust and other Jewish themes, and his website is full of blogged articles in support of Israel and its policies. As I reviewed these various topics, I was looking for possible "ulterior motivation" behind Yeagley's overtly pro-Jewish views, such as messianic messages and a hidden conversion agenda, and I couldn't find any. In fact, as a sign of possible "higher" approval for Yeagley's Torah-teaching endeavors, his introductory video is ironically immediately followed on YouTube by an inspiring video lecture by Rabbi Zev Leff of Moshav Matityahu in Israel, which is aptly entitled "Torah Learning Is Everything."

Finally, based on how anti-Semitic bloggers regularly attacked him on the Internet, you can rest assured David Yeagley was a true friend of the Jews, maybe the best Comanche friend our people have had since...well...since Chief Bad Eagle!

Dr. Yeagley lost his lengthy battle with cancer on March 11, 2014, at the age of sixty-three. His website, www.badeagle.com, formerly contained many items of interest to the Jewish community. Those interested in the details of the life of this extraordinary American writer, activist, and composer could find them there. It

---

* David Yeagley, "Shiurim Torah (Bereshith) Genesis 1," YouTube video, March 10, 2012, http://www.youtube.com/watch?v=VI1xLQdKooE.

was a site well worth visiting. Unfortunately, as of this writing, the site has been taken down and only a Wikipedia article and this biographical piece are the sole monuments to one of the most intriguing Comanches of all time.

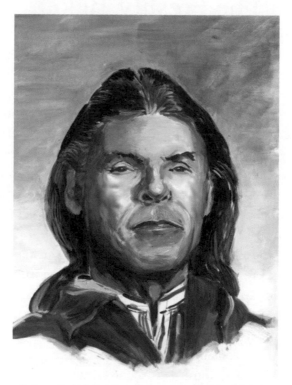

Professor David A. Yeagley, 1951–2014, Comanche Friend of the Jews.
Drawing by Norman Sonne

The Freshly Baked
Mountain Mashgiach

Vacations in the Catskills were a popular mainstay of the 1960s. Some of these small mountain towns provided the setting for memorable times shared by the hundreds of Jews who traveled there. There are so many great stories from those summers, and the one that follows is among my favorites.

On July 5, 1965, Jack Rabinowitz, his parents, and his five-year-old sister drove up the Rip Van Winkle Trail from the New York Thruway, past Palenville, Haines Falls, and Tannersville into Hunter. They unloaded their belongings into their small rental cottage on the Perlow property near the center of town, and within a day or two, Jack had fully reacquainted himself with the old gang of teenagers he had befriended the previous summer, riding his green, three-speed Raleigh sport touring bike down Main Street toward the famous Hunter Synagogue for prayer services. There were, however, some significant differences from the previous year. Jack, now fifteen years old, was a responsible junior in high school with expanding interests. His parents gave him more authority around the house and expected a greater display of maturity on his part. Jack wanted more independence and freedom from parental supervision.

To achieve his goals, Jack decided he would need an independent source of income. Not that his parents were not generous in meeting any reasonable request, it was just that as a teenage boy spending the entire summer in Hunter, New York, it would be advantageous to have a steady source of income derived from non-parental sources. Jack would have to find some kind of paying job or jobs. During his first week in Hunter, he secured a weekly job giving Hebrew lessons to the ten-year-old grandson of the owner of the town's main department store. The boy was an eager student, but it didn't pay very well, so Jack looked elsewhere for supplementation.

"I heard the Hunter day camp is looking for counselors," Jack's mother said to him.

"Not really what I want to do: chasing little kids around, telling them what to do. It's like being a watchdog. Boring," Jack countered.

After two days of getting nowhere, the door of opportunity finally opened. After morning prayers, Jack's friend Aaron told him that the Hunter bakery was looking for a *mashgiach* to supervise the limited run of kosher products they produced each week. It involved working roughly six hours a week over two or three days, the pay was good, and, best of all, you got to work in a bakery. The job didn't require rabbinical training, just enough understanding of Hebrew, knowledge of the laws of separating challah from the dough, and sufficient manual dexterity to attach the "Kosher Pareve" stickers on the finished product. Jack jumped at the chance and sped directly to the bakery on Main Street, just down the road from the synagogue.

Twenty minutes later, Jack was in the kitchen of his bungalow, telling his mom about his good fortune.

"I've never been on the inside of a real bakery – it should be fascinating."

"Just think," his mom said, "you'll be providing kosher bread to hundreds of families in the mountains!"

Jack's friends were duly impressed when he told them of his new job, though some joked that they would never again eat a piece of bread from any bakery that hired him. But, all kidding aside, they were a little jealous of him, Jack thought.

Jack was scheduled to start his job the following Wednesday. On the allotted day, he got to the bakery early for orientation. Eddie, the chief baker, led him through the swinging kitchen doors, and Jack found himself in a large warehouse-shaped room filled with shiny stainless steel machinery with white powder and flour floating thickly in the air. Most noticeable were the large conveyors separating the prepared dough of various types into the required shapes and sizes. Workers stood by to take the pieces of dough that came off the conveyors and prepare whatever type of bread or rolls were being created at that particular time. On that day, submarine rolls were on the menu, and in no time Jack was learning how to fold the dough into the required shape. He tried his luck on one or two rolls while the pros effortlessly tossed out six or seven perfect ones each. They laughed at Jack's efforts and he half-heartedly joined in.

"I feel sorry for the poor person who ends up with the submarine roll I prepared!" he said to no one in particular.

Eddie motioned to Jack to follow him to a section in the back of the room away from the conveyors. There, in a large, low vat sat the main object of Jack's attention: a huge mass of grayish-white, viscous mixture that bore a close resemblance to quicksand or oatmeal. It was quite thick; occasional bubbles rose to the surface of the blob, creating the illusion that the mixture was alive, belching flour into the surrounding air. Eddie explained to Jack that rye bread, the staple kosher product made at the bakery, was a mixture of rye flour and wheat flour to give the finished loaves a lighter color. The dough in the vat contained the mixed flours along with a sourdough starter that facilitated fermentation of the dough and aided in causing the bread to rise before the baking began. Jack was amazed at the intricacy of the process.

"You've got to be a scientist almost to figure out how to prepare bread," he said to Eddie.

"Not really, Jack; bakers have been making these breads for thousands of years. It's pretty simple to prepare them these days. There are plenty of variations today. We make the most basic bread for the kosher market. Now, we're going to start baking shortly, so do your thing now!"

Jack reached for the pad where he had marked out the blessing he was required to recite over the dough. He gingerly grabbed a fistful of the gelatinous dough from the vat, walked over to the large oven, recited the blessing, and tossed the dough into the fire. The workers then rolled the vat toward the conveyors where other workers started to load armfuls of the dough into the cutting funnel. After a minute or two, roughly equal portions of dough descended the conveyor toward the workers standing ready to roll the dough into individual loaves. The finished loaves were placed on sheets where they could rise. After that, they would be loaded onto racks for transport to the ovens. The whole process, including the baking, took under three hours. Once the loaves were removed from the ovens, they would cool, following which Jack was to place the stamped stickers on each loaf, indicating that the bread was baked under kosher supervision.

Following his first bread run, Jack was congratulated by the bakery staff. He was paid his per diem by the bakery owners and was soon on his way home for lunch.

Back home, Jack had a big appetite for the casserole his mom had prepared.

"It's pretty amazing how a bakery works, mom," Jack told her. "A lot of coordination of activities is necessary, and the workers move about their jobs quickly. They can turn out dozens of rolls in no time!"

"I would guess it's actually a lot harder than it looks," his mom countered.

Jack returned the next day for another rye bread run and repeated his work the following week. After four rye bread runs and several more attempts at mastering Kaiser roll preparation, Jack was getting bored with the routines of bread *hashgachah*. The third week at the job proved to be his downfall, and it had nothing to do with rye bread, sourdough, or rolls.

Jack's Achilles heel proved to be jelly doughnuts, confections renowned for their pastry-like consistency and sweet surprise fillings. Early on, Jack had questioned Eddie about when and how jelly doughnuts were filled with their delicious filling during the cooking process. Eddie informed him that the jelly doughnuts prepared at the Hunter bakery were a once-a-week job, and that the doughnuts were deep-fried but could be baked if desired. The jelly was the last piece of the puzzle. The bakery used an advanced injection system to force the jelly into the doughnuts; this consisted of a two-pronged needle-like device that shot a measured amount of jelly into each doughnut when you pressed it against the needles.

"But you really shouldn't touch that machine, as it can be quite temperamental and sometimes jams up," warned Eddie. "The jelly doughnuts, containing eggs as they do, are not certified kosher anyway, and you should stay away from them."

Jack heeded Eddie's warning at the start, until one day during his fourth week on the job. During a break in the bread-baking process that day, Jack forgot himself and grabbed two jelly doughnuts from a freshly baked tray and walked over to the electrically powered machine. As he pressed the doughnuts against the machine, it jammed in the "on" position. The bakery prep area was soon covered with the sticky reddish mixture that squirted without stop from the jelly machine. Rows upon rows of bread, rolls, cakes, and cookies were quickly ruined, and Jack sadly found himself being shown the door. Luckily for those who required kosher supervision, Jack's friend Aaron was quickly hired to replace him. Luckily for Jack, the bakery didn't charge him for the damage he had caused.

Years later, in looking back on his brief tenure as a bakery *mashgiach*, Jack confessed admiration for the toil and creativity of those who worked in bakeries. Though Jack never served as a *mashgiach* again, he certainly ate his fair share of baked goods during the remainder of his life – all baked goods, that is, except jelly doughnuts.

A Jewish Guide
to Board Games

Teddy and Mila/shutterstock.com

Whether it's Chanukah or we're celebrating a birthday with a friend or family member, there always seems to be an event that might require just that special gift of a game. I'm talking about the non-electronic types that we used to spend hours playing, the favorites of Americans for generations. Let's briefly analyze these games to better understand why they remain perennials and see what lessons may be learned by our eager Jewish youth from playing them.

GO TO THE HEAD OF THE CLASS. Parents' favorite...kids, not so much. Prepares boys and girls for competitiveness in the classroom and in life, not to mention the correlation with Trivial Pursuit, SAT, and achievement scores later in life.

CANDY LAND. Positive prep for early dentist visits; negatives include probable early tooth decay and an onset of type 2 diabetes; favorite game of Big Pharma. Involves the uncomplicated pleasures of life, teaches that little effort is required to achieve a spectacular sugar high. Requires limited counting skills and no reading skills. No strategy whatsoever needed. Never too young to learn that in life the winner can often be predetermined by a mere shuffle of the cards.

CHUTES AND LADDERS. Early exposure to the literal and figurative ups and downs of life, this game stresses how little careful planning has to do with success and achievement in life and how much luck is involved in outcomes. Invented in ancient India, where it was called Snakes and Ladders, it focused on the virtues and vices to advance up or slip down the board of life.

THE GAME OF LIFE. Live your life from cradle to retirement home in a matter of hours instead of years. Play at parenting, working, and paying the mortgage and taxes, not to mention insurance premiums and utility bills, all from the comfort of your living room. Known to cause depression in child prodigies.

MONOPOLY. Capitalism 101. Practice going in and out of jail for white-collar infractions or landlord violations. A "Pardon" card would be preferable to a "Get out of jail free," since we all know there are no free lunches in this world. Early reality check: teaches pre-teens there's a real chance they're not going to grow up to be tycoons and reinforces the Torah lesson that "by the sweat of their brows, they'll eat their bread"!

STRATEGO. Why go to war and face bodily harm when you can stealthily bring your adversary to surrender his flag? Stresses short-term memory development, so you remember where your opponent placed his important pieces.

SORRY. What can you say about a game where the best part consists of drawing the desirable "Sorry" card that allows you to send anyone you want back to the start of the game as many times as you can? Only truly vengeful types will enjoy playing this game of chance.

ADVERTEASING. A relative newcomer to the board game field, this game consists of matching products with their familiar advertising slogans or jingles. Will appeal only to non-cynical bar and bat mitzvah age or older. First exposure to ironies and other flaws of medical advertising; beware of side effects. These medications may cause more harm than good; the tummy ache you're trying to cure may morph into an ulcer!

SCRABBLE, CLUE, CHINESE CHECKERS, AND CHESS. These games will only help to increase your vocabulary skills, find lost objects, solve murders, and plan ahead – worthy achievements, but in no way comparable to ruling the world or devouring your favorite ice cream. Favors those who can think ahead and anticipate their opponent's moves.

Despite the popularity of the foregoing games, the really challenging board games involve mathematical reasoning and probability skills possessed by very few. That's why they're not particularly fun to play. Chances are that if you receive a Backgammon set, for instance, the gift donor never personally mastered the game himself. Think about it: Is it really fun to traverse a board with your pieces, moving to open spaces on the throw of a pair of dice? Only the mathematically inclined among us would take pleasure in such a pursuit. Backgammon was invented by the Greco-Romans and remained popular with medieval Europeans, so if you want to play a really old game, this one's for you.

Whichever of these board games catches your fancy, the biggest problem you'll face over time will be avoiding the loss of critical game pieces. In order of importance:

- Try not to lose the spinner that determines how many spaces you advance on your turn. Dice of course can substitute for the spinner, but I'm pretty sure you'll misplace one or both of the dice in fairly short order.
- Game pieces are important as well; in some cases, losing a game piece means the game is over, but you can often fashion a substitute.
- Finally, the "money" required in several of the games discussed, if lost, can't really be replaced, unless you're willing to substitute the contents of your wallet (I'm speaking to parents now!).

Assuming you avoid any of the mishaps mentioned in the previous paragraph, you should have hours and hours of fun playing with your friends and family. Good luck! But please check with your local rabbi as to the halachic implications of playing any or all of these games on Shabbat or *yom tov* (holiday).

An Oil Crisis

Warning! The following story has nothing to do with Saudi Arabia, OPEC, or the price of a gallon of gas at your favorite service station. It's really a story about my childhood friend Jakey Rabinowitz and the time he came close to violating a certain biblical proscription and nearly upsetting the cosmic balance in the process.

Jakey was the kind of kid your parents would always tell you they wished you were more like: an A student, well groomed, polite, and helpful. Truth is Jakey was a phenomenal student; he was almost a year younger than anyone else in our high school class, yet he was taller than most and extremely bright. The only thing wrong about him was his rebellious streak, which he somehow kept hidden from most of the adults in our community. The guys, however, were witness to several of his schemes and pranks, and on several occasions he barely escaped the punishment that was due him. There was, for instance, the time in biology class that he gave samples of his rare blood type to a number of his classmates to submit as their own during a blood-typing experiment. (They were afraid to use the lancet to draw their own blood.) To this day, our teacher still hasn't figured out how half our class had B Negative blood type.

One time, however, Jakey overstepped the line, and the results could have been disastrous. It was just after Yom Kippur. Jakey and I spent a lot of the fast day standing at the back of our synagogue on the Upper West Side in New York, philosophizing as only smart-aleck fifteen-year-olds can.

"I regret only one thing," Jakey said to me, "and that's being born in our time and not two hundred years from now."

"What are you talking about?"

"If we'd been born two hundred years from now, all the major diseases would have been conquered, and people would be living healthy lives of at least one hundred years."

I couldn't refute Jakey's logic, but I was a realist, I guess, and since we were alive now, we couldn't do anything about being born in the future. A *gabbai* walked past us with his finger on his lips, so we broke up our impromptu session and headed back to our seats to pray.

I caught up with Jakey in Riverside Park the following Shabbat. He told me to drop by his house the following morning, as he had a "chemistry" project he wanted to work on with me.

"I've decided after much thought to create something meaningful. It's something we studied about in school, and I want to submit it as our joint science project," Jakey began. "I don't know whether to use it for our chemistry class, our Tanach [Hebrew Bible] project, or both."

I wondered what could possibly qualify as both a chemistry and a Tanach project.

"Do you remember when we were learning about the construction of the Mishkan [Tabernacle] in the desert, how Moshe was given a recipe to confect the *shemen hamishchah* [oil of anointment]?

"Moshe was instructed to create this special oil to anoint the Tabernacle, its walls, and all of the priests. When the Israelites entered Canaan, they used the oil to anoint their prophets and kings. Supposedly, the oil that Moshe created lasted a very long time, since they never totally used up that oil and just kept adding to it."

"Is he crazy?" I thought. Had Jakey forgotten that the oil is supposed to be used to anoint the Messiah and that it's a sin to reproduce the exact oil that Moshe mixed?

"Jakey," I said, "no one is supposed to prepare that recipe exactly as Moshe did in the Torah; if you happen to succeed, the consequences could be dire. Please think of another project. Also, there isn't even agreement among the sources about some of the ingredients," I protested.

But Jakey was too caught up in his project to listen to me and change his mind.

"It would be so easy," Jakey continued. "All we need to do is mix the ingredients set out in the parashah and prepare several batches according to the different viewpoints of the rabbis. The batch of the rabbi whose view is correct will reproduce the 'winning' oil."

The notion of the next king of Judah or Israel walking around Manhattan seemed incredible to me, not to mention a newly anointed Messiah shopping at Zabar's!

My objections didn't shake Jakey's determination to proceed; in fact, he had already purchased the "ingredients," which he began to spread out on his parents' large dining room table. First, he put out the four ingredients agreed on by the authorities: thirteen pounds of pure myrrh, six pounds of sweet cinnamon, thirteen pounds of cassia, and about a gallon of pure olive oil. The fifth ingredient, called *kanneh bosem*, was the tricky one: most authorities identified it as a sweet cane grass, but the Rambam and other Rishonim had differing opinions. The volume of olive oil to be used was also subject to dispute. All these differing opinions made me feel a little better about Jakey's project. How likely would it be that he would get the mixture exactly right?

For the next several hours, Jakey mixed and matched until he completed four "likely combinations." They were all quite thick, with a brownish paste-like consistency, given the overwhelming proportions of spices and herbs to the olive oil. What Jakey, as smart as he was, had not quite figured out was how to test his anointing oil. His baby brother and his pet malamute ran in the opposite direction as he approached them with a cupful of mixture in hand.

"Jakey," I objected, "you don't need to test it! It's enough that you put it together. We're sure to get a good grade just by demonstrating what we did."

After a while, Jakey had to agree there were too many risks in concocting the actual anointing oil. The biblical proscription was punishable by lashes, which neither of us wished to contemplate. If we had produced the "real thing" among our samples, who knew what the consequences would be if we anointed someone, intentionally or otherwise? Accordingly, we placed a small amount of each sample in separate small vials and disposed of the rest. The next day, we presented to our Tanach and chemistry teachers the results of our work and, happily, our efforts were rewarded with A's all round.

Sometime later, I asked Jakey if he had really been tempted at any time to "try out" the anointing oil on someone, just for the heck of it.

"Actually," he said, "I was tempted to try it out on myself, but I thought it wouldn't do to be called a 'self-appointed' Messiah."

Looking back, I thought he used the term "self-anointed" and not "self-appointed," but, if you think about it, they pretty much mean the same thing.

Some fifty years have passed since the above anecdote with Jakey took place. It has been a long time since I have spoken with him; sadly, I'm not certain where he lives or what he does. But I was surfing the Internet recently when my eye caught the following online advertisement: For the inexpensive price of $4.70 a bottle, you can acquire today from Ein Bokek Cosmetics a quarter-ounce bottle called "Light of Jerusalem Anointing Oil," described as a "blend of frankincense, myrrh, cinnamon, and cassia with virgin olive oil to form a product reminiscent of biblical oils." The bottle is fashioned in the ancient style for "authenticity." "Miraculous formula," the ad continues. In small print it concludes "Results not guaranteed."

Five glowing endorsements from around the globe accompany

the ad. I think Jakey would have been proud of me for starting Ein Bokek Cosmetics some years ago, the company his experiment had inspired. It's made me a lot of money, even though it's debatable if our product has yet transformed the world. But who knows what's possible in the future? While it's generally agreed the Messiah has yet to appear on the Upper West Side, it's been rumored the reigning King of Judah resides in Riverdale.

Belmar Tale –
A Chain of Daddies

An old Jewish proverb says that a person can never have too many guides on his life's journey. The real difficulty lies in knowing which advice to take and which to ignore. Sometimes things cannot be proven with scientific accuracy but simply have to be taken on faith – just as the young child who grew to trust his father in the following story did.

A seven-year-old boy is spending the summer of 1957 at a beachfront hotel on the Jersey Shore. It's early August and the weekend is approaching. Waves crash ashore and the ocean appears broad and overpowering. The penny arcade, already old, with games for a penny, newly rigged for five or ten cents, stands mute opposite the wooden boardwalk. The electronic shooting (gunnery) showcases vintage games of World War II, begging to be played, their photoelectric sensors registering hits or misses as enemy aircraft dart like ghosts across the glass panel erected before the player. The old guesthouse annex, gabled, with creaky steps leading up to a covered porch, sits perched at the corner of the sand-strewn street angled toward the ocean. Two withered wicker rocking chairs await the boy and his father, who climb the stairs and sit together, dressed in their Shabbat clothing, awaiting the evening services.

"Daddy, can I ask you a question?"

"Sure," the father replies.

"How do we know that all the stories in the Torah are true?" asks the boy. "And how do you know that we're really Cohanim?"

"Those are good questions," answers the father. He ponders his response for a moment. "Well, I learned these stories from my father when I was your age, and Grandpa was taught these same stories by his father when he was a boy, and so on over all the years back to the time of the Bible: many daddies teaching these stories to many sons such as you. Maybe a hundred daddies back! And a daddy wouldn't lie to his son. So that's how we know they're true!"

"Also," his father continues, "my daddy told me I'm a Cohen and his daddy told him the same, all the way back to Aharon Hacohen!"

The boy listened to his father's explanation carefully, trying to take in the distances in time these stories had traveled to reach him on that porch, where he sat rocking, facing the timeless ocean.

Here on the shores of the mighty Atlantic, an important moment in Jewish tradition has been repeated, the transmission of our ancient lore and belief system. The father has been awaiting his young son's first questioning of the Torah knowledge he had acquired at home and in school, his son's first doubts or, more accurately, desire for tangible proofs that what he had learned had in fact occurred. Thirty-six years earlier, the boy's father had sat on the European shore of the North Sea in Knokke, Belgium, a seaside beach resort nestled near the Dutch border, asking his own father these same questions. The response was the same that day in 1923, Jewish tradition being transmitted through the "chain of daddies" to another Jewish child.

Our Belmar boy's grandfather had himself been born in southeast Poland in 1868, in a town with no massive body of water, no seashore to launch his Torah dreams. Yet it is not inconceivable that his father, Rabbi Mordche the vinegar maker, told his son of the "chain of daddies" proof sometime around 1875.

Rabbi Mordche's father had been a Torah scholar in Poland; he had authored several commentaries on portions of the Babylonian Talmud. In an introduction to one volume, he listed the names and occupations of several of his ancestors dating back to the early 1700s, more tangible flesh-and-blood "daddies" to add to the 1957 chain of transmission.

Back in Belmar that Friday evening in 1957, the boy and his father sit at their hotel dining room table, which glistens with polished silverware and gleaming Kiddush cups. The boy feels a strong connection with his father that night, a closer kinship with the Jewish people than he had ever felt before. He senses that one day he might be called upon to relay the "chain of daddies" story to his own children. He smiles to himself as he sips some sweet wine from his Kiddush cup.

In the years that follow, the boy will be exposed to many alternative theories of where he came from and where his right place in history might be. Despite the sophistication of these ideas and their superficial attractiveness, the boy will not forget that Friday afternoon conversation with his father in Belmar. Remaining firmly rooted in his mind, it will guide him throughout his life, reminding him of who he is and all that he can be. As luck would have it, one day he too would add his own new links to the chain of daddies, his own sons reacting with the same joy and recognition that he had done as he transmitted to them the lessons he had learned from his father that summer day long ago in Belmar.

Uncle Malcolm, Travel Advisor

There was a time when Jake Rabinowitz was at a crossroads, when his life was not in perfect balance. Today, he is near the top of his profession, with a happy wife and three admiring children. A large home with no mortgage and many charitable deeds complete the picture of Jake's full life. But Jake remembers when it was not like that at all, when a chance meeting with his Uncle Malcolm sent a clueless Jake in the direction of success and happiness.

Malcolm Maiglich, Jake's only maternal uncle, lived on the West Side of Manhattan or, as he liked to call it, New Mesopotamia, that island of active life between the Hudson and East Rivers. His place of employment was a storefront on 87th Street and Broadway, where he plied his trade as a travel agent, helping his clients sort through available vacation destinations (both domestic and international), book reservations, and the like. He also kept a selection of somewhat out-of-date guidebooks for the most popular destinations. He couldn't really compete with the large travel agencies, the AAAs of the world or the large book chains, but it was a living and it met his needs. Despite residing alone in a fairly sizable rent-controlled apartment on 90th and Columbus Avenue, and maintaining a fairly isolated social life, Jake's uncle possessed some rather special people skills. He was charming and readily put people at ease. He often joked that he had an "elevator personality," meaning that if he entered an elevator with a stranger on the ground floor, he would know his new friend's life story in detail by the time they exited a few floors later.

But such friendliness didn't extend to all members of his family. Sadly, Malcolm had never been particularly close with his sister or her children, including Jake.

Yet there was the time about three years earlier, on a particularly chilly late fall day, that Jake scheduled an appointment with his uncle to plan a winter break getaway for Jake's family. Preliminary discussions narrowed down the options to Disney World or Miami. After some time, Malcolm and Jake reached a joint determination that Disney World offered the better value. Jake seemed troubled, however, nervous and hesitant to totally commit. Malcolm sensed that something serious was bothering his nephew.

"Are you OK?" Malcolm asked.

Jake paused, fingered the Disney brochure laid out in front of him, and began. "Uncle Mal, it's my job – my work, I mean. I'm frustrated about the direction of my life, actually – my professional life, that is. You know I work here in the city at a good job as a DKK attorney."

"Is it a matter of money; do you need something to tide you over? I'm single, you know, and have put a nice sum aside that I'd be happy to help you out with."

"Oh, no, Uncle Mal, that's so generous of you, but it's not really necessary," Jake said. "I bring a fairly large paycheck home every two weeks from DKK, and Esther works as a teacher. It's just that I feel unfulfilled by my job as a litigator, like there must be something more to life. I spent years studying hard to get to where I am and now that I've arrived at my current position, it's as if I can't see myself doing this for the rest of my life," he faltered. "I really shouldn't be bothering you with all my personal problems – you must have some of your own."

"It's not a bother at all. I've heard your lament often. You've ended up in the business of providing legal services and you're thinking, 'Well, if I'm working in a business, there are a lot of other businesses after all that I'd prefer to be engaged in!'"

"That's exactly right," said Jake. "I mean, the first day I started working in my firm, they presented me with a thick pad of time sheets on which I was to record, in eighth of an hour segments, all activities I undertook on a given day. Please believe me that in all my years of higher education, including law school, I had never *heard* of time sheets nor given a thought as to how clients are billed. I was a true idiot savant when it came to the practice of law! After all, I was the first lawyer in the family, and I saw myself as a direct successor to Clarence Darrow, Louis Nizer, and Perry Mason!"

"Jake, how many years have you been practicing? Seven, eight?"

"Eight," Jake responded.

"Your disillusionment with your chosen profession could be said to be 'right on schedule.' Last week, I had a young medical student planning a winter cruise to the Bahamas. What he really wanted was to discuss his unhappiness with life as a young resident – his frustration with the long hours, and his future as a doctor. He, too, is facing a future of government-regulated healthcare, that spider's web of limits and rules and just so many details that have nothing to do with helping people live healthier lives. And the week before, a CPA dropped by and he too lamented his career choices. You, Jake, and those other two all had so much in common – young, ambitious, hard-working, and unhappy!"

"Well, what did you advise them," Jake asked.

"I reminded them that they have a lot more control over their lives than they could ever imagine. I invited each one, as I invite you, to come as my guest to my apartment for dinner at their convenience, where I discussed a specific plan of action for them in more detail. I invite you to do the same."

Jake had been listening to Malcolm's remarks with interest, and he agreed to take his uncle up on his offer. He did so with a mixture of relief and trepidation; he had been under a lot of pressure at work and desperately needed a friend to confide in. He couldn't afford to reject any offers of help.

Malcolm buzzed Jake in a little before 8:00 on the designated evening. Jake entered the apartment through a sizable foyer; it was a one-bedroom affair with a fairly spacious living room-dining room arrangement. They sat down facing each other on the tan-colored couches, a coffee table between them. The walls of the large room were covered with oil paintings and woodcrafts.

"I bought a sampling of some Chinese foods for the occasion," Malcolm began. "I hope that's OK."

"That's fine," said Jake. "Esther is expecting me back in about an hour."

"Take a look at some of my paintings, Jake. You might find them interesting," Malcolm said as he walked to the kitchen to prepare the food.

Jake rose from the sofa and turned to the nearest grouping of artwork. He immediately noticed that the artist appeared to be Malcolm himself, if the large "M" inscribed in the lower left-hand corner meant anything.

"Yes, I am the creator of all the artwork you see," Malcolm shouted from the kitchen, anticipating Jake's question.

The first group of paintings were brightly colored images of various handicraftsmen arranged sequentially across the main wall of the room. They were plainly framed, the lightly tinged wood contrasting nicely with the intense hues of the subject matter. Jake's eyes quickly scanned seven pieces comprising the group, seemingly in no particular order. Malcolm had painted a potter at his wheel, a mason grasping a stone, a welder embracing a piece of iron, a seaman steering the wheel of his ship, a glazier shaping a piece of colored glass, a draper dealing in cloth, and finally, a silversmith hard at work at his craft. The seven figures appeared almost lifelike in detail, animated in the artificial light in which they were bathed. Jake felt that the images seemed to shift as he stared at them, sometimes almost moving about before his eyes.

"Interesting paintings, aren't they?" Malcolm interrupted Jake's reverie. "Care for an eggroll?"

Jake took the offered treat and sat down again on the sofa. "You have great artistic skill," Jake said. "Why aren't you painting professionally? You're very good!"

"The paintings you've been studying are the only subjects I feel qualified to put on canvas," Uncle Malcolm answered. "They contain the sum total of all I believe in and think worthy of preserving."

Malcolm and Jake sat down to their dinner, following which Malcolm got down to the substance of this meeting.

"Those paintings, you may have noticed, describe several different labors where humans appear to have some freedom of action, but in reality I believe everything in life is divinely decreed. It's the illusion of freedom that each worker possesses, but our momentary desires matter far less than the divine plan. You may be disillusioned by your current career. I'm therefore telling you that if that plan permits, you can choose without fear to take your life in another direction. Of course, change may bring uncertainty, temporary loss of some income, and friction with loved ones, but that doesn't mean it won't ultimately prove the wise course to take."

"I'm not sure I agree that everything in life is divinely determined; and even if it is, how will I know that I won't live to regret changing my profession?" Jake countered.

"You simply won't know for sure. But if you're a believer, remember that two very wise men, Isaiah and Jeremiah, both believed that every professional who ever lived was merely 'clay' to be shaped by the Almighty, all Hashem's handiwork. Remember that even though your ultimate fate is predetermined, you still have an active part to play in the outcome. For if you choose to do nothing about your current situation, you will only have yourself to blame."

Jake thought long and hard about what his uncle told him. He glanced up at the pictures on the wall.

"I'm just not sure what to do," Jake said.

Malcolm took a slightly different approach.

"Look at it this way. In our modern times, we question more

and more what the meaning of life is. We strive and strive, follow all the guidelines our elders set out for us, achieve a certain status in our chosen profession, and question whether, in the end, it's worth it. What exactly does it mean to be a success, we ask. You alone can decide that answer, Jake. Take all your inherent skills and instincts, your genetics, add all your acquired knowledge, and do the best you can. The rest is up to chance. Remember, also, that the one with the largest bank account, the most 'toys' at the end of his days, is not necessarily the 'winner'!"

Before he headed out, Jake studied the paintings one last time.

"Now I remember what inspired these paintings; it's that prayer from the High Holy Days, isn't it?" Jake asked "That was your 'being shaped from clay' reference, wasn't it?"

"Guilty on all counts, Jake!"

Back on Columbus Avenue, Jake walked slowly toward his apartment two blocks downtown. Jake knew Uncle Mal was right to place the emphasis on luck in the equation of Jake's future success, professionally or otherwise. As the moon came out, Jake held fast to the small painting Malcolm had given him as a present. It was a silver etched drawing of the words "Mazal Tov" on a light blue background, and Jake knew he'd hang it in a prominent place in his apartment and in his heart.

Jack Is Jilted

Doors open and close. Opportunity knocks and is gone just as quickly: mere clichés or the essence of human experience? Consider this episode from the life of Jack Rabinowitz back in 1976. It was registration day at City College, and Jack drove up to the college in Harlem with his close friend Mark. Jack's own registration at Columbia wasn't scheduled for another week, but he drove uptown to hang out with Mark because there was nothing else going on that day.

Parking on Convent Avenue, Jack saw Rebecca almost immediately in the crowd of students milling around in irregular groupings in front of the registration hall. She acknowledged him briefly with a nod. They exchanged a few words of greeting, but without any particular warmth. Their respective friends nearby didn't know how close they had been over the last few years. Jack had felt their relationship slipping away over the past few months and he wasn't eager to continue the conversation; it was just a little too painful to be in Rebecca's presence after the adventures they had shared.

"Good luck," was the best he could come up with as they parted.

Mark left Jack at the entrance to the hall, promising to take no more than half an hour to register. In actuality, it took more like an hour, during which time Jack sat on a comfortable bench reading a book he had brought along just in case he got bored.

"All done," Mark announced. "Just have to go to the bookstore to pick out the required texts. Shouldn't take too long."

Jack accompanied Mark to the store about three blocks away. Students lined the street in front of the store, old and new friends meeting up for the first social event of the new semester. Inside the bookstore, there were row upon row of texts laid out on shelves, tables, and the floor, with printed signs highlighting courses by subject and number. Mark headed for the math section at the rear of the store, while Jack stopped in front of the humanities section to riffle through the pages of a title that caught his eye. He returned the volume to the shelf, turned, and saw a girl standing to his left with a look of frustration in her remarkable eyes. He had seen her talking to Mark earlier, so without hesitation, he asked her if she needed help finding something.

"It's all so confusing," she said. "So many books, and so many people!"

"I couldn't agree more," Jack offered. "I saw you talking to Mark before. I'm one of his oldest friends. Like I said, do you need any help?"

She had been unable to locate the books required for her Freshman English course, and for good reason: "Those books aren't in yet. They're on order," the clerk informed them.

Jack helped her gather the other books she required, playing the gallant gentleman by offering to help her carry them to the checkout line. As they waited together to pay, he impulsively asked her if he could call her up sometime and perhaps take her to a movie. He felt justified in doing so, since it was apparent Mark knew her and that was enough of an introduction for Jack at the moment.

"Sure," she said. Jack scribbled down her number on a random piece of paper and placed it in his wallet. He helped her outside with her bags of books, left her with some friends, and joined Mark for the return car ride back to the West Side.

It didn't take Jack long to call up the girl for a date. Vivian answered on the third ring and then, after he reintroduced himself, they agreed on a day and time for their first date. A movie and maybe something to eat was the modest program, but Jack was happy to have taken the initiative that day in the bookstore. She lived in Washington Heights, near the George Washington Bridge and the northern Port Authority Bus Terminal. He took the subway uptown to the Heights that first late afternoon and walked along Fort Washington Avenue until he reached her building. Hers was the last one on the avenue, almost projecting out onto an outcropping of Manhattan granite running alongside the upper level of the bridge itself. The six-story building had an ancient elevator that creakily rose to the top floor where Vivian lived with her parents and older sister. He walked down the corridor to her apartment, saw the *mezuzah* on the doorpost, rang the bell, and waited. He could hear voices inside.

"I'll get it – it's for me!" the voice said.

Vivian opened the door. She seemed shorter than Jack remembered. She was dressed casually in a blouse and skirt.

"It's a little chilly. You might want to take a light coat in case it gets cooler later."

"I'll be back by 11:00 or so," she shouted over her shoulder to her father, who appeared in the background. "Bye."

As they made their way outside, Jack looked at her. He liked how she looked, her blue eyes clear and her long brown hair tied back.

Their first date went as expected. They talked about school, which had recently begun for both of them, about their first college classes, those they liked and those they didn't. The subway ride downtown was uneventful, dinner at Lou G. Siegel's expensive, and the film somewhat overdone. It was Hollywood's take on the Broadway hit *Camelot*, and none of the actors who had the major parts – King Arthur, his queen, Guinevere or Sir Lancelot – could sing a note. Everyone in the audience waited for Lancelot to sing "If Ever I Would Leave You," at which point *they* wanted to leave the theater!

As they walked along Fort Washington back to her apartment,

the wind from the Hudson was brisk, blowing her hair in that violent way only people who live along the river would recognize. They said goodnight at the door and Jack began the trek back home happy and looking forward to their next date.

The next time, Jack took Vivian to one of his favorite places, Madison Square Garden, to watch his beloved New York Rangers play ice hockey. Vivian was genuinely taken with the exciting, colorful game, and they followed up the match with a ride through Central Park, enjoying the night air.

Over the next two months, as midterms began at school, Jack and Vivian saw each other only twice, conversing more frequently on the telephone. As New Year's Eve approached, Jack asked Vivian out for the big evening, planning dinner and a show followed by a visit to Times Square to usher in 1968 with thousands of others. She accepted the invitation without hesitation. On New Year's Eve, Jack prepared for the date with special enthusiasm. At around 5:00, as he was shaving, the phone rang in Jack's apartment. His father answered and called him to the phone.

It was Vivian. "I'm so sorry, but I can't make it tonight, Jack; I haven't felt well all day and my parents don't think it's a good idea for me to go out tonight, the cold weather and all."

"You're kidding, Vivian. "

Jack was so surprised that he couldn't hide his disappointment on the phone.

"You're sure?" he said finally in a weak voice.

She confirmed that the date was off, and all Jack could do was sit there unhappy at this last-minute change in plans.

"Well, I hope you feel better. Get some rest tonight – and tomorrow's an off day, you know," he meekly offered. "By the way, I bought you a little gift of the new Cat Stevens album you said you wanted to get."

Jack paused and then got an idea.

"I could bring it by your house tomorrow morning if you like.

Sort of make a comfort call to help you get better quicker and bring the album with me."

The offer surprised her so that she didn't know what to say. Jack's offer was reasonable enough if she was really sick. Jack himself wasn't sure whether or not Vivian was going out after all on another date that night, only that she wasn't going out with him! He firmly reiterated his offer to see her the next day.

"I'll see you tomorrow around 10:30. Meanwhile relax and feel better."

Vivian responded with a weak "OK" and hung up the receiver.

"You're not going to believe this, Dad," Jack informed his father. "But my date for tonight just got cancelled. She said she's sick, but I'm not sure. I'm 'all dressed up and nowhere to go,' just like the song."

Jack dried his tousled hair and thought for a moment about whether Vivian was getting ready in her apartment for her New Year's Eve date with someone else. At that moment, he realized their relationship had probably come to an end, and, for an instant, he felt that sickly feeling he always felt when someone he liked broke up with him. The feeling lingered. He'd take her the record album the next day as a parting gift of sorts. It was the "adult" thing to do. If she really wasn't sick, at least his visit the next day would require her to spend New Year's morning pretending she were so!

"Aren't the Rangers playing tonight at home?" his father interrupted any thoughts of revenge Jake harbored toward Vivian. "Maybe we could get some last-minute tickets, good seats, since it's New Year's Eve," he offered.

Within two hours Jack and his dad were sitting against the glass at the old Garden watching their favorite team go at it with the Maple Leafs, the sting of rejection having, for the most part, left Jack.

The next morning, Jack rang Vivian's doorbell promptly at 10:30. Vivian's mother ushered him into the living room, where

Vivian sat on a sofa covered with a blanket. Through the window, Jack could see the nearby eastbound lanes of the bridge, traffic sporadically passing by at high speed on the way to the Bronx and ultimately New England. Jake sat down after passing Vivian the neatly wrapped Cat Stevens album he had promised her. She seemed very pleased with the gift.

After a half hour, Jack got up, said goodbye, and left. He felt he had accomplished little with his visit. He imagined Vivian getting up right after he left, relieved that he was gone, and going about her business without a care.

Jack and Vivian did not go out on another date following the New Year's Eve fiasco, but that wasn't the last time they saw each other. Two years later, Jack was studying in Jerusalem for his junior year of college. One Friday evening, he was dining in a popular downtown restaurant (he had prepaid for his Shabbat meal, as was the custom in Jerusalem at the time) when he happened to glance at a nearby table. There sat Vivian with two female companions. For a moment her remarkable eyes met Jack's and he thought she was inviting him to speak to her. Jack, two years older if not wiser, declined to take up the invitation. If Vivian was interested in renewing their relationship, Jack was not. He nodded politely in her direction and without hesitation exited into the cool night air of Jerusalem.

Herman's Last, Best Chance

Everyone is born with a unique set of skills, or so the wise men say. Even though most members of the Orthodox Jewish community frown on such activities, in Herman Schwartz's case his talents sadly lay in the field of gambling. From his youth, Herman displayed an unusual interest and skill in every sort of game of chance. By age fourteen, he had become adept at almost all types of gambling, and soon graduated to underage visits to local casinos in the company of older friends. It didn't hurt that he looked older than his age. As he got older, he frequented pool halls and other places of dubious reputation where he bet on games with the local players.

When he was eighteen, Herman began to study the stock market. Utilizing the small inheritance he received from a deceased aunt, he soon mastered the intricacies of Wall Street speculation. He did reasonably well as a student and ultimately parlayed his knowledge of the rules of probability into a job as a bookkeeper in the Garment District.

Herman's parents, Julius and Fran, were not very happy with their only child's gambling obsession, nor did they like the company he kept on the Upper West Side, where they lived. But Herman was a headstrong young man, and so rather than pushing him away by taking a stand against his hobby, they chose to overlook it. There were debates among the rabbis on whether gambling was prohibited outright by the Torah or just frowned upon because it led to other more obvious shortcomings. His parents merely prayed he would one day outgrow his interest in gambling, either through "growing up" or running out of money to spend on such foolishness. But somehow Herman always seemed to have more than enough spare change to feed the kitty. By the time he was twenty-one, Herman Schwartz was among the most talented and experienced all-purpose gamblers in New York.

There was one singular area, however, where Herman was unwilling to take any chances at all. Considering he was generally willing to bet on anything at any time – a "regular risk taker," they called him in his neighborhood – even Herman couldn't quite explain it – he simply could not or would not take a chance on love! Over the years his aversion to dating, even of the blind-date variety, concerned his parents, as they felt his settling down with a proper mate would be the most direct path to curing him of his gambling habit. Herman, on the other hand, felt quite the opposite was true: meeting and marrying, in his view, were a very bad bet, a surely losing proposition.

Now, it wasn't a matter of his looks. Herman was a fairly good-looking fellow, about six feet tall with clear blue eyes and a shock of curly blond hair. His slightly crooked smile somehow meshed with a set of almost perfect teeth – an orthodontist's nightmare, he used to call them. He dressed well, though he had a preference for wearing colorful vests, a sartorial touch tied to his gambling habit. No, there was nothing on the surface that could explain Herman's aversion to the opposite gender: this gambler simply would not take a chance on love!

Gamblers are a secretive lot, so it was possible that Herman had formed relationships outside the view of his friends and family. But the latter thought not. He was so busy with his gambling, it appeared he didn't have the time to develop any meaningful ties with other humans.

"It's just a matter of his meeting the right girl," his mother would often opine to her husband. "Maybe he should spend some time at a resort over a holiday where many people go to socialize. Are you listening to me, Julius?"

"Yes, I'm listening. Herman should go to the mountains and socialize!"

"I didn't say the mountains. He could go to Florida, out west, or even Europe, anywhere he could meet a nice girl."

After months of pressure, Herman finally relented and agreed to travel to British Columbia out in western Canada, where he would spend the Passover holiday at an expensive resort. His parents were pleased that he was at least trying to meet someone. Before he left, however, he warned them (half seriously) that he would soon have to move from New York because he had "dated everyone in the city who's available!" He also swore to them that he would never marry anyone who lives with her parents. Subject to that and several other provisos, he promised to be sociable while out west.

A week later, Herman was enjoying the fair weather, comfortable accommodation, and the ambience of his Windermere Lake, British Columbia resort along with five hundred other guests of various ages. After several days, he found himself mildly attracted to one Malka Klein, an unattached young woman from Brooklyn who didn't really reciprocate his interest. Herman had brought some books along to read in case he got bored, and by day six he was ready to begin page turning. Before starting the Grisham novel at hand, he decided he'd be better off first getting in some exercise to shed the few pounds he had put on in the dining room. So, off he went to the scenic forested grounds surrounding the hotel for a short jog along a mountain trail.

About ten minutes into his run, he stopped in his tracks: there, a mere twenty feet in front of him on the side of the trail, stood a grizzly bear. Herman had unintentionally interrupted the bear from devouring the carcass of a small animal he had just killed. The bear, in no mood to share his meal with Herman, reared up on his hind legs in a menacing posture, claws at the ready, close to seven feet tall! Herman, forgetting all he had been taught by forest rangers over the years, could not repress the urge to run away from the bear – exactly what you're not supposed to do when confronted with an attacking grizzly!

Before the bear could cover the short distance between them, a shrill, high-pitched sound pierced the air, the sound of a loud whistle aimed at stopping the bear in its tracks. Luckily, the sound had the desired effect, as the startled bear turned tail and scampered off into the brush. Herman turned around to find Malka removing a police whistle from her lips.

"I've been trying to catch up with you for a while," she said.

"I'm glad you did," a shaken but relieved Herman responded. "I'm especially glad you brought that whistle!"

"I never go out on these mountain trails without it – bears and wolves, you know."

Herman thought for a moment how lucky he was that Malka had showed up when she did. When she later told him that she lived at home with five siblings and her parents, Herman decided that wasn't the obstacle he had previously thought it might be to a relationship. He was being honest with himself: his luck had almost run out that day on the trail, and henceforth he would bet on Malka being his sure thing.

The following week, he brought her home to meet his parents.

"Mom and Dad, I want you to meet Malka. She saved my life last week in Canada. A grizzly almost made a meal out of me, but Malka luckily showed up in the nick of time!"

Herman's parents didn't quite understand what Herman was talking about. As she looked at her son, however, Herman's mother knew that it might at last be time to send out invitations to a simcha.

"Julius, go get stamps, lots of stamps from the post office, you hear?"

A Guide to
Jewish Relationships 1 -
Meeting Your Intended

I had originally planned to call this piece "A Humorous Guide to Jewish Relationships," that is, before mistakenly asking for advice from the special people in my life.

"There's nothing funny about Jewish relationships, honey, and besides, you know nothing about them!"

"You met Mom when you were twenty years old and were married at twenty-two and a half; how can you know what it's like to be single at twenty-six or dating at twenty-eight?!"

So began my dear wife of forty-plus years and my five children when I told them I was writing about the funny side of Jewish relationships. They were ready to disqualify me from the outset and torpedo any possibility that my efforts to write the definitive essay on the subject would succeed. Working clandestinely, however, I hid from them all evidence of what I was writing. My secret mission complete, you (hopefully) happily hold in your hands the fruits of my labor.

The Torah describes the lives of the husbands, *avot*, which of course include the lives of their wives, the *imahot*. Multiple wives was the norm for the *avot*; sometimes they found their wives on their own, other times marriages were arranged by matchmakers, a phenomenon that is still recognized in our time among the *charedi* (ultraorthodox) population in particular. Along the way, from ancient to modern times, Rabbeinu Gershom placed a ban on having multiple wives. Legendary failures to achieve *shalom bayit* (peace in the home) in two-wife homes led to negative consequences for Jewish communities around the world, prompting Rabbeinu Gershom to issue his famous decree outlawing the practice. The fact that many wealthy men could and did successfully support multiple wives in Sephardic Jewish communities centered in Muslim-ruled lands was of no consequence to Rabbeinu Gershom, whose ban has led, even in our time, to the situation that many women never find husbands and reproduce.

According to research on the subject, most Ashkenazic husbands during Rabbeinu Gershom's time in fact married only one woman at a time. However, Ashkenazic men who traveled extensively to Sephardic communities did wed local women and raise families far from "home," often without divorcing their first, Ashkenazic wives.

It is currently speculated that it was toward these itinerant Ashkenazic husbands that Rabbeinu Gershom aimed his decree. The net effect of this marital ordinance, however, even if directed at a relatively small number of Jewish males, has, as pointed out, been far-reaching to our times. "All the good ones are taken" would not be the end of the *shidduch* (arranged marriage) conversation today as it frequently is, were it not for the ban. Since our rabbinate does not appear ready to endorse polygamous Jewish marriage any time soon, single marriages will remain the ne plus ultra of Jewish relationships.

How we go about meeting our *bashert* (soul mate) differs broadly among the various sects of the Orthodox community. At the more liberal end, dating is an offshoot of the socializing that takes place between both genders, who often share educational and recreational activities, supervised and not. These activities extend from schooling, Shabbat groups, summer camp experiences, and supervised trips abroad. This is where many Orthodox meet, date, and get married.

The *charedi* sects frown on mixed-gender interactions before marriage, but have a recognized matchmaking process that leads, for example, to the familiar, ubiquitous *shidduch* date, otherwise known as hotel lobby encounters. Those traveling on holiday in Israel or Brooklyn, for example, have seen these young couples sitting demurely, sipping a cold drink, while engaging in exploratory conversations with each other.

Whether by means of an official matchmaker or a family friend suggesting a "blind date" candidate, detailed data gathering is often an integral part of the process. The young man and young lady in question will create a list of desirable and undesirable qualities that meet their standards (or not); some of the important characteristics are listed here and are not mutually exclusive:

- Tall/short
- Wants to make aliyah/doesn't want to make aliyah
- Wants spouse to work/doesn't want spouse to work
- Seeks a *yeshiva bochur* (yeshiva student)/prefers a professional type
- Prefers a family of means/prefers good character and *yichus* (laudable ancestry) above all

Candidates for a date with some young ladies or men are vetted more thoroughly than prospective Supreme Court justices! It is no wonder that many remain in search of a mate for numerous years. The Orthodox community should do a better job in making it easier for Orthodox men and women to meet in proper social settings that are conducive to relationship development. Teas, lectures, mixers, weekends all are tried and true methods of allowing people to meet in pleasant social surroundings. The fact that these venues worked in the past does not mean they have lost their usefulness.

Finally, I should point out that Jewish dating uniquely encompasses a modification of the customary American numerical ranking of desirable mates. I refer to the use of the number ten to express the highest degree of desirability. Among Jews, clearly such rankings are woefully inadequate in choosing a mate. In its place, knowledgeable Jewish males have recently substituted a thirty-point system consisting of ten points for *seichel* (intelligence), ten more for *to'ar* (beauty), and ten points for *middot* (personality). This grading system clearly leads to better choices and almost guarantees that the young man will meet a woman smarter than he is, the secret to a long-lasting, happy relationship.

A Guide to
Jewish Relationships 11 -
The Jewish Wedding

Meeting, falling in love, and getting engaged are but parts of the formidable task facing our children. They must survive – no, overcome – that test of tests known as the Jewish wedding. Let's explore that institution in all its complexity and splendor. I caution all parents of brides and grooms to also be prepared to face this hurdle, or, really, a series of hurdles and challenges that only the hardiest will overcome without scars. I set out a brief list of the key features that one should look out for in planning and executing a successful wedding. Hopefully, they will help you avoid many of the pitfalls, so that you'll still be on speaking terms with the *mechutanim* (in-laws) and each other long after the simcha is over.

You must choose a venue and hire a caterer. Cost is the most obvious factor in deciding on these components. The tricky thing is what I call "intelligence gathering." How much is the other side willing to pay, and how much are you willing to spend? To determine the relevant figures requires the diplomatic skills of a veteran negotiator, as most people are hesitant to discuss finances with relative strangers. It's a feeling-out process that should take you about two months to resolve. Be prepared to find that by the time you make up your mind, your top three choices for dates for the affair and your favorite venue will have already been taken by someone else. It's a given!

Once a caterer and venue are chosen, you'll start to divide up the responsibilities of choosing a photographer/videographer, a florist, and a musician. Once you go through the list of obvious choices recommended by your best friend or your Aunt Chani, you'll narrow the field to one or two and choose the least expensive one who can do the best job. At this point, the father of the bride and the father of the groom have lost all interest in the wedding and tell their spouses to contact them only when the bills have to be paid. This is a good strategy on the fathers' parts, since they thereby spare themselves the agony of participating in the most tedious part of the wedding preparations.

In place of the ubiquitous tuxedo or dark suit worn by the males, the females of the Orthodox species will spend much time choosing and refitting the dresses that will be worn by the wedding party, all this after selecting the all-important color scheme. Fathers are not needed (or wanted) at this stage of the proceedings! After the effort expended to determine what the ladies will wear, something as insignificant as choosing the *kibudim* (honors) is easy by comparison.

As the wedding nears, the mothers and the caterer choose the menu, leaving the fathers with limited veto power. However, at this point the fathers must be careful to protect the family fisc from one particular charge that can sink the enterprise: the per-person liquor charge. While excessive drinking has traditionally not been a major problem of the Orthodox community, sophisticated drinking has been increasing in our circles. "Open bars" are deadly to the pocketbook. Hopefully, fiscal sanity will prevail and you'll avoid the most egregious charges.

When the great day arrives, feel fortunate if your promised musicians actually appear and perform as contracted and their sound system works. With God's help, your photographer will produce a reasonable facsimile of a photo album within two years of the event. Assume the floral arrangements you slaved over will be perfect (they usually are), but they are the most ephemeral part of the event and will be forgotten until you're reminded of them once again when you go through your long-awaited album or video.

Minor additional criticisms aside, you'll have a great sense of satisfaction once your affair is over; but don't think your job is over. You have a whole week of *sheva berachot* (wedding blessings) to prepare and/or attend!

Fare Exchanges –
Two Civics Lessons on Wheels

It's Friday afternoon in wintertime. You work in lower Manhattan, and Shabbat is starting shortly after 4:00 p.m. How do you ensure you'll get home in time for candle lighting? Or you're late for an important meeting uptown. Faced with time pressures, if you're smart, you'll choose the subway instead of a cab. Logic and experience have taught you that traveling underground will be the quickest, if noisiest, way to arrive on time. You'll avoid all surface traffic, not to mention inclement weather. But be aware of what you might be giving up by going underground.

In addition to foregoing door-to-door service, choosing the subway will deprive you of the one key element of a cab ride that well elevates it over the subway: the cabbie conversation. There's nothing like a talkative cabbie whose insights are well worth the extra minutes and money you'll lay out to reach your objective. Given the number of immigrant cabbies, you'll often find yourself able to teach a newly minted American a meaningful lesson about life in the USA, something you will not be able to do if you take other means of conveyance. These lessons may be simple confirmations of everyday truths, but every so often profound insights can be exchanged. On this score, two particular incidents in my travels stand out as exemplary.

Haitian Protest

On my way to a conference last spring, I found myself hailing a cab in front of Madison Square Garden. I soon found myself shoehorned inside the cramped interior of a taxi ably driven by one Jacques Delisle, a mixed-race native of the island nation Haiti. Monsieur Delisle spoke French-accented English, and I attempted a few French phrases I learned from my Belgian father and had perfected through four years of high school and college study. I soon ran out of French expressions, so we continued in English.

"Do you like it here in America?" I asked him.

"You know, it's not the easiest life here, not like people believe. America has problems too; things are far from perfect."

I was taken aback by his ambivalence at living here. I thought about it for a moment and decided to pose the following rhetorical question to him: "Jacques, I think there are some important differences between life here and life in Haiti that should make you more appreciative of this country."

"Less of a difference than you'd think," he countered.

I continued, "Let's imagine you and a group of your Haitian friends go down to the Grand Place in Port-au-Prince, your capital city, with placards in hand and begin to protest, shouting, 'À bas le gouvernement' [Down with the government]. What do you suppose would happen?"

I responded for him. "An unmarked car or truck would roll up, you'd be forced into the vehicle by the secret police, driven off, and never seen again.

"Now contrast that with America. You and your protesting Haitian friends make your way to the corner of 42nd Street and Fifth Avenue, in front of the New York Public Library. You'll be armed with a bullhorn and placards, and you'll distribute protest handbills declaring, 'Down with the government.' Unlike the deadly results of the Haitian protest, in New York, assuming you're behaving in a peaceful manner, the worst thing that will possibly happen to you is that you'll be ignored!"

At my last remark, Jacques looked over his shoulder at me and smiled, his white teeth actually reflecting the sun that had just emerged from the cloud cover.

"You make a very good point, *mon ami*, a very good point!"

Cairo Campfire

It was a cool October day when I boarded a large Checker cab on the corner of 38th Street and Broadway. I was on my way back to my law office on the Upper East Side. The driver's license card stapled to the plexiglass divider in front of me identified him as one Moustafa Ibn Omar, #IL-23576.

In an ecumenical state of mind, I greeted him with my regular Arabic greeting: "*As-salamu alaykum.*"

Mustafa responded in kind, "Do you speak Arabic, perhaps?"

"Not really, I know how to say 'yes' and 'no,' and I know my name in Arabic, Yussuf Ibn Mussah, but that's all. Where are you from?" I asked.

"Egypt, from Cairo to be exact," he responded. "I arrived here more than eight years ago."

We exchanged pleasantries for several minutes, after which I decided to begin a more controversial line of discussion on the Middle East.

"Mustafa [we were old friends by this point], let me ask you, in a thousand years from now, which modern Egyptian leader do you think will be best remembered?"

"I have no doubt," he said. "It will be Gamal Abdel Nasser, of blessed memory!"

Mustafa had chosen the quintessential nationalist leader who tweaked the twin colonial powers, England and France, nationalized the Suez Canal, and waged relentless, if ineffectual, war on Israel. Nasser's death from a heart attack at age fifty-two and his life as a diabetic evoked sympathy from his people, if not from vast multitudes outside of Egypt.

I didn't agree with my Egyptian driver, but I thought I'd take a soft approach to make my point.

"I beg to differ, Mustafa. I believe the leader who will be remembered a thousand years from now will be Anwar Sadat," the leader who addressed the Knesset and carried the power and dignity of Egypt to Israel to achieve peace and recognition with its erstwhile foe.

"Sadat, how can you say that?" he exclaimed. "Sadat was a midget compared to Nasser." He was obviously unimpressed with Sadat's peaceful accommodation with Israel.

"Didn't Egypt regain the Sinai, not to mention a good deal of its lost prestige through Sadat's efforts?" I pressed.

"He was a traitor to our cause; I'll say no more!" Mustafa gritted his teeth as he spat out those words of indignation.

We were approaching my destination just a few blocks away. I hesitated for a moment, and a final thought occurred to me: "Mustafa, I am still convinced that Sadat will in fact be the Egyptian leader who will be remembered one thousand years from now, and not Nasser."

"Because?"

"Because he'll be remembered around the campfires of *my* people. The surest way to be remembered in history is to be remembered in *Jewish* history!"

At this point, the cab ride was over. I paid the fare, tipping Mustafa a little extra for his silent acceptance of my final comment, and stepped out into the cool afternoon.

Davidic Generations – A Sober Reflection on the Wealth Triad

Science often seeks to find patterns in the way we live. Some are more obvious than others. Such patterns, when they are recognized, can be of great use to individuals and societies alike. As a teenager, I learned of one such life pattern, one that involved family wealth, which I called the "wealth triad." It was a most persistent and useful pattern of oft-repeated familial behaviors that have been part of the human experience since earliest times. As I will demonstrate, this triad has long been part of Jewish tradition as well and finds its ultimate source in the Tanach.

How exactly does the wealth triad work? Old Far Eastern sources declared centuries ago that family wealth lasts for only three generations. There is the generation that earns it, the next generation that maintains or expands it, and the third generation that fritters it away. This pattern correlates to a corresponding knowledge drain from one generation to the next that is supposed to account for the inability to retain family wealth previously accumulated for longer periods of time.

The wealth triad was known in more modern times as a common literary convention. James Fenimore Cooper, noted American novelist and author of *The Last of the Mohicans* (1826), primarily about American life after the Revolutionary War, prefaced one of his earlier novels – *The Pioneers* (1823), which concerned the rigors of American life in the 1790s – with a unique reference to the triad. He noted that the wealthiest citizens of that time were typically the grandchildren of the indentured servant class who themselves had served under the thumb of the wealthy old-money Dutch patroons who originally settled upstate New York three generations earlier. Cooper points with great irony to the fact that the grandchildren of these once-wealthy Dutch were now employed by – and largely lived under the economic thumb of – the descendants of those formerly indentured servants.

More recently, British author John Galsworthy made a successful career writing generational sagas that allow the reader to follow one family through time, dramatizing the ups and downs of fortune that impact the vivid characters he delineates (*The Forsyte Saga*, 1922). James Michener also included triad generational sagas in most of his well-designed works (*Hawaii*, 1959; *Centennial*, 1974; *Texas*, 1985; and *Mexico*, 1992).

I was first exposed to the existence of the wealth triad phenomenon during my junior year of high school. We studied the Book of Kings and learned the source and paradigm for the triad. It was through the interactions of the family of one David, son of Yishai, from the tribe of Judah, that the true scope of the triad was revealed. David, a shepherd boy, whose potential greatness went unrecognized even by his father, came to establish a kingdom with its capital in Jerusalem. With much blood on his hands, David was not permitted to build the First Temple in that city, but he lived long enough to see his chosen heir, Solomon, ascend to the throne. This son was recognized as one of the wisest men to have lived, and David surely had the peace of mind that Solomon would follow in the ways of God and carry David's line further. Solomon was in fact quite successful in carrying out his father's dream, but at the expense of more religious laxity than David would have liked, as well as excessive wealth accumulated by Solomon, measured in horses and chariots, not to mention wives and concubines.

The temporary result of Solomon's rule was to expand the borders of the Davidic Kingdom to its largest extent ever. Unfortunately, it was not to last. Solomon was hardly in his grave when his son, Rechavam, ascended the throne in Jerusalem. The country was facing a serious fiscal crisis, and the new king called for a meeting of his council of advisors. Attending were an equal number of Rechavam's younger, less experienced advisors and the late King Solomon's older, trusted councilors. The agenda turned to whether the fiscal crisis should be met by raising taxes on the already overburdened citizens of the monarchy. The older advisors recommended that Rechavam tread lightly; they advocated that he not raise taxes until the people had a chance to draw closer to their new king. Rechavam's young advisors counseled otherwise.

"Tax the people now," they clamored. "Let them know from the start who's the boss!"

Without hesitating, Rechavam followed the advice of his contemporaries and raised the taxes significantly.

The effect of the king's actions was immediate: ten tribes "voted with their feet" and promptly seceded from the kingdom. They formed a breakaway Kingdom of Israel headed by the charismatic Yeravam ben Nevat. Rechavam was left with the rump Kingdom of Judah, joined only by the tribe of Benjamin.

This sudden and profound division in the recently established kingdom of David and Solomon had shocking implications for the Jewish people. The two states were weaker than the unitary kingdom had been, and religious practice suffered as well, leaving the Jews prey to their surrounding enemies.

How could such a state of affairs have come about in such a short period of time? David had been such a strong leader, a man of war, possessing many talents, including political instincts and judgment. His son Solomon's reputation for wisdom was unequaled in his day. Yet none of those qualities ensured the kingdom's continuity even a generation beyond Solomon! In modern parlance, David's kingdom suffered from a serious lack of succession planning.

If, for a moment, you think the triadic problems that impacted David's family are just so much ancient history with no possible relevance to today, think again! For the wealth triad has become almost emblematic of modern Jewish families. Take the following pattern, for example: Grandpa flees Europe in the 1930s or '40s, goes to America with no possessions but his tallit and tefillin. Over the remainder of his life, he develops a trade/profession, even a chain of successful stores or a business empire. As a result, his sons live quite different lives from their father, their material needs well taken care of. Grandpa sees that his children are trained in the religious traditions he was taught, attending the finest *yeshivot*, *batei midrash*, and even, on occasion, top secular universities. This first generation on American soil continues in Grandpa's ways, expanding his wealth and giving charity generously, while enjoying the fruits of the founding generation's labors. Grandpa may lack the refinements of the second generation, he may speak English with an accent and never quite become "Americanized." Still, he is beloved, and is missed when he passes away.

It is in the third generation that we frequently see the familiar breakdown, the confirmation that the wealth triad pattern is alive and well. The "wealth" that we see dissipating in the third American generation is not merely measured in dollars and cents, but in values of a more spiritual nature. Similar to their parents, the second generation sends their children to *yeshivot* and gives them the training they themselves received. Sadly, something is missing in the home and, soon enough, the results are clear. The third generations may physically resemble their grandparents, but that's where the resemblance ends. The grandparents knew the value, almost the necessity, of hard work to ensure success – they knew how to make a buck. Their grandchildren know how to utilize an ATM machine. In the course of three generations, the wealth triad rears its head in our times. You name the modern Jewish community, and it has seen this phenomenon time and again.

Yet some don't believe in the inevitability of the triad; they argue that not all families manifest these patterns, that in some families, the third generation is more devout than previous generations. They further argue with some justification that within the same family and generation individuals will differ in their behavior, some steadfastly maintaining traditions, while others break with the past. As a result of these considerations, but in light of the example of the Davidic generations, all each of us can do is *try* to ensure that "wealth," spiritual and material, remains to be enjoyed by our families and communities far into the future.

PART IV
LINKED TALES OF THE LOWER EAST SIDE

An eight-chapter memoir of the late 1950s and early 1960s wherein we follow Joey and friends through several memorable school adventures in a changing, historic New York City neighborhood.

How It All Began

Joseph Rotenberg

During the late 1950s, Orthodox Jewish parents in Manhattan had only a handful of options when selecting schools for their children. The schools ranged from the so-called Modern Orthodox day schools, such as Ramaz, Manhattan Day School, Soloveichik, and Salanter with their Mizrachi/Zionist orientations, to the more traditional *yeshivot ketanot*, represented by Chofetz Chaim, and the oldest of all, the Rabbi Jacob Joseph School on the Lower East Side, popular among the Agudist (ambiguously) Zionist wing.

Life at these two types of schools differed significantly. The first group was co-ed, while the others were all-boys schools. Those on the religious right thought that the more liberal, co-ed schools were no better than Jewish prep schools, placing their students on an assimilationist track. In the stories that follow, we will trace the adventures of one child who, for better or worse, was exposed to both types of schools during his formative years.

Joey was born in December 1949, the fourth of five children to his naturalized, stockbroker father and his native-born, homemaker mother. His three older sisters attended the Ramaz School on the Upper East Side, and when the time came for Joey to begin first grade, his parents decided, for convenience purposes, to send him there as well. During his first three years at Ramaz, Joey did well in both his Hebrew and English subjects, made many friends, and, overall, received a first-rate elementary education. When he reached fourth grade, however, several of his more right-wing relatives began to suggest to Joey's parents that a switch to an all-boys school would be appropriate at this time. Their arguments ran from "this will make Joey into a man" to "I'm afraid you're raising a fourth daughter" by keeping him at Ramaz. Partially yielding to this outside pressure, Joey's parents enrolled him in the all-boys summer Camp Agudah following third grade. Joey's attendance at a *frum*, strictly Orthodox camp, while attending coeducational Ramaz, was a bit of a culture shock, but he tolerated the experience very well.

After he returned from his second summer at Camp Agudah, however, Joey received some news from his parents that did not sit so well with him.

"Joey, Daddy and I think that now that you're nine years old and a big boy, you're ready to attend an all-boys school," his mother told him. "The school we have in mind is the Rabbi Jacob Joseph School on the Lower East Side. It's called RJJ for short and we hear it's a great school. Some of your friends from Manhattan Day School will also be attending this year. The school is downtown and you'll be taking the subway there each day. They have a cafeteria where you can buy your lunch and snacks, and we'll give you an allowance you can use for your meals."

It was a lot for Joey to absorb. At first, he was very upset that he'd be leaving his Ramaz friends. But, of course, he could make new ones at RJJ, and it might be fun to travel on the subway to school. So Joey bravely bottled up any nervousness and conflicting emotions he might have felt and accepted his parents' decision without too much fuss.

As September approached, Joey's dad took him on some dry runs to the school. His father was not leaving it to chance that Joey would make it to school in one piece. Accordingly, on two occasions in August he took Joey in hand and together they boarded the IRT Number 1 train at 103rd Street and Broadway.

"Now, remember, you take this train six stops to 59th Street and Columbus Circle; you get off there and walk to the 59th Street IND station where you must pick up the D train going downtown. You'll take the D train 10 stops to East Broadway. You'll get off there, go up the stairs, around the corner, and in the middle of that block, Henry Street, is your new school. It's just that easy. At night, you just reverse the steps you took to get there. To be on the safe side, I'll write out the directions so you can't get lost. Keep them in your briefcase so you'll know where they are."

The first time he climbed out of the East Broadway train station with his dad, Joey noticed several elderly people slowly shuffling along the sidewalk. A vendor selling Gabila's knishes, with their trademark waffle-like covering, stood not more than ten feet in front of him. A large automat, filled with diners, occupied a corner retail space. Above the automat rose the offices of the famous Yiddish-American newspaper the *Jewish Daily Forward*. Mesivta Tiferes Yerushalayim, the yeshiva of the famous *posek* (Jewish legal decisor) Rabbi Moshe Feinstein, took up a big chunk of East Broadway to the left of the subway station. A Good Humor ice cream truck was parked across the street as Joey and his dad covered the short distance on Rutgers Street to Henry Street.

"This place doesn't seem so bad," Joey thought, as he liked knishes and ice cream, though not necessarily together.

Joey and his dad turned left at the corner of Henry Street and made their way down the block past a playground on the corner dedicated to the memory of Rabbi Jacob Joseph's grandson, a captain in the US Marines who had fallen in the Pacific at Guadalcanal during WWII. Finally, after another hundred feet or so, they passed the entrance to the RJJ Mesivta high school building, and ultimately that of Joey's new school. After this test run, Joey's dad reported to his mom that Joey already seemed familiar with the route and that he foresaw no problems once school began.

The first day of school approached, and Joey collected all his school supplies, organizing them carefully in his shiny new, tan leather briefcase. On the morning of the first day of classes, Joey's dad surprised him by accompanying Joey down to school. As they entered the building that day, the principal informed them that Joey would be placed in fifth grade for secular studies, but be held back for another year in fourth grade for Torah studies because of insufficient exposure to Chumash while at Ramaz. That assumption may have had as much to do with the attitudes of the RJJ administration at the time toward the more liberal institution Joey had attended than Joey's actual abilities. Joey was not at all happy to hear he would be repeating fourth grade in his Hebrew studies, but as events would turn out, he'd ultimately make up for that demotion.

The ride home from school that day was uneventful, even though it represented Joey's first "solo" run. He met another Westsider whom he knew on the subway platform, they compared notes and managed to ride uptown to their respective destinations. Joey felt a real sense of accomplishment when he arrived home safely. It had only taken thirty-five minutes and he was now officially a commuter at the tender age of nine!

As we'll see ahead, not every trip would be as trouble free for Joey.

Open School Day

Joseph Rotenber

Joey's first task at RJJ at the start of fifth grade was to meet his new classmates and hopefully make some new friends to replace those left behind at Ramaz. Luckily, there were a number of other boys who were transferring from Upper Manhattan day schools and were in the same boat as Joey. From the first day of school, Joey and Norman hit it off, and they would share the same desk in the same classroom for secular studies for the next four years. Joey and Norman formed a bond that would keep them friends for over sixty years, a cherished school-day friendship that truly lasted a lifetime. The twosome became friendly with two other classmates, Gary and Michael, both of whom lived on the Lower East Side, close to RJJ. The final member of their group, Sammy, was one of the few boys at RJJ from Brooklyn. He had a likeable personality that complemented their group.

Orienting to a new school was a bit of a challenge for Joey, but so was adjusting to the demands of entering the more challenging environment of fifth grade. RJJ had some stark contrasts in store for Joey when compared to his plusher life at Ramaz. Take, for example, the simple matter of lunch. At Ramaz, the food service consistently produced varied, high-quality food for its students. At RJJ, eating a well-balanced diet was more a matter of luck than design. If you so chose, you could bring your RJJ lunch from home. Joey tried that for a while, stuffing one or two sandwiches, egg or tuna usually, into his briefcase. But when he got to school with a daily allowance in his pocket, he was often tempted to sample the local restaurant or deli for sustenance, rather than eat what he had brought from home. There was also a well-stocked candy store on the corner of Henry Street not far from the school that offered Devil Dogs, Yankee Doodles, chocolate milk, and potato chips in great supply, not to mention baseball cards.

It got to the point that in the face of all this alimentary temptation, Joey would often forget that he had brought lunch to school with him. It was only days later, when he got a whiff of the inside of his briefcase, with its distinctive sulfuric odor of rotting eggs, that he would remember his uneaten lunch and gingerly retrieve the flattened mess from between his school papers, quickly disposing of it in a nearby trash can.

RJJ was proud of its school-run cafeteria and touted it as a cheap food-service option. It needn't have bothered. It simply couldn't compete with the vast array of better choices in the immediate neighborhood: restaurants, delicatessens, and specialty food stores. Managed by a nondescript woman named Fanny, with long, disheveled hair and nondescript dress, who toiled in a darkened room, the cafeteria specialized in greasy French fries served in small brown paper bags and potato "nik," a kugel-like confection that was tolerable when hot but was often served cold. You never wanted an end piece when it came to potato "nik," but you had no say in the matter. Fanny's cafeteria also served a limited number of forgettable entrees, such as spaghetti with tomato sauce, but RJJ connoisseurs knew to stay away from these dishes.

As the weeks passed, Joey established a routine when it came to things both inside and outside his classroom. He quickly learned that life at RJJ was in fact rougher and potentially more dangerous than he had been used to at Ramaz. He had more unsupervised time, for example, and he used his recess period to explore the diverse neighborhoods around the school. Italians, Puerto Ricans, and Chinese New Yorkers all had their enclaves not far from Henry Street, and, along with Norman, Joey became familiar with these mysterious parts of his new world. Henry Street was a mere four blocks away from the FDR and the East River, and the mighty Manhattan Bridge cast its large shadow over RJJ's world as it wound its way toward Brooklyn across the water.

Things were different from Ramaz in the classroom as well. He found his fourth-grade Hebrew class to be somewhat unchallenging, but his rebbe was kindhearted. In his English classes, Joey learned from his friends several activities that made the time pass more quickly. Since the school day began at 8:45 a.m. with Hebrew studies, and secular studies ended at 6:15 p.m., there was great incentive to develop some plan to survive the occasional boredom of the lengthy sessions. Joey and Norman mastered "spitball baseball," an ingenious game in which the player would create a baseball "field" out of a piece of 8 × 11 loose-leaf paper. You would draw a horizontal line across the middle of the page. Above that midline, you would draw rows of individual, equal-sized boxes in which you would write baseball terms such as "ball," "strike," "pop out," "fly out," "single," and "home run." You'd make sure to list every possible situation to allow for a realistic outcome. On the bottom half of the paper, you would draw a baseball diamond with bases. You would roll up a small piece of paper into a spitball, place it on home plate, and with your index finger flick the ball onto a vacant "box" on the upper half of the page. In this manner Joey and his friends played entire "seasons" of baseball during class, even using professional baseball team lineups to add to the fun. Joey's teachers never appeared to notice what Joey and his friends were doing, or they didn't care.

On a more educational note, Joey and Norman engaged in what could best be described as battlefield "reenactments," which could also be conveniently played at your desk. For this activity you would take a piece of paper from your loose-leaf binder and draw a map of a famous battlefield, setting up in stick figure fashion the field positions of two competing armies. The "soldiers" would be armed; you would include artillery, tanks, and so on within your drawing, as well as bomber and fighter aircraft. On other occasions, you would recreate naval battle scenes with battleships, planes, and aircraft carriers. Once drawn, the player would begin to "activate" the battlefield by tracing a linear "line of fire," leading to the victory of one side or the other. In this fashion, Norman, a Civil War buff, and Joey, more into medieval clashes, successfully reenacted many famous battles from Gettysburg to Agincourt and Marathon to the Battle of Midway, all while their classes were in session. Their parents may not have approved, but the boys learned a lot from those reenactments.

By the time Joey's mom made her way downtown to Henry Street for open school day in December during his first term at RJJ, Joey was already deeply committed to his new school. As she nimbly worked her way through the sea of rubber balls bouncing off the stoops that lined the brownstones adjoining the school during recess, Joey's mom spied him near the candy store; it was lunchtime and he was eating what looked suspiciously like a Devil Dog. Joey saw her, swallowed quickly, and ran to greet her.

"Let's eat at the school cafeteria," his mom suggested. "I've heard such good things about it."

Joey rolled his eyes, but added, "Sure, if you want to."

He had little appetite, for he'd already had his lunch.

Adventures on the D Train

Joseph Rotenberg

By the time Joey started sixth grade at RJJ, he had become quite adjusted to his new school. With a year of subway travel under his belt, he was used to his routine on the IRT and IND lines from the 103rd Street and Broadway station on the West Side to the East Broadway station a block away from Henry Street and RJJ. Attending the oldest Hebrew day school in North America meant it was *old* – the building and facilities had seen better days, and the school was perpetually underfunded. But it also meant a yeshiva educational tradition dating back more than fifty years, thousands of graduates helping lead their communities into the future, establishing the foundations of Modern Orthodox Judaism. Of course, not all the graduates necessarily reflected well on these traditions and on the school itself, but nobody was perfect, nor was any institution. Rumors abounded at the school that as varied characters as beloved US Senator Jacob Javits and infamous gangsters of the '30s and '40s, such as Louis "Lepke" Buchalter, head of Murder, Inc., who notoriously met his end at Sing Sing prison, both attended RJJ in their youth. Joey took this to mean that an RJJ education didn't guarantee any particular outcome. It was up to the individual *and* the institution working together to achieve anything worthwhile.

Entering sixth grade, Joey was not focused on where he stood in the broad history of RJJ. He simply wanted to get through the school year as quickly and as painlessly as possible. So each day he grabbed his subway card and his briefcase, which was stuffed with his loose-leaf binder and his lunch, prepared and wrapped lovingly by his mother. His leather briefcase, a luggage-like carrier popular among students, required some arm strength to lug up subway stairs and around the train. Even empty of books it weighed a ton; with a typical, thick textbook or two added, it became almost impossible to move without great effort. When school began at RJJ, a year earlier, Joey had immediately developed calluses on the hand that held the briefcase – a physical reminder at the time that he was attending school much farther away from home than in the past. Now, as a sixth-grader, the books he carried were even heavier, so his calluses had nowhere to go but grow!

A two-block walk to the IRT station began the half-hour trip downtown to school, a trip involving a change of lines at the 59th Street station where the IRT and IND D lines meet. Joey hoped to get a seat on both trains. Standing (and not falling) on a subway ride is an art in itself; ten-year-old Joey couldn't reach the straps designed to help steady taller passengers, so he made a beeline for the poles, which allowed him to hold on. As time passed, Joey became more and more adept at balancing himself through the twists, turns, and sudden stops of a typical subway ride, a skill that was later to prove useful in mastering the sports of skating and skiing.

The subway rides to and from RJJ played an additional part in enriching Joey's school experience. RJJ ran charity drives several times a year, and all students were encouraged to participate. Each student was given a *pushke*, or cylindrical charity box, in which to collect donations from the public. Based on how much you raised, a student could win prizes or premiums listed in a booklet distributed to the students at the beginning of the drive. Students of all ages were encouraged to solicit donations widely, and it was common for the students who traveled by train to walk back and forth through the subways cars, shaking their *pushkes* noisily. Joey had few inhibitions and jumped right into the routine. Imagine the scene: a chubby, red-cheeked ten-year-old, wearing a heavy winter coat and a hat with Chinese-style woolen earflaps, shoving his *pushke* in front of dozens of strangers on a subway train, weary passengers trying to ignore him. His collection routine never varied that year, but pickings were slim; mysteriously, he was able to fill up three large *pushkes* during the main charity drive. Apparently, some secret donors at home were dropping sizeable donations in the *pushke* while Joey wasn't looking. By the time the school year ended, Joey had even mastered the art of counting the contents of the charity box without breaking it open; a dexterous use of a butter knife did the trick, but Joey always felt a little bad about removing the contents, even if he carefully returned every penny into the *pushke*.

The subway experience also played an important part in developing the imaginations and decision-making skills of RJJ students. Take, for example, the sixth-grade Latin America social studies project. Each student in Class 6-1 had a month to come up with a project proposal and another two weeks to create a finished project. Joey loved these projects, and he immediately seized on the idea of building a diorama of a Peruvian or Andean village. He quickly visualized the scene: adobe-type huts made of clay built on a clay foundation, figures of a farmer and his family working their paper crops, with small animals made of puffy cotton material completing the scene. All would be constructed in the empty core of a medium-sized Macy's box. A written report would accompany the diorama. It took Joey all of the two weeks to complete his project, and he looked forward to the following Monday when he would transport his "village" to school.

On the appointed day, Joey entered the subway station with his arms full. He had strapped his book bag to his shoulder, but had barely enough carrying capacity to support the diorama. He managed to get a seat soon after entering the car, but the vibration in the older train was not helpful. By the time he reached East Broadway at the end of his trip, the Peruvian village was in shambles and Joey was near tears.

At lunch, he came up with a solution of sorts. There was no time or materials for a repair job, and so Joey did the next best thing. In place of the sign he had written at home on the side of the diorama announcing "Peruvian Village Scene," Joey substituted another sign declaring the diorama a "Peruvian Earthquake Scene"! Miss Wachholder, his teacher, was dutifully impressed and gave him an A for his work, wisely never revealing to him if she had suspected anything.

The D train was the scene of another unfortunate incident for Joey. There was a time after school when Joey mistakenly boarded the D train heading in the wrong direction, only to disembark at York Street, the first stop in Brooklyn. Unfortunately, that station didn't allow for free transfers to the Manhattan-bound side, and Joey had no money left after having bought a snack for the ride home. Desperate, without a moment's hesitation, Joey did what countless straphangers had instinctively done before and after him when faced with a similar challenge – and all turned out all right. Joey's first effort at begging was successful, as the kindly token clerk on the other side of the tracks permitted a sobbing Joey to board the correct train free of charge.

The final connection that the subway had to Joey and others who used it to travel to and from school concerned that favorite contraband material of pre-bar mitzvah RJJ students: fireworks; specifically, the low impact firecracker, not the more powerful firecrackers or fireworks that are rightfully banned from use by non-professionals. The D train became the favorite method of schoolboys to "smuggle" their patriotic fireworks and sparklers from the Lower East Side to home. As noted elsewhere, the Jewish neighborhood surrounding Henry Street where RJJ was located abutted directly on Chinatown to the west. It was only a matter of a few blocks from the yeshiva and you'd be transported to Shanghai for all intents and purposes. By the time Joey and Norman were in sixth grade, they had, on several occasions, explored adjacent Chinatown, frequenting in particular a certain penny arcade not far from their school. The Chinese proprietors looked bemused at these young Jewish boys, with their skullcaps on their heads and tzitzit hanging out, but good businessmen that the Chinese were, they said or did nothing to discourage their patronage.

On one occasion in late spring, the owner of the arcade asked Norman and Joey if they were interested in fireworks. The boys thought fireworks would be just perfect for the Fourth of July, but since they were going to summer camp that year and fireworks were considered contraband and would ensure them a ticket home, they decided not to buy them. Years later, when Joey was in high school, he returned to Chinatown and located a source of firecrackers near his old school. He secreted them under his shirt and carried them home on the subway, nostalgically boarding at the RJJ East Broadway station he had learned to love those many years before.

The Science Project

Seventh grade at RJJ posed some new challenges to our familiar crew: Joey, Norman, Gary, Michael, and Sammy, along with their 7-1 classmates, who were now in junior high school. More was expected of them, academically and socially, as they started their bar mitzvah year. Among the academic challenges were more complex school projects, some joint efforts among two or three students, and other, often more difficult, solo efforts. Of all the projects required of the seventh-graders, none was more demanding than the science fair. However strong a student's academics, the fair required him to come up with an original idea and execute it. This wasn't science in theory, this was science in practice.

Our group of students got decent enough science grades, but none of them could be considered scientifically gifted. Joey, for example, read a lot of books on scientific topics, but unfortunately didn't have an original thought on the subject. For his project, he chose to build a machine that would generate static electricity. It sounded simple enough. He went to the public library on the Upper West Side and took out a book with directions on how to create such a device.

"Daddy, it'll be easy to build this. All we have to do is get the materials listed in this article and follow the instructions. It'll be a snap!" Unlike Joey, his father was very handy; Joey talked a good game when it came to school projects, but Joey had learned early on that reliance on his dad was usually a safer bet in these situations.

The concept for Joey's generator seemed simple enough. Create a glass wheel-like plate, which could be turned by some sort of crank or handle to rub against a leather strop, thereby creating a friction source that would generate static electricity. Joey's dad located a glazier in the neighborhood whom they contracted to build the glass wheel. The leather strop was more difficult to find, as was the handle to crank the glass wheel. In the course of a week, however, Joey was able to put all the required items together. When assembled, the device produced plenty of groans – but no electricity!

As finally constructed, Joey's generator was flawed in several ways. The glass wheel was more than an inch thick; the handle, made of thin copper wire, was too light to turn the wheel with any degree of force; and the leather strop against which the wheel was supposed to rub hardly made contact with the glass. If mankind was relying on Joey's device to generate electricity, it was going to be very disappointed. The science fair was only a week away, and Joey had to think quickly to save his project and his grade. There was no time to build another model, instead, Joey came up with the idea of calling his device, "Early Unsuccessful Prototype of Static Electricity Generator." In light of what followed at the fair, Joey's entry certainly paled in the face of the other entries.

On the day of the fair, the students of 7-1 brought their projects to school in a variety of packaging. Joey's machine was fairly compact, so it didn't pose too much of a problem on the subway. The seventh-grade homeroom was emptied of all desks and chairs; in their place were tables on top of which up to three projects would be displayed. Joey set up his generator near the center of the room between what looked like a model of a volcano and a prototype of an irrigation system. His classmates were all busying themselves with their projects as Mr. Salmon, their science teacher, sharpened his pencils before officially opening the science fair and beginning his inspection of the student entries.

Soon, all was ready. Krasner, the volcano builder, had taken his assignment literally, fashioning a funnel-shaped mountain out of papier-mâché, packing it with a small charge of thermite and triggering mini-explosions on the quarter-hour, to Mr. Salmon's chagrin. Each explosion was followed by a trickle of a red, lava-like substance that looked suspiciously like Heinz ketchup.

On the other side of the classroom, in contrast to Joey's non-working model, stood Willig's homemade Van de Graff generator, a shiny aluminum canister that stood four feet tall. Willig was as close to a science whiz as 7-1 possessed. But if he was a scientist, he was surely a mad one. Willig's generator produced and stored ten thousand volts of static electricity! No one, including Willig, was aware of this fact. As Mr. Salmon approached within a foot of the generator, the hairs on his head stood up, porcupine-like, in all directions; a six-inch spark arced from the side of the genera-tor and struck Salmon squarely in his arm. An even larger spark jumped from the generator across the two-foot gap between the tables, striking Krasner's volcano and igniting the remaining store of thermite. No lava flowed after the explosion tore into the mountain, exposing the wooden table underneath.

Sadly, no amount of electricity from Willig's generator could bring Joey's contraption to life, however. It took Mr. Salmon half an hour to recover from his Van de Graff incident. Despite his injuries, however, he showed an attitude of forgiveness to Willig and Krasner by giving them A grades for their respective science projects. Joey wasn't quite as fortunate; Salmon gave him a B-, which, under the circumstances, was quite acceptable; Mr. Salmon having been "disabled" by Joey's classmates and thus unable to examine closely Joey's nonfunctional generator.

"I should have shocked him," Joey told his father that night, trying to rationalize his low grade.

Wine, Kiddush, Flame, Havdalah, and Time

We've followed the adventures of Joey and his friends as they grew from fifth-graders at RJJ day school until graduation four years later. This story recounts the circumstances under which Joey skipped a year of Hebrew classes at RJJ as a result of his excelling on his year-end final exam, one unexpectedly attended and observed by the Torah sage Rav Ahron Soloveichik, *zt"l*, of Skokie, Illinois.

When Joey arrived at RJJ to start fifth grade, you may remember he was informed by Rabbi Ginsburg, the Hebrew principal, that he would have to redo fourth grade in the Hebrew department to compensate for the lack of sufficient training in pre-Talmud studies during his previous four years at Ramaz. It wasn't an ideal situation for Joey, but he did as he was told and spent that year and the one following in fourth and fifth grades respectively, while completing fifth and sixth grades in his secular classes. As a result of that demotion, Joey began his third year at RJJ in Rabbi Goldberg's sixth-grade Talmud class, still a year behind his proper track.

The yeshiva was studying tractate *Pesachim* of the Talmud that year, and the chapters chosen for intense review were the first, which covered the laws of *bedikat-* and *biyur chametz* (checking for and destroying leavened products in one's possession), and the last, which covered the rules and rituals of the Seder night. These were topics with which your average ten- and eleven-year-old RJJ student was quite familiar, and Joey was no exception.

Rabbi Goldberg was short, his handsome face decorated with a neatly trimmed but bristly blond mustache. His outstanding physical characteristic was his fiery disposition, and he ran the class dictatorially, broaching no break in military-like discipline. He enforced his rule, aptly wielding a large, unforgiving ruler he kept at his side, ready to deter wrongdoers with a swift rap on the knuckles. Joey feared the punishment his rebbe could and did mete out to those who provoked him and stayed as far away from that ruler as he could during that year.

In this environment, students who wanted to learn actually found an ally in Rabbi Goldberg. Joey was among the group that benefited most from the strict environment. Among the other students who shared the classroom with Joey at various times were Moshe and Eliyahu Soloveichik, sons of Rav Ahron, *zt"l*, who resided on the West Side at the time, and were also nephews of Rav J.B. Soloveichik, *zt"l*, of Boston. They too spent the year dodging Rabbi Goldberg's ruler. As the year progressed, Joey found his interest and success in Rabbi Goldberg's class increasing by leaps and bounds. Joey realized that this was his last real chance to show the administration that he finally belonged in his age-appropriate Hebrew class. As June approached, it would take a stellar performance on Joey's final *bechinah* (examination) to clinch the deal.

Rabbi Goldberg suggested to Joey that he carefully study the lengthy seven-part *machloket* (dispute) contained in Arvei Pesachim, the last chapter in the tractate. It involved a discussion between both Tannaim and Amoraim about the proper sequence of blessings to recite when the Pesach Seder falls on a Saturday night. The dispute essentially arises from the fact that Shabbat typically ends with the recitation of Havdalah to usher in the new week. (Havdalah consists of a combination of a prayer over wine, a lit candle, spices, and the recitation of the Havdalah blessing itself.) But this particular Saturday night is also the beginning of the second night of Pesach, which in the normal scheme of things would require the recitation of a blessing on wine, a recitation of the Pesach Kiddush, and a recitation of the *shehecheyanu* blessing of thanksgiving that we have lived to celebrate the occasion or *zman* (time). The problem facing the rabbis was whether it was most appropriate to first end the Sabbath with the recitation of Havdalah or to first usher in the new Pesach holiday eve and then complete the Havdalah.

The Gemara lists the disputants roughly as follows: On the side of the Havdalah "firsters" are Shmuel, Rabah, Marta, Rav Shmuel, Rebbe Yehoshua ben Chananya, and Abaye; on the side of the Kiddush "firsters" could be counted Rav, Levi, Rabanan, Mar ben Rabanah, and Ravah. The foregoing rabbis differ somewhat in the sequencing of individual blessings within the Kiddush and Havdalah blessing complexes.

The Rashbam (Rabbi Shmuel ben Meir) in his commentary on the Gemara details all the various legal positions taken by the aforementioned scholars, but required almost six hundred words to lay them out completely. It should be noted that Rashi's commentary on the final chapter of the tractate is missing, and the commentary of the Rashbam (Rashi's grandson) has been substituted. The Rashbam, though a worthy commentator, lacked the terse prose of his grandfather and expressed himself in a more detailed, expansive style.

When Joey's turn came to be examined by the *rosh yeshiva* (yeshiva dean), he surprised everyone, including himself, by flawlessly reciting from memory the Rashbam's explanation of the Gemara in question. When he finished, ten minutes later, Joey saw Rav Soloveichik nodding approvingly in his direction. That vision stayed with him forever.

Joey remembered at least two other things from that memorable day at RJJ. First was the great joy he felt at being told he could skip seventh grade as a result of his performance and begin eighth grade the next fall in both his Hebrew and English classes. Second, he never forgot the conclusion in tractate *Pesachim* that the proper order of blessings on a Pesach which begins on a Saturday night is "wine, Kiddush, flame, Havdalah, and time," Ravah's view.

As an interesting footnote to this episode, quite coincidentally, Joey, now a man in his sixties, recently found himself at a wedding where by chance he sat next to a tall, bearded man with a pleasant demeanor in the mostly empty chuppah chamber prior to the wedding ceremony. They engaged in conversation and soon discovered they had much in common. The man turned out to be none other than Rav Eliyahu Soloveichik, Joey's classmate at RJJ fifty-five years earlier. They discussed many things before the ceremony began, but, most importantly, Joey recounted the time that Rav Eliyahu's exalted father had "approved" of an eleven-year-old *yeshiva bochur*'s recitation of a Rashbam, and thereby helped him, by his mere presence, to advance in his studies.

Joey wondered to himself if Rav Eliyahu actually remembered him and the events of that day, but the mere mention of his father brought a warm smile to Rav Eliyahu's face, indicating to Joey that at worst his story brought back pleasant memories to his classmate of his now deceased father of blessed memory.

Spring Fever

Joseph Rotenberg

The onset of spring brought unrestrained joy to the hearts of the seventh-graders at RJJ. Situated as it was on Henry Street in the heart of the Jewish Lower East Side, RJJ was home to over six hundred students from Manhattan, the Bronx, and Brooklyn. The seventh-graders, particularly the students in the highest academic track, 7-1, couldn't wait to shed their heavy coats; they dreamed of longer days, baseball, and ultimately, summer vacation. But of course, there were still many days of school until the end of June, and our familiar group of students – Joey, Norman, Gary, Michael, and Sammy – contrived to figure out ways to make the time fly with minimum study effort.

That year, 7-1 was assigned a Mr. Handelman as their English and homeroom teacher. He was an odd-looking, gaunt fellow, about 6'3", with black-rimmed glasses and a matching black Ivy League cap topping his balding head. He wore that cap throughout the day, never once removing it. Handelman had some other notable habits: he spoke with a thick Brooklyn accent and traveled to and from school in one of those tiny foreign cars that opened with a hatch and into which he barely fit.

Handelman's classes were thorough, if not particularly inspiring. The students of 7-1 were assigned several writing assignments, compositions that went through several drafts, the best of which were read to the class at large upon completion. Sprinkled among these occasional literary "masterpieces" on traditional topics such as "What I Did on My Summer Vacation" and "My Favorite Person" were memorable efforts by Willig, who would, it seemed, recite each time he was called upon, an almost identical story about attending a baseball game at the Yankee Stadium, changing only the score of the game and the opponent. Handelman either didn't listen to Willig's recitation or he didn't care about the redundancies, or both.

Handelman was a stickler about spelling, of all things. Yes, even though they were seventh-graders in junior high school, every week Handelman read out loud lists of long words with unusual endings, requiring the students to record those words in their notebooks. To this day, these Handelman lessons are the only reason many of those 7-1 students know which English adjectives end with "-ible" or "-able." On balance, Handelman's classes bored the heck out of 7-1, with only his occasional silly grin making up for his monotonous delivery.

Once spring rolled around, it became more and more difficult for the students of 7-1 to pay attention in Handelman's class, and spitball throwing increased in intensity. Joey's mother was active in the Mizrachi women's organization on the Upper West Side, and Joey found out that soon after Passover his mom would be hosting a spring luncheon for Mizrachi at their home. Joey planned his strategy early because he wanted to make up some excuse to stay home and partake in all the goodies that his mother would be serving. He decided he would need to try a test run, and so the following Tuesday he woke up complaining of a terribly sore throat – there was no possible way he could go to school. He didn't have a fever, but his mom thought he looked a little flushed and so she permitted him to stay home on condition that he rest in bed.

"I don't want you watching TV all day, Joey!" she directed.

"No, mom, I can hardly move," he responded.

His mom had a lot of shopping to do that morning, so Joey had three solid hours of unsupervised time at home before she'd return. He walked into the living room where the black-and-white television console sat. He drew the curtains, opened the double windows fronting onto 101st Street, and caught the sounds of spring on the gentle, warm breeze that blew in from Riverside Drive.

Joey reached for the *TV Guide*, picked out a Western on channel 9's Million Dollar Movie and watched for about a half hour before realizing he had seen the film twice before. He flipped the dial to the other channels, but this was the pre-cable era and there were few choices.

"I hate soap operas, and that's all that's on!" he protested.

At 11:30, he noted a Merv Griffin show would be starting. The show involved the host introducing new talent he had discovered. Compared to watching soaps, Griffin's show might be interesting. Joey used the intervening fifteen minutes to make himself a sandwich in the kitchen. By the time the opening credits of *Talent Scouts* began rolling, Joey was back in front of the tube. The first act was a young singer from Queens who sang two current hits, but Joey wasn't impressed. After a couple of commercials, Griffin introduced the second act.

"You're really going to like this next performer; he's a local guy, a comedian who has attracted some attention recently in comedy clubs. Ladies and gentlemen, may I present..."

Joey gasped, nearly choking on his sliced egg sandwich: on the screen in front of him was none other than his homeroom teacher!

"...Stanley Myron Handelman!"

The camera turned, and there before the eyes of the studio audience, thousands of viewers at home, and Joey in his living room, stood Mr. Handelman, black Ivy League cap, black-rimmed glasses, and goofy laugh. He told jokes for about ten minutes, shook hands with Merv Griffin, and left the stage.

"No one is going to believe what I just saw," Joey exclaimed out loud to himself. Handelman hadn't been nervous at all and performed like a seasoned professional. "He was no Red Skelton or Bob Hope," Joey reasoned, "but he was pretty good nonetheless. For a homeroom teacher, he was great!

"Maybe teaching us in 7-1 is not his main job," Joey thought. "Maybe it's what he does between comedy performances."

The next morning back at school, Joey told the gang what he had seen the previous day. Norman and Sammy didn't believe him at first, but when 7-1 convened in homeroom after lunch, Joey led a delegation of his friends up to the front to congratulate their teacher on his performance the previous day. Handelman smiled sheepishly and instructed the boys not to forget to hand in their book reports, which were already two weeks late.

In the weeks that followed, Handelman's class didn't seem quite as boring to his students. Everyone in 7-1 continued to write down his lengthy spelling words, work on grammar problems, and compose compositions. But secretly, they all were waiting expectantly for Handelman to break into his standup comedy routine just once. It never happened that school year, and the following year the boys advanced to the eighth grade. Handelman, known for his subtle, brainy brand of humor, graduated to two decades of Hollywood fame and fortune with Dean Martin and Johnny Carson. Joey never forgot his bout of spring fever that year; he recalled it every time his RJJ homeroom teacher, black cap, black-rimmed spectacles, and goofy grin, appeared on the screen.

The Snowball Fight

Joseph Rotenberg

When winter comes to New York City it often brings memorable snowstorms that wreak havoc on our schedules for work, school, and play.

Back in the late 1950s, the students of the Rabbi Jacob Joseph day school on the Lower East Side were far from immune to the consequences of a coating of snow blanketing Henry Street, thereby momentarily turning the grime of the neighborhood into an almost unrecognizable winter wonderland. Our regular crew of friends – Joey, Norman, Michael, Gary, and Sammy – were now in eighth grade and at the apex of the pyramid of their school. Opened in 1903, and named in memory of the short-lived only chief rabbi of New York, Rabbi Jacob Joseph of Lithuania, their school had educated three generations of Orthodox Jewish boys, mostly Manhattan-born and bred. Housed in a tenement on Henry Street and soon joined by an adjacent high school/

seminary building, the RJJ Lower School housed approximately six hundred students from grades K–8.

The school sported classrooms, an office, a small synagogue, an antiquated gymnasium, and a cafeteria that had somehow evaded inspection by the local health board. Given the state of the school building – classrooms occupying one of four former bedroom apartments on each of six floors, no lighting on the steep staircases between the floors, and limited outdoor facilities shoehorned between decrepit and often garbage-strewn buildings – it was a miracle that a fairly significant amount of learning actually took place there and that the building did not come crashing down on its student body as they stampeded down the narrow staircases to recess outdoors.

The student population came mostly from Manhattan, but RJJ had quite a diverse group of students, many of whom were exposed to a kind of class warfare at a very early age. The school tracked students in both Hebrew and secular English subjects. There were two official Hebrew tracks, the first of which purportedly translated the subject matter from Hebrew into Yiddish, the second, Hebrew into Hebrew. In reality, no one on the teaching staff was fluent in modern Hebrew, so this second track was effectively Hebrew into English.

The students were tracked in English subjects as well, using a numerical ranking of 1 to 3. The students in 8-1 were considered academically advanced in comparison to their other classmates. Those in 8-2 were considered less so, though in actuality they were pretty much equal to those in 8-1, but less motivated to do their homework or achieve high grades. The students in 8-3, however, were altogether in a different class from those in the other two sections. Class 8-3 contained the misfits of RJJ society – students who inspired fear in their teachers, boys and young men who bore all the marks of future delinquency.

Normally, interaction between the classes was limited, but on special occasions, usually competitive ones, the class sections came together, often with disastrous results. One particular winter activity stood out in this regard, namely the intramural snowball fight. Now, at this time in American history, the Vietnam conflict was warming up, the Cuban Missile Crisis and World War III had just been averted, and the nuclear Cold War was raging. Nevertheless, none of these worldwide conflicts had as big an impact on the lives of our protagonists in Class 8-1 as hand-to-hand, armed snowball combat against the hooligans in 8-3 had. Our familiar members of 8-1 were by no means cowardly. It was just that the 8-3 crowd didn't play by any civilized rules. To most participants, snowball fights consisted of running battles where combatants threw the eponymous balls of snow at marauders from the enemy classes. Not so with the boys of 8-3, who were known to hurl pieces of ice covered with a thin layer of snow to inflict maximum damage. Worse yet, if you were unlucky enough to be captured by members of 8-3 during these skirmishes, you faced the dreaded "face-rub" with ice shards.

Yes, indeed, these snowball fights were frightening. Joey was so apprehensive the night before these scheduled bouts that he would dream up excuses to avoid going to school. He wouldn't admit to his parents why he felt too sick to leave his bed, but, in the end, he would usually get up slowly and get ready for school. On such mornings he would give his mother a particularly long, wistful farewell at the door, worrying about how he would look at the end of the day when he returned home from the battlefield at Seward Park. His mother always wondered why he skipped breakfast on these wintry mornings, but it was simple: he had no appetite when faced with the upcoming dangers. Joey's morning Hebrew classes would fly by, with frequent stolen glances at his watch ticking off the time until recess when last-minute strategies would be discussed and tactics finalized.

At last, the lunch bell rang. The men of 8-1 deployed in five groups of three and set out for the Seward Park "battlefield" adjacent to Henry Street and RJJ, across East Broadway. Normally, they would have set up their base near the now-empty playground, using those natural objects – slides, monkey bars, and swings – as protective barriers from behind which they could shelter and throw their snowballs in safety at their onrushing foes from 8-3. But before they could position themselves behind their chosen barricades, the enemy from 8-3 surprised them with a barrage of ice weapons and quickly took three prisoners, including Joey, into their custody. The other 8-1 combatants retreated, leaving their three comrades behind. Joey determined by his watch that there were still twenty minutes of lunch break to go. Unfortunately, one of his captors noticed Joey's shiny watch as well.

"Take off the watch," he growled.

Joey couldn't believe this was happening to him, but, like a robot, he began to open the black watchband.

"You can't take my watch!" he suddenly cried, unwilling to part with the new watch he'd received as a birthday present from his parents just weeks before.

"Who says?" replied his captor.

Joey made a break for the entrance to the park and the freedom of East Broadway, but he slipped on an icy patch of sidewalk just as he was making his escape. He glanced at his watch and saw that the crystal had cracked against the granite, and his hand was bleeding. His captor was upon him in a flash, preparing to smash him in the face with a particularly nasty combination of ice and snow.

"What are you kids up to?" shouted a little old lady carrying an enormous umbrella in her hand.

"Let that poor fella go, if you know what's good for you," she added.

At that last remark, the felon from 8-3 withdrew, leaving Joey, now sitting up on the ground, wounded but safe.

"Aw, it's the end of lunch break, anyway; you were lucky this time, four-eyes," was the best his 8-3 captor could muster, as he crossed East Broadway and headed around the corner to school.

Joey limped back to class, hungry, but with no time to eat the lunch his mom had prepared. He scarfed down the Devil Dog she had included instead. Back in school, Norman and the rest of his classmates didn't talk about the ignominious defeat they had just suffered at the hands of 8-3. Joey was simply happy he had survived another snowball trip to hell and back. This time he had barely escaped his ordeal as a prisoner of war. His treasured watch could be repaired, the wound on his hand would heal, but he was sure his parents would never quite understand the perils he endured at RJJ every time it snowed.

Punchball Follies

Joseph Rotenberg

The school calendar at RJJ had run its course to early June. The eighth-grade class would be graduating at the end of the month, but there were several more important dates than graduation remaining on the calendar. First, there was the overnight class trip to Washington, DC, during graduation week, and there were always final exams and *bechinot* to prepare for. But by far the most important event was the annual senior punchball tournament held between the three sections of the eighth grade.

Punchball was the main athletic activity at RJJ. It's a game seldom played today, but in its time the game was a favorite of RJJ students and Jewish youngsters throughout the metro area. Even baseball greats such as Jackie Robinson, Yogi Berra, and Sandy Koufax played the game growing up. Played with a round, pink-colored, hollowed rubber ball (usually manufactured by the Spalding company), the game mimics baseball in its rules: four bases, an infield, an outfield, nine or ten fielders as the norm. What makes the game different is that there is no pitcher or catcher involved and, most particularly, no bat is used to strike the ball. Instead, the batter stands at home plate and tosses the ball in the air or bounces it on the ground, and strikes the ball with his fist, thereby putting it into play. The fielders do not use gloves.

Each June, several eighth-grade sections would hold tryouts among class members to choose teams to compete in a winner-take-all tournament to be held at Hester Street Park's largest asphalt ball field. This particular year, the tryouts were very well attended, and Joey, not exactly known for his punchball prowess, estimated he had no chance of making his 8-1 team, certainly not as a starter. Each squad consisted of eighteen students, so it was not impossible, but Joey was considered an abysmal hitter, having a reputation as the player most likely to strike out even though he was "pitching" the ball to himself. The one saving grace he had was that he was a decent fielder; he was a lefty and would occasionally play first base in intramural pickup games played with the less gifted athletes in 8-1.

Following the tryouts on a cloudy day, Joey got the news from Norman that he had made the team as the third-string first baseman. Someone had obviously pulled some strings on Joey's behalf! Of course, this meant that he would almost assuredly not get to play, which was fine with him. There were some terrific players on his team; and who needed the pressure, he thought. Also, the field on which this game was played was enormous by punchball standards. You needed an outfielder's arm to make the throw from third or short, and the bases seemed almost eighty feet apart.

The first game class 8-1 played was a quick demolition of class 8-2 by a six-run margin. As he had expected, Joey did not get into that game. Class 8-3 also defeated class 8-2 by a similar margin, and the championship game was scheduled for the following day between the two rivals. Joey thought how great it would be to drive in the winning run against his longtime foes, his implacable enemies from many (not soon to be forgotten) winter fights.

The sun shone brightly on the field as the game commenced the next afternoon; 8-3 got out to an early lead, but Joey's team battled back to tie the game at 3–3 in the fourth inning. No one scored over the next three innings. In the top of the eighth, however, Mr. Lehrer, who ran the gym program, insisted that all players who had not yet played an inning in the field during the tournament be inserted as substitute fielders. This meant that Joey was going into the field to play first base at a critical juncture of the championship game. The starting infield was otherwise unchanged.

To say Joey was nervous was the understatement of the year. After two popup outs, it seemed 8-1 would get out of the eighth inning without any damage. Unfortunately, that was not to be the case. The third 8-3 batter slammed a hard ground ball to Gary at shortstop, where it was fielded perfectly. Gary, who possessed a cannon of an arm, threw a hard strike to Joey at first base. Joey saw the ball heading straight at him, cupped his hands to receive the missile, and squeezed his hands together as hard as he could to hold on. The ball, however, had a mind of its own. It hit the back of Joey's hands and boomeranged out of his grasp, flying across the diamond back toward where Gary stood at shortstop. The runner was safe and came around as the first of three runs scored by 8-3 in the decisive inning.

Not surprisingly, no one spoke to Joey for the rest of the game. He lost his last chance to strike a blow against 8-3, and there would be no other opportunities. Joey always felt that the other first basemen might also have failed to catch that particularly hard throw he had bungled, but, as in life, no one would ever know for sure.

"Good try," Norman offered the next day at school. "It was a tough throw, and we didn't score enough runs anyway."

Joey appreciated Norman's kind analysis. It was good to have friends at times like this.

PART V
ON HOLIDAY

A Tale of Two Rabbis

In the last two decades or so, fiction writers have rediscovered what might be called religious cryptography. I'm talking about finding hidden meanings in familiar biblical texts: secret codes and esoteric symbols revealing ever more secret mysteries about the origins of life on our planet. Once upon a time, such studies were the staple of every living hermit or social outcast who could find someone to listen to his ravings. The Talmud and Jewish lore have their share of tales of demons, false prophets, monsters, and other supernatural creatures. I'll confess to a healthy skepticism at one time concerning all these mystic goings-on, but for sure, many of these tales are good box office draws, and I suspect we haven't seen the last of the *Da Vinci Code* and its ilk.

Below is my contribution to the genre – a tale of two rabbis that may cause you to frankly wonder about the connections between our day and the ancient past; it certainly turned me into a believer that there is a whole lot we don't understand about the world in which we live.

Rabbi Past

Rabbi Judah ben Beteirah was a master of the Mishnah who lived about 1,900 years ago. He lived quite an unusual life by any measure. He was probably one of the few individuals whose life spanned both the destruction of the Second Temple by the Romans in 70 CE and the final suppression of the Bar Kochba revolt by Rome in 134 CE. His survival – the fact that he was

neither killed nor enslaved during his life, which was the fate suffered by tens of thousands of his countrymen – may be attributed
to his abandoning Jerusalem soon after the destruction of the
Temple. He fled north to a town called Nisibin, located today in
southeast Turkey. While present-day Nisibin is near the center of
the ISIL-Syrian-Iraqi conflict replete with beheadings and mas-
sacres, at that time, Nisibin was a dusty, sleepy Roman village far
from world events. During his exile there, Rabbi Judah became
something of a local celebrity. The Syrians or Arameans (as they
were known then) came to respect him and often took his counsel
on important common matters.

Our story focuses on one particular event that took place in
the rabbi's life, a tale recounted in the Talmud in tractate *Pesachim*, where the laws of Passover are generally discussed. As the
Talmud recounts, one day, Rabbi Judah became aware of a Syrian
neighbor who was bragging that he traveled up to Jerusalem every
year to partake in the ritual sacrifice at the Temple for Passover.
This was clearly prohibited by Jewish law. Rabbi Judah asked the
Syrian to confirm this violation, and the Syrian boasted that he
could trick even the most careful participant into sharing his holy
offering with him.

"I eat of the best and they never know it," the Syrian proudly
exclaimed.

Rabbi Judah was quite upset by this confession and decided
to turn the tables on the Syrian. "Have you ever eaten from the
tail of the sacrifice? It's simply delicious – a true delicacy." Rabbi
Judah was counting on the Syrian being unaware that the fat-filled
tail of the sacrifice was *never* eaten, but instead burned on the altar.

"No, as a matter of fact, I've never been offered it," replied the
Syrian.

"Well," said Rabbi Judah, "next Passover you must ask them to
give you the tail to eat."

When the holiday next approached, the Syrian ascended to
Jerusalem and followed Rabbi Judah's instructions exactly. No

sooner had he requested the tail, when the Temple officials point-
edly asked him, "Who told you to ask for the tail?"

"Rabbi Judah ben Beteirah," the unsuspecting Syrian responded.

The officials wondered for a moment how it was possible
that Rabbi Judah would offer such advice. They immediately
investigated, discovered the Syrian's true identity, and took the
necessary steps to ensure that he wouldn't eat from the Passover
sacrifice ever again.

To this point, the story of Rabbi Judah and the ill-fated Syrian
has all the elements of the proverbial wise man tricking the wrong-
doer who lacks all the necessary information to make the correct,
"safe" choice. But it's the next phrase in the Talmud, following the
punishment of the Syrian, that's most intriguing for what it may
foreshadow in our day. The Temple officials send a message of
thanks to Nisibin: "Peace be with you, Rabbi Judah ben Beteirah.
Even though you are in Nisibin, in the distant Diaspora, your net,
spread wide, reaches us in faraway Jerusalem!"

Rabbi Present

Rabbi Menachem Leibtag is an internationally acclaimed Bible
scholar and lecturer, especially noted for his work as *rosh mesivta*
(yeshiva dean) at Yeshivat Har Etzion and lecturer at Midreshet
Lindenbaum in Jerusalem. Several years ago, a Jewish man in
Teaneck, New Jersey, found himself in a bit of a quandary. He
had been asked to prepare a scholarly talk on the occasion of
the sixtieth anniversary of the State of Israel; time was running
short, and he was sorely lacking ideas to pull off his assignment.
The man struggled to come up with a meaningful concept, when,
in a last ditch effort, he Googled a website created by Yeshivat
Har Etzion. On the site, he uncovered a treasure trove of Israeli
Independence Day addresses and lectures given by Rabbi Leibtag.
Cobbling together some of Rabbi Leibtag's thoughts on the
subject with other sources he found, the man was able to meet
his deadline and gave a very satisfactory talk (at least in his own

mind!). Imagine how surprised the man must have been when, just two weeks later, he received a notice from his shul that the scholar-in-residence on the upcoming Shabbat would be none other than Rabbi Menachem Leibtag himself! The man wanted to personally thank the rabbi for his "assistance" with the Independence Day talk, and as the weekend approached he thought hard on what exactly he could say to the rabbi.

Friday night arrived, and the man despaired of finding something meaningful to say to Rabbi Leibtag, other than *"Shabbat shalom"* and "thanks." Just when he had given up all hope, the man stood up from the couch where he had been sitting and exclaimed to his wife, "I've got it; I remember a story from *Pesachim* that's right on target. I know *exactly* what to say to Rabbi Leibtag tomorrow. This is incredible!"

His wife looked at him as if he had lost his mind.

"Go to sleep so you won't be late for shul; stop worrying what you're going to say to Rabbi Leibtag!"

The next morning Rabbi Leibtag addressed more than four hundred congregants at the close of Musaf services. Following the speech, the man worked his way through a throng of people until he stood alone in front of the rabbi. He nervously recounted to Rabbi Leibtag how he used his online materials to construct his own speech, and then remembering Rabbi Judah and the Temple officials, he blurted out, "Peace be with you, Rabbi Leibtag, for even though you are in Jerusalem, your net – [the Internet] – spread wide, reaches us far away in the Diaspora!"

In that singular moment, Rabbi Judah's almost two-thousand-year-old Nisibin tale took on a modern, digital life of its own. In truth, Rabbi Leibtag is today recognized as a pioneer of Torah education via the Internet. What's most intriguing is how that fact may be viewed as completing a link foreshadowed in the days when the Temple still stood. Two rabbis, past and present, connecting Jews in a worldwide Torah *net*work!

A Call for Unity -
The Hunter Shul

What could YU, Breuer's, the Bluzhever Rebbe, and the Slutzky family possibly ever have had in common?

As wise King Solomon teaches us in Megillat Kohelet, there are times when it's preferable to separate, and times when it behooves us to come together. In each of our lives, as well as in the lives of our Jewish communities, there are those events that unite us and those that seem to pull us apart. We are all familiar with the often polarizing conflicts that have arisen in the recent Jewish past between various factions, organizations, and individuals: left versus right, Mizrachi versus Agudah, Yeshivish versus Modern Orthodox, Ashkenazi versus Sephardi, and *charedi* versus everyone else. Then there are the geographical divisions: Litvak versus Galitzianer, and Yekke (Jew of German descent) versus non-Yekke. Finally, a historic schism came to these shores as an import via Ellis Island: European Jews brought us Chassid versus Misnaged (one who opposes Chassidism).

From the foregoing list, it would appear that Orthodox Jews throughout American history have been at each other's communal throats more often than not. The following tale emphasizes, however, a happier time in the past when *achdut* (unity) prevailed in Modern Orthodox American Jewish life. It also illustrates that opportunities occasionally present themselves for us to learn lessons from our fellow Jews even if we have to cross age and geographic barriers to do so. Prepare to consider one of those special times of year in the American-Jewish calendar when Jews unite as a community: summer vacation!

Yes, summer vacation is when American Orthodox Jews seem to bury their differences in the interests of ensuring they can find a minyan to pray with, kosher food in reasonable proximity, and comfortable accommodation for large families. Once found, these locations are returned to year after year, and friendships are renewed with people you only socialize with when on vacation. Between July 4 and Labor Day, fellow vacationers become steadfast neighbors. If you're lucky, summer week after summer week you can forget about where you come from and put away all September thoughts until you start reciting *L'David* during davening. Some of these summer escape destinations have taken on an almost utopian aura, lifelong memories of happy moments, and rites of passage that only become more firmly fixed in one's recollection as time passes. Every so often, one or two of these locations rise to the level of legend, where historic figures in Jewish history rub elbows with commoners, the learned with those who still have lots to learn. My story is about one such place, a sleepy hamlet tucked under tree-lined mountains just 128 miles from New York City.

The village of Hunter, New York, stands 1,800 feet above sea level at the foot of the second-highest mountain in the Catskill Mountains, Hunter Mountain. For approximately 150 years the area around Hunter Mountain, at an altitude of four thousand feet, has attracted visitors for its natural beauty, cool summer nights, and hiking possibilities. The last fifty years have also seen the development of all-year ski facilities that set the standard for the southern part of New York state. Hunter's virtues have attracted its share of Orthodox Jews for more than a century, which has led to the listing of the Hunter Synagogue, located on Main Street, on the National Register of Historic Places. The synagogue was constructed between 1909 and 1914 through the efforts of, among

others, the noted Jewish-American businessman and philan-
thropist Harry Fischel, who built a stately seven-gabled home in
Hunter for his extended family to spend their summers away from
New York City. Accompanying him was his son-in-law, Rabbi
Herbert S. Goldstein, founder of the Institutional Synagogue on
116th Street in Harlem and inspirational leader of the fledgling
Modern Orthodox community.

Without the lifelong efforts of these two men, the Orthodox
world as we know it would be much different. Rabbi Goldstein
was the only man to serve during his lifetime as the head of the
Orthodox Union, the Rabbinical Council of America, and the
now-defunct Synagogue Council of America. He introduced
many people to the idea of kosher food supervision, and he inno-
vated the now very familiar OU kosher certification. He was also
instrumental in creating the concept of the synagogue center (the
synagogue as the center of communal Jewish life, with educational
programming and services supported by membership dues).

By the 1930s, Hunter was Rabbi Goldstein's summer refuge
from his busy communal schedule, as it was for his father-in-law,
Harry Fischel. By the time the latter passed away in 1948, no one
could have predicted what Hunter and its shul would come to
mean within a generation to a broadly diverse Orthodox Jewish
community.

The 1960s saw Hunter becoming a summer haven for Jews to
relax with fellow Jews, specifically those who wished to avoid the
large, boisterous hotels of the Borscht Belt of Sullivan County. The
latter establishments claimed to be located in the "heart" of the
Catskills. As any amateur geographer (or anyone who could read
a map) knew well, those hotels were nowhere near the Catskill
Mountains, which ranged west from the Hudson River and ter-
minated way short of Sullivan County. The "real" Catskills were
truly mountainous, rocky, with fast-moving streams and major
reservoirs serving even faraway New York City.

Hunter and its twin village, Tannersville, began to attract a new sort of Jewish visitor, namely those hardy folk who followed the traditions of Rabbi Samson Raphael Hirsch and the Frankfurt, Germany, community: Breuer's of Washington Heights. Leading this group to Hunter was Rav Naftoli Friedler with his wife and large family. Rav Friedler founded the *beit midrash* of the Breuer's yeshiva/*mesivta* and served as its first *rosh yeshiva* in 1958. Originally trained at Gateshead Yeshiva in England, Rav Friedler brought many Breuer's families north to Hunter each summer for at least a decade.

Alongside the Breuer's group came members of the growing Yeshiva University family of teachers and students. Among them were future *roshei mesivta*, including notable Talmud scholar Rabbi Yehuda Parnes, later *rosh yeshiva* of Lander College, who was equally adept at helping a student understand a complex Tosafot or on occasion assisting his sons on a baseball diamond or basketball court.

Alongside Rabbis Friedler and Parnes, the Hunter summer community was blessed in particular with the annual presence of a true Chassidic great, the Bluzhever Rebbe, Reb Yisroel Spira (1889–1989), notable Holocaust survivor and leader of a vibrant Brooklyn community. His presence in the Hunter shul every summer day was inspiring to young and old.

In contrast to these rabbinic lights were those many Jews who lived observant lives, but did not necessarily consider themselves steeped in learning or training. From the 1920s, for example, the Margareten family of matzah fame called Hunter their summer home. The Slutzky family not only developed the Hunter Mountain ski lodge and lifts during the 1960s, but were the main year-round supporters of the Hunter Synagogue. Rounding out the summer community were several dozen families of *ba'alei batim* (working folks) without any particular affiliation, simple Orthodox Jews from the New York Metro area, happy to join in this annual summer escape.

The net effect of this varied *kehillah* (congregation) was that on an ordinary summer Shabbat morning in the Hunter synagogue you might find me, a fifteen-year-old *ba'al korei* (Torah reader), grandson of Gerrer Chassidim, reading the Torah with a German *trop* (cantillation) to a minyan consisting of, among others, the Bluzhever Rebbe, Rav Naftoli Friedler of Breuer's, Rabbi Parnes of YU, the Margaretens, Rabbi Reichel of the West Side Institutional Synagogue, and members of the Slutzky family. Jews of so many different stripes were all praying together in tranquility on those days, with mutual respect and devotion and a real sense of community.

The most meaningful of the rituals performed over those summers in the Hunter shul were undoubtedly those special situations that took place midweek when the teenagers and young adults of the community were called upon to participate in greater numbers than on weekends. The weekly routine of fathers leaving Hunter after the weekend and returning to the city to go to work put the onus of daily minyan attendance squarely on the younger male residents and the relatively few older male members who remained in Hunter during the week.

In 1965, I recall a particularly memorable midweek Tisha B'Av Eichah (Lamentations) reading that brought the younger elements in Hunter directly in contact with the Bluzhever Rebbe, one of the few adults to attend the reading that night. His inspiring presence bridged any gaps that might otherwise have existed between the different types of Jews who attended. It was as if the Rebbe saw each Jew as equal, and his wartime experience led him to consider all external, factional labels of little importance.

That particular August evening, the small group that gathered at the end of Ma'ariv (evening service) to hear Megillat Eichah moved to the front of the shul where the Bluzhever Rebbe sat in his familiar mizrach seat. The Rebbe spoke mostly Yiddish, and most of the boys did not. He smiled in their direction and indicated that they should approach him and be seated. The young man chosen to read the megillah knew little of the Rebbe's wartime suffering, how the Rebbe had witnessed countless horrors and had lost his wife and children. In fact, throughout his years of incarceration, the Rebbe had often lifted the spirits of his fellow inmates by secretly performing important Jewish rituals and ceremonies. Many have recounted how the Rebbe obtained matzah, lit the menorah, and pronounced blessings in Bergen-Belsen at great risk to his life. To the young Jews who sat before him that night, the Rebbe seemed a passive figure, smiling and nodding in their direction. What thoughts must have crossed his mind of Tisha B'Avs long ago, of skeleton-like figures surrounding him, tears in their eyes as they recalled ancient and present losses of incalculable measure?

Now, in 1965, the Rebbe saw before him a different audience: young, strong Jewish men who knew no oppression, who knew the return to Zion, and who venerated their elders, who had suffered through the bitter war years. Did the Rebbe in any small way feel redeemed by the experience of hearing the haunting melody of the reader, the poignant words of Yirmiyahu enunciated by free Jewish voices in a country that had granted him refuge? Or did he feel simple thanks to Hashem that he had survived to reach that day? No one spoke much after the Ma'ariv *kinot* (mournful poems) were completed. Whatever he felt at that moment, clearly the Rebbe saw only fellow Jews before him – not Chassidim, Misnagdim, Ashkenazim, or Sephardim. The Rebbe thanked the reader with a *"yasher koach,"* walked slowly down the aisle of the shul, and was helped into a car that took him to his bungalow.

The high degree of humility and modesty that characterized the Bluzhever Rebbe is further illustrated by an anecdote recently told to me by my cousin from Toronto. Apparently, my uncle Alex, the best fisherman in Hunter, had been planning a fishing trip to a location not far from town, a spot that had, in the past, never produced a satisfactory number of fish. Alex approached the Rebbe prior to his outing.

"Can the Rebbe give me a blessing so that I might have a successful fishing trip?"

The Rebbe thought for a while and then responded to Alex with, "*Vi'yidgu la'rov b'kerev ha'aretz*" (And may they proliferate abundantly like fish within the land).

Alex thanked the Rebbe for his blessing and headed out to the reservoir. Hours later, Alex arrived at shul for Ma'ariv. Following the service, he approached the Rebbe.

"So how did it go, Alex?" the Rebbe him asked in Yiddish.

"Don't ask, Rebbe, I didn't catch a thing!"

Without hesitation the Rebbe said, "That should show you just how much *my* blessings are worth!"

Maybe Hunter wasn't a utopia for all the Jews who called it their summer home, but sharing time there with the Bluzhever Rebbe and others certainly raised the awareness of many of the common features of their existence as Jews and the superficial, and ultimately insignificant, nature of their differences. It can be safely said that we need more "Hunters" in our future and fewer divisions among our people.

The Reforms of Rabbi Amnon - No Changes Required

Among the numerous prayers recited in synagogues on the High Holidays, few have the impact of Unetaneh Tokef ("Let us now relate the power... of this day's holiness"). The chazzan and the congregation alternately chant the refrain that "on Rosh Hashanah [our yearly fortune] is inscribed and on Yom Kippur it is sealed." In the prayer, we ask Hashem, rhetorically, among other things, "Who shall live and who shall die, who in his time, and who in an untimely fashion?"

The origins of this prayer are well known. Supposedly, Rabbi Amnon of Mainz was brutally assaulted by the Bishop of Mainz for failing to appear at the appointed time for a dispute between the bishop and the rabbi, and for failing to convert to Christianity as the bishop, his former friend, commanded. Rabbi Amnon died a Jew while publicly reciting Unetaneh Tokef on Yom Kippur. Tradition has it that sometime later Rabbi Amnon appeared in a dream to Rabbi Kalonymus ben Meshullam of Mainz, to whom he dictated the words of the prayer verbatim. The latter circulated the prayer throughout the Ashkenazic Jewish world, and it became an integral part of the High Holiday service. Today, some scholars question whether the story of Rabbi Amnon's martyrdom is factual and simply attribute the prayer to Rabbi Kalonymus. Nonetheless, whatever the source of the prayer, it has become an integral element in the striving for repentance essential to that time of year.

Each year, as I participate in this communal recitation, I think about those who may have passed on during the year and what fate might await me in the year to come. But I also often consider the changes that have taken place in the world over the year and ways in which this lofty prayer might be modified to better address man's concerns going forward.

Part of the problem I have in understanding the thrust of Unetaneh Tokef relates to the concept contained in Parashat Nitzavim (Deuteronomy 29:28) and included at the end of the Vidui to the effect that "the hidden are for Hashem, our God, but the revealed are for us and our children forever, to carry out all the words of the Torah." This verse is generally interpreted to categorically refer to hidden "sins" and revealed "sins," though the reference is merely implied from Moshe's warnings to Israel that precede this verse (29:15–27). The verse clearly requires that, as Jews, we must do all we can to fulfill all the mitzvot and avoid all the sins we possibly can, fulfilling commandments and obeying proscriptions that have been immutably passed down from Moshe at Sinai. That hasn't changed from generation to generation. However, as the years advance, many of God's secrets, the secrets of the natural world, for example, have been revealed to man in increasingly rapid fashion. Talking of the world today with its digital advances, novel medical treatments and devices, and genomic discoveries as "unchanged" or "unchanging" from the world of the past would be met with loud denials by any thinking person.

Today, we are fortunate to have artificial hearts, the tools available to restart stopped hearts, the ability to transplant organs such as kidneys and livers, and many other previously unimaginable life-saving devices. It wasn't that long ago that life was much more precarious. Even as recently as one hundred years ago, people faced countrywide crop failures throughout European

Jewish communities: no wheat, rye, or grain of any kind over vast stretches of England, France, Germany, Italy, Austria, and Russia. Today, generally such extensive, prolonged famines are happily a thing of the past. In America, we are blessed with agricultural wealth never even dreamed of by our ancestors. Even though I know this to be true, I still repeat the part of Unetaneh Tokef that asks, "Who [will die] from famine?" While I know obesity would be a much more likely cause of my demise and those of my fellow congregants, I'll forgo the urge to add that phrase under my breath. I'll continue to stick to the original text until my rabbi instructs me otherwise, despite my sensibilities that the Jews of today may need to ask some new/additional questions of God.

An extremely capable colleague of mine, by the way, interprets Unetaneh Tokef quite differently and does not feel compelled to change anything in the recitation of the prayer. He believes that the whole point of the prayer is that despite all the changes in our lives and the revelations uncovered by mankind, we are still at the mercy of Hashem, especially at this time of year. He feels quite certain that all the so-called advances of mankind do not change this basic premise that we are ultimately faced with the challenge of doing *teshuvah* (repentance) to attempt to attain God's forgiveness.

Finally, as I contemplate the High Holidays, I am struck by the question of the desirability of possessing prophetic powers. Often in life or in literature, when people dream of obtaining the power to know the future, they imagine the wonders they will be able to achieve if for even a moment they could know with certainty what the future will bring. Tales of Wall Street windfalls and racetrack triumphs fill the speculative fiction. But of course the power to see the future is a double-edged sword. Everyone wants to foresee the good that will happen to them, their friends, and their loved ones. Few, if any, wish to know the sad news that awaits them; those details can be left to the future, thank you! In light of the foregoing, the next time you recite Unetaneh Tokef, please reflect on the opportunity you have to ask God to grant you and yours the best year possible, an opportunity worthy people of faith throughout the world would be glad to possess and make use of.

I Have a Confession to Make - Two Yom Kippur Notes

Yom Kippur on the High Seas

We often speak of how fortunate we American Jews are to live in an affluent community, to be able to practice our religion free from oppressive governments, repressive societies, and hostile neighbors. All this is true, but it can lead to religious practice that stretches the bounds of propriety. Take, for example, the exotic Jewish holiday vacation packages regularly offered to our communities through the media: "Spend Succoth in Nairobi: Nine nights in a safari setting complete with *arba'ah minim*. Sleep under the stars and hear our scholars-in-residence discuss topics of interest." Then there is Passover at a ski chalet: "Take your pick of British Columbia or the Bernese Alps. Spend chol hamoed visiting the house where Albert Einstein lived while discovering his theory of relativity."

I confess to traveling on occasion to Jerusalem to celebrate the major Jewish holidays, but that's different. Travel away from home on Succoth, Pesach, and Shavuot is one thing, but travel away from home on Yom Kippur is much more unusual. Only once in my life will I confess to having spent Yom Kippur away from home, and since I was only six years old at the time, I don't consider myself responsible for that extravagance. Besides, there is actually some halachic support and precedent for where my parents, siblings, and I spent Yom Kippur that year.

In 1956, my father decided to return home to Belgium for the first time since he had fled Europe in December 1940. He booked all six of us on a seven-week vacation to Europe that involved transatlantic ocean travel. We traveled to Europe on the British ocean liner *Queen Elizabeth,* and the trip home on its sister ship *Queen Mary.* As the calendar worked out that year, we boarded the *Queen Mary* two days before Yom Kippur, which meant we would be spending the fast on the high seas somewhere between Iceland and Greenland. I remember overhearing that the Cunard Line management had arranged for special Yom Kippur services to be held in the first-class lounge for those passengers who wished to participate, a major concession since almost all the Jewish travelers were booked in tourist (third class)! The fast aboard ship was somewhat unique, since many passengers were suffering from seasickness and had no appetite to eat anyway, so in that regard they didn't feel the deprivation they might otherwise have felt.

I recently discovered that just three years before, two young Lubavitcher Chassidim made the same *yom tov* crossing on the *Queen Mary.* On that occasion, they received a wiregram on board the ship sent by the Rebbe in which he instructed them to conduct services for their fellow passengers and to wish all a *g'mar chatimah tovah* (to be sealed in the Book of Life)!

Vidui

Vidui or confession – we all have to face that chilling word when Yom Kippur approaches. Confessing is a process nobody likes to undergo. As we mature, we develop a sense of responsibility for our personal actions and omissions, but no one really enjoys reviewing his past failings, nor the possible failings of one's neighbors, even for the purpose of atonement. Think about it the next time you are reciting the Al Chet portion of the Vidui. Here, you have listed before you category upon category of sins that people may have committed during the previous year.

Interestingly, in this prayer, we seek atonement for the sins that we have collectively committed. I don't know about you, but I am often struck by how few of these categories apply to me, even to the extent that I think, "What kind of a person could possibly do such a thing?" Then I stop in my prayer "tracks" when I reach a sin that describes my iniquitous behavior precisely. At that point, I'll spend a serious amount of time reviewing my personal failings, and ask God for the strength to stop repeating that behavior. "But it's a victimless crime," my *yetzer hara* (that inner voice we all recognize) will whisper in my ear. Despite that rationalization, I know there are no victimless crimes, for I am at minimum a victim of my own shortcomings and, even more so, bear some responsibility for the sins of my colleagues. Unfortunately, having spent so much time on my particular sins, I have to hurry to finish the collective Vidui before the cantor begins the repetition of the Amidah.

Detecting the Elect –
A Worthwhile Endeavor?

Eskemar/Shutterstock.com

The Talmud cryptically teaches us that in every generation thirty six righteous people "greet the Shechinah," the Divine Presence. From this arcane reference has emerged the belief that at all times in history there are thirty-six unique people in the world upon whose existence the world depends. If any one of them, man or woman, were missing, the world as we know it would end. These special people have been known in history and legend as the *lamed vav* (thirty-six), *lamed vavniks*, *tzaddikim* (righteous ones), or the *tzaddikim nistarim* (hidden righteous people). Essentially, it is believed by Jewish mystics and others that these thirty-six lives are conducted in such a way as to justify to God that mankind is fulfilling God's purpose in creating man in the first place.

It is believed that man is created "in the image" of Hashem. Therefore, man must manifest those qualities, sensitivities, and behaviors that reflect the Divine. It would seem pretty clear that, at a minimum, these thirty-six people would be charitable, kind, and caring toward their fellow man. It is also clear that above all a *lamed vavnik* would be humble, humility being the basis of the selflessness required to fulfill his task on earth. Total anonymity, even to themselves, would be among the other primary characteristics of the elect.

Throughout history, those persons accepting or believing in the legend have often attempted to identify who, among their neighbors, might possibly be a *lamed vavnik*. During recent times these speculations have led to a veritable flood of fictional works on the subject. In the period 1958–2013 alone, for example, there have been no fewer than twenty-one different works of art: novels, films, television programs, short stories, and even comic books whose themes have centered on detecting, defending, and befriending one or all of the extant *lamed vav tzaddikim*. From Andre Schwarz-Bart, French author of the seminal novel *The Last of the Just*, to the Coen brother's recent cinematic offering, *A Serious Man*, the legend has captivated audiences around the world.

Unfortunately, these fictional works haven't solved the question of how to detect the elect, and for a very good reason: because humility is the central component of the makeup of a *lamed vavnik*, he or she will always be unaware of being a "special" person. It is widely believed, in fact, that if someone claims to be among the elect, that very claim would disqualify him from that status! Making things even more difficult from a detection standpoint is that most of us know more than a few people who appear to be selfless, kind, and caring. They can't *all* be *lamed vavniks*! Yet often at a Jewish funeral you will hear a eulogizer declare that the recently departed, given his virtuous character, was clearly one of the *lamed vav*. Even Menachem Begin famously stated at the funeral of Rabbi Aryeh Levin, noted *tzaddik* of Jerusalem and spiritual leader of the Irgun, that Rabbi Levin was considered by many to be a *lamed vavnik*. Begin questioned the existence of such a group of thirty-six people since, in Begin's words, "there could not possibly be thirty-five other people in the world like Levin!"

Before turning to a possible solution to our detection dilemma, it would be fair to ask why one would need to know the identity of the *lamed vavniks*. The answer given by most experts is that knowledge of their identities would permit the community to protect the *lamed vav* from forces that might wish to harm them and us. That such destructive forces exist in the world at all times is sadly evident to anyone who follows current events. An even deeper question concerns why we even need the *lamed vavniks* to preserve the world in the first place, given all those many wonderful, caring souls that already inhabit our world and are not among the elect.

After considering all aspects of this problem, it seems that the very notion of thirty-six anonymous, concealed mystics existing to emerge in times of crisis to save the world is supposed to have a transformative effect on all of us who are *not* among the elect. Sharing our lives with such perfect souls should force us to live a better life, a life of goodwill toward all with whom we share the planet. Maybe the existence of the elect is designed to teach us all to "aspire to become *lamed vav*-like," as a rabbi from Denver once wrote. If the existence of thirty-six hidden *tzaddikim* in each generation would possibly lead to self-improvement of people at large, what could be a better result?

In the end, spending hours trying to determine if that rather shabbily dressed person you pass every day on the way to your bus stop or Dunkin' Donuts is one of the *nistarim* may be a waste of time. Even if you've convinced yourself that he was one of the elect, you'd be bound to keep it to yourself, according to the legend. The person would be bound to deny it, even assail you for making such an absurd accusation. Rather, it may be preferable instead to simply treat him nicely and go on your way. Expecting miracles often leads to disappointment.

Purim Lament - Seeking Poppy Seed Hamantaschen

ChameleonsEye/Shutterstock.com

It's been going on for years in Teaneck: a dastardly conspiracy to prevent me from consuming at least one large poppy seed hamantasch to properly celebrate Purim. March comes around, Adar Aleph, sometimes Adar Bet, and this classic Purim culinary treasure, this classic hamantasch, so delicious with a cold glass of milk, is nowhere to be found! During this festive time, local bakeries bake enormous quantities of small, wheat flour, cookie dough hamantaschen made with all sorts of fillings: fruits, preserves, nuts, and so on. But the poppy seed–filled variety seems to have fallen on hard times.

In actuality, one would think that this "original" would be increasing in popularity. After all, its contents are derived from the poppy plant that produces in its seedpod and stalks the well-known opiates morphine, codeine, and cocaine. While the poppy seed itself doesn't contain a drug-level content of these opiates, its use is outlawed in some countries because ingesting poppy seeds causes some to fail drug tests. Poppy seed bagels and muffins are known to give these false positives, but I haven't personally heard of anyone carrying a poppy seed hamantasch in his luggage being stopped by the authorities at the Canadian or Mexican borders.

I have confronted the local kosher bakery in Teaneck often in the last several years about the need to produce poppy seed hamantaschen at this time of year. The responses I've received fall into two categories:

- "We had them briefly last week, but we ran out." (It's two days before Purim, so why don't you bake some more?)
- "People really don't like *mohn* [German/Yiddish for poppy seed] very much; the other varieties are much more popular." (Infuriating! You can serve cholent without potatoes and call it cholent, but it isn't cholent. Similarly, hamantaschen have the word *mohn* in their name, so you shouldn't be permitted to delete the poppy seeds and still call it hamantaschen!)

I'm fed up with receiving boxes of hamantaschen for Purim *mishloach manot* (food gifts) and having to sift through them for hours to locate a single poppy seed variant. The bakery industry long ago recognized that the black poppy seed fillings made for a nice contrast with the lighter-colored dough, so they came up with a substitute dark filling to confuse the poppy seed lovers, namely, prunes. How many of us, unsure what the filling is, bite into what we hope is a poppy seed hamantaschen only to discover we've bitten into a prune-filled one or a date-filled one? I don't know about you, but that drives me crazy. Did they actually think that we wouldn't be able to tell the difference?! (Apricot and raspberry-filled varieties offend me less, because those fillings can be traced to ancient times.)

What is clearly needed is some sort of pledge on the part of our bakeries to promote resumed consumption of poppy seed hamantaschen, to return it to its primacy among fillings. If they fail to act, much to my dismay, I feel compelled to organize a boycott of those establishments until such time as they produce adequate supplies of poppy seed hamantaschen.

Suburban Scandal -
The Afikomen File

Gilya/Shutterstock.com

A recent investigation by elements in the American Jewish leadership has uncovered some irregularities among many observant families concerning an ancient Passover practice. The problem has nothing to do with eating egg matzah on Passover, mixing matzah with liquids (*gebrokts*), eating chocolate-covered matzah, or overdosing on macaroons. Nor does it involve examining your romaine lettuce maror under an electron microscope (you'll find something, I assure you). Finally, the issue in question has nothing to do with eating the minimum volume of matzah at the Seder or drinking the four cups of wine or grape juice. Those laws are pretty closely observed to everyone's satisfaction.

No, I refer to the custom of children hiding the afikomen and only returning it to their parents in exchange for the parent's promise to buy them a specified gift.

This custom dates back to antiquity, but in recent years the number of parents who have reneged on the promised bounty has increased geometrically. The problem has mushroomed, particularly in affluent Jewish suburbs in the New York Metro area.

Rabbi Pinchas Schwartz of Bnei Tefillah in Crescentville, Connecticut, was part of a rabbinic commission that studied this problem, and he spoke with me at length about his group's findings.

"At first we thought it was a small, innocuous problem. You know, when younger kids – five, six, or eight – steal the afikomen, we discovered they often fall asleep during the meal and don't even participate in the bargaining. If they do, they often forget by the next morning, so the parents get off scot-free," Rabbi Schwartz explained. "But in other cases, there's outright deception involved on the parents' part. Older kids pilfer the matzah in good faith and bargain for a present only to discover their parents or grandparents never intended to honor the promises they made to ransom the cracked pieces of matzah."

Whether or not the parents ever intended to fulfill their afikomen contractual obligations, the sheer number of "reneges" is estimated to be in the thousands.

Rabbi Schwartz reported that in his community, many youths have protested both in school and at home against these breaches, and there's been talk of bringing their elders to a *beit din* (rabbinic court). Pro bono legal clinics are considering bringing a class action suit in federal court to redress the losses suffered by countless youngsters in the community.

"You know, we have many lawyers in my shul, and while they're not particularly litigious, they feel that an easy case of promissory estoppel can be made on behalf of most children who are scammed by the afikomen swindle," Rabbi Schwartz said.

The investigative commission noted in their report that the afikomen issue has caused frequent rifts among families, as illustrated by the following anecdote. The Rosenblum family from an unnamed town in northern New Jersey held a Thanksgiving dinner at their home this past November where, following the turkey course, several grown-up children asked their father to explain what ever happened to the backyard swing set that he supposedly promised them many years earlier as an afikomen present. It's reported that Mrs. Rosenblum, his wife, took the children's side in their protest against Mr. Rosenblum.

"I don't remember agreeing to that," said Mr. Rosenblum, emphatically denying his children's claims.

The issue has become a polarizing one. In light of the movement to hold parents accountable for their inactions regarding afikomen promises, groups of parents are binding together to defend themselves. Rabbi Schwartz has noted this growing counter-trend. "There are parents forming associations advocating that the entire afikomen process be overhauled, asserting that the cause of parents' reneging on afikomen promises is directly related to increasingly excessive demands on the part of children at the Seder table.

"I heard of one youngster in Florida demanding an all-expenses-paid vacation to Europe; another wanted a car. How can parents afford such extravagance?!"

Renowned New York child psychologist Andrea Bird thinks that the phenomenon of parents not fulfilling promises is a complex one, and we may never find an exact cause or solution.

"Is it that most parents promise at the Seder table with the intention of never following through, or is it all about the moment when the deal is struck, and it's all anti-climactic after that?" Bird wonders.

Regardless of the cause, Bird stresses the positives that may arise from the current impasse.

"Ultimately, the fact that even our youngest children get enthused about bargaining over the afikomen guarantees that thousands of Jewish consumers will enter the population over time as 'wise shoppers,' skeptical of deals that seem too good to be true. Every cloud does have its silver lining!"

PART VI
OBSERVATIONS OF AN ORDINARY MAN

Choose Your Airline
Seat Carefully

In his sixty-two years Jack had traveled rather widely: sightseeing trips to Europe; adventure treks through the Yukon, the Alps, and the Rhone Valley; family expeditions across the US Continental Divide; and sunny drives down the Pacific Coast Highway. He'd seen strange places and even stranger people in his time. But nothing compared to the unusual encounter that took Jack by surprise two years ago on an outbound flight to Israel: on that startling occasion Jack came face to face with a fellow passenger who happened to be both an honest-to-goodness Jewish-American princess (archduchess, to be exact) and an heiress of the infamous Romanian Vlad the Impaler (that's Dracula to you). As outlandish and unbelievable as this may seem, everything that happened to Jack in this story is true; he swears to it, and I never question Jack.

On this particular occasion, Jack boarded a United Airlines direct flight from Newark to Tel Aviv. He was traveling solo because his dearly beloved had to stay home to prepare for their son's wedding later that month. He had lost the debate, and so, if he wanted to go, it would be alone or not at all! His seat was on the right side of the center seating area in the business class cabin. He was quite prepared for the ten-hour flight, the noisy humming of the engines, and, quite particularly, the comfortable bed his cushioned, convertible chair would transform itself into. Upon boarding the aircraft, he located his seat (6D) easily, lifted his hand luggage into the open bin above his head, and quickly sat down on his pillow and blanket to permit later arrivals to attend to their needs. There was only one thing he still needed to do, and so he politely asked the nearest cabin attendant to bring him some water so he could take an overdue dose of medicine.

The requested water arrived shortly and was placed on the raised armrest between Jack's and the adjoining seat. At the same moment, a tall woman with very pale skin and dark, straight hair that framed her face stopped at seat 6E to claim her place on the flight. She caught Jack's attention with her rapid actions in preparing for takeoff, arranging her hand luggage overhead and below in record time. Just as she prepared to sit down, however, Jack moved his left arm to reach for the cup of water and knocked it over. The contents spilled out in the direction of the woman, who was able to avoid getting drenched by her quick reactions. Jack rose to wipe off the spill, aided by a towel that was provided to him. He apologized to the woman twice for his clumsiness, and in a moment or two everything was under control. She acknowledged his apology coolly, with a slight nod of her head. Jack felt himself obliged to introduce himself to his neighbor, strike up a conversation (during which he apologized a third time for nearly spilling water on her), and inquire about the object of her trip to Israel.

The woman gave him a comprehensive profile: "I was born in Israel," she said. "I'm going to visit my mother in Holon. My sister lives near my mother; I try to visit her every year. My mother is nearly ninety years old and has slowed down a bit. I've lived in America for many years."

The woman also told Jack that her husband was an architect and her daughter a young lawyer working in the entertainment industry. Jack responded with his life story, a rehearsed tale that took several minutes to complete. The woman seemed interested in what Jack was saying, but after another moment or two, Jack and the woman turned from their conversation toward their own affairs: Jack arranging his dinner tray and the woman turning off her electronic devices.

Half an hour passed, and a light dinner was served. Jack ate his kosher meal while the woman ordered from the regular menu. After the attendants deftly cleared away the last dishes, utensils, and packaging materials in which his meal had been wrapped, Jack raised his serving tray and sat back to relax.

The woman suddenly addressed him. "You know, I am a princess," she said.

Jack was taken aback for a moment.

"Really? That's very interesting. What do you mean exactly?" he countered.

"My husband Roderic is an heir to the throne of the Austro-Hungarian Empire. Our family name is Lothringen-Habsburg. I am his second wife."

Jack was a student of history and knew a lot about the former empire that collapsed after World War I. At university he had studied the detailed honor codes of that empire and the duty, if challenged, to defend one's honor. All he could think of as the princess spoke to him was that he had nearly spilled a cup of water on a royal Habsburg princess in circumstances that would have required him to fight a duel had any Austro-Hungarian soldier witnessed the event.

"There are many heirs to the imperial throne last held by Franz Joseph," the princess continued. "My husband is actually fortieth in line to the throne. Also, since I am a commoner, our children don't count in the succession, and my titles won't be inherited by the children."

The princess described in detail what life was like when the "royal family" got together on annual occasions. "Roderic's mother was a royal princess of Romania, heiress to the throne of that kingdom. When the Communists took over the country in 1947, they confiscated all the royal property, and the family went into exile. In 2006, the new Romanian government welcomed my husband and me back to the country and restored most of our holdings."

At this point, Jack felt somewhat honored that the princess was comfortable in telling him her story in such detail, but his eyes were getting heavy and the time had come to get some rest.

"All of this is fascinating," he finally said to end their conversation.

Before he could fall asleep, Jack took out his iPad to confirm the princess's story through an Internet search. Swiftly, he found Roderic Lothringen among the heirs to the Austro-Hungarian throne, but he found that he was also thereby the ousted heir of the Kingdom of Lombardy in northwest Italy. "Quite a celebrity!" Jack thought. One particular item, however, caught Jack's eye. Bran Castle, the family property overlooking Brasov that had been returned to Roderic and his princess bride in 2006, had a famous previous owner, none other than Count Dracula of Transylvania. Apparently, Bran Castle was one of three castles ruled by Dracula while he ran roughshod over the population in medieval times. Jack soon found pictures of the archduke and his wife – Jack's neighbor – at a 2006 ceremony at the castle. Jack concluded that the occupant of seat 6E was indeed a princess, as she claimed, a Jewish princess!

Jack drifted off to sleep without shutting off his iPad. Soon, he began to dream misty dreams of a verdant countryside, a valley filled with glistening vines, wooly sheep, and friendly, smiling farmers. Looming darkly above the valley stood a castle, sandstone in color, with red-roofed eaves atop its turrets and towers. Jack found himself moving inexorably toward the castle and suddenly found himself inside a somewhat narrow, dimly lit corridor decorated with ancient wall paintings. He heard the shuffling of feet, and before him appeared a caped figure, face shrouded in darkness. Jack ran away from the figure, who followed quickly behind him. Jack ran faster still, but the caped figure continued to gain on him. Around one last turn, Jack found himself at a large, oaken door. There was no escape. The figure edged toward him and bent forward. Jack let out a shriek and all was dark.

Jack awoke to the gentle shaking of the steward.

"Are you all right, sir?" he asked "You let out a scream, so I ran over to see if you were all right. You were probably having a nightmare."

"I think I'm OK," Jack offered. He sighed. "Wow, everything was so real."

Apparently, none of the passengers, including the princess, had reacted to Jack's outburst. Soon, Jack realized why. He looked around the cabin and noticed that the crew had been offering light beverages to the passengers. He must have been sleeping for a while, since they had already passed his seat. Something made Jack glance to his left. He turned to see the princess finishing what he believed to be a glass of bright-red tomato juice. Jack hurriedly turned away. He couldn't even glance at the princess for the rest of the trip. At the end of the flight, he and the princess exchanged the briefest of farewells, after which Jack rushed off the aircraft without looking back.

Be Careful What
You Wish For

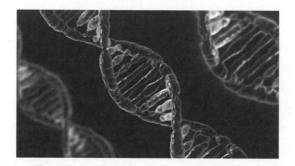

Of all of the novelties the 1990s brought to America and to American Jews in particular, few were more consequential than the preoccupation with one's ancestry, where one came from. We Jews have always been concerned with our *yichus*, so this latter-day general fixation with one's predecessors didn't seem unusual. The differences this time were the digital tools now at our disposal: entire websites dedicated to ferreting out every last record both here and abroad to allow us to painstakingly recreate our forebears' lives, at least from the last two centuries or so. Those investigative tools were now just a mouse click away. You might ask how this development could possibly have any negatives. Short of finding out you're a direct descendant of some unworthy, unsavory personage, what could possibly go wrong? The following tale will give you great pause before you rush out and provide that DNA sample. Join me as we meet Jason Block in a cautionary tale.

    Jason is a forty-nine-year-old stockbroker who lives with his wife and four children in suburban New Jersey. The year is 1999, and Jason has just purchased a book entitled *Abraham's Seed* at his local Barnes and Noble. Over the next two weeks, Jason works his way through the book and, in the process, learns of a joint program being sponsored by the University of Haifa and the University of Arizona that promises to analyze a person's paternal and maternal DNA, compare the data to others around the world who participate in the study, and maintain an ongoing online database that participants can access freely. So fascinated is Jason by the study that he informs his wife that he's thinking of signing up.

"All it involves is ordering a kit from Family Tree DNA, swabbing the inside of your cheek, and sending the sample back to them," Jason tells her. "Then they contact you with the results!"

"And how much does all this cost, Jason?"

"Just $300 for the basic testing of your paternal DNA and another $250 for your maternal DNA. There are other charges for more advanced tests. They can even tell you if you're a Cohen, as they apparently have their own DNA subgroup."

"But you know you're a Cohen, Jason, so why do you need to take a test, and what if the test shows you're not one?"

"I'm sure there's a margin of error anyway, honey, so I think I'm going to order a kit. You and your dad should also test yourselves."

"Whoa, if you want to do this, that's one thing. I'll wait to see what happens to you. This is your project!"

Jason orders his kit, follows the directions carefully, and within two weeks, receives a document stating that he in fact is a Cohen and that his parents were descended from one of the most populous groups of European Ashkenazic Jewry, whose descendants today populate not only the United States, but Russia, Poland, and Germany as well. Jack is impressed by the reported results, as he had not informed the testers of his Cohen status. After coaxing his wife for two weeks, she agrees to have herself and her father tested. Soon, the greater Block family's DNA is analyzed, and to their great surprise they find they share remote chromosomal roots with people residing in Scandinavia and Scotland, of all places. All very entertaining, for sure, until one night three months later when Mrs. Block sees an email addressed to Jason from someone in California.

"Jason, this fellow says he recently joined the Family Tree program, and according to the information listed on the website you are very closely related to him," Jason's wife tells him. "In fact, there's a 90 percent probability that you and he are related within the last two generations. He says he wants to talk to you; here's his number if you want to call him back."

Jason is tired and thinks of delaying a call back until the next day, but something compels him to dial the West Coast number without delay. Jason thinks that maybe this person had some medical purpose in contacting him. Perhaps he's suffering from a disease and needs to find a close relative for an organ transplant or such? The phone rings twice, and the male voice at the other end is a mellow baritone. The story he tells Jake is remarkable and, frankly, disturbing.

"My name is Roger Grabner, I live in San Jose, and I sell exercise equipment. I recently sent in a sample of my DNA to the Family Tree people to try to locate any ancestors or relatives I might have on my father's side. You see, I was adopted at birth and raised in a traditional New Jersey family. Only two years ago, I discovered that my natural mother had been an unmarried Holocaust survivor who gave birth to me sometime in 1952. She suffered severe emotional problems from her war experiences as well as the circumstances of her pregnancy. As a result of her disabilities, she was institutionalized in Creedmoor Hospital on Long Island soon after my birth and died there in her mid-forties. I never met her, but I've spoken to members of her family who still live in the area."

Jason listens sympathetically to Grabner's tale of woe, but is somewhat confused as to why Grabner has reached out to him.

"What a sad story. I wish you only good things, but how can I help you?" Jason asks.

"You see, no one seems to know who my father was. My natural mother's relatives couldn't provide me with any details as to his possible identity. Some thought he might have been a soldier; others remembered her traveling on a cruise after the war where she met a young man, but they didn't know any details…"

"…So you're using the DNA testing to try to find someone, anyone, who might lead to finding your father," Jason finishes Grabner's thought.

"Exactly, and you turned out to possibly be that missing link!"

"You're aware of course that there is a significant chance we are not at all related despite the similarity of our DNA profiles," Jason responds.

"Yes, I am aware of that possibility. Nevertheless, I've accessed information about your family on the Internet and there are some intriguing hints that your father, or more likely one of your uncles, may be my father!"

"Wow, that's a lot to take in in one late night's conversation, wouldn't you agree?"

"Sure. Look, I'm not saying anything with certainty. I'd just like to communicate with you from time to time regarding clues I come up with that might help me in my search. I'd like you to confirm or reject any evidence I find."

"I guess so, but I'm afraid we may never find out the truth of your father's identity. In my opinion, it's very unlikely we're cousins. Certainly based on what I know of my father and uncles, I can't imagine they fathered a child out of wedlock. That's crazy."

"But not impossible, you'd have to admit," counters Grabner.

"I'd like to sleep on this for a couple of days, if you don't mind," Jason finally says.

"I'll email you the information I've already accumulated, if it's alright with you," Grabner says.

"Sure," Jason reluctantly answers, feeling sorry for the Californian orphan who might actually be his relative.

"Goodnight, cousin," ends Grabner to Jason's resigned sigh.

In the weeks and months that follow, Jason dutifully sifts

through multiple detailed emails, records, and notes forwarded to him by Grabner, which could shed some light on a connection between Grabner's mother and a Block male, but no conclusive link can be established. Jack begins to feel that he was too dismissive of Grabner at the start. Just imagine if you had been trying for a lifetime to find your blood relatives and now you seem on the brink of discovering that long-lost relative. Several curious suggestive pieces of information remain that give even Jason a hope that the decisive link might be proven. Of Jason's uncles, only one is still alive at this time. He had been married at the time of Grabner's birth to a refugee from Berlin who was active in charities involving other German-Jewish refugees. Grabner's mother was from Berlin as well, which might have forged a link to Jason's uncle.

At Grabner's urging, Jason invites him to a family wedding where Grabner meets his other putative "relatives." Grabner convinces one of Jason's cousins to send a sample of DNA to be analyzed by Family Tree. Ultimately, at Grabner's request, Jason's uncle, as the last surviving member of his generation, agrees to submit a sample as well. As far as Grabner is concerned, this is the ultimate test, because it can be compared directly with Grabner's own profile. The results are fairly compelling in that alleged father and son share 3,750 out of 3,975 alleles tested.

Within two months of the test, Jason's uncle unfortunately passes away, he and Roger having never met.

"Roger, even though the test results are very similar, in no way can you conclusively say that either my father or my uncle was in fact *your* father," Jason says to Roger in what ends up being their last conversation, sometime after the funeral. "No geneticist would accept that as definitive."

Despite Jason's dismissal, Grabner refuses to say die and continues to this day to refer to Jason's uncle as "Dad." According to Grabner, Jason's uncle might never even have been aware of the pregnancy or Grabner's birth. Jason, for that matter, every so often compares a picture of Grabner at age two with one of his cousin's pictures at around the same age, and darned if they don't bear a resemblance to each other. As unlikely as it appears to be, they *could* be related to each other, Jason always concludes, but that doesn't mean they *are!*

Some things are best left unresolved.

Confessions of a
Campus War Profiteer

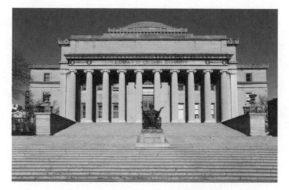

Have you ever imagined yourself deeply involved in a crisis, a battle for survival, a moment that tests your courage, your resolve, your will? Would you be the one to fall on the grenade, to block the knife, to rally the troops to victory? Or, when tested, would you scramble or slink away in a cowardly fashion? Mercifully, few of us are so challenged, but rather live a lifetime of minor ego scrapes and bruises. Below, however, is a story of a Jewish student who, like Zhivago, didn't want to let some small bothersome thing like a national upheaval or revolution interfere with the life he had planned for himself. He was one of many. Unlike Zhivago, my friend Jack, in his mind, became a true war profiteer.

"We all want to stack the deck in our favor occasionally."

So began my friend Jack as we sat on the porch of our cabin overlooking Lake Sebago in New York last summer. The fireflies blinked on and off in that random pattern we knew so well from prior talks under the August moon. The slight breeze coming from the lake was a welcome relief from the heat of the day.

"You remember back in our college days?" he asked.

Who could forget such a time?

"I was in school at Columbia in 1968," Jack continued, "when the students took over Hamilton Hall and locked the dean in his office. All hell broke loose, but it was damned entertaining if you didn't have an interest in the outcome."

I asked Jack, "How is it possible that you didn't feel more of a sense of involvement with the issues that concerned the protesters: the war, the police violence, the sense that the Establishment didn't give a damn for the Bill of Rights or the residents of Morningside Heights, et cetera?"

"I'll tell you why," he replied. "I simply felt that the student protesters were in the wrong, that however valid some of their arguments were, their end – stopping the war, for example – didn't justify the means they employed to achieve their goals. Shutting down the school for weeks and depriving those who wished to attend classes of that option created a deep sense of anger and opposition among the majority of students who were not protesting."

Jack opened a bottle of Diet Coke, sipped some of the bubbly drink, and continued to speak of that time long ago in Morningside Heights.

"OK, in the beginning, I'll admit there was a real sense of excitement and empowerment because the students were able to stop the school routine in its tracks. We actually joked among ourselves that our pedestrian ID cards that had previously allowed us to merely borrow library books and class materials had been magically transformed into 'passports to adventure.' You see, you couldn't get onto the campus without that ID card, as the police limited access to students and security personnel. Even the press couldn't get in."

"How long did it last," I asked, "before the police broke it up, I mean?"

"About a week, and it ended early in the morning with hundreds of arrests and plenty of injuries."

"Did it accomplish anything in the end?"

"Well some of us profited from the student action, me more than most."

"What do you mean?"

"Well, one of the major results of the student protest was the creation of a Student Senate that would represent the students' point of view in any future decision making on campus policies. The first order of business when the dust settled was how to deal with the remainder of the spring semester. There were about five weeks to go when the protests started, and four remained when they ended. Within two days, the school decided that classes would not resume, and all students and teachers would go on early vacation. No final examinations would be scheduled, either."

"So you lost an entire school semester as a result of the protest?"

"Not exactly," Jack said. "The Student Senate decided to propose several alternative options, essentially leaving it up to the students to decide which one was most desirable. You see, they recognized that most students had not protested and shouldn't be arbitrarily forced to lose the semester credits. After all, there had been nine weeks of classes prior to the closure."

"What were the options?"

"First, you could take all your classes pass/fail. Second, you could take an incomplete and finish the course in the fall. Third, you could start the class anew in the fall. Fourth, you could take your midterm grade (assuming there had been a midterm exam) as your final grade."

"Wow, so what did you do, Jack?"

Jack hesitated for a while, then said, "Well, I've never told this to anybody 'cause I feel a little uncomfortable about it. I chose the last option for all my classes."

"So what? That doesn't sound so bad. Why are you so self-conscious about it?"

"Well, it's like this. That semester I had taken a required intro-ductory biochemistry course. They used a programmed text to teach us how to draw increasingly complex molecules. Now, I wasn't a science major by any means, but through this text I had mastered some pretty heavy science. When you finished the text, you could spit back a great deal of knowledge. But it was a lot like they say about Chinese food: an hour after you close the text, you can't remember anything!"

"You mean an hour after you eat Chinese food, you feel hungry again?" I corrected.

"Exactly," Jack continued.

"Well, this bio course had a midterm scheduled for the last week in March, and our teaching assistant dutifully informed us that it would consist of a two-hundred-point examination with an extra credit question worth twenty additional points. The exam was a tough go, I recall. All of us left Schermerhorn Hall feeling numb.

"A week later we returned to get the midterm exam results. Of course, the professor waited until the end of his lecture to return our exams. Actually, the professor took off after the bell and left his assistant to deal with us nervous students. The assistant told us that, based on poor performance, she had to curve the grades. She grabbed a piece of chalk and listed the letter grades vertically from top to bottom on the large blackboard. Next to each letter grade she listed the number of students who received that grade following the curve. Most students stopped looking after they saw that one student had received an A+ on the test!

"Moments passed and the assistant stopped writing on the board.

"All I could think of was how my test score was probably disas-trous. I slowly descended the amphitheater steps and approached the desk. In a moment, I found my exam paper and couldn't suppress my joy. There, on the top of my paper, was an A+ inside a circle. Next to the grade was a raw score fraction of 199/200.

Nineteen points of extra credit made up for twenty lost points on the basic exam.

"I was ecstatic," said Jack, "and almost flew home to West End Avenue, my feet barely touching the ground."

"Impressive, Jack," I said, "very impressive!"

Now clearly Jack's achievement on that bio midterm exam was a wonderful accomplishment in its own right. He told me his mother would not let him throw the exam away and kept it as long as she lived. But, as a result of the student protest weeks after the exam, it took on even greater importance.

"I have to confess I took that A+ on my midterm and used it to claim an A+ as my full course grade."

"Don't be so hard on yourself, Jack. While you might consider yourself a profiteer of circumstances, or an opportunist, just remember how the *leaders* of the protests ended up. Almost without exception those radicals became capitalists! I wouldn't accuse them of selling out in the end; let's just say they became realists and turned into the parents they treated with such disdain during those hectic college years. To paraphrase Mel Brooks's two thousand-year-old man: '[They] mocked that which [they were] to become!'

"You profited from your hard work, Jack, and from your diligence, and you have nothing to be ashamed of. It's carpe diem, friend. Students seized buildings, but you seized the day."

Rory and Winston -
Rory's Lost Weekend

Rory was born in northeast Pennsylvania about ten years ago. How he came to Teaneck is part of this story; how he never became friends with Winston, a longtime Teaneck resident, is another, equally important part. By far, however, most people are interested in how and why Rory and Winston fell out with each other, how a potential friendship could sour so quickly, and how proximity could lead to contempt. Sometimes, as in this case, no definitive explanation can be given for how things turned out. Sad to say, sometimes things just happen despite the best intentions.

Rory's natural parents were rather famous (in their circles): long-term residents of the Pocono Mountains, East Stroudsburg, Pennsylvania, to be exact. When Rory was born, he joined a large group of relatives who resided in the Stroudsburg area. From his birth, it was apparent that Rory's parents could not afford to keep him and would put him up for adoption as soon as possible. Early on, Rory's parents thought a responsible home, a Jewish home, would be ideal for Rory, who had shown signs of curiosity and courage. Through mutual friends, a family from Teaneck, New Jersey, with several children of their own expressed an interest in adopting Rory. The family visited Rory at his home, got to know him, and soon decided to formally adopt him. After the necessary papers were completed, the Schiffs drove out to Pennsylvania to collect Rory. He seemed sad on the trip east to New Jersey, but the Schiff kids did their best to cheer him up. After a short while, Rory seemed to warm to the Schiffs, and they arrived home in Teaneck as one happy family.

As chance would have it, Winston Bronstein was out on the street at the exact moment Rory stepped out of the Schiffs' car. Winston did not exactly greet Rory with open arms. In fact, he let Rory know he was not welcome on Winston's turf. As Rory ran behind Mr. Schiff for protection, Winston had to be restrained. The Schiffs scooped Rory up and ran inside their home while the Bronsteins steered Winston in the opposite direction. Since it was getting late and Rory had been up at the crack of dawn, Mrs. Schiff prepared Rory's bed and calmed him by gently rocking him to sleep. As soon as she placed him down, however, he opened his eyes and sort of smiled, even winked at her. Rory would clearly not be easy to put to bed!

Now, what you have to know about Mr. Schiff is that he was a very organized individual; he ran a very tight ship at home. As he sat in the family den reading the paper, he heard Rory in the next room giving Mrs. Schiff, the sweetest and most patient of women, a hard time. Mr. Schiff bristled a bit for a moment and suddenly rose, went over to the large bookcase opposite his recliner, and reached for a large loose-leaf binder wedged between two volumes of *The Midrash Says*. The red binder contained several articles and notes concerning behavioral training for the young that Mr. Schiff had collected to prepare his family to raise Rory. Mr. Schiff reached for one article in particular. It was titled "How to Establish Male Dominance in the Home." It started simply enough:

> When training your new arrival, it is most important to establish who the boss is going to be, who the alpha male will be. You cannot assert yourself too early in establishing that you will be setting the rules in the house and all must obey. The earliest step you should take is to stare firmly in the trainee's

eyes, making sure you maintain your gaze until inevitably the trainee will avert his.

That seemed simple enough, so Mr. Schiff turned to where Mrs. Schiff was struggling to put Rory to sleep.

"Rory, look at me," shouted Mr. Schiff. Rory looked up from where he was sitting on the ground and peered at Mr. Schiff.

"Keep looking at me, Rory," Mr. Schiff continued. Rory continued to look in Mr. Schiff's direction, almost smiling at him in a curious, crooked way.

"That's good … keep looking."

Mr. Schiff kept at this charade for about a minute, but he was finding it hard to maintain his pose and his poise. Finally, reluctantly, he averted his gaze from Rory, who reacted with a sort of chuckle at having bested Mr. Schiff at his own game. Rory followed Mrs. Schiff to her favorite sofa in the adjoining living room, and in a short while, perhaps from the excitement of his triumph over Mr. Schiff, Rory was gently snoring on Mrs. Schiff's lap. Mr. Schiff was chagrined.

The next morning, the Schiffs rose at eight and prepared to attend services at their local synagogue. It was Shabbat and they planned to leave Rory at home with a sitter. They were concerned that Rory was not yet toilet trained, and they feared the babysitter would balk at seeing to his needs. Soon after arriving at the Schiffs' home, however, the sitter advised them that she was experienced in handling "new arrivals," and that they could go to the synagogue as planned.

As the hours away from home passed, the Schiffs couldn't wait to return and to take Rory out to show him off to their neighbors. The Schiff kids ran ahead and dressed Rory in a fine suit of clothes, combed his hair, and led him outside.

"Be careful, kids! Look out for cars! Make sure you stick close to Rory!"

Rory frolicked on the front lawn of the Schiffs' home, alternately playing with his new siblings and several toys that littered the lawn. Couples strolled by on the adjoining streets, returning, as were the Schiffs, from synagogue services.

"Did you like the rabbi's speech today?" one matron asked Mrs. Schiff, just as she was restraining Rory from following a red ball into the street.

"As usual, he started out strong, and then my lack of sleep took over."

"Rory is so cute," opined Mrs. Field from down the block, "and I love his outfit!"

Just as Mrs. Field was bending down to give Rory a kiss, Winston Bronstein came down the block to see what all the commotion was about. As soon as he spied Rory, Winston raced in his direction at full speed. He collided with Rory (what you might call a blindside hit), who went flying onto his back. Parents, siblings, and friends immediately intervened and separated Rory and Winston, who were soon eyeing each other menacingly, holding them back from mauling each other further. The Schiffs were concerned. This was the second time in as many days that Winston had made his intentions clear to run Rory off the block. Rory was even more concerned. Winston's demeanor made it clear that, at least in his view, there wasn't enough room on the block for both Rory and Winston. From Rory's brief history with Winston, Rory felt that Winston's bite might be worse than his bark, and since Winston's bark was hideous, Rory couldn't imagine what his bite felt like. Rory hoped the Schiffs would protect him from Winston now and in the future. But he feared Winston might waylay him when the Schiffs were not around.

For the moment, the danger passed when the Bronsteins finally removed Winston from the scene, after making a show of punishing him for his unneighborly moves on Rory. And just when everything had calmed down, another near calamity took place. Around the corner of the Schiffs' house appeared a small, white-tailed rabbit attracted by some of the edible plants emerging in the Schiffs' front garden. In a flash, Rory became the aggressor, running after the rabbit and chasing him into and across the street. Rory's siblings gave chase as well and caught up with Rory just as a car was turning onto the street across which Rory had dashed. The rabbit made his escape under the fence into a thicket, and Rory accompanied the Schiffs back into their home for Shabbat lunch. It was quite an eventful morning!

After the meal, Mrs. Schiff sat down next to her husband in the den. He had been unusually silent during lunch.

"What's wrong, dear? Is it something I said?"

"No, not at all; it's just I think we might have made a mistake adopting Rory."

"He's so cute, dear," she replied, having instantly fallen in love with him. She was secretly devastated that her husband was considering giving up Rory.

"Raising Rory is going to overwhelm me! I never realized how much work is involved. He doesn't listen to me, but he loves you and the kids. It would be one thing if everyone would lend a hand in raising him, but you're all going off to work and school every day, and I'll be forced to quit my job and stay home with him! It's a full-time job in itself!"

"Well, it was you who wanted to adopt him in the first place!"

"Yeah, well, I thought when it came to it, everyone would pitch in. Now I see that you all want to play with him but not get involved in the hard part of raising him. And then there's Winston who, frankly, frightens *me*, not to mention Rory."

"I don't know what to say; the kids will be very disappointed."

"Not to mention the adoption folks who asked us numerous times if we understood the difficulties in adopting Rory," Mr. Schiff added. "It won't be pleasant confronting them."

"You'll be doing this by yourself if that's what you decide. I'm not facing those people," his wife insisted.

Sunday morning came, and it was a very somber one in the Schiff house. No birds tweeted that morning. A few clouds flecked the mid-spring sky as the Schiff children said their goodbyes to Rory. Mr. Schiff loaded up the gray Ford Edge with Rory's mea-ger belongings and checked the auto gauges for the trip back to Stroudsburg. As Mr. Schiff was adjusting his mirrors, none other than Winston Bronstein happened to come by on his morning constitutional. Rory's oppressor seemed to sense that something important was up at the Schiff house.

"Winston is sniffing out another opportunity to harass Rory," thought Mr. Schiff, "but I won't let him!"

Mr. Schiff stepped on the accelerator just as Winston made his move. Rory, in the back seat of the Ford, was sad to leave his new friends after such a short stay. He wasn't quite sure why things hadn't worked out with the Schiffs, but he was happy to be rid of that Winston fellow, who just then got a mouthful of engine exhaust for his efforts that morning to attack Rory. As Winston coughed and squealed in discomfort, Rory quickly turned around to look out the broad, rear window in one final glance back at his Teaneck home. As he did so, his flea collar, loosely hanging around his neck, fell silently to the floor of the vehicle.

The Elusive Third Purchase

Dennis Fishman was happy. His life seemed quite in order. After five years of college, four years of medical school, and an internship at a prestigious Midwest hospital, he had joined a growing orthopedic practice in the suburb of Degart, outside Chicago. At thirty, his professional prospects seemed excellent. However, his major interest in life was not medicine. He did diligently carry out his responsibilities at the office, at the hospital, at the clinics where he worked, but medicine held no excitement for him except as a means to an end.

Every weekday morning at 9:15, wherever he might be, Dr. Dennis Fishman would break out in a cold sweat. He would fidget with whatever happened to be in his hands, worry written on his face. The good doctor was not suffering from an attack of malaria. Rather, he was preparing to call his stockbroker. The "market" was about to open! Nervously, Dr. Fishman would seek out a quiet corner in his workplace with a secure phone line, a safe place from which to reach across space and link himself with the action he craved.

Harold Schwartz of Price and Chase was Dr. Fishman's investment guru. A second-generation broker, he had been in the business for fifteen years. Married with four kids, Schwartz had met Fishman several years earlier at a summer resort while waiting for the dining room to open. A short conversation at that time had led to several profitable trades in the newly opened Fishman account, and the relationship was established. Fishman knew very little about Schwartz, and he preferred it that way. In fact, he had told Schwartz the week they met that he was glad he really didn't know him well, so that if Schwartz were not to look after Fishman's affairs carefully, Fishman would be able to pull his account away from Schwartz without the slightest hesitation – just another example of a late-twentieth-century relationship of trust.

In reality, Fishman might have been very interested to know one particular detail about Harold Schwartz. For some time, Schwartz had been living a life of not-so-quiet desperation. His bills were piling up, his creditors had his phone numbers memorized, he would not be buying or leasing any new – or used – cars for the foreseeable future. Schwartz did not remember exactly how he had gotten into his present fix; he simply knew that he was having the damnedest time making ends meet. Nevertheless, Schwartz's personal financial problems did not necessarily disqualify him from advising others on where to invest their funds. Strangely, Schwartz's own success or lack thereof in personal investing bore little relation to how well his clients did. It was Schwartz's lifestyle that was doing him in: some months he cut down his expenses, but income was down; other months, business was good, but expenses rose unexpectedly. Whenever he had a really great month, Schwartz could guarantee it would just enable him to pay off amounts in arrears. The thought of two solid months in a row never occurred to him.

"Mr. Schwartz's office, good morning," the secretary intoned. "Oh, Dr. Fishman, how are you? Harold's on another call, but I'll let him know you're on the line."

"Doctor, how are you?" interrupted Schwartz. "You're calling about Steinway Amalgamated? It hasn't gone down. I know. Still holding at fifty-one. Well, your put options have two weeks to run. I know. If Steinway doesn't drop below forty, the options will be worthless. My sources say that Steinway is due for a big drop; they're heavily committed to these annuities where they're paying double-digit interest to the holders. Now, with interest rates dropping, they'll never be able to earn enough to pay off their obligations. They're going down!"

Schwartz didn't really have any special "sources" on which he was basing his play. The only "inside information" he had going for him was what he had inside his head. Fishman liked the story; it made sense to him. He had agreed two months earlier to buy one hundred put options on Steinway Amalgamated, giving himself the right to sell ten thousand shares of Steinway for a period of three months at fifty. The options cost Fishman five thousand dollars; if, and he hoped when, the stock dropped to say, forty, he could pocket one hundred thousand dollars.

"Sometimes you come up with good ideas, Schwartz. I'll call you later on to see how it's doing."

Schwartz put down the receiver. He chuckled to himself as he recalled his first conversations with Fishman. "I want to make money, lots of money – you've got to give me winners, under-stand?" Over time, Schwartz wasn't sure if he had made money for Fishman. It always intrigued Schwartz that the reason people stayed with their brokers often had little to do with how well they did financially. For some, their broker was "the son they never had"; for another, a friend, a confidant with whom to discuss the latest news in business or politics. "I'm even a psychiatrist," thought Schwartz, "practicing without a license, no less!"

Over the next two weeks, the shares of Steinway Amalgamated remained high. Fishman's options weren't working out so well. Schwartz counseled patience.

"How come the stock hasn't gone down?" barked Fishman.

"Look, it should be lower than it is. It might be prudent at this point to buy some longer-term options right now – say, running another three months, until July – and sell the options you now hold."

After a moment's hesitation, Fishman, sighing deeply, agreed to the switch. True, he was taking a loss of three thousand dol-lars on the first trade, but if Steinway collapsed before July, he would make enough to cover the loss as well as the additional five thousand dollars he was using to buy the new July options. What the heck, it was only money, and Fishman had this great urge to succeed.

Schwartz was soon disappointed when Steinway Amalgamated continued to refuse to go down in price. For weeks, it hovered between fifty and fifty-two dollars a share, condemning Fishman's second options purchase to the same fate as his earlier one. Fishman was getting increasingly testy on the phone.

"Meanwhile, it hasn't budged from where it was on the day I bought those damn options," Fishman argued.

"There's nothing I can say," Schwartz said. "I mean, I'm as distressed as you are about the situation. I don't know why it hasn't gone down. I guess the company is handling its cash flow crisis better than expected."

The day before Fishman's July put options were to expire, Schwartz reached him at the hospital.

"Doctor, I realize we've got only one more day till your options expire, but," Schwartz sighed nervously, "I think you should –"

"I know what you're going to say, Schwartz, but no way am I going to put another penny into any recommendation of yours. I'm not buying any more options on Steinway Amalgamated today or ever. I'm finished with this crap!"

"I'm sorry you feel this way, but I can understand how frustrated you feel. I am too!"

"Look, you're a nice guy, but I'm taking my business elsewhere. You won't be seeing me again."

Fishman hung up the receiver and shrugged. "I'm getting some education in the market. Why am I always so unlucky?"

Schwartz was disappointed. He had staked a lot on the Steinway Amalgamated collapse, and all that had fallen was his relationship with Fishman. "He was a good client; I could have gotten referrals from him if I had succeeded," Schwartz thought self-pityingly.

It was October that year when the news broke: Steinway Amalgamated reported it was having trouble making certain loan payments, and the rush to sell was on. Within days, analysts were urging their clients to sell. The reason for the turnaround in the company's fortunes was the inability of Steinway Amalgamated to pay its annuity holders' interest in the required amount. By November, the company was in bankruptcy.

Schwartz took the news badly. He calculated that with Steinway dropping to two dollars a share from fifty dollars, Fishman would have netted some five hundred thousand dollars, obviously more than enough to recover the fifteen thousand dollars in total costs he would have put in had Fishman made the third purchase of options Schwartz desired him to make.

"That damned third purchase," Schwartz thought. "It's never made. I can never persuade anyone to make that third purchase if they've lost money on the prior two trades!"

Schwartz thought back to his college days, to something he had learned many years earlier in an experimental psychology course. It hadn't seemed important then, but time and experience as a broker had taught Schwartz that it was one of the most important lessons in human psychology an investment advisor, or any other person for that matter, could learn. In that class Schwartz and his fellow students would spend their Wednesday lab sessions training their assigned pet rats to press a bar when a light shone in the cage in order to obtain a food pellet. After weeks of conditioning the rat to press the bar to obtain the food, the students would reverse field and administer an electric shock to the rat each time it pressed the bar in response to the light. Sooner or later, the rats got the idea that hunger was preferable to pain, and they ceased hitting the bar when the light came on.

This negative reinforcement was not the end of the experiment, however. The final phase consisted of reconditioning the rat's behavior, fancy words for seeing if you could coax the rat to resume hitting the bar again to obtain food. The thing was, as

Schwartz and his fellow students discovered, you could, with some effort, get that rat to hit the bar again; he had some capacity to forgive and forget. But – and this is what Schwartz was convinced of – "shock" the rat a second time and he's never going to come back! Fishman's departure as a client of Price and Chase was thus perfectly understandable. Fishman, like the rat, had lost heart when there was much to be gained with a little more faith.

Fish Tales –
An "Unorthodox" Guide

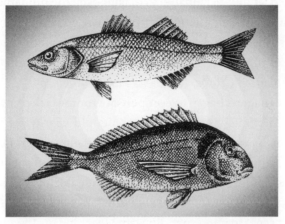

Camek/Shutterstock.com

Among Orthodox Jews, aquatic sports, outside of swimming, can't be counted among the most popular participant sports. Sailing, competitive rowing, and sculling are simply not pastimes commonly pursued in our circles. With few exceptions, and leaving summer camp aside, unless you're a direct descendant of the tribe of Zevulun, it's unlikely you'll be obsessed by these waterborne pursuits. There is, however, one water-related activity with universal appeal, and the Orthodox can be counted in numbers among the aficionados. I speak of course of fishing, of which there are many varieties: lake fishing, ocean fishing, stream fishing, shore fishing, guided fishing, andself-guided fishing, to name just a few.

As a young Jewish boy growing up on the island of Manhattan, I could view the Hudson River from my bedroom window on upper Riverside Drive. On occasion, I would spy large ocean-going vessels, barges, and fishing boats slowly gliding over the grayish-blue waters that separated my island home from the cliffs of New Jersey. I wondered where those ships were bound, how long they had been at sea, and what adventures the seamen on board had experienced. I read novels about the dangers of sea voyages undertaken by whaling crews, fantastical tales of mermaids, sirens, and sea monsters. But I had to face the sad fact that I was a confirmed landlubber, unable to master even the fundamentals of swimming. This put a serious crimp in my youthful plans to run away to sea as a cabin boy, a career goal firmly planted in my mind by a series of realistic Disney films such as *Kidnapped*, *Treasure Island*, *Robinson Crusoe*, and *Swiss Family Robinson*.

As a teenager, I began to compensate for my lack of swimming skills by spending as much time as I could *near* water with my uncle Alex, an expert fisherman, during the summer months when I visited him in Hunter, New York. Born in Antwerp, Uncle Alex served as a young courier in the resistance during World War II and played semi-professional soccer when he came to America. He didn't seem to mind spending time teaching me the rudiments of mountain stream fishing for trout, skills that were difficult to master and required a great deal of patience.

From my uncle Alex, I developed my love of fishing and learned the important skill of baiting your hook with live bait. Don't laugh! You'd be surprised how many very brave people are unwilling and/or unable to place a wriggling night crawler (read earthworm) on a small hook. From these beginnings, I began to read about the sport, realizing that, as in other things in life, I'd only get better if I actually *practiced*. By the time I got married and started a family at the age of twenty-five, I decided to overcome any latent fears I had of drowning while at sea and embarked on a series of fishing expeditions that took me far from local waters. I wanted to set a somewhat braver model for my children than the rather nervous adolescent I had been.

I recount for you some of these adventures below, stressing the lessons I learned so that you may avoid some of the problems I encountered and better prepare yourself if you should choose to take to the water on a fishing trip. Two preliminary matters you should be aware of. First, like most of us, you likely possess seasickness genes and will suffer from mal de mer as soon as you hit open water. Second, you should note that the ocean neither loves nor hates those who sail upon it; it is merely a force of nature in or on which you can often successfully recreate, navigate, surf, or swim. But always be aware that the ocean can swallow you up in an instant, experienced sailor and novice alike.

The first fishing expedition of note that I participated in was a Memorial Day Atlantic Ocean party boat charter in Belmar, New Jersey, along with three friends from Teaneck. The advantages of embarking on a sizable ship with thirty other stalwart fishing novices to try your hand at catching fluke and bluefish is that you'll find you have plenty of company, and as you know, misery loves company. Unfortunately, you'll have a better than 50 percent chance of chucking up your breakfast, which you shouldn't have eaten in the first place. You were probably the brave one of your group who didn't take the recommended Dramamine dose, and so you'll be quickly introduced to the blessings every Jewish sailor learns to recite sooner or later if he engages in ocean fishing.

You didn't know there was a *berachah rishonah* (initial blessing) and a *berachah acharonah* (concluding blessing) that one should always be prepared to recite when on such a trip? In fact, on setting out you should intone the following blessing: "Please bless this enterprise with success, much fish to bring home, good weather, and smooth sailing." Upon reaching the fishing zone, whether or not you or any of your fishing companions are capable of standing up and actually fishing, you will be moved to recite the following: "Please return me safely to shore; if You do, I promise to lead a more righteous life and to never embark upon such a trip again!" The latter is usually recited when the declarant has taken refuge below deck and is performing natural childbirth breathing (the real reason husbands should accompany their wives to Lamaze sessions!).

The Belmar expedition was followed by a Boca Raton, Florida, fishing idyll, where six hours among friends produced zero fish, but less seasickness. Next, I hired a professional guide to engage in flat fishing off the shallow waters near Flamingo, Florida. A red tide obscured the fishing ground, so the guide diverted to Cape Sable, the southernmost point of the continental United States on the Gulf of Mexico, where we fished the mangroves offshore and caught two seven-foot blacktip sharks and several smaller fish and encountered ocean-going mosquitoes the size of sparrows.

The Florida outing was followed by an early morning trek in April to the middle of the broad Delaware River, where I, guided by a Grizzly Adams type, fished for shad on their annual spring run up the center channel of the river between New Jersey and Pennsylvania. After landing nine of these shiny, razor-thin ten-pound fish in a matter of minutes, my arms felt like they were about to fall off! Over the following years, I also fished freshwater lakes, large and small, for lake trout (Lake Ontario several times, Lake Minnewanka in the Canadian Rockies), bass, pickerel, perch, sunfish (primarily at Camp Lavi on the shores of Fork Mountain pond in Wayne County, Pennsylvania), and carp (including a nine-pounder caught within two hundred feet of Route 17 South in Paramus near the Fashion Center!). I've also attempted fishing in the charming though unproductive winter waters off San Juan, Puerto Rico, in the Caribbean.

All the foregoing was mere preparation for facing the ultimate fishing trip of a lifetime in the North Pacific waters off Ketchikan, Alaska, known as the salmon-canning capital of the world. Rising at dawn, we left our cruise ship for a fishing excursion dressed like Gorton's fishermen from Gloucester, Massachusetts, complete with waders held up by suspenders, rain boots, and raincoats with head gear. I motored out offshore on a twenty-foot boat with two other fishermen, Californians, guided by a seventy-four-year-old sailor at the controls. We weighed anchor in three hundred feet of water in the Pacific Channel, and over the next two hours I caught two sea bass, a scorpion fish (kosher!), and three twenty-five-pound halibut.

The two Californians failed to catch anything until one swung his rig toward me while exclaiming, "Look, I've caught some kind of jellyfish!" He smacked the jellyfish into my cheek and chin before dropping his rig on the deck of the boat. My face became numb immediately and then started to redden and throb seriously, the pain lasting for several hours. Back on board the Norwegian Pearl, I consulted the ship's doctor, who informed me that had I been stung by the South Pacific variant of the jellyfish that had struck me, I probably would have died! I thanked him for that information and the vinegar treatment he provided me with, and ran to tell my wife about my brush with death! The fishing guides filleted the ten pounds of usable fish I caught in the Pacific, flash froze the tasty morsels, and sent the package ahead to Teaneck, where, upon my return, I placed my prized catch in our freezer to parcel out on special occasions. Two months after my return from Alaska, to my everlasting chagrin and anger, a lengthy PSE&G power outage destroyed the remaining five pounds of Pacific treasure!

So what exact lessons can I convey to you from my fishing experiences? Every parent, I'm told, prays that his offspring will be a bigger and better version of himself. That dream unfortunately runs smack into the belief we Jews have that *"ma'aseh avot siman l'banim"* (the deeds of fathers foreshadow the future deeds of their sons). And so it happened recently when my son Efrem set out for the first time on a sunny Florida fishing trip off Fort Lauderdale. Like his father before him who went out from Belmar those many years earlier, Efrem faced the wild chops of the Atlantic and prayed for deliverance to the same God who spared his father. He returned safely to shore after several hours, but he felt the earth spinning many days after his return to dry land. It is unclear whether he'll ever repeat his high seas adventure, though I'm guessing he will after enough time has passed. Smooth sailing and good fishing!

Something to Worry About
or The Procrastinator

A car drives into downtown Newark. Its driver is lost and pulls over to seek directions from a passerby. He has stopped in front of a large medical center and gets out of his car at a no-parking sign. It is a sunny day with a brisk, chilly wind. He sees a woman standing not far off and motions to her.

"I am lost, unfortunately," he says. "Could you possibly help me with directions?"

The woman approaches until she's no more than three feet away, and only then does he realize how disfigured her face is. He shrinks from her as she's almost on top of him.

"I'll help you if you help me; you see, I've got the plague!" she cries, seeking to embrace him.

The man lunges away and soon other people begin to turn and walk toward him, the woman leading the pursuit. The man attempts to return to his car and hurry off as the crowd begins to overtake him. He notices that each of his pursuers is facially disfigured, grotesque figures, some with eyes missing and others with almost blank manikin-like stares upon their twisted faces. The man fumbles with his car keys. He drops them, and as he bends to search for them, he is overtaken by two of the terrifying creatures, whose icy hands grasp him. He blacks out as the image of the Newark street fades.

"Where am I?" he asks himself in the next moment as his eyes open. The familiar surroundings of his bedroom are the first things he sees.

"I must have been dreaming again. Yet it seemed so real."

A moment more in bed and then the man rises to start his day. Within minutes he has forgotten his nightmare and focuses on the tasks before him on this Monday in late March. He is due in the office at just before nine, so he has plenty of time to get downtown; the digital display on his alarm reads only 7:10.

In a matter of minutes, he showers, dresses, eats breakfast, and emerges from his apartment onto the now busy street in front of him. He heads toward the bus stop, and soon he is sitting back enjoying the ride, gentle enough to rock him to sleep for a few moments. He doesn't dream this time, however, and he is jostled enough to be reawakened just before his stop.

The man descends from the bus and, joining a herd of workers, enters the wide doors of 300 Broad Street. His office is on the twentieth floor of this steel and glass tower. Disturbingly, he can't remember the name of his employer; he vaguely knows he is working as an attorney for this law firm but can't recall when he started his employment. He has a feeling that he has been assigned various tasks by the partners in charge of his department, but has failed to complete any of those tasks. Worse, he has forgotten exactly what those assignments are. Surely the partners must be aware that he has been totally derelict in his duties! Yet here he is walking around the office, schmoozing with his coworkers and the secretaries, just a regular Joe, charming. They all must know that he hasn't done any work in a long time – so long that he can't remember when he last worked on his forgotten assignments.

A feeling of dread overcomes him as the minutes pass. He recalls that back in his college days he had similar feelings about courses he took where he neglected all assigned readings until he faced the terror of a final exam for which he was totally unprepared. Then it was a course in Napoleonic history, now it is law firm work. How, he wonders, will the firm be able to bill the clients on whose behalf he is working. But, again, who are those clients and what are the legal matters he is supposed to be working on? He tries to steady his nerves; there has to be an answer. Yes, he'll ask the assigning partners to review with him what he is supposed to be doing for them. But he has to be subtle about it; he can't ask them directly. Somehow, he'll have to address them obliquely. But he realizes this approach is doomed, because he can't recall the names of the clients assigned to him in the first place.

He is now in a state of panic: "I'll have to wait until the partner contacts me, requesting that I submit my work. But it's been so long since any partner has done that. Maybe they themselves have forgotten. Yes, I've been here so long with little interaction, it's likely they've forgotten me too. Then I guess I'm free and clear, no worries, just that unending sense of dread as I walk the corridors of the office, exchanging chitchat with my colleagues. This could go on forever, but how likely is that?"

After several more moments he sees a group of partners slowly emerging from a large, glass-enclosed conference room. They begin to converge on him, their now-visible, disfigured faces mocking him as he is discovered for the charlatan that he is! The light fades again.

"One hundred four degrees, nurse, no improvement yet. Let's hope the antibiotics work."

The young doctor writes down some notes on the patient's chart and quickly walks out of the infectious diseases ward.

"Nasty thing, this plague, very nasty!"

It Happened One Night
on Turner Classic Movies

The man sat in front of the large screen TV set, enjoying the images of George Clooney, John Turturro, and Charles Durning cavorting before him in their 1930s attire. The former two were dressed in overalls, only slightly better fitting than the prison garb they had disposed of after they made their escape from the Mississippi prison farm in which they had been serving time doing hard labor. Durning, as incumbent governor Pappy O'Daniel, was harmonizing with the Soggy Bottom Boys in a chorus of "You Are My Sunshine" to the delight of a boisterous political rally. Thick Mississippi accents filled the air and projected into Jake Rabinowitz's New Jersey living room, where Jake sat comfortably with his legs up on his favorite recliner. A couple of years earlier, Jake had seen the movie *O Brother, Where Art Thou*. He had enjoyed its part-fantasy, part-folksy spirit and especially loved the music, being one of the few Jewish fans of bluegrass in his community.

Some time passed as the main characters sorted out their lives, "Baby Face" Nelson was apprehended, and the political process in Mississippi was put back in its proper place, order restored.

At some point, Jake noticed Ben Affleck on the screen, his Mississippi accent not quite as sharply inflected as Durning's and Clooney's. Softer, like something one might hear in St. Louis or Kansas City, Missouri. Affleck's clothes as well seemed a bit more modern than what the others had been wearing. Affleck was concerned about something that had not bothered the other characters. A police detective entered the scene, and she seemed bothered by the answers she was getting (or *not* getting) from Affleck. After a couple more minutes, Jake wondered where Durning and Clooney had gone, along with the rest of the cast and their Mississippi accents.

Jake shouted to his wife in the adjacent kitchen, using *his* best Mississippi accent, "Ah don't know what's goin' on heah, muh dear, but Ben Affleck seems to be in a bit of trouble," Jake said. "Very strange. It seem his wife is missin' and the po-lice think he's involved with the disappearance. Ah still don't know what's happened to those fellows in Mississippi and how we got to what looks like modern times!"

"I can't really hear what you're saying, Jake," she finally shouted. He heard her loud and clear, but she still couldn't hear him over the sound of the running water.

Back on the screen, Ben Affleck now had a more serious look of concern on his face than before; the cops had discovered troubling evidence that seemed to connect him to his wife's disappearance, and they suspected foul play. Affleck denied involvement in any plot to harm his wife. He realized he had to escape the surveillance of the police if he were to establish his innocence. He accordingly excused himself to go to the bathroom and, exiting the building through an unguarded window, slid out to his back yard, jumped a fence, and left in his car without being detected.

"He sure could have used the help of Clooney and Durning to solve this mystery," thought Jake. "I'll bet Affleck's wife planned her disappearance on purpose; she set up her husband. Wow!" Jake was still confused, though. What did all these characters have to do with each other? Why were some speaking with a Mississippi accent and others with a Missouri accent? Why were some dressed in 1930s garb and the others in current fashion? Affleck's car was the last straw – the Acura Sport he made his escape in looked quite modern, while the vehicles available to Durning and company appeared to be at least eighty years older!

It finally dawned on Jake that he must have fallen asleep during the last ten minutes of the Clooney-Durning film and slept through the first ten minutes of the Affleck film. The transition seemed almost seamless to him.

"I went from *O Brother, Where Art Thou?* to *Wife, Where Art Thou?* as if they were connected." Jake took the controller in his hand and hit the Info button. The Affleck movie was titled *Gone Girl.*

"I guess that describes my wife as well," Jake said to himself, noticing for the first time that the water was no longer running in the kitchen sink. He, like Affleck, had been abandoned by his wife, who had quietly left the kitchen seeking refuge from her eccentric husband.

"I finally figured it out," Jake shouted to no one in particular, returning to his New Jersey accent.

From the floor above, a distant, muffled voice could be heard, "What did you say? I can't hear you clearly," said his wife.

"It's not important, dear," Jake shouted back, as he turned to watch Affleck confront *his* rediscovered wife on the large TV screen.

A Celebrity Is Just
a Table Away

During my student and professional life, I've had the fortune of frequently running into celebrities. I don't seek them out in any systematic way – maybe I'm just lucky. At the request of some of my friends, but with some hesitation, I've decided to record several of my more memorable celebrity encounters from over the years. I will also reveal some of the general rules or principles you can follow to increase your chances of meeting celebrities, should you so desire. I make no promises nor give guarantees that you'll be successful if you follow my guidelines, but doing so should increase your chances of a celebrity sighting. You'll also learn that there are occasions when recognizing a celebrity can present unexpected dangers.

1. Move to New York City and Dine Out Frequently

I grew up on the Upper West Side, an area known over the years to attract entertainment types and intellectuals. During the 1950s, '60s, and '70s, when it came to dining, Orthodox Jews had a narrow choice of kosher dairy restaurants from which to choose. You could dine at Steinberg's dairy restaurant on 82nd Street and Broadway or at Famous Dairy restaurant on West 72nd Street off Broadway. My parents dined at both of these places frequently, and would often take me with them. As I grew older, I occasionally stopped at these places on my own. Until the late 1970s, CBS TV operated a broadcast studio on Broadway and 81st Street. This brought many actors to the neighborhood, and they apparently favored Jewish-style food. For example, Walter Matthau was frequently seen dining at Steinberg's, a favorite haunt of his.

Then there was the evening in 1960 when, aged ten, I accompanied my parents to dinner at Steinberg's and discovered I was sitting almost directly across a small table from an actor I had seen on TV just the night before. I had been watching the famous *Untouchables*, an exciting television drama about Eliot Ness and his federal agents fighting Al Capone in the 1930s. In that particular episode, a criminal character had attempted to inform on Capone, only to disappear under mysterious circumstances. Imagine my surprise the next night at Steinberg's when sitting right across from me, alive and well, was none other than the "rat" who informed on Capone (noted character actor Murray Hamilton, who went on to play the mayor of Amityville in the *Jaws* movie series, among thirty-eight other memorable roles in many famous films).

Also at Steinberg's, dinners often involved visits from famous composer and Jewish folk artist Rabbi Shlomo Carlebach, a family friend who would pull up a chair and converse with my parents for long periods of time.

Lunches at Famous further downtown led to encounters over the years with other major award-winning actors such as Lee J. Cobb and Jason Robards, each of whom turned out to be quite friendly and even seemed pleased to be recognized by a well-behaved fan. (Or were they simply great actors?)

2. When in Israel, Dine at the Best Hotels

When I spent my junior year of college at the Givat Ram campus of the Hebrew University in Jerusalem, I rented an apartment in the quiet residential neighborhood of Kiryat Shmuel. After a strenuous week of studies, I looked forward to Motzaei Shabbat (Saturday night), when I could head to Ben Yehuda Street to socialize with friends, take in a movie, or just stroll down the avenues full of Jerusalemites. As time progressed, I occasionally chose a more sedate activity for Saturday night, namely, heading for the famous King David Hotel to dine in the hotel's dairy restaurant, just off the lobby. The menu was a delightful nod to American-style eateries, and the food and service were first rate; it was also pricey, which is why as a student away from home, I didn't eat there all that often. What really stood out about the restaurant, however, was its location. On my first or second visit I discovered that the King David Hotel lobby was *the* meeting place for the most important Israeli leaders and politicians of the period when they were in Jerusalem.

My first such encounter took place when one Saturday night in 1969 Abba Eban sat down at the table next to me. I tried to act nonchalant, but got excited when several minutes later Golda Meir came in with an aide, sat down next to Foreign Minister Eban, and ordered some tea and a piece of cake. On a later visit, I was ushered into the restaurant and shown to a table adjoining Moshe Dayan, eye patch and all. After that visit, I began to take my dates there, hoping to be able to celebrity-watch and impress my companion. Of course, whenever I went there with the express purpose of meeting celebrities, they never showed up. The ability to "rub elbows" with the highest echelons of society, including the most important political leaders, may be unique to Israeli society. Although I'm guessing that unbeknownst to me, every time I dined in close proximity to Eban, Meir, and Dayan, they weren't as "alone" as I might have assumed at the time.

3. Seek Out Israeli Hotel Room Upgrades *during Likud Party Caucus Season*

When my wife and I checked into the Jerusalem Plaza Hotel on King George Street in Jerusalem during the summer of 2004, we were pleasantly surprised to be told by the familiar desk clerk that we were entitled to an upgrade for our two-week stay.

"How would you like to stay in one of our penthouse suites, Mr. Rotenberg?" the clerk asked us. "You've been a frequent visitor with us, and we're happy to offer you this opportunity at a good rate."

We agreed to the upgrade, took the special elevator to the designated floor, and were soon looking out the window to the most spectacular view of East Jerusalem we had ever seen. This was a two-hundred-foot-high perspective that only eagles experienced, and we even rose early the next morning to record on our cameras a sunrise unequalled in our experience.

I had work to do the next day, and my wife stayed behind in the room to freshen up. When I returned to the hotel later that afternoon, my wife told me of an interesting encounter that had taken place between her, Prime Minister Ariel Sharon, and Bibi Netanyahu. I recalled reading in the morning paper that the Likud Party was meeting in Jerusalem that week to go over party caucus issues. What I didn't know was that they were meeting at our hotel, and not only that, they were meeting on the penthouse floor conference room next door to our suite.

"At about 12 o'clock I was leaving our room," my wife told me, "when right in front of me appeared Sharon and Netanyahu, who were leaving the Likud meeting and waiting for the elevator to take them to the street. I was in the process of closing the door when both politicians looked past me into our suite. They noticed the view from our room, and Sharon immediately asked both Bibi and me, 'Who do you have to know to get *that* room?'"

All three laughed at his remark. Apparently, Sharon had no fear of heights.

4. Make Plans to See the Stanley Cup

Back in 1981 I worked for a broker-dealer in Manhattan requiring that I carpool into Midtown Manhattan on a daily basis. Seven of us hardy Orthodox Jewish souls from Teaneck shared the costs and the traffic delays. On one mid-February, Monday morning commute, one of the passengers mentioned that over the previous weekend he had seen the Stanley Cup on display at the newly opened Glenpointe Hotel.

"You're a big hockey man, Joe, why don't you check it out?"

"I probably will, though I doubt it'll still be there," I responded.

I promptly forgot about the Stanley Cup until I arrived home late that afternoon. I remembered just in time to convince my wife to let me take Jeff, aged six, and Michelle, aged four, to the hotel to see the famed chalice.

Without bothering to change out of my dark three-piece suit and gray felt fedora, off we went to the Glenpointe, the kids excited at the prospect of seeing the cup. We parked in the large lot in front of the hotel, and fighting brisk winds, made our way into the lobby. No one stopped us as we walked hand-in-hand into a side lobby that led to a room in which the desired sports objects were on display. There was the Stanley Cup, shining silver and all, surrounded by every trophy the NHL gave out annually, maybe ten large trophies in all. And no one was around except us! In a second I realized where we were. I had forgotten that the NHL all-star dinner was scheduled to be held that night, hosted by the newly formed New Jersey Devils hockey team. We had obviously walked into a privileged room in which no civilians were permitted. Yet there we were, looking like we belonged.

Before I had a chance to exit, I was approached by a smiling, tuxedoed young man, who offered me his hand.

"Hi, I'd like to introduce myself; my name is Wayne Gretzky," he said firmly.

"It's a pleasure to meet you," I responded, trying not to show any nervousness.

He obviously thought I was there in some official league capacity, and I wasn't going to disabuse him of his mistake. In the next ten minutes, literally two dozen players, coaches, and NHL general managers entered the room and began to form two lines from which they would enter the adjacent grand ballroom for formal introductions to the guests seated inside. As they stood in formation, the players studied us carefully, some I assume wondering who we were and what we were doing there, but most not caring. Jeff and Michelle were scurrying around asking for autographs and snapping photos as future proof that we had been there. Within twenty minutes of our entering the room, it was empty of all personnel, the NHL regalia left alone once again.

We arrived home happy with how things had turned out. After all, we had the documentary evidence we needed to establish to our family and friends that we had been NHL All-Stars, for an evening at least.

5. Get a Job at an Entertainment Law Firm

At one point in my career I worked as a tax attorney in New York. During the six years I plied that trade, I found myself employed at the firm of CGLO & L, a well-known entertainment law firm in Midtown Manhattan. In this field of law, a firm typically represented either the management side or the labor. CGLO & L was a bit of a hybrid, being foremost a labor shop, including the Actors' Equity Association labor union among its main clients, but also representing well-known producers, directors, writers, and actors. Several of the firm's clients were in need of tax counsel, not a regular service CGLO & L provided, so I was hired by the firm to help resolve the tax issues that had recently arisen. I had no previous experience in dealing with entertainment industry types, but I was no stranger to the field, having grown up on a steady diet of movies and television shows.

My first months at the firm were uneventful, consisting of meetings and phone conversations with accountants and IRS agents. Sometime in December of my first year at the firm, I was called in to meet two new clients, both well-known performers in their fields. First, I was introduced to Mikhail Baryshnikov, a gifted Russian ballet star who had recently defected to the West. Baryshnikov shook my hand so firmly he nearly fractured several of my fingers! He wasn't tall, but was very athletic and charming. I was assigned the task of incorporating him and setting up various retirement plans on his behalf.

The following week, I was presented by my supervising partner to a thin woman with long, straight blond hair and a noticeably angular face. I guessed she was about thirty years old. Her name was Meryl Streep, and over her illustrious career she would go on to win three Academy Awards for acting. She had just married after the death of her boyfriend, actor John Cazale, who played Fredo Corleone in *The Godfather* movies. Similar to the Baryshnikov case, I was assigned the task of incorporating Ms. Streep and providing a vehicle for her retirement planning.

In subsequent months, I met Anthony Quinn and Theodore Bikel at the office, as well as the expatriate producer Charles Schneer, he the less well-known Jewish producer of many classic fantasy films such as *The Golden Voyage of Sinbad, Jason and the Argonauts*, and *Clash of the Titans*.

The most notable celebrity encounter that took place during my time at CGLO & L occurred on a rather dreary Tuesday morning in March when I arrived at the office somewhat delayed by heavier than normal traffic. The corridor leading to my small shared office was narrowed by thick black cables that stretched the length of the passageway from the main entrance. Large klieg lights lined the same corridor. Suddenly, a short, dark-haired figure appeared at the other end of the passage, striding purposefully toward me, head down. As he approached, I recognized him as none other than well-known motion picture star Dustin Hoffman. We greeted each other with a series of hellos, and I pointed out that I was heading to my office; he said he was there to "make a movie." I wished him good luck and assured him that I was sure it would be a success. I subsequently found out from colleagues that Hoffman and Meryl Streep were filming an interior shot that day for a scene in their upcoming film, *Kramer vs. Kramer*. The scene in question takes place in a lawyer's office, so what better location to film it? Given the good wishes I gave Hoffman that day in our chance meeting, I take no small measure of credit for the ultimate success of the film winning the Academy Award for Best Picture in 1980.

6. Buy a Ring-Side Seat to the Big Apple Circus

This technique can be a bit of a budget buster, and you'd better pray you don't have an obstructed view or an inordinate fear of elephants, but you might find yourself sitting next to someone such as Mary Tyler Moore, as happened to me many years ago. She introduced me to her new doctor husband. A friendly human being, she engaged with my daughter throughout the entire show. She will be missed!

7. Choose an Italian Barber but Speak Softly

Back in the 1980s I worked in the investment field in Manhattan, and among my habits was a monthly haircut appointment, usually *erev Shabbat* (Friday afternoon), with my favorite barber, Nino. A native of Sicily, he was a short, stocky fellow with salt-and-pepper hair and a well-trimmed, thick moustache. I don't recall now how I met him, but I followed Nino from place to place over time through his various job shifts in midtown. By 1990, he was employed in a mezzanine-level shop just off 3rd Avenue between 48th and 49th Streets, a quick escalator ride up from the lobby.

Nino always wore a smile when I came for my monthly haircut, and a visit with him was frequently memorable. For example, I recall a framed autographed glossy publicity photo of Jerry Lewis he kept hanging on the wall next to the barber's chair.

"You know, Joe, Jerry Lewis had some strange habits," Nino told me. "I normally cut his hair in his hotel suite when he came to New York. Did you know he never wore the same pair of socks twice?"

"That's very interesting," I said to Nino, calculating in my head that at the time Lewis must have had an annual sock budget of $1,300. "I guess he avoids any issues of missing socks this way, putting on a new pair each morning, plus, he saves on washing and drying."

On another occasion, I arrived for my appointment with Nino a little late and entered the cubicle while the previous customer was buttoning his shirt and placing his well-cut Italian suit jacket on his shoulders. My sudden entry surprised him, and he turned quickly to confront me, staring at the folds of my suit jacket. I smiled and moved to the side to allow him to leave. He had dark hair and wore striking black-framed glasses. He looked tough.

When the man left, Nino motioned for me to sit down in the chair. He knew of my interest in matters Sicilian and my curiosity about mob-related history.

"Lucchese," Nino said, without elaborating. I took it to mean the fellow who had preceded me was a member of the Lucchese mob, one of the five New York mafia families. Apparently, Nino had not only trimmed the fellow's hair but his chest as well. In addition, from his reaction at my sneaking up behind him, he might have thought for an instant that I had been sent to settle some old mob score. Nothing could be further from the truth, and soon he was just a memory.

Two weeks later, however, something happened to me at Nino's that proved I had not learned my lesson from my first mob "encounter." The evening before my barber appointment, I had watched the conclusion of the highly regarded PBS series *The History of the Mob in America*. It was such a well-done production that I was feeling quite Italian that day as I got comfortable in Nino's chair. Ten minutes passed. "From now on, Nino, I want you to call me Don Giuseppe," I said in my finest Italian-American accent.

Nino gasped and nearly stuffed my mouth with a nearby towel; he held up two fingers to his lips in silent warning.

What had I done wrong, I wondered.

Nino finished up my trim, and I put my jacket on to exit to the cashier. When I emerged, I saw that the next customers had arrived and were sitting silently off to the side. Immediately to my left was a fairly large white-haired gentleman wearing glasses. Behind him sat an even larger, younger fellow, who eyed me carefully as I paused in front of them. Finally, almost in front of me, sat a woman, maybe fifty years old, neatly dressed and smiling like a Cheshire cat. Her mouth, that is, was smiling, but her eyes seemed blank, shark-like. I had seen that face somewhere before; it was quite familiar, but I couldn't place it immediately. Then, suddenly, it came to me: that was the smile of Carlo Gambino, well-known head of another of the famous five families of the New York Mafia; in this instance, the Gambino smile was presumably marking the face of his daughter, a quintessential, if middle-aged, Mafia princess.

I had to think fast, and without hesitation I stiffened up, made a little bow in her direction, smiled, and hurried out of the shop. My years of watching *The Godfather* had taught me how to behave properly, and my show of respect enabled me to escape to spend Shabbat in the safety of my home surrounded by my loved ones. I never returned to Nino's.

Rabbi Sure's Last Stand - The Botwinick Case

You could call Rabbi Shaya Sure a creature of his times. Like many whom he spiritually guided, he was multitalented, possessing a special knack when it came to publicity and self-promotion. He lived in an age when no member of his flock was satisfied to be a specialist, a master of one set of skills or one profession. He ministered to several doctors who considered themselves financial experts, merchants who claimed to be philosophers, and butchers who listed Olympic wrestling as their favorite pursuit. Some attributed Rabbi Sure's acumen in public relations to his having been raised in Hollywood, but there are many other Los Angelenos who didn't possess his formidable skills.

The following story concerns an episode later in Rabbi Sure's life when it would be claimed by some that the good rabbi lost his special talents and, like Samson of old, his unusual strengths failed him. This sad state of affairs caused the rabbi no end of trouble. Curiously, multitalented individuals such as Rabbi Sure often run into multifaceted controversies. His problems began simply enough and involved a young boy with unusual qualities of his own.

Many children get caught up in the fantastic tales they read in the books they find hidden on family bookshelves, in attics, closets, and other secret places in which humans have always hidden written material they once devoured with their eyes and minds but no longer have any apparent need for. These could be stories written by the Brothers Grimm or Hans Christian Andersen, or *Tales of the Arabian Nights* and sagas of savage Norsemen, dragons, and sea monsters. Add to these the Jewish fables of archdemons such as Ashmodai: wild, unexplored regions where the river Sambatyon thunders through unfamiliar canyons, stopping its churning only on Shabbat. What possible impact could these tales have on an impressionable young man or woman, what effect on their states of mind as they grow from young readers into maturing adolescents?

Most children outgrow the Peter Pans, the Golems, and the monsters (Jewish and non-Jewish) of their youth and learn to laugh at those things that disturbed their sleep in the past as they approach adulthood and begin to distinguish them from those objects truly worthy of their concern. But not every child is successful at leaving those early terrors behind. David Botwinick appeared to be one such child.

For all intents and purposes, David appeared to be a perfectly normal boy growing up in Monsey, New York, one of four children born to a family that struggled to feed, educate, and house their growing brood. David's parents did the best they could to teach him the proper Torah values, and he loved them dearly, as they did him. It was David's teachers at school who first noticed David's "gift," if we can call it that, when, every so often, David would sit in class with a vacant stare on his face, unresponsive to his teachers' questions. These spells would not last very long, and David would soon be himself again, but the school administrators felt that David's strange, repeated spells disrupted his class and had to be dealt with. Thus, they invited David's parents to the school for a consultation, along with David and the school psychologist, to "get to the bottom of this," as Mr. Klein, the lower school principal, characterized it.

The meeting with the school psychologist proved that David was quite intelligent, socially well-adjusted, and far from unruly.

The meeting didn't uncover any particular basis for David's spells, and so no course of action was recommended at that time. "Watchful waiting" was the agreed-upon prescription. Several weeks passed, and sadly the episodes increased in frequency with the added feature that David, at the height of his trance, could be heard uttering the words, "He's coming!" This new behavior created quite a stir among his classmates, and once again David's parents were called on the carpet to discuss David's behavior with the school administration.

"We believe it would be better for all if David left our school and was home-schooled going forward," Principal Klein concluded at the end of the meeting. "Perhaps when his condition improves, we can reconsider his attending school again."

The Botwinicks were saddened by the school's decision, and that might have been the end of the story except that a reporter for a local paper, the *Airmont Arrow*, happened to be visiting the school at just that moment. David was sitting in the hallway in front of the principal's office when he went into a trance, culminating with the repetition of the phrase "He's coming!" three times. The reporter, a Mr. Golumb, had never seen anything like this before, and he asked the Botwinicks if they cared to explain. They did and added that they didn't know what David's words signified.

"Perhaps he's a clairvoyant in some way," Golumb offered. "It doesn't seem fair that the school is suspending him for something he can't control."

Golumb then did what any good reporter would do. He promised the Botwinick family that he would write a feature about David's case and try to rally the community to have him reinstated. The Botwinicks were unsure about accepting Golumb's proposal.

"We don't want to make trouble, you know," said David's father. "It's really a private matter, don't you think?"

Golumb disagreed. "Your son may have a special gift in that he can see the future. Who knows whom this 'he' is, the one he says is 'coming'?"

Golumb didn't wait for approval from David or his parents on running the story. Instead, he headed for his office and soon convinced his editor of the merits of featuring David's story in the following week's edition of the *Arrow*.

Now, many worthy stories are printed regularly in periodicals, but fall flat and fail to impress the public. David's tale was one of those rare stories that had legs. Though hidden on page eight among ads for legal services, food emporia, and cemetery plots in Israel, the story of the boy with the mysterious message resonated among the readership as few stories did.

Two weeks passed, and the case of David Botwinick spread like wildfire through the wider Jewish community until even national publications carried the story of the young New Yorker who forecast the coming of some mysterious stranger. Other media outlets from the news press, radio, and television and cable news got wind of the story of the precocious Jewish boy. Crowds gathered at the Botwinick home on Poplar Street. Local police were called in to supervise traffic around the home. Events took an important turn when a local rabbi of some importance arrived unannounced at the Botwinick residence one evening, forcing himself past David's surprised parents and presenting a plan to exclusively represent David before the curious public. Rabbi Sure cautioned the Botwinicks that unscrupulous, unnamed individuals would be looking to exploit David and would make a media circus out of his condition.

"Only I can protect David from these types, and I assure you, I'll do everything to see that he grows up unaffected by publicity," Rabbi Sure insisted.

The Botwinicks didn't know what to say to Rabbi Sure, who, as was his habit, took their silence as consent. Accordingly, the next day, Rabbi Sure, who was very well connected with publicity and public relations, introduced himself to local New York radio and television and cable outlets as the "exclusive" representative of the Botwinicks and thus began a month-long campaign to promote

David as a psychic phenomenon, perhaps calling for the imminent arrival of the Mashiach (Messiah).

Rabbi Sure didn't proclaim this message directly; he just left listeners with the impression that this was the case. Soon, people of all religions and denominations got on the Botwinick band-wagon, and David and his family were showered with offers of free vacations, computers, and grocery provisions. Who knows how long this might have gone on, except that after several weeks had elapsed with no apparent Messiah, skeptical voices began to be heard among David's previously adoring public. Matters then took a turn for the worse when David's trances miraculously ceased. His parents didn't want to believe that he was "cured," but after a week passed without a recurrence, they were overjoyed. They arranged for David's reinstatement with Principal Klein and all of the Botwinicks' friends and relations shared in their happiness.

Everyone except Rabbi Sure, who made as quick an about-face from his previous association with the Botwinicks as could ever be imagined. At his last interview on the subject a week later, the rabbi was quoted by a reporter from the *New York Post*: "I knew from the very start that David's trances had nothing to do with the Mashiach. Maybe he was suffering from a real medical condition, but it was apparent to all that he wasn't the real McCoy!"

Life returned to a greater degree of normalcy for the Botwin-icks, who were happy to be out of the public eye. David never had a recurrence of his "spells," and went on to become a model student and fine young man in every respect.

Rabbi Sure didn't emerge from the Botwinick affair in quite the same shape. People who had closely followed his career began to feel he had somehow lost his way, that the novelty of his approach was wearing off, and that his frequent public appearances were being met by public reactions of "Not him again!" rather than with the adulation he had received in the past. Rumors began to spread of erratic behavior on the rabbi's part.

The reality was much simpler, if less dramatic. Rabbi Sure him-

self underwent something of a transformation, toning down his
public persona and spending more time with his large family and
engaging in less public, and, ultimately, more meaningful rabbinic
pursuits. In the end, the lesson learned by all was one worthy of
the prophet Isaiah himself, who lived twenty-five centuries earlier:
knowing how to convey a message and how to publicize that message well will never be as important as the quality of the message
itself. Most importantly, the messenger should never, ever confuse
his importance with that of the message he seeks to convey.

On that score, one elderly neighbor in Monsey had this to say
after reading an account of the Botwinick case: "Our community
needs a rabbi who is *celebrated* for his character and actions; I don't
think it needs a *celebrity* rabbi!"

Back to America - Notes from a Returning Vacationer

Two weeks abroad on an annual summer vacation can be somewhat disorienting when you return stateside. My recent trip to Israel, which my wife and I spent based in Jerusalem, overlapped with both the Republican and Democratic conventions. These distinctly American events were in fact global in their impact. Given a seven-hour time difference, we watched the afternoon sessions with great interest and were awakened early morning by the primetime coverage. Rather than rely on the commentators and panels spinning their skewed webs of misinformation, we closely followed the commentary on WhatsApp provided by our five children and their spouses, who seemed to make much more sense than the aforementioned professionals.

During this time abroad we were asked by many friends, acquaintances, and even strangers in Israel whom we would be voting for in November. The inquisitors seemed to know that their question would be difficult to answer. Though not American, they were aware that the two 2016 presidential candidates seemed uniquely unsuited for the office to which they aspired. Both were considered untrustworthy by close to 70 percent of the electorate.

One candidate seemed to possess the seemingly contradictory qualities of "putting his foot in his mouth" on alarmingly numerous occasions while simultaneously stubbing his toe with an inane remark. The other candidate, while serving in several elected and appointed governmental positions, had not distinguished herself particularly in any of the former tasks, had arguably disgraced herself as Secretary of State, and may have been guilty of at least misdemeanors in her conduct of that office. Her assertions of innocence on the latter charges and claims of exoneration from any wrongdoing were just the latest in a litany of falsehoods and half-truths emanating from that candidate's campaign. Taking responsibility for one's actions or inactions sadly seemed to be a quality lacking in both candidates.

So there we were in Israel, being questioned on our opinions on the upcoming election. You can only imagine how quickly we tried to change the subject. A shrug of our shoulders, a look of bemusement, following which we asked our questioners some questions of our own on a different topic. Soon our trip came to its end, and as we drove to Ben Gurion Airport on the morning of our flight, we wondered if the conventions we had observed from afar had in some significant way changed the landscape in the United States. Remarks from the Republican candidate had almost singlehandedly converted his lead of three points in the race to a deficit of ten, if you believed the polls. And, as we landed on the runway at Newark Liberty Airport twelve hours later, it appeared the party of Lincoln was in a death spiral.

I was home for just twenty-four hours when I got the first inkling that despite the conventions, nothing meaningful had changed in America over our vacation. I was sitting in my recliner catching up on the financial markets when my cell phone rang, and a voice at the other end informed me, "You've been selected to receive a special offer of home improvements. Please stay on the line so we can collect information from you so we can best assist you."

"I don't have need of any such services," I interjected. Only then did I realize I was talking to a prerecorded message.

A second voice – this time a live caller – came on the line: "We provide many kinds of home repair services: roofing, siding, painting, heating, cooling, plumbing, et cetera. Which ones appeal to you?"

"We made a large home renovation last year, in fact," I vainly tried to interject.

The caller would not be stopped.

"We use the best contractors available. And our prices are most reasonable. We also provide financing at low rates. Does that appeal to you?"

"Not really," I weakly replied, my jet-lagged mind clouding my response. "I don't need your services, thank you. I don't want your services either."

"You're absolutely certain we can't help you?" she countered.

At this point sarcasm and fatigue took over.

"Only by hanging up," I said.

Abruptly ending the conversation, I looked at the screen only to discover my favorite stock was now down an additional 2 percent. I was inclined to blame the decline on the distraction of the unsolicited phone solicitation.

"Back home in America, nothing new here," I thought.

I got up five minutes later to make some lunch when my phone rang again.

"Hello, this is your lucky day. We have determined that you may be among a select group of people whose debts may be eliminated because your lender has violated the Fair Lending laws. Press 1 to hear how we can help you eliminate your debt. Press 2 to have your number placed on the 'do not call' list."

I was feeling confrontational at this point so I pressed 1. After some seconds, a live caller began her spiel in a friendly tone. "Good afternoon. Is this Joseph *Rottenberg* I am speaking with?"

"Actually it's *Rotenberg*," I corrected.

"So sorry, *Mr. Rothenberg*, I'll make a note of that.

I didn't correct her this time.

"What exactly is this call about? The message said you can eliminate my debt totally. Is that right?"

"Absolutely. Eliminate your debt," the caller insisted.

"Now, you don't mean you're just proposing to *refinance* my debt, like charge me a lower interest rate than I'm now paying. You mean paying off my debt for me?"

"Exactly!"

"Wow, this must be my lucky day," I crowed.

"It sure is, *Mr. Rosenberg*," she continued. "By the way, how much debt do you owe at this time and what interest rate are you currently paying?"

"Why do you have to know what my current interest rate is? I thought you said you're going to pay off everything at this time."

"Yes. By Christmastime, you won't owe anything. Santa Claus is going to make you a present of all that you owe."

"Wait a minute," I said. "Santa Claus is going to make *me* a present. I'm not so sure. You see, I'm Jewish. Do you really think Santa is going to pay off all *my* debts?"

The caller insisted. "By Christmas you won't owe a penny. Santa will pay it off even if you're Jewish!"

Maybe the caller knew something I didn't, but I politely ended this call: "Tell Santa not to bother. I'm sorry. I'm not interested."

I quickly returned to my recliner, tired from the back-and-forth of the two calls, now finally feeling as if I were safely back in America. Though the electoral times were hazy and confused, as long as the law allowed humorous and annoying unsolicited phone calls in equal proportions, it would remain the country that I loved.

The Contortionist

Ah, how true that we're living in a time of great innovation! If we review the past century and a half, we see that the Orthodox Jewish community has had to adjust in quick succession to the introduction of the telephone, the radio, the airplane, television, personal computers, cell phones, and the ubiquitous Internet, to name but a few. Our scholars, rabbinic and lay, have struggled mightily to fit these inventions into the context and fabric of our traditional lives. Legendary leaders such as the Chasam Sofer, *zt"l*, the Chofetz Chaim, *zt"l*, and Rav Moshe Feinstein, *zt"l*, all in turn penned responsa and essays wherein they attempted to come to grips with how exactly these transforming discoveries would appropriately fit within our Jewish lives. Suffice it to say that these great thinkers reached remarkably similar conclusions as to how we, as Orthodox Jews, should relate to these new tools.

The public's reactions to these devices became predictable. Many initially viewed the innovations in question as veritable "tools of the devil," devices that if permitted in the home would pollute the religious and moral atmosphere. Total bans of newspapers and telephones, for example, greeted their arrivals in eastern Europe during the late nineteenth century as did the introduction of the radio, television, and movies (not to mention the personal computer, cable television, and the Internet) over the last half century. Happily, in time, the Modern Orthodox community from the leadership to the laymen recognized the essential truth that each of these man-made discoveries or creations was morally neutral, that it was man who infused them with positivity or negativity, and moved the debate as to the *morality* of using these devices to a more appropriate sphere. As a result, it became clear that the telephone, for example, was neither evil nor good, that it could be used to convey the most sublime messages, such as "It's a boy," "We're engaged," and "I passed," but also to convey messages of hate and obscenity. This duality is inherent in the nature of all creation and bears remembering whenever we consider how we should relate individually and communally to technological innovation.

Several nights ago I happened upon an on-demand showing of one of those summertime television competitions, this one generously titled *America's Got Talent* (I'm not responsible for the atrocious grammar, but *America* Has *Talent* apparently isn't as catchy a title, hence the slang). This loose talent competition consists of a series of acts ranging from stand-up comedy to singing and dancing to novelty acts. Among the latter are performers who present less conventional fare, including acts that can often be kindly referred to as "sensational" or "bizarre."

On this particular night, a tall, slender gentleman appeared on stage clad in a dark gray business suit and tie. On his head he wore a black *kippah*, essentially invisible against his black hair. He introduced himself to the four celebrity judges and began his performance. Over the next five minutes, the man amazingly twisted his body into an unrecognizable shape, astounding the audience with his flexibility, dexterity, and double-jointedness. At the end of the performance, he appeared to be a third of his original size and quite capable, assuming he had the proper postage, of "mailing" himself home in a standard UPS or USPS box! As he rearranged himself and returned to his original shape, the Jewish contortionist stood up to the loud applause of the audience and the approval of all four judges. He was rewarded with an invitation to the next round of the competition some weeks hence. He thanked everyone, smoothed his suit, and walked gingerly off the stage, his *kippah* still in its original place, not having moved a bit despite his exertions.

As I thought briefly about what I had just observed, it struck me as a perfectly appropriate, almost representative act for an Orthodox Jew to perform in 2016 on primetime, nationwide television. The concept of Jewish contortionism after all is so rich in symbolism in our times that no other act could have had an equal impact. Just think about how we, as modern Jews, learn to twist and bend ourselves to accommodate modernity and innovation in our lives. What are the possible consequences of these repeated acts of almost inhuman flexibility? What becomes of our religious principles? Like our talented TV contortionist, are we almost unrecognizable at the end of our day in the outside world? How successful exactly are we in *bending* our principles, without *breaking* them altogether?

I suggest that as we continue to interact with the broader world and with innovations to come, we, as Orthodox Jews, as *contortionists,* remember to infuse our actions with the morality and spirituality that they might otherwise lack, never for a moment forgetting that it is we who ultimately determine whether those actions work for good or for evil. Being flexible while adhering to principle is the worthy challenge that we must be willing to undertake.

Epilogue - Mapping
Timeless Travels

Link (our worker from the prologue) finished reading *Timeless Travels* in December of the year in which he discovered the volume among the debris of the construction site in Teaneck. As it happened, as he approached the final pages of the book, he noticed a thin, folded, yellowing piece of lined paper wedged inside the back cover. He unfolded it only to discover what appeared to be a key of some sort, characterizing each story or essay in the collection as based on fact or speculation on the author's part. Link couldn't determine whether this list was the work of the author of *Timeless Travels* or some later reader, but, for whatever it's worth, it is included below as an aid to current or future readers and a chance to compare their impressions with the author's reality.

There were four categories listed.

Pure, speculative, or historical fiction: *On the Road to Jerusalem; Jerusalem Tale: David King's Singular Journey; Homolka Hesitates; The Avenging Statue or the Last Victim of Hiroshima* (the statue does however exist as described); *Samovar or the Magic Teapot; Suburban Succah; An Oil Crisis; Uncle Malcolm, Travel Advisor; Herman's Last, Best Chance; Rory and Winston: Rory's Lost Weekend; The Elusive Third Purchase; Something to Worry About or The Procrastinator; It Happened One Night on Turner Classic Movies; Rabbi Sure's Last Stand: The Botwinick Case.*

Creative nonfiction: *Golden Days: Gaza 1967 Remembered;*

From Moscow to Riverdale: A Spy among Us; Food for Thought; The Inquisitive Swiss; Highway 49 and the Vision Quest; Torah and Teepees: A Comanche Friend of the Jews; Fare Exchanges: Two Civics Lessons on Wheels; A Call for Unity: The Hunter Shul; Choose Your Airline Seat Carefully; Confessions of a Campus War Profiteer; Jack Is Jilted.

True stories (told essentially as they happened): *Jerusalem Tale: A Modern, Mystical Moment; Sinai Journal; A Winter's Ride Like No Other; Jerusalem Tale: High Gear, Low Gear, No Gear; The Amazing Mrs. Webster; A Letter from Lisbon; Iranian Nuclear Fallout: A Twice-Told Tale; In Memoriam: Heroes of the Skies; The Petrovs Speak!; The Name; The Ambiguous Reward; The Freshly Baked Mountain Mashgiach; Belmar Tale: A Chain of Daddies; Linked Tales of the Lower East Side (all eight stories); A Tale of Two Rabbis; Be Careful What You Wish For.*

Essays and satires: *A Jewish Guide to Board Games; A Guide to Jewish Relationships (parts I and II); Davidic Generations: A Sober Reflection on the Wealth Triad; The Reforms of Rabbi Amnon: No Changes Required; I Have a Confession to Make: Two Yom Kippur Notes; Detecting the Elect: A Worthwhile Endeavor?; Purim Lament: Seeking Poppy Seed Hamantaschen; Suburban Scandal: The Afikomen File; Fish Tales: An "Unorthodox" Guide; A Celebrity Is Just a Table Away; Back to America: Notes from a Returning Vacationer; The Contortionist.*

Author's Note

The book you hold in your hand (or the personal electronic device on which you are presently reading my words), *Timeless Travels: Tales of Mystery, Intrigue, Humor and Enchantment*, reflects a lifetime of research, observation, and study of the Jewish people, primarily in the United States, but throughout the world as well. If you've read the book, you know I have chosen to take a multi-genre approach to my subject, and in its pages you will have found stories of several kinds: fiction, creative nonfiction, memoir, history, and essay. As with life itself, many of the stories are infused with humor and irony.

The unabashed aim of my book was to inform and entertain its readers, a goal shared by all writers. Given the multifaceted nature of the book, the hope is that its stories will appeal to a broad range of readers of all perspectives. The topics covered ranged from the timely to the timeless, uncovering little known events and personalities that have impacted on the American-Jewish world of the last century or so. My work also attempted to recreate that world as accurately and as broadly as noted Yiddish writer Sholem Aleichem did more than one hundred years ago in his famous stories describing the Russian-Jewish experience. In that sense, *Timeless Travels* can be thought of as a continuation of the stories of Tevye and his neighbors, with their children, grandchildren, and great-grandchildren peopling my stories in far-off America and other environs distant from Anatevka.

In fact, as you read the stories you will have traveled as far and as wide as the Jews themselves, through time and space, from locales in the United States, ranging from New York and New Jersey to Colorado, Montana, and Florida, and from Portugal, France, Belgium, Switzerland, Czechoslovakia, Russia, Ukraine, and Poland to Israel (ancient and modern), Morocco, Egypt, and the Sinai Peninsula. Hopefully, throughout, you were joined by interesting characters – historic and contemporary – as your companions.

The literary influences reflected in the book are as extensive as the travels themselves. Youthful attachment of the author to the works of Poe, Hawthorne, and Twain, later exposure to Bellow, Hemingway, Singer, Steinbeck, and Michener may have been reflected, if only indirectly, on the preceding pages, as were the short works of the Russian school: Pushkin, Gogol, Dostoyevsky, and Chekov.

The book's format followed the 1950s work of the late Harry Golden, who, in his popular collections, *Only in America* and *For Two Cents Plain*, introduced Jewish culture to many non-Jewish Americans for the very first time. Hopefully, that format has helped me to portray accurately the modern American Jew, who today is as much at home in the halls of the Ivy League, the corridors of power in Washington, the corporate boardroom, and the theater as he is in the *beit midrash* and the synagogue. Aside from entertaining and informing the reader, it is hoped that *Timeless Travels* will contribute to the general public's deeper understanding of the American-Jewish experience.

Several general themes run through the stories. First is the notion that in the face of challenges the American Jew has demonstrated contortionist-like resiliency in "bending, without breaking" when it comes to principles of faith and adherence to traditions. In the American-Jewish experience, as in life in general, extraordinary things happen to ordinary people with some frequency. Most of the characters you have read about in these stories demonstrate remarkable adaptability and courage in the face of the difficult life challenges they face. It would not be surprising if you come away from the book confirming in your mind that the contemporary American-Jewish subculture overlaps substantially with the mainstream, secular American experience. In significant ways, the melting pot has worked its magic on the children of Israel in America. Finally, and more generally, the book highlights the intrigues large and small that color the lives of ordinary people and most importantly the humor that infuses all of life, which makes the tragedies and hardships we all face a little more tolerable.

Five years ago when I began to write the stories and essays that comprise this volume, my goal was simply to recount a number of tales my father had repeated to me over our life together. My father, Maurice Rotenberg, was a quiet, gentle man whom I loved greatly, and he permitted me to find the voice with which I have written this book after so many years. Most memorable among the many stories he told me was the tale of his escape to America from war-torn Europe in 1940. As I prepared to write his history, I recalled another story he recounted to me, about a Portuguese tobacconist whose honesty amidst all the selfishness and treachery of war stood out like a beacon. I joined these separate tales of my father together in "A Letter from Lisbon." This fusion led to similar stories, each with a hopeful lesson to be learned.

With the experience gained from writing about my father, I soon expanded my efforts to writing fiction as well, a uniquely satisfying adventure. This in turn led me to a writing form I had assiduously avoided since college, namely, essay writing, several examples of which are contained in this volume. Finally, sprinkled throughout the book as well are several travelogues in which I have taken the liberty to add occasional observations of a social and political nature. Those travel tales acted as a "vacation break" from the routines of life, but even when you, dear reader, were "on the move" through the pages of the book, it is fervently hoped you found plenty of humor and enchantment along the way to add to your enjoyment.

If you have any further questions, please see the epilogue that precedes these notes for clarification.

I hope you had a pleasant trip!

Joseph Rotenberg
Teaneck, New Jersey
February 1, 2017

Acknowledgments

Many individuals contributed directly and indirectly to the writing of this book. First, I would like to thank all who helped edit the manuscript: Dassi Zeidel of Teaneck, New Jersey; Cole Gustafson and Erin McKnight of Kevin Anderson & Associates in New York and Nashville; and the editorial staff at Gefen Publishing House in Jerusalem – Lynn Douek, Project Manager; Gayle Green, Editor; Kezia Raffel Pride, Senior Editor; and, of course, thanks to Gefen's Ilan Greenfield for his guidance and advice. In addition, several gifted friends read the manuscript and offered meaningful comments. In particular, Professor Jenna Weissman Joselit of George Washington University was very helpful in this regard. Professor Jeffrey Gurock, who holds the Libby Klapperman Chair in American Jewish History at Yeshiva University in New York, was most gracious in writing the foreword to the book; his contribution cannot be overstated. My wife Barbara Rotenberg, a very talented writer, helped edit many of the stories in the collection. Also, the detailed comments I received from Ruth Rollhaus Lehmann of Suffern, New York, a friend of many years with great editing skills, proved invaluable.

The photographic genius of my niece, Melissa Taub, is responsible for the illustrations that accompany many of the stories. She has great taste! At the time of this writing, Melissa has just been chosen by the Israeli Ministry of Absorption to receive the 2017 Yuri Stern Prize granted annually to the best immigrant artist in the category of photography. She can be reached at melissataubphotography.com.

In compiling many of the tales I often relied on friends and family members for their recollections and insights. I ask forgiveness in advance if I left someone out: Azriel Chelst; Jeffrey Rotenberg; Michelle Rotenberg; Jonathan Rotenberg; Daniella Rotenberg Wittenberg and Scott Wittenberg; Ariel Rotenberg; Lesley Anne Solte (a great-granddaughter of the amazing Mrs. Webster who helped me in telling her bubbe's story); Lenny Fuld; Rabbis Sholom Baum and Duvie Weiss of Congregation Keter Torah, Teaneck, New Jersey; Dr. Yvette Vogel; Dr. Isaac Herschkopf (himself a great writer and an inspiration to me from our days together in high school); Robert Pachner of California; my devoted associate Cathy Sheerins of New Jersey; and my beloved *droog*, Alex Solovyev, the "Kharkovite," on whom I have relied for background material on all matters Russian. I also thank Eddie and Malka Phillips of Givat Mordechai in Jerusalem for their friendship and inspiration. Eddie is the Israeli artist known as "Ben Avram" whose colorful artwork graces the cover of this book and surrounds me daily as I write and work.

Special thanks goes to the entire staff of the *Jewish Link of New Jersey*. Its publisher, Moshe Kinderlehrer, and its editor-in-chief, Elizabeth Kratz, both encouraged me over the last three years to contribute my stories to their wonderful paper on a regular basis. I value greatly your friendship and insights.

One more mention of my best friend and unswerving supporter (though heaven knows I try her often!) would be appropriate. My wife Barbara, to whom this volume is dedicated, deserves much of the credit for its creation. She has accompanied me on our life's travels for more than forty-five years, and without her I'm nothing. Thanks for everything!

Finally, I would be remiss if I failed to mention my debt to my late parents, Ruth and Maurice Rotenberg of New York, and my late in-laws, Grace and Julius Rosenzweig of Woodmere, New York, for their many kindnesses and unwavering support of my efforts over the years.

JR